Arcamira

Arcamira

Hannah Sandoval

COSMIC EGG
BOOKS

Winchester, UK
Washington, USA

JOHN HUNT PUBLISHING

First published by Cosmic Egg Books, 2019
Cosmic Egg Books is an imprint of John Hunt Publishing Ltd., 3 East St., Alresford,
Hampshire SO24 9EE, UK
office@jhpbooks.com
www.johnhuntpublishing.com
www.cosmicegg-books.com

For distributor details and how to order please visit the 'Ordering' section on our website.

Text copyright: Hannah Sandoval 2018

ISBN: 978 1 78904 262 7
978 1 78904 263 4 (ebook)
Library of Congress Control Number: 2018958571

A CIP catalogue record for this book is available from the British Library.

Design: Stuart Davies

UK: Printed and bound by CPI Group (UK) Ltd, Croydon, CR0 4YY
US: Printed and bound by Thomson-Shore, 7300 West Joy Road, Dexter, MI 48130

We operate a distinctive and ethical publishing philosophy in
all areas of our business, from our global network of authors to
production and worldwide distribution.

Contents

To Lottie, to fill your world with stories. May you have
Andromeda's heart, Atalanta's spirit, and Felicity's audacity.

Chapter 1

Vampire Ball

Atalanta yanked the pearl-encrusted comb down the length of the auburn hair that ended at her hips. Each tangle she met and each accidental scrape to her pointed ears brought a curse from her mouth. She tried to draw comfort from her surroundings. Sitting on a rock in the elf palace's enormous orchard and brushing one's hair was much more enjoyable than sitting at a vanity. The Arcamirian sun filtered through the treetops, filling the place with green light. Multiple varieties of stone fruits weighed down the limbs.

Atalanta gave the comb one more pass and then tossed it aside as a lost cause. She reached up and plucked a peach from the limb just above her head without having to stand up. She bit into the fruit, sending the juice running down her arm to stain her silver silks. She looked at the mess she'd made and shrugged. Her father had requested that she "untangle that wild horse's mane" before she made her appearance in the High Court. He had said nothing about maintaining her dress.

She itched to go riding or perhaps challenge Malik to a bit of swordplay or archery. She was not so sure she liked coming of age. As a child, she had yearned to be bigger, so she could fight great battles and rule her kingdom alongside her father. Her father had taught her to handle a sword, ride a horse, and use her magic. He had awakened the need for adrenaline, for excitement. He had encouraged it, and now he wanted her to comb her hair and wear her silks and be a dignified elf of the court because she was "becoming a fine elvish woman." If court and political pomp went along with becoming an elvish woman, she wanted no part of it. And why should the change be so instantaneous? She'd only turned seventeen yesterday. Why should a birthday mark

1

the end of free-roaming through the woods and castle dressed in leathers and pants and the beginning of dull, polite talk with the High Court, dressed in delicate dresses? Why seventeen? It seemed so soon. Her father was nearly three hundred. She was still a babe by comparison.

She flicked the peach pit into a nearby bush with a fast, practiced movement.

The bush shook. Atalanta's high, pointed ears flicked toward the sound. She must have hit a rabbit with the pit. She rose to coax the animal out, her hand outstretched, sensing the earth from the bottoms of her bare feet to her fingertips, and froze. It did not feel right. Her heartbeat quickened.

"Come out, whatever you are," she said, her hands clenched in fists at her sides, her green eyes fixed on the bush.

A squat deformity leapt from the depths of the foliage with a battle cry. The creature was no bigger than a human child, but with the muscles of a man. Its spine protruded and curved, and its knees seemed permanently bent so that it waddled toward her. Two necks sprang from its hunched back, carrying two heads, each with its own nose, mouth, and bulging, singular eye. The two heads yelled in unison, revealing large tongues as big as a dog's, but decidedly human.

Atalanta pressed her back to the rock and let out a cry of disgust. She side-stepped the creature easily as it barreled toward her at a clumsy, waddling run. It pulled up just short of smashing into the rock and turned to face her, identical snarls on both its heads. Atalanta bent her knees in a fighting stance and reached for her sword hilt. Her fingers met nothing but the soft, silver silk of her dress. She looked down at the useless dress with gritted teeth.

The monster lunged, and she placed a strong kick to one of its jaws. It should have sent the creature flying and broken its jaw, but the muscular beast only took a step back and grunted.

As Atalanta placed her foot back on the ground and made to

take off toward the palace, she stepped on the hem of her dress and stumbled. Her ingrained balance ensured that she did not fall, but before she could recover, the waist-high beast grabbed a handful of her long, freshly combed hair and yanked.

Hair ripped away from her scalp and something in her neck popped, making her gasp in pain. With its free hand, the beast grabbed her ankle and toppled her. She planted her hands in the earth as she fell, saving her head and chest from impact. She tried to whip her legs around to take the creature's out from under it, but it snatched her hair at the crown and tightened an arm around her neck. She struggled on the ground, her feet kicking up grass as she tried to stand and free herself. She clawed at the beast's arms with her nails, raking bloody lines in the flesh. She jabbed at its eyes over her shoulder, but the heads parted and danced away from her fingers. She put her hands on the ground and tried to push herself upright, but the creature was too strong, and its flexed bicep was cutting off her air. Her vision was slipping, her lungs screaming.

"Sleep, little elfling," said the creature, both mouths speaking in unison so that the words echoed in her ears as she slipped into darkness.

* * *

Andrew's sword caught the sun as the blade crashed to the ground.

"Come on, Andrew, you can do better than that," said Michael, a taunt in his voice and in the curl of his mouth.

Andrew looked at his older brother's bulk with an unspoken complaint. Michael's muscles shaped his mail into firm hills. He stood a full foot higher than his brother, and his shoulders had twice the berth. He was a near spitting image of their father, right down to the large, somewhat crooked nose and flaming hair.

Andrew favored their mother, with slender shoulders, lean muscle that was lost under his mail, and jet-black hair that he kept shaggy. The family resemblance could be found in their father's blue eyes and sharp jaw.

Panting, with his hands on his knees, Andrew looked over at his sisters, still locked in a duel. Andrew's twin, Andromeda, was clearly winning. It was all Felicity could do just to block Andromeda's flurry of attacks. The large lock of inky hair that had fallen loose from her braid and into her eyes didn't seem to impair her vision.

Their grey-haired training master, Archimedes, had his eyes fixed on the girls, for which Andrew was grateful. But if he let his twin outshine him, he'd never hear the end of it—not from her, but from Michael and Archimedes. He picked up his sword and resumed his stance in front of Michael. His breath was still coming too fast. The broadsword was a constant, tiresome weight and felt awkward in his grip. Michael, on the other hand, breathed easy, and tossed his sword from hand to hand. Andrew had a sudden urge to spit.

"Try it again," said Michael. "You need to learn how to disarm your opponent. If it comes down to a battle of stamina, you'll lose."

"Who made you training master?" said Andrew.

Michael lashed out with a vicious downward stroke that vibrated Andrew's arms when he blocked it. With an angry grunt, Andrew pooled the last of his energy and tried the combination one last time. On the final, upward thrust, Michael's sword slipped from his hand. Andrew whooped and punched the air, suddenly revitalized.

"Good," said Michael, "but don't let hubris get the best of you."

Michael's dulled broadsword smacked Andrew across the chest in a bruising blow.

"Don't let your sword dangle in the grass," said Michael.

Andrew struggled for air and gritted his teeth in a snarl. He dropped his sword and rammed his shoulder into Michael's chest. Michael's heavy mail tipped him off balance, and the two boys grappled furiously on the ground.

Archimedes came trotting toward them, not looking all that concerned. Despite his age, the retired general was still built like an ox. He plunged a hand into the fray, balling a chunk of Andrew's hair at the scruff of his neck. Andrew did not cry out, but his jaw muscles flexed as if holding in a scream. Archimedes gave Michael's midsection a good kick.

"Get up."

Michael did as he was told. Archimedes tossed Andrew away, and the sixteen-year-old hung his head and eyed the training master like a wounded animal.

"Michael, you're not the master here. You understand?"

"Yes, master."

"Andrew, you start a cheap scuffle like that again, and I'll beat you black and blue."

"And I'll wear each bruise with pride, master," said Andrew with a wolfish grin.

Archimedes' hand whipped out and struck Andrew across the face.

"Don't get smart with me. You're not princes on this training field, boys; you're soldiers, and I'm your commander. No special privilege here. Sass me again and you'll be working the stables the rest of the day."

"Yes, master," said Andrew, going red at the neck.

"It might improve his smell," said Felicity.

The dark-blue eyes fixed on Andrew beneath Felicity's fair lashes were the only proof that Felicity was an Avalon, and they ensured the false rumors of Queen Isabelle's possible adultery remained little more than whispered market stall gossip. The origins of her thick blonde curls were a mystery, as was her voluptuous figure. Queen Isabelle was tall, slender, small breasted, and slim hipped. Andromeda was her spitting image. Felicity, however, was of average height, slim in the middle, and round on both ends. She did not share her sibling's pale, burn-prone skin either. Her skin was a buttery gold that turned the color of perfectly baked bread in the summer.

Though there were four Avalon siblings, Felicity was the true middle child, with the attitude to back it up. At eighteen, she was two years the twins' senior and two years Michael's junior. She was aware of the rumors surrounding her birth and of the way most men stared greedily as she passed, and she scoffed openly at both.

"Even after a whole day in the stables, I'll still smell better than Sir Barroth," said Andrew, referring to a young knight who had caught Felicity's eye of late.

At Felicity's wide-eyed disbelief and feral snarl, Andrew smirked and said, "What? You thought no one knew?"

"Take it back, imp," said Felicity, flicking her rapier's thin blade under Andrew's chin.

Archimedes' horsewhip cracked down on Felicity's wrist, and she dropped the blade with a wounded cry of outrage.

"No archery today for you three," said Archimedes, pointing at Michael, Andrew, and Felicity. "You're running the course until I've sweated all the fight out of you. I've had it with your childishness."

"What about her?" said Felicity, jabbing a thumb at Andromeda, as Michael and Andrew groaned.

The course was a battle scenario of Archimedes' own invention. Enemies made of corn sacks were rigged with levers and pulleys to move about the course, which was made up of obstacles like chicken wire and a large hill of overturned pig troughs that had to be climbed with care. Worst of all, it had to be run as quickly as Archimedes desired, and if a trainee didn't go fast enough, they were assured of some sort of projectile whizzing at their head from the training master's considerably strong arm.

"She hasn't made me consider murder yet today," said Archimedes. "And she put you in the dust, Felicity. If it was a real battle, you would have been dead three times over. She could probably do the same thing to Andrew, too."

"Not if I had a rapier," said Andrew, lifting his chin to preserve his dignity. "I don't like broadsword. It's too cumbersome. I can't move properly."

"Rapier's are for woman and children," said Archimedes. He paused to spit from a hole between his yellow teeth. "Broadsword is a man's weapon. You're a man, now, are you not?"

Andrew flushed, but kept his head high. "Yes, master."

"Then learn to use a man's weapon. You'll use the broadsword when you run the course."

"Master," said Andromeda.

It was the second time she had spoken, but her soft voice had been drowned out by her sibling's complaints and her master's outrage.

"Yes, Andromeda?"

"I wish to run the course as well," she said, pushing the annoying strand of loose hair away from her grey eyes. "I don't wish for special treatment."

"It's not special treatment," said Archimedes. "It's fair treatment. You're practicing archery. That's my word, and my word goes. Grab your bow. The rest of you, collect your breath and meet me at the course. If you dally too long, rest assured I'll let you know it."

When Archimedes was safely out of earshot, Felicity rapped Andromeda in the shoulder with her middle knuckle.

"Baby Andromeda always gets her way," said Felicity with a disgusted sneer.

"If I had gotten my way, I would be running the course," said Andromeda, rubbing her shoulder.

"Sure," said Felicity. She adopted a soft, mouse-like voice

and said, "Oh, please, master, I wish to run the course because I'm the perfect warrior. You may fool him, but you don't fool me. You've gotten your way, just like you always do."

"Leave her be," said Andrew, stepping between the two girls with his armor centimeters away from Felicity's. "You can't blame her for being better than you at everything. It's not very hard to do."

"I would very much like to see you prove it," said Felicity through gritted teeth.

"Quit it, both of you," said Michael. "I won't be getting a lashing because you two can't get along. I'll drag you to the course if I must."

Felicity smacked Andrew across the face with her curls as she turned to follow Michael. Andromeda grabbed Andrew's hand as he made to follow them.

"You know, Archimedes shouldn't call rapiers women's weapons just because he's useless with one," she said.

"Archimedes isn't useless at anything," said Andrew, shoving his twin playfully. "But thanks."

* * *

The Avalon's palace was an ancient masterpiece of polished stone rising into a half dozen towers. Inside, every wall was hung with dense tapestries, vibrant paintings, and elaborate ironwork that had adorned the passageways for centuries. The four siblings walked down a long, arched hallway, headed for their rooms in the east wing.

"That old man loves throwing walnuts far too much," said Felicity, massaging a welt on her neck. "He ought to have been a squirrel."

"I think he's more of a dragon, myself," said Michael.

"More like a grouchy old troll," said Andrew, scratching at his shaggy black head like a dog.

"I'm going to have Cecelia draw me an extra hot bath before the ball," said Felicity.

"The ball!" said Andromeda. "Ugh, I forgot all about that dreadful thing. I suppose Mother will make me wear a corset."

"Stop complaining, Andromeda," said Felicity. "At least you won't have any bruises underneath your corset. I shall have at least three. Though, I could give you some if you don't want any special treatment."

Andrew clenched a fist, but Andromeda just sighed softly and kept her grey eyes on the tapestry at the end of the hall. Felicity appraised her with sly, sideways glances. The scowl lines between her soft brown brows vanished into her forehead, and she breathed a small sigh of her own.

"Don't look so dreary, Andromeda," said Felicity. "Balls are fun. Dance with a boy. I'm sure if you're wearing a corset, you'll get plenty of offers."

"If I'm to decide between a boy and breathing, I shall choose breathing every time," said Andromeda.

But it seemed that Andromeda's governess had other plans. After a bath that was far too hot, a great deal of rib-cracking corset tugging, and a quick meal of braised lamb and cranberries that she could hardly eat for the terrible compression of her stomach, Andromeda stood next to her siblings in the palace ballroom.

It was the largest and most spacious room in the castle. Its floor was the only one in the castle made of polished wood rather than sanded stone. Hundreds of the human realm's lords and ladies drifted gracefully across it in their finery. The floor was hardly visible through the mass of colorful silks and satins and the stampede of polished shoes. At intervals around the room, giant, gilded mirrors three times the height of a man were fixed into the walls, making the room look and feel as though it was full of thousands rather than hundreds as the mirrors reflected both the dancers and themselves in endless tunnels. Between the mirrors, broadswords, bows, and maces hung on the wall, fixed into wooden coats of arms of all the noble human families. A spiral staircase led to an upper balcony where even more people looked down on the dancers. The balcony wrapped around the room's entirety and was supported by white marble columns. Vines made of pure gold wrapped around each column, the leaves reaching for the balcony as though it was sunlight.

The siblings stood near the far wall, in front of the crimson and silver banners that bore the Avalon family crest: an eagle with a sword clutched in its talons. Their parents, King Markus and Queen Isabelle, sat in thrones just behind their children. They had started the dancing, as was customary, and then had returned to their thrones to observe their court, but their eyes were actually locked on their children. They leaned toward one another over a wooden table laid with wine and goblets for their refreshment, secretly commenting on who had danced with whom and wondering if Andrew or Andromeda would dance at all without prodding.

Felicity scanned the crowd for someone who met her standards. In her royal-blue satin dress with a skirt made of hundreds of bows and her diamond tiara, she was rather imposing in her beauty, and very few young men approached her. Six brave souls out of dozens had asked her, but she had turned them all down with a wrinkled nose.

Andromeda stood next to her in a long-sleeved deep-crimson dress with buttons up the back, holding her waist where the dreaded corset was squeezing her. She made it a point not to catch anyone's eye and stood slightly behind her siblings. Her hair was pulled up in a braided arrangement, held back by a glittering tiara, but she wished that the annoying lock that usually fell in her eyes was back in place tonight.

Michael looked more dashing than imposing now that he had exchanged his armor for a soft white tunic and a black overcoat embroidered with golden eagles. He had already asked three girls to dance, and all had accepted.

Andrew's coat was dark-blue and embroidered with silver wolves, but he looked uncomfortable. He watched many girls, but never moved from his twin's side to ask any of them for a dance.

"I don't see the point of these balls," Andromeda whispered into Andrew's ear.

"Me either, but there's no escaping," he replied. "Mother loves them."

Andromeda sighed and watched as an extraordinarily tall man with slender limbs and sharp features approached Felicity and held out a hand for a dance. Andromeda waited for Felicity's sniffed rejection. This pale man was far too lean for Felicity's taste. She often remarked that she had no interest in a man she could easily pummel, and preferred thicker built men, usually with dark hair and short beards. This man was also a little too old for her fancy as well.

The man said something Andromeda didn't catch. Felicity curtsied and took the man's hand. Andromeda went slack-jawed as Felicity followed him into the crowd of dancers. Perhaps she did not know her sister as well as she thought.

Michael shifted over and stood between Andrew and Andromeda.

"You two better dance with someone or Mother will pick someone for you," he said. "She and father have been pointing at the two of you and whispering with their heads together."

"Damn," said Andromeda.

"Since when do you curse?" said Michael with mild admiration.

Andromeda made a face at him, and Michael laughed and retreated.

Andrew stepped in front of Andromeda.

"Would you care to dance, dear lady?"

He did an over dramatic bow and held out his hand. She

laughed, curtsied, and put her hand in his.

The twins spun around the dance floor, doing all the steps their mother had taught them during their much dreaded lessons as children. Andrew kept spinning Andromeda much too hard on purpose. He held her in the proper form, with one upheld hand in hers and the other on her back, and whipped them around in dizzying circles. The rush was exhilarating, but disorienting. When he released her back and spun her out from him, she collided with another dancing couple, and she and the other woman crashed to the floor in a tangle of satin and metal hoops.

Andromeda tried to stifle her laughter as she apologized to the much older woman, but Andrew had no such qualms.

"Hush," she said through a snicker as she returned to him. "You'll get us into trouble."

He held up his hand in answer, and she took it.

"Not so hard this time," she said. "This corset already makes me short of breath. I may faint if you make me any dizzier."

"You're Archimedes' prized warrior, and yet you lose a battle to a corset?" said Andrew.

She pinched him in the ribs and he straightened out, leading her at a pace that actually matched the music. Andromeda looked over Andrew's shoulder into one of the mirrors. She saw her own smiling face and Andrew's shaggy black hair. Then, just as Andrew was about to turn her in another direction, she caught sight of Felicity's golden curls.

She dug her nails into Andrew's shoulders and planted her feet in order to keep her eyes on the mirror.

"Ouch, Andromeda! I'm keeping pace with the music. No need to draw blood."

"Andrew, look," said Andromeda, her voice a harsh, frightened whisper.

Felicity held her hands out in front of her as if they were resting on someone's shoulders, but she was dancing by herself.

Andromeda and Andrew turned their heads from the reflection in unison and found Felicity in the crowd. She was dancing with the tall, pale man whom Andromeda had seen ask for her hand. Felicity looked into his eyes with a dazed, slack-jawed expression.

"It can't be," said Andrew. "Can it?"

Andromeda turned back to the mirror, and Andrew followed suit. Felicity turned on the floor by herself. The twins looked back, eyes fixed on the man with his arms around their sister.

"Vampire," they echoed.

"What do we do?" said Andromeda, her usually quiet voice reaching a high, squeaking timbre.

Andrew scanned the room, as if the answer might appear on the walls.

"We have to get her away from it," he said, nodding as if to affirm the solution to himself. "It can only keep her in a trance if it maintains eye contact."

"You have to be the one to get her. It will be harder for it to put you in a trance."

"Why?"

"You're a boy," said Andromeda, giving him a familiar scolding look for not remembering his tutoring. "I'm going to alert the guards. Try not to let it know you've discovered it, and don't look it directly in the eyes."

Andrew watched her dash into the crowd, knocking guests aside with her hoop skirt. He slowly turned back to Felicity and the vampire, suddenly feeling like his bladder might give way. He maneuvered through the crowd and held out a shaking hand to tap the vampire on the shoulder. The vampire froze so quickly that Andrew's eyes traveled past it before he realized it was no longer moving.

"Pardon me, sir," Andrew said, a noticeable quiver in his voice.

The vampire slowly turned his head and fixed on Andrew

with deep, dark eyes. Andrew quickly looked at the vampire's chin instead.

"I'm afraid I need to borrow my sister for a moment. The king and queen need a word with her."

"I'm not sure your sweet sister wishes to be ... borrowed," the vampire said in a strange, lilting accent that sounded eerily like the ancient Arcamirian the young royals had been forced to learn since they were children in order to read the old scrolls.

Across the room, Andromeda had nearly reached the ballroom doors where armed guards were posted outside when she spotted Michael holding a pretty girl in a pink dress close enough to stunt the movement of their dance. Andromeda snatched Michael by the arm, making him release the girl in surprise. Andromeda ignored the daggers the other girl shot her way and said, "Michael, I need to speak with you, *now*."

Michael's jaw tightened in anger for only a moment before he caught sight of Andromeda's wild eyes.

"What's wrong?" he said, allowing her to lead him away, much to the dismay of the young maiden in the pink dress.

"A vampire has Felicity in a trance," she said.

Michael's laugh was nearly a bark.

"A vampire? Are you sure it's not just a nobleman who hasn't seen enough of the sun?"

"Michael, please. It has no reflection! Andrew is trying to get her away from it. You have to help him."

Michael's face lost all color. He gripped Andromeda's arms a little too tight.

"You're serious."

"Yes!"

"Where are they?"

Andromeda pointed back toward the middle of the dance floor.

"Alert the guards, but tell them not to do anything until I

signal them. If it really is a vampire, it could snap her neck and suck her dry before they could even get near her."

Andromeda swallowed hard at the thought and nodded. Michael released her arms, and as she ran for the door, he ran to grab one of the swords mounted on the wall. He freed a broadsword from its wooden mount and started winding his way through the crowd with it held up by his head in a ready position. The dancers that he passed stopped to watch him go, whispering to one another and shifting uneasily.

In the center of the dance floor, Andrew watched as Felicity blinked rapidly and then opened her eyes wide as if coming out of deep sleep. The vampire's threatening gaze was fixed on Andrew, daring the young prince to challenge him again, but his trance required eye contact.

"Felicity?" said Andrew, seizing his chance. "Come with me. I need to speak with you a moment." He held out a tentative hand toward her.

"What?" said Felicity, blinking at her brother.

"Stay with me, my sweet," said the vampire.

Felicity jerked and, still encircled in the vampire's arms, looked up at him. She sucked in a sharp breath, preparing to scream, and then she shivered from head to toe. Her body went limp and submissive. Her eyes glazed over again.

Andrew clenched his hands into fists, but there was nothing he could do. He was unarmed, and no match for a vampire's strength and speed. He scanned the crowd looking for Andromeda and the guards, wondering how long the vampire would keep up his charade. Andrew figured the vampire had hoped to lure Felicity out of the castle under a trance and avoid the guards, but now that he was discovered, he might unleash his fury at any moment.

There was no sign of the guards, but Andrew's eye caught on a flash of silver and red. It was Michael, shoving his way through the crowd with a deadly look on his face and a sword in his hands. Andrew averted his eyes, so as not to alert the vampire.

"It would be wise to let her go," said Andrew, keeping Michael in sight.

"Why is that, puny little prince?"

"Because my brother is much bigger than I," said Andrew.

The vampire's brow pulled down in a frown just as Michael slammed into his shoulder from behind, knocking Felicity free of the creature's arms. Michael grabbed Felicity around the waist with one arm, picked her completely off her feet, put her behind him, and then faced the vampire with broadsword brandished.

As the three siblings watched in horror, the vampire's face began to change. All of his teeth grew sharper and larger. His canines grew down to kiss his bottom lip. His jaw enlarged with sickening pops and his lips curled back to accommodate the vicious, toothy maw. Black claws the size of lion's teeth grew from his nailbeds, overlapping his fingernails, and ripped away his tunic and overcoat. His black, bat-like wings, folded to his back like a second skin, now had room to unfurl from his shoulder blades. When he lifted his head and grinned at the siblings, a forked tongued hung from his mouth. He let out a horrible, screeching growl like a wild cat in a brawl.

Felicity, fully out of the trance, shrank back and tripped over her dress. She hit the floor and screamed so loud it made the vampire flinch.

Hers was the first of hundreds. The crowd began to shift like a living, pulsating thing as people ran for the exits, shoving each other aside, not stopping to help the fallen, but instead trampling those in their way.

Michael's pale face was drained, but he set his jaw and held his sword higher. He looked at Andrew, whose mouth was open in a cry he could not find a way to voice.

"Andrew, take Felicity and run!" said Michael, making Andrew shift his eyes from the vampire. "Find Andromeda. Get them both out of here! The guard's priority will be Mother and Father."

Andrew grabbed Felicity's hand and helped her to her feet. With one last worried look at their older brother, they battled through the stampeding crowd together.

Outside, Andromeda had just given the palace guards Michael's message when she heard the blood-chilling cry of the vampire.

"Damn the signal," said Andromeda. "Get in there, now!"

The guards drew their swords in a cacaphony of steel sliding out of scabbards. The doors to the ballroom burst open and a wave of screaming lords and ladies came spilling out.

"Wait!" said Andromeda, arms out to halt the guards as they moved to press through the crowd.

Her mind raced back to all of the books she had ever read on vampires. They had to be stabbed with stakes, shown a crucifix, or sprayed with holy water. Swords would not do. The crowd parted around the armor and shields of the guards, who were peering into the ballroom.

"We aren't equipped to fight a vampire. Those swords will be of no use. You'll be slaughtered."

"Princess," said one of the guards, "Their Majesties are inside. We have pledged our lives to protect them, and we shall."

"I understand," said Andromeda. "I only mean that you shouldn't engage the beast. Concentrate on getting everyone to safety. We'll hunt down the vampire and kill it another day."

"Aye, Princess," said the guard.

The others pounded their swords against their shields and forced their way through the stampede of oncoming guests. Andromeda followed in their wake to find her siblings.

The guards headed toward the thrones, but Andromeda kept her course toward the vampire, whose wings rose above the crowd. A man elbowed her in the ribs and knocked the wind from her. A woman slammed into her shoulder. Andromeda was finding it hard just to put one foot in front of the other. Felicity and Andrew nearly collided with her, too.

"Andromeda! Thank God," said Andrew, clutching a stitch in his side.

"Where's Michael?"

"Fighting the vampire," said Felicity, her voice shrill and unrecognizable.

"What?" said Andromeda. "We have to get him out. He'll be killed! What's he fighting it with?"

"A broadsword," said Andrew, his eyebrows questioning the relevance of the question.

"A sword!" said Andromeda. "He can't fight a vampire with a sword! He'll be torn to ribbons."

Michael blocked a swipe from the vampire's claws with his sword. The steel sang with the impact. He was already wearing down from dodging and fending off the vampire's fast, powerful blows, but he countered with a quick, expert swipe of his own. He caught the vampire's arm just above the elbow, cutting down to the bone.

Michael's triumphant smile drooped as the skin knitted itself back together before his eyes. The new skin smoothed over without even a scratch. Michael was unscathed as well but weakening. Every blow that he blocked from the vampire made his arm ache, and if he failed to block one of the vampire's attacks, his skin would not grow back.

"Michael, run! The sword's no good," called a voice behind him.

He turned his head at his youngest sister's frightened warning and saw all three of his siblings running toward him through the significantly thinned crowd.

A powerful blow struck his right temple. Four claws scraped his head as he flew backward. The sword flew from his hand, and he landed hard on his back. Blood trickled from his head.

Felicity's frightened face appeared over him.

"Felicity, run. Get out of here," he said, his head throbbing.

Before the words fully formed, the vampire materialized behind Felicity and swatted her with the back of his hand. The blow knocked her to the floor with such force that she skidded sideways across the polished wood where she lay motionless.

The vampire crouched over Michael and opened his lethal jaws. The putrid stench of rotting flesh and blood fell like a heavy blanket over Michael's face. The long, forked tongue fell out past the giant teeth as the vampire moved his head in toward Michael's neck. Michael closed his eyes, unable to look death in the face.

There was a shriek of pain. Michael's eyes flew open to see the vampire cringing and writhing. A sword pierced his body, but no blood spilled from the horrendous wound.

Michael felt hands under his arms pull him backwards, away from the beast, and he looked around to see Felicity, a nasty swollen bruise discoloring her high cheekbone.

The vampire turned to face its attacker, wrenching the sword from Andrew's grip. Andrew retreated, gaping at his handiwork.

Michael rose to his feet, his head swimming.

The vampire reached and grabbed the sword hilt protruding from his lower back and pulled it out with a horrible squelching of disturbed flesh and the scraping of steel on bone.

Michael looked away, fearing he might vomit, and realized that Andromeda was nowhere in sight. He hoped she had reached safety with their parents.

The vampire held up the broadsword with one hand as easily as if it was a child's wooden toy and observed it with a sneer of distaste before throwing it aside. The wound began to heal itself as the vampire stepped toward Andrew.

After calling her warning to Michael, Andromeda had veered off toward her parents' thrones, an idea forming in her head. On her way, she snatched a sword and dagger from one of the coats of arms. The king and queen were nowhere in sight—whisked away by the royal guard. Andromeda upended the small wooden refreshment table, smashing the pitcher of wine and splattering the thrones with crimson.

Andromeda used the sword to hack off one of the wooden table legs. She sat on the floor, her dress belling out around her, and began sharpening one end to a point with the dagger. When it was sharp enough to give her finger a good poke, she looked back across the ballroom to find it empty save for her siblings and the vampire. All of the doors were open, but no one was in sight.

Amidst the chaos, the guards had not realized the royal children had gone after the vampire instead of fleeing for the exits. They would realize their mistake at any moment, but Andromeda feared they would be too late.

The skin of the vampire's bare stomach was healing itself, and he was advancing on her twin. She gripped the newly carved stake in her hand and ran for her brother as fast as she could pump her legs.

She was not fast enough.

The vampire leapt at Andrew and pinned him to the ground, digging his claws into Andrew's shoulders. Felicity's scream mingled with Andrew's cries of pain, and Michael scooped up the fallen sword.

Andromeda did not stop running.

As the vampire lowered his head to Andrew's neck, she plunged the wooden stake into the left side of his back, using her momentum to put her full body weight behind it. The stake did not go all the way through, but it did its job.

Spent, ancient, black blood oozed sluggishly from the wound to the heart. The vampire threw back his head in a final, beastly cry of anguish before he fell to the side with a crash. His skin turned ashy gray. Cracks appeared like veins, and then the entire body crumpled in on itself until there was nothing left but a heap of ashes.

Andromeda stood over the pile of ash, panting. Andrew slowly got to his feet and locked eyes with his twin.

"Thank you," he said breathlessly.

Felicity curled her lip in disgust.

"He turned into ash!" she said as if it was the most lewd and disgraceful of sins.

"Vampires are undead," said Andromeda. "Don't any of you read the old books?"

Andrew shrugged.

"I don't have time to read," said Felicity with a sniff.

"Their disease allows them to live eternally if they feast on the blood of others. The blood sustains their bodies because their own hearts no longer pump blood through their veins. But they aren't indestructible. The last bit of their own blood is stored in their heart. If they are staked in the heart and that blood is spilled, they become what they truly are: a corpse." She looked down at the mess on the floor. "Not all of them turn to ash. This one must have been very old."

"I never thought I'd see one," said Michael, the sword drooping from his hand and blood flowing from his head wound. "They're supposed to be extinct."

"There have always been stories of one or two coming out every now and then in the Northern villages. I just thought they were stories, though," said Andromeda. "The people are going to—"

Andromeda stopped, her eyes on Michael. She went to his side. He was incredibly pale and supporting himself on the sword. His hair was matted with dark blood.

"Andrew rip the sleeve off your tunic," said Felicity, coming to hover beside Michael. "I need to stop the bleeding."

As Andrew obeyed, Markus and Isabelle ran into the room, guards hot at their heels.

"Oh my darlings," said Isabelle, trying to touch all of her children at once, "you're hurt." She whirled on the guards. "Next time there is a threat to the castle, you get our children out first or I'll have all your heads."

"No need to threaten the guards, dear," said Markus. "They did what they were charged to do."

"Well, I have a new charge," said Isabelle, flicking a loose strand of raven hair, much like the one always bothering Andromeda, out of her eyes.

"Yes, Your Majesty," said the Head of the Guard.

"Michael needs a physician," said Felicity, wrapping Andrew's sleeve around Michael's head as a bandage.

"Take him to Britton immediately," said Markus.

Two guards rushed to drape Michael's arms over their shoulders.

"Andrew is bleeding too," said Andromeda.

"Go with them, son," said Markus.

"I'm going, too," said Isabelle. "Someone has to make sure that old boar doesn't patch them up without milk of poppy like he did when Andrew broke his arm."

When only Markus and his girls remained in the room, he stared down at the pile of ashes and ran a worrisome hand through his thick, red beard.

"My God," he said in an awed voice. "It just walked right in. Makes one wonder how many more are still amongst us."

The rest of the night was chaotic and tiresome. The four siblings had to tell their story over and over. First, to their parents, then to the new general, and finally to Archimedes. Britton stitched Michael's and Andrew's claw wounds and soothed Felicity's cuts and bruises. All four of them were thankful to fall into their beds and drift into uneasy sleep.

Vampires entered all of their dreams.

* * *

In the fortnight following the vampire attack, many things changed around the castle. Archimedes began training the young royals to fight not only humans, but mythical creatures as well. They had to learn to fight with a sword in one hand and a stake in the other. They had to learn new methods of fighting airborne enemies. They all carried a crucifix and a bottle of holy water with them.

King Markus believed that if vampires were still roaming Arcamira that his kingdom should assume that their diseased cousins, the werewolves, were still roaming somewhere deep in the woods. Thus, all arrows and swords had a layer of silver melted over the steel.

Guards were put on heavy night watch, for that was when both vampires and werewolves stalked the earth.

The villagers hung garlic and crucifixes on their doorframes and barricaded their doors at nightfall.

Thus, when the elfin messenger rode into Barion, the large village that encircled the Avalon's palace, he was met with a small army of guards, shuttered windows, and empty streets.

Each guard he passed fixated on the pointed ears sticking out from the elf's waist-length blonde hair, and their eyes widened. None of them had ever seen an elf in person. By the time he reached the castle gates, he had an entourage of gawking guards following close behind.

"Are you going to stand there gaping, human, or are you going to let me in?" said the elf, lifting his head to address the gatekeeper. "I have an urgent message from my king, to be delivered as quickly as possible to King Markus."

The gatekeeper fumbled with the lever used to lift up the gate.

The elf rode under the spiked metal before dismounting his palomino in one fluid movement. He was met by two more stunned guards. One took his horse and the other escorted him to the castle doors. When the giant oak doors were pushed open by four guards, the elf and his escort walked through the stone brick castle to the council room where the king and queen met with nobles and peasants alike. Two golden thrones overlooked the chamber and the pews lined up for guests and council members.

The guard offered the elf a seat on one such pew and rushed to fetch the king and queen.

When Markus and Isabelle were both sitting on their thrones, the guard assumed his post at the door.

"Who are you and what message do you bring from your king?" said Markus.

The elf produced a scroll from his tunic. The tunic was very dirty and travel worn and his blonde hair was matted and filled with leaves, but still his beauty was beyond human capacity. He seemed to glow with an ethereal energy.

"My name is Glaiden, and I have traveled a fortnight to deliver this message," said the elf.

He approached Markus' throne, his movement unrealistically graceful, and placed the scroll in the king's hand. Markus unrolled it and his eyes skimmed the elegant handwriting in dark green ink. The queen left her throne to read along with him.

To the great King Markus Avalon of the human realm,

I hope this message finds you in good health and that your kingdom fairs better than mine. My only living child and heir, Atalanta, has been taken by a beast I have never heard of before, if the servant who claims to have seen it from a window is of sound mind. She claims it was a two-headed cyclops with a hunched back. My elves are still searching for it, but the beast has left barely a trace. I did not wish to break our treaty and sanction search parties on your domain without permission, but some of my best scouts believe they've found signs of my daughter and her captor near your Northern border. I am writing to ask for permission to cross this border. Any search parties of your own would be appreciated and remembered as well.

My Atalanta is a mere babe of around your daughters' age. I am asking for your help as a fellow king and father. Please aid me in the search for my daughter.

King Zanthus Galechaser

"The poor child," said Isabelle. "Markus, we must help."

"Guard," said the king, "fetch my scribe."

When the scribe had arrived with quill and parchment in hand, Markus dictated his reply.

To my ally, King Zanthus Galechaser of the elfin realm,

My queen and I are grieved to hear of the kidnap of your precious daughter. You have my consent to send your search parties over my borders. Not only will I send out search parties of my own, but I also extend my hand in alliance to give you the full resources of my army if the trouble should escalate. I hope it does not come to that, but I will keep that promise all the same. Strange things have happened here as well. A fortnight ago, perhaps on the very same day as your Atalanta's capture, a vampire attacked my daughter, Felicity, at a ball. My four children managed to slay it, but it has left my people shaken. I fear there may be trouble brewing in Arcamira.

King Markus Avalon

Chapter 2

Archimedes' Gifts

"Why didn't you wake us?" said Felicity, her arms crossed tightly below her bosom, her breakfast of eggs, porridge, and blueberries congealing in front of her.

The family was seated at one end of the sprawling, oak, dining table. It seated over one hundred lords and ladies at feasts and events, but most of the time only the western side was utilized, the family seated next to each other with Markus at the very head.

"What need was there to wake you, child?" said Markus, after swallowing his bacon.

"Perhaps to let us see an elf," said Felicity her eyes wide to emphasize what she thought was obvious.

"We don't gawk at guests, dear," said Isabelle. "Especially not the elven king's personal messenger."

"I wasn't going to gawk," said Felicity, her mouth a small 'o' of outrage.

"Please," said Andrew, only partially under his breath, "I'd put my gold on you drooling all down your front."

Felicity's right arm drew back for a punch, but Markus reached over Michael and grabbed her fist.

"Heaven's sake, Felicity!" said Isabelle in her best scolding tone. "At the breakfast table? Don't make me regret allowing you and your sister to train with the men."

"Bloodying his face won't do any good to stifle his tongue," said Markus, a mirthful twitch playing at the corner of his mouth. "Best to remain ladylike."

Felicity held up her chin and narrowed her blue eyes at Andrew as she lowered her fist. She sniffed and said, "Do you think the attacks are connected, Father?"

"As unlikely as it seems, I suppose it's possible since King Zanthus believes Atalanta's kidnapper crossed our border," said Markus, scratching at his red beard. "I've always considered him astute and level-headed. Sometimes too level-headed, as if he's bored with it all, but I suppose that comes with living for a few hundred years. He's rather shaken now, though, and I admit that troubles me."

"If the vampire and the cyclops creature are connected, is someone else behind the attacks?" said Michael. "I've never heard of vampires allying with other creatures."

"I've never heard of a two-headed cyclops," said Andrew.

"What's the motivation?" said Andromeda. "Who would want to kidnap princesses and why? I would suppose it has to do with leverage against Arcamira's two great kings, but why hasn't Zanthus received demands if that's the case?"

"Slow down," said Markus, a rumbling chuckle shaking his wide chest. "I haven't got the answers; I only just learned of the questions."

"We need to train harder," said Andromeda, mostly to herself.

"Enough with training," said Michael, slamming a fist down on the table hard enough to make his goblet wobble. "We should be joining the search parties. It's time for action, not practice. I don't want to stay locked up in the castle like a child anymore."

"I'll not have it," said Isabelle, needing only the sharpness of her voice and blaze of her eyes to convey her passion in place of a fist. "It's far too dangerous; you're all too young."

"I'm twenty," said Michael, puffing out his substantial chest. "I've been called a man for two years now. I'm not too young. It's time I took up all my duties."

"I'm not too young, either," said Felicity. "I just turned eighteen last month. We've been training for something like this since we were ten."

"What good is our training if we don't use it, Mother?" said Michael. "How can we call ourselves rulers and protectors of our people if we sit back and let good soldiers go out and brave the unknown without us?"

"These are not normal circumstances," said Isabelle, chewing at her lower lip. "The true enemy is unknown, and there are evils involved that our kind has not truly faced in over a century. You only just began to train to fight the Diseased Ones."

"We aren't children anymore, Mother," said Felicity, her arms crossed once more.

"I say we let Felicity and Michael go," said Markus, making Isabelle pale and look at him with desperate eyes. "They speak the truth; they're adults now. We must let them make their own decisions. We will send them in a party with our best men. Andrew and Andromeda will stay here and continue their training."

"What?" the twins yelled in furious, echoing unison.

"You heard me clearly," said Markus, a warning etched in the set of his jaw.

"That's not fair!" said Andromeda. "We're just as good as they are."

"We aren't children," said Andrew. "We should be allowed to go, too."

"You are children," said Isabelle. "You will obey your father and stay here."

"We have as much duty to the people as they do," said Andrew. "We're of no use here. You promised Zanthus to send your best after his daughter. We are the best. We have better training than most of the soldiers. We've been trained exactly like all the knights."

"I'm a better sword fighter than Felicity," said Andromeda, earning herself a deadly look from Felicity that promised later retribution. "Just ask Archimedes. If she's allowed to go, I should be."

"Your sword skills are not in question here," said Markus, "your maturity is. My word is final. I'll hear no more protest."

Silence fell over the table, and Felicity gave Andromeda a wicked, triumphant smirk over her porridge spoon.

Andrew scraped his own spoon along the bottom of his bowl and mumbled, "We'll just go after them."

"What was that?" said Markus, each word slow and enunciated.

Andrew studied his food.

"We'll go after them anyways," said Andromeda, startling the whole table with the uncharacteristic strength of her voice and the proud set of her shoulders. "Even if you lock us in our rooms when they leave. Eventually, we'll find a way to go after them. And I think you know it." She looked directly into her father's face without the slightest hint of fear, but also without defiance. She was calm, steady, reasonable. She addressed her father as a peer. "So, the question becomes whether we are safer going along with the party or chasing after them by ourselves in the Northern Wood."

Andrew looked terrified for his twin's wellbeing. Felicity's cheeks were red with anger. She seemed the only one to think Andromeda would get her way this time. Michael's bottom jaw hung slack on its hinge. Isabelle's face was blank until she looked to her husband. Then she looked worried.

Markus leaned back in his chair to study his youngest daughter. He met her gray eyes with his blue ones. She was the only child not to inherit the trait, but she was like her father in other ways. They both shared a calm demeanor and the ability to logically and knowledgably address problems under pressure. Markus's relationship with Andromeda had always been more adult than those he shared with his other children. Inherently curious, she often came to him with questions he actually had to puzzle over—questions of morality and theory that sparked serious discussion. The question she had put before him now was defiant in nature, but mature in delivery. Her point was clear; now he had to decide whether or not arguing with it was the correct choice.

"The answer to your question is obvious," said Markus, a smile gently curving his mouth. "The real question is whether I'm going to indulge it at all."

"I think it would be unwise not to," said Andromeda, "considering the consequences."

"You will stay with at least two members of the party at all times," said Markus, keeping his face stern as Andrew's and Andromeda's lit up. "You will follow orders, not give them. You will not engage in combat of any kind unless absolutely necessary. If you do find the elven princess and her captor, you will hang back while the rest of the party engages. I will give the party leader instructions to send you back to the castle with an escort if any of these rules are violated. Do you understand?"

"Markus!" said Isabelle, her thin, black brows slanted at a dangerous angle. "You can't be serious!"

"I think they're ready, Isabelle," said Markus, gentle but authoritative. The king's word was law, and not even the queen could go against it. "They've been properly trained, and they are right; things like this are their natural royal duty."

"They're children, Markus!" said Isabelle, tears shimmering in her eyes. "Our children. Would you really cast them out into unknown danger?"

"Let me speak with your mother, children," said Markus.

The siblings nodded obediently and moved the remainder of their breakfast down to the other end of the long table.

Markus then leaned in to his wife, gently sweeping aside her hair to wipe a tear from her cheek as he whispered in her ear. "There are only hints that the beast and the princess are even in our lands. It's highly unlikely they will find anything, much less the enemy they seek. I think it best if we indulge their desire for adventure now, instead of in certain battle. Letting them go may very well serve to wipe away some of the imagined excitement and glory of such things. Long, uneventful rides in the woods aren't exactly what they're dreaming of, and that's most likely exactly what they're going to get."

"Do you really think so, or are you only trying to quiet me?"

"I truly do."

Isabelle bit her lip and squeezed her husband's hand. "All right."

"I expect you to train twice as hard today," said Markus, raising his voice to reach his children. "You only have three more days to prepare yourselves for your first quest."

Andrew sloshed wine from his goblet as he raised his arm in victory.

"Oh, thank you, Father, Mother," said Andromeda. "We won't let you down."

Michael watched the twin's celebration with amusement and shared excitement, but Felicity scowled.

"Precious Andromeda gets her way again," she hissed.

* * *

The day before the search parties were to head out, Archimedes summoned the four siblings to the weaponry.

It was a long traipse into the older, danker portion of the castle where the floors and walls were made of thick, square, gray stone. In the center of the weaponry, stone-topped tables laden with short swords, knives, daggers, and arrows stood in neat rows. The walls were covered with broadswords, rapiers, shields, spears, and bows hung up on iron settings. All steel weapons had recently received a layer of silver, and even in the slim ray of light coming through a single, small window, the weapons shone.

"You four already have daggers, swords, shields, all the basics, so you won't be needing any of those," said Archimedes, looking pointedly at Andrew who was reaching up to grab an ornate shield adorned with the Avalon eagle. "You'll be needing some of the old weapons—those used for killing the Diseased Ones. We don't have many left in acceptable shape, but I managed. You might also need to restock on arrows. Oh, and I almost forgot; you'll be needing new armor."

"Oh good," said Felicity, "my mail doesn't fit me right anymore."

"I've been wanting a new breastplate," said Michael. "I was thinking of having garnet's put in place of the eagle's eyes."

"No mail, no breastplates," said Archimedes. "Vampires and werewolves move like nothing you've ever seen ... well, I guess now you have. Mail is too restrictive. You need something lighter."

With a flick of his first two fingers, he directed them to the farthest table where four sets of black leather shirts, breeches, and arm coverlets lay. Andromeda leaned in closer, and her nose wrinkled.

"A corset," she said, looking betrayed. "That's your idea of armor? An infernal corset!"

"Shut your gob or I'll shut it for you," said Archimedes, his gruff snarling voice not to be questioned. "These are my own design, and it cost the King and Queen a small fortune to have these made for you. Though I suspect after the attack at the ball that money was no object to your improved safety. The very night of the attack, they set me to work commissioning and designing nearly everything I'm about to show you. So be grateful."

"Pardon my insolence, master," said Michael, "but that vampire was brutally strong as well as fast. How is boiled leather going to protect us?"

"God above! If your parents knew how daft you all were, they wouldn't be letting you go out on this search, I guarantee it. You think boiled leather costs a fortune, boy?"

"So what is it?" said Michael, crossing his large arms and furrowing his brow to show his distaste for being insulted.

"The best lightweight armor in all of Arcamira. That leather you're wrinkling your noses at is elvish, made from their legendary stallions and imbued with their magic. It is far more flexible than ordinary cow leather, and considerably harder to penetrate. Still, a bloodsucker or moon mutt will still get through it. That's why there's a layer of dwarvish chain mail inside."

The siblings looked at the leather armor with newfound respect. Andromeda traced the smallest, slimmest set with her fingertips. Michael uncrossed his arms. The dwarves had died out nearly five hundred years ago, and their underground and cavernous homes had been raided by every other race in Arcamira. Few artifacts were left. The Avalon's had two full sets of dwarvish armor, but due to the small stature of the pieces, they were kept in the treasury instead of the armory.

"It was taken from the sets in the treasury," said Archimedes. "It took a dozen metal workers to figure out how to detach the pieces. The plan was to rework it into shorts and breeches, but no one could figure out how, so they just slapped it in the leather and stitched it up. Still, it'll do the trick. And it isn't a corset." He shot Andromeda a look. "It ties in the back, yes, but there's no ribbing, and no need to tighten it until you can't breathe. The boys' tie the same way. No need to fret."

Andromeda smiled sheepishly and fiddled with her hair.

"Thank you, master," she said. "It's wonderful."

Following her lead, the other siblings conveyed their thanks. Archimedes grunted in welcome and moved to the next table where a small array of strange weapons was laid.

Michael picked up a leather arm guard normally used for archery that had a strange contraption fixed atop, much like a simple, miniature crossbow. He turned it side to side in his hand. On the underside, where it tied over the arm, there was a pocket filled with thin wooden stakes tipped in silver. Michael tapped the tips with his finger. Archimedes held out his hand, his fly-away brows raised expectantly. Michael handed it over.

"This is my own invention, as well," he said. "Of course, I

had to have the smiths make it. Not much good at that sort of thing myself. Notch the stake in the hollow of the bar, just like you would a crossbow. When you pull back the string to set it, you will see a thin steel bar emerge from the leather at your palm. Clench your fist to push the bar and loose the stake."

The siblings leaned in to examine the contraption, but Archimedes handed it back to Michael.

"Try it out," he said. "I had you in mind when I designed it. You fight heavy handed with your broadsword and shield. It gives you power, but hinders your speed. This will give a quicker kill method. It will also be handy if you are disarmed."

Michael followed Archimedes' instructions, and sure enough, when he pulled back the string, there was a faint whir and click noise within the arm guard. A thin bar the length of Michael's palm slipped out of the folds of the leather. Michael aimed at the open window and made a fist. The arrow loosed from the mechanism with a whoosh and hurtled out the window.

"Thank you, master."

Archimedes nodded and picked up one of four identical silver cylinders. Two small buttons were placed on opposite sides of the cylinder. Archimedes pressed the two buttons at the same time and a long, silver stake popped out with the high, melodic ring of metal on metal. They all jumped in surprise. Archimedes chuckled.

"No need to worry about sticking yourself with these, but if you press both buttons at the same time, you'll stick anything else."

He handed one to each of them.

"This is for Andrew," said Archimedes.

"Oh, thank you, master," said Andrew. He'd been eyeing the silver crossbow the entire time. He had always had a penchant for archery that far surpassed that of his siblings.

"The smiths melted down dwarvish metal to make the string. The same that's in your armor. You will need to wear a full glove to pull it back, or you may end up with bloody fingers after a few shots. The mechanisms are far more powerful than an ordinary wooden crossbow. It will shoot farther, faster, and truer. With silver-tipped arrows, you can take down a moon mutt as easily as an ordinary wolf."

Archimedes watched Andrew cradle the bow like a child, and smiled. With a flourish, he picked up the next item on the table. It had the base and trigger of an ordinary wooden crossbow, but at the end was not an arrow but a large metal hook. Strangest of all was the large reel of cord protruding from the side.

"Felicity," he said, picking it up, "I have never forgotten the day you jumped from the top of the stables as a child and managed to break only your wrist. I carried you to the physician and asked you what in blazes you were thinking and you looked at me and said, 'I'm going to fly, master.'"

Felicity smiled, a rosy blush coming to her cheeks.

"This may get you as close as you've ever come, my dear. When the trigger is pulled it shoots out this hook, along with an elvish horsehair cord wound in this reel. It will hold your weight. You can use it to scale mountains, swing yourself across gaps, climb to the top of trees or rooftops—anything you wish. It does take a while to wind back up, though, so keep that in mind."

Felicity surprised everyone by flinging her arms around Archimedes' neck. The training master's grizzly eyebrows flew up in shock as Felicity's golden curls tickled his face. He cleared his throat, his face softening an inch, and patted Felicity on the shoulder.

"You're welcome, child."

Felicity stepped back with a somewhat embarrassed smile and took the grappling hook from Archimedes.

"And now for Andromeda's gift," said Archimedes after clearing his throat one more time.

The last object on the table did not look like a weapon, and

Andromeda's eyes narrowed as she picked up the ornate bracelet.

"It is beautiful, master," said Andromeda, unable to fully hide her disappointment.

"It is much more than a beautiful ornament, child," said Archimedes. "This treasure has been kept in the vaults for centuries, used every now and then by a member of the royal family, and then hidden away again. It was a spoil of war back before the alliance of elves and men. No one remembers exactly when or where it was taken. It is imbued with old and powerful elfin magic. It allows you to sense the thoughts and feelings of animals. All elves have the power to some degree, but the magic contained in this bracelet is not ordinary, even for elves. I'm sure you can think of ways to make it useful in battle. I decided to give it to you because you've always been extra fond of animals."

Andromeda held the bracelet up to her eyes in reverent awe. Thin gold and silver vines wove together in a perfect ring. She looked to Archimedes open-mouthed, temporarily robbed of speech.

"Put it on," said Archimedes with a grin.

Andromeda had never been fond of bracelets or any jewelry that dangled in her way. She pushed the bracelet up near her shoulder to wear it as an armband.

No sooner had she let go of the band than her brain was assaulted by a rush of conflicting emotions and snippets of thoughts. She clapped her hands to her ears to muffle or silence them, but they were inside her.

"Andromeda? Andromeda, are you all right?"

Andromeda heard her twin's voice through a tunnel. She was feeling scared, hungry, happy, sad, and confused all at the same time. Half her thoughts didn't make any sense. She had to get back to her hole. She was anticipating the taste of mouse. She shut her eyes and doubled over.

Someone grabbed her wrist, and she cried out. Suddenly, all of the alien thoughts and feelings vanished. When she opened her eyes she was face to face with Michael. The bracelet was in his hand.

He chucked her under the chin. "All right?"

She nodded and swept her hair back behind her ear.

"I thought something like that might happen," said Archimedes.

"You could have warned me," said Andromeda.

"I thought you should experience it once," he said with a shrug.

"What did it do?" asked Andrew.

"I can't fully explain," said Andromeda, shaking her head. "Lots of voices and feelings all jumbled together. I supposed I was sensing the creatures outside." She looked at Archimedes. "How am I supposed to control it?"

"Simple focus," said Archimedes. "Concentrate as if you were in battle facing a single opponent. Focus on what you want to hear. The magic will do the rest. You'll need practice. It's like building a new muscle. Try again."

Andromeda took back her bracelet and pushed it into place. She was better prepared for the wave of feeling and sound, and it did not seem so loud or frightening, merely confusing. She walked to the window and looked out. She spotted a sparrow perched in a tree and concentrated with all her might. The other thoughts faded to whispers and her chest swelled with the little bird's happiness as he sang.

"It's absolutely wonderful!" she said.

Her concentration broke and the river of alien emotion spilled from its bed. She yanked the bracelet off and knitted her brow in frustration.

"In time, child. In time."

* * *

"Do you think the elf princess is even still alive?" said Andrew.

"She'd better be," said Felicity, "or else we're just going to be riding around aimlessly in the woods."

The four siblings rode side by side, just behind their parents, at the head of the small party of twelve that would accompany them into the forest, along with three knights who would serve as the king and queen's escort back to the castle. The search party consisted of handpicked soldiers, huntsman, and trappers, assembled for their various skills in fighting, tracking, and survival. Markus and Isabelle had insisted on travelling to the edge of the Northern Wood to see the party off. They had already been on the move a full two days, but were expected to reach the wood before midday. Other parties had headed out with them, but had branched off in different directions to cover the entirety of the Northern region of the Avalon kingdom. Most would be entering the woods and systematically heading toward the mountains.

"There's a good chance that's all we'll be doing anyway, whether she's alive or not," said Michael. "I hope she is, though, and I want us to be the ones to bring her back. Maybe then we won't have to haggle with Mother and Father the next time there's a call to arms."

"Even if we don't find Atalanta, our journey may not be so uneventful," said Andromeda. "The Northern Wood is still a wild territory. There's only a handful of settlements in the entire region, and it backs up to the mountains. Those haven't been inhabited by anything friendly since the days of the dwarves."

"You think there could be werewolves still living in there?" said Andrew.

"Why not?" said Andromeda with a shrug of her slender shoulders. "They used to rule it. If the vampires aren't truly extinct, who's to say the werewolves are?"

"Now I wish I hadn't asked," said Andrew, swiping his shaggy hair off his brow with a nervous hand.

"Why?"

"There's a full moon tonight."

"I'm more scared of goblins than werewolves," said Felicity with a shudder. "They aren't extinct."

"Did you say something, dear?" said Isabelle, turning in her saddle.

"Nothing of importance, Mother."

The siblings fell silent, and Andromeda took the time to practice using her bracelet, as she did in every spare moment. She chose to focus on Andrew's black stallion and found that his tail swishing and head bobbing was an attempt to impress Felicity's mare.

She could now wear the bracelet at all times, and only utilize its power when desired ... for the most part. Every now and then a particularly strong feeling would break through—a jolt of terror from a pursued hare, a burst of joyful triumph from a predator that landed its prey.

As they crested a hill and looked down onto a flat plain, the woods finally came into view on the horizon, the treetops rich with dark foliage at the height of summer. The mountain range in the far distance was a blur of gray stone and fluffy clouds, and the woods wrapped around it like a cat curling up against its master's leg. Markus stopped his horse and turned to face the party.

"This is where we leave you," he said, his eyes on his children.

"Come down so I can bid you a proper mother's farewell," said Isabelle, sliding from her mount.

Her children obeyed, and Markus followed suit. Isabelle embraced them each in turn, tears glittering in her eyes. She stepped back, and after a few false starts said, "Be safe, darlings."

Markus slapped both his boys on the shoulder and embraced both his girls in a singular bear hug.

"Yes, be safe, but enjoy it," he said with a wink. "Youth has its sweet advantages. One day other responsibilities will keep you from adventure, so enjoy it while you can. I know you'll make me proud."

Michael bowed his head in a gesture of respect, and his siblings followed his example.

"Remember, you obey Sir Gregor's orders, or you'll be sent back home," said Markus, as they remounted. "He is commander of this party."

"I will care for them like my own, Your Majesty," said Gregor.

The siblings turned to look at their newly enforced parental figure with a varying mixture of defiance and resignation. He was completely bald, but he made up for it with a massive black beard that touched his chest. He was the only knight in the search party, and was thus the most richly dressed of the men. His family crest—a brown bear rampant on a field of forest green—was emblazoned on his shield. A brown bear fur was draped over his horse's flank. In midsummer the Northern region was pleasant during the day, but could turn chilly in the night.

"See that you do," said Isabelle, brushing her tears away with swift, rough strokes of her hand.

Gregor bowed as best he could on horseback.

With a last blown kiss, Isabelle nudged her horse and her escort knights broke off to follow her.

"Farewell," said Markus with a wave and a smile. "Enjoy your first quest. You'll remember it forever."

"All right, let's move on," said Gregor, when the king and queen were a fair distance. "Time is of the essence for the princess. I believe she would appreciate swift horses and chastise complaint."

With that he kicked his stallion and set the pace at a canter toward the woods. The pace was short lived. The wild forest had no need for the pathways of men, and once they were a mere fifty paces into the dense trees, they were forced to rein in their horses to a trot.

The forest contained more evergreens than the siblings had ever seen. Pine needles cushioned the footfalls of their horses and sent up such a strong aroma it tickled the nose. Massive oaks and other deciduous trees towered overhead as well, mingling with the evergreens in a dense canopy that dimmed even the midday summer sun. It was significantly cooler, and some of the men shrugged on their furs. The forest was alive with the rustling and chirruping of forest creatures.

Andromeda scrunched her eyes and nose.

"Lots of chatter?" said Andrew, taking notice.

"Yes. I may have to take it off for a while."

"You should keep it on and practice shutting them out," said Michael. "It's going to be like this the whole journey, and I think it would be wise for you to keep it on. It could be of use if anything unsavory attempts to sneak up on us."

"If she shuts them out, how will she hear them if there is danger?" said Felicity.

Michael's brow furrowed.

"I'll figure something out," said Andromeda.

Ahead of them, Gregor slowed his horse to a fast walk.

"How are we to make any progress at this pace?" said Felicity. "I thought time was of the essence."

"Moving quickly isn't of much use if we pass over a footprint or some other sign of her whereabouts, princess," said Gregor.

"What exactly does a two-headed cyclops' footprint look like, Sir Gregor?" said Felicity with a cocked eyebrow.

"His two heads will have little effect on his step, my lady," said Gregor, turning to fix Felicity with a hard look, "but his small stature and hunched spine will. His prints will be child-like and his gait stunted."

Andrew snickered at Felicity's abashed look, and she swatted him with her horsewhip.

By the time sunset drew near, with no sign of a monster of any sort, it was too dark to continue. Fortunately, one of the huntsmen had managed to take down a deer along the way. Gregor halted the party in a small clearing by a stream, and everyone began to lay out their bedding and help set up the fire to prepare the venison. By the time night had fully fallen, Gregor cut off the first hunk of meat from the spit, and the party settled down for venison, bread, and cheese.

"I hope it gets more exciting than this, or I may die of boredom on this so-called adventure," said Felicity, daintily eating pieces of bread she picked off the loaf.

"Be careful what you wish for, Your Highness," said one of the huntsmen. "Tonight's a full moon. I'd rather spend a hundred dreary days out in this wilderness than have one encounter with a werewolf."

"You truly believe there are werewolves still in this wood?" said a trapper in a derisive tone.

"Why not?" said Andromeda.

The trapper faltered for a second as he turned his attention from the huntsman, but soon his lip regained its condescending sneer.

"They're extinct, Princess."

"It wasn't long ago that vampires were believed extinct, but I saw one with my own eyes," said Andromeda. "Why should it be so foolish to think werewolves still roam here?"

"Because I've seen just about every inch of these woods with my own eyes," said the trapper. "I've trapped and skinned every sort of creature in these woods since I was boy, and I've never come across scent or sign of a moon mutt. They're gone. Hunted down to the last pup."

"Just because you haven't seen one, doesn't mean they aren't there. Can you see every inch of the wood all at once?"

The trapper opened his mouth to retort, but Gregor's black boot crashed into the pine needles between the trapper and Andromeda.

"Werewolves or not, everyone will be taking turns on guard tonight. You can be first, Macon. If you can keep your eyes open as easily as your mouth, you shouldn't have a problem."

"Don't I get a partner?" said Macon, eyeing Gregor as if he was imagining putting a fist to his jaw. "Easier to stay awake that way."

"You're too right," said Gregor with a disturbingly cheery, yellow-toothed grin. "You get the pleasure of my company tonight."

"Oh, lovely."

* * *

The full moon was directly overhead when Andromeda's torso shot up in the midst of sleeping bodies. The forest that had teemed with the sounds of life was completely silent save for the occasional snore. Even the air was still.

"Felicity?" said Andromeda, shaking her sister by the shoulder, her whisper high-pitched and strained.

"What?" groaned Felicity, swatting Andromeda's hand from her shoulder.

"Felicity, the animals."

"What about them?"

"They're running. All of them."

Felicity propped herself up on her elbow, searching her sister's face in the moonlight.

"It's probably just a coyote or something," she said, but she did not sound totally convinced.

"Felicity, it's all of them! There's even a bear clearing out about four furlongs away from here. I can sense whatever it is they're afraid of, Felicity. It's like … like a big shadow, and it's angry. Really angry. It feels different from all the other animals. I can't totally get a sense of it. I think it might … might be a werewolf."

Felicity sat up like a puppet whose string had been yanked.

"You're sure?"

"Are you both all right?"

Felicity and Andromeda looked directly upward, following the sound of the familiar voice. Andrew peered down at them from his perch in the tree they were laying beneath.

"Andromeda says the animals are running from a werewolf," said Felicity, a tremble in her voice.

"Are you sure?" said Andrew, raising his crossbow.

"I think so," said Andromeda.

"Michael, wake up," said Felicity, smacking him in the shoulder with a backhanded swing of her arm.

He grunted.

"Something the matter?" said the huntsman they'd spoken to at supper. He was walking toward them from his watch post on the other side of the clearing.

"Michael, wake up," said Felicity, shaking him with both hands now.

"What?"

"Werewolf, Michael, werewolf," said Felicity, her eyes wild.

"Werewolf?" said the huntsman, his hand going for the sword at his belt.

He was halfway to the siblings when the snarl emanated from the trees on his right. He whirled to face the sound just as the beast leapt from the dark of the dense wood. Nine feet tall and covered in shaggy gray fur, it stood up on its two back legs like a man and wrinkled its muzzle in a teeth-baring snarl. Tattered shreds of a tunic and breeches hung from its body. Beneath its fur, muscles of a man flexed as it crouched down and faced off with the huntsman.

The man drew his sword and took a step back. The sword shook in his hand. The werewolf pounced with its jaws wide and collided with the huntsman, swatting his sword away with a swipe of its black claws. The open jaws clamped shut on the huntsman's throat and ripped the esophagus, sending blood spurting over its wrinkled muzzle.

The whole camp was on their feet or scrambling out of their

blankets, drawing weapons and screaming. Michael was wide awake now, and helped his sisters to their feet, pulling them around behind the tree where Andrew was perched.

The werewolf threw the bloody carcass aside and eyed the company. Then, with fangs dripping blood, it threw back its huge head to howl at the moon.

Chapter 3

The Hybrid King

"Andrew, shoot it!" said Michael, craning his head to see into the branches.

"No need to yell!" said Andrew from his perch, the arrow already back and ready to fly.

The werewolf crouched on all fours, preparing to spring at Sir Gregor, the only man brave enough to approach it with broadsword brandished high. Andrew readjusted his aim and loosed the silver-tipped arrow. The werewolf let out a clipped yelp as the arrow pierced its eye and embedded in the soft tissue of its brain. It took one stilted step before crashing to the earth, muzzle first.

Andrew slung his legs over the branch and dangled for a moment one handed, his silver bow in the other, before landing on the ground in a crouch. Andrew gave his siblings a nervous smile and a shaky chuckle. He held up the bow and said, "Remind me to thank Archimedes again."

Andromeda let out the breath she'd been holding in a loud gust. Michael clapped Andrew on the back.

"My little brother, the werewolf slayer," he said. "Who would have guessed?"

Felicity cleared her throat to ensure Andrew's attention before chucking him under the chin.

"Still the best shot in the kingdom," she said.

Andrew held himself straighter, a grin dominating his face.

As Michael and Felicity moved to join the rest of the party gathering about the werewolf carcass, Andromeda imbued her own thanks on her twin by brushing his wrist with her fingers as she passed him. As children, the simple gesture had solidified as a sign of affection, thanks, and comfort between them. They did not feel each other's pain or constantly speak in unison as some twins were rumored to, but they had formed a silent language known only to them.

"Do you think we should keep the head for Father?" said Andrew as he took a few rushed steps to catch up to his twin. "It's a far better trophy than that elk I killed last summer, and he mounted that in the dining hall."

"That might turn out to be a little more gruesome than you're imagining," said Andromeda.

"Why?"

"Take a look," said Andromeda.

They had reached the throng around the werewolf. Andrew elbowed his way in, and Andromeda followed in his path.

An extremely hairy, middle-aged man with large yellow canines growing over his lips lay dead on a bed of fur in the grass, hardly covered by the destroyed remnants of his clothing. But even as the crowd watched, some of the hair on his back and legs was shed and blew off in the breeze. His teeth shrank before their eyes until they were no longer fangs, but ordinary canines that fit easily in the slack mouth. Andrew's arrow was still embedded in his right eye, oozing blood and goo.

Andrew paled, his Adam's apple rising and falling in a gulp. He jumped when Gregor clapped him on the shoulder with his massive, callused hand.

"Great shooting, Your Highness," said Gregor. "That's a man's kill. You may just have saved my life."

"Macon wasn't so lucky," said one of the men.

The poor hunter lay next to the werewolf carcass, throat gashed and eyes wide in terror.

"We should bury them," said Andrew. "Both of them."

"The wolf, Your Highness?" said one of the soldiers. "He doesn't deserve the honor."

"When the moon isn't full, he's the same as you and me," said Andrew, rounding on the soldier, his face suddenly vicious and his hands clenched in fists. "The moon disease makes him not himself. How would you like to lose control of yourself in the night—to hardly remember what you'd done when the disease takes hold?"

It seemed that Andrew had not forgotten all his lessons.

"We'll bury them, Andrew," said Michael, gently pulling Andrew away from the bewildered soldier. "Right here in the clearing. It's as good a place as any."

Howls answered Michael's words. Howls from all directions. The echoes made it impossible to tell how close. Heads snapped up and recently sheathed weapons returned to every hand.

"Werewolves are attracted to the howls of their own kind," said Andromeda, her knuckles white on the hilt of her rapier.

"How many?" Michael asked her. His voice was steady, but his eyes darted around the clearing. He gulped, making his Adam's apple bob in his throat. "How close?"

Andromeda steadied her breathing and closed her eyes. Only her siblings and Gregor paid her any mind. The rest of the men were busy forming a sloppy ring around the camp, shouting to each other.

"Should we run?" said a lanky huntsman standing behind Felicity.

"We'll be slaughtered," said a soldier at Gregor's elbow.

"There's five approaching fast," said Andromeda.

"Five?" said Gregor, his mouth a dark O in the middle of his beard. "I didn't think there were even five still alive."

"How does she know that?" said the nearest trapper.

"Yes," said Gregor, an eyebrow raised at Andromeda, "how do you know that?"

"This elvish bracelet—" she began, pointing to the band on her arm.

"What do we do?" said one of the men, his panicked shout cutting off Andromeda's explanation.

"Get on your horses!" shouted another. "The horses are our

only hope of outrunning them."

Gregor blinked at the words and looked around to find his men untying their frantic horses from the trees. "What? No, we need to form a unit," he said.

The men mounted, still yelling to each other.

"Hurry up. They sound closer," one said.

"Every man for himself."

"Halt!" said Gregor.

A trapper went flying by him on horseback, and Gregor snatched for the horse's reins and missed by centimeters.

"I am commander of this unit, and I said halt! You'll be picked off." The last horse tail disappeared into the dark around the clearing, and Gregor stamped his foot. "Fools! Cowards!"

"They—they're leaving us!" said Felicity, her breathing shallow, her voice on the verge of panic. Despite her creeping terror, she kept her rapier raised and her feet in the proper stance.

"What do we do, Sir Gregor?" said Andromeda, her eyes wide and child-like.

"There's no helping them now. We'll only put ourselves in danger," said Gregor, running a hand roughly through his beard. "My duty is now to you four alone. We stick together here in tight formation. Come, get back to back by the fire. If the moon mutts are anything like regular wolves, they may be wary of flame."

They wordlessly obeyed him, huddling by the fire, backs pressed against each other and weapons held at the ready. The screams started soon after, followed by a chorus of howls, yips, and barks. Even the horses were screaming. The hellish sounds seemed to come from every direction.

"Fools. Damned fools," Gregor muttered each time a scream ripped through the night, but the words were melancholy rather than harsh.

"Andromeda, have any of the wolves been injured?" said

Michael when some of the noise settled.

After a few moments of concentration she said, "I'm not sure. They are harder to access than other animals. I suppose because they are only part animal. I feel only rage when I try to sense them. There are still five, though. All still alive. And … I think they smell us. They are regrouping and coming this way."

"You wouldn't happen to have another of those contraptions, would you?" said Gregor, nodding his head at Andromeda's bracelet.

"Sadly, no. But your sword is going to be a better asset now. They're nearly here."

"Steady, children," said Gregor. "Keep your heads clear."

"Andrew," said Andromeda, the words an urgent hiss, "in front of you. Shoot now."

Andrew could see nothing in the pitch around the moonlit clearing, but he loosed an arrow anyway. There was a whine and a snarl from among the trees.

"Not dead," said Andromeda.

The werewolf crashed into the clearing, running lopsided on all fours, an arrow deep in its shoulder. Andrew fought to steady his shaking hand, and let another arrow fly. The werewolf skidded along the ground on its nose, an arrow in its chest.

"Three approaching together," said Andromeda. "They're splitting off. They're going to surround us. Coming fast."

The crash of foliage echoed from three sides. Andrew shot blind again, but there was no answering whimper.

The wolves crashed through the trees all at once, two with shaggy black pelts, the other a scraggly brown. Gregor met one of the black wolves head on with a war cry. He brought his broadsword down in a sweeping arc and imbedded the silver-washed blade in the beast's skull.

Andrew notched an arrow to take aim at the second black wolf, but it was upon him too quickly. The beast lunged with its deadly jaws, and Michael knocked Andrew out of the way, his sword raised flat side out in a defensive position. The wolf's teeth clamped on the blade and it wrenched the weapon from Michael's grip, slicing its jowls with the razor sharp metal. It bared its teeth in a bloody snarl and swiped at Michael with a clawed paw more like a giant, furry hand. The blow hit Michael square in the chest. His armor protected him, the claws leaving marks in the leather, but he was knocked on his back. Michael stuck out his arm, board-straight, and loaded one of his silver-tipped stakes. The werewolf lunged for his throat, but Michael clenched his fist and sent the stake through its brain. It collapsed on top of him.

At the same time, Andromeda and Felicity met the brown wolf with rapiers drawn. It went for Felicity first, barreling onward like it meant to ram her. It launched itself toward her with its powerful back legs and flew through the air, claws and teeth out. Felicity held her ground. With an upward slash of her sword, Andromeda sliced the lunging beast's belly from the side, and Felicity jumped out of the way as it crashed to the ground. As soon as it hit the grass, it found its footing and whirled on the sisters in a crouch, snapping wildly with its teeth. Even crouched on all fours, the beast's head was level with the girls' chests.

The two girls moved in together, but Andromeda suddenly stopped, a hand pressed to her head. The werewolf fixed its yellow eyes on her, and Felicity took advantage of its distraction and plunged her blade into its neck just as Andromeda screamed, "Gregor, look out!"

Gregor, who was running for the brown wolf, broadsword raised above his head, locked eyes with Andromeda just as the fifth and final wolf—a gray, mangy, half-starved thing—leapt from the trees and collided with him. His sword went flying, and he hit the ground hard enough to concuss himself. The wolf tore into his neck, spraying blood across Gregor's beard, the grass, and its own muzzle. It whimpered when Andrew's arrow struck in the back of its neck, but it kept eating without looking up. Michael's sword cracked its skull, and at last it ceased, but it was far too late for the knight. Much of his face was gone.

Felicity crouched next to him and put a hand to her mouth to stifle a gag.

"If they were hungry, why didn't they eat those cowards?" said Felicity, standing up with angry tears in her eyes and a tight jaw. "Why weren't they enough?"

"Werewolves don't kill to eat," said Andromeda quietly. "They kill out of rage."

* * *

Atalanta huddled in the corner of the stone cell. She used a sharp rock she'd pulled loose from the floor to carve yet another line in the wall. By her count, she had been here for a little over a week.

The cell was dank, musty, and smelled of mold. The only source of light was a small, circular window almost two heads above her. Even on tiptoe, she couldn't see out. A large door made of vertical iron bars held her captive. Atalanta's muscles ached for exercise. Her eyes longed for sunlight. For an elf, it was the worst form of torture. Her very blood ached for nature, but the only nature in her cell was a few rats and numerous bugs.

She peeked into a small hole in the back of the cell to check on the rat family who were her only source of comfort. She could see nothing in the dark crevice, but she could sense them inside when she pressed her hand to the wall. She was certain there were three babies.

She heard footsteps approaching. Odd. She had only just finished the small meal of stale bread, half-rotted fruit, and small bowl of water that was carefully pushed between the bars three times a day.

She walked to the door to press her forehead to the bars and look down the torch-lit hallway. The burly man trudging toward her was the only source of social interaction she'd had throughout her whole captivity, and he wasn't much of a talker. He bore the same sour expression—which seemed permanently stamped on his face—amidst long, scruffy, brown beard and shoulder-length, matted hair. He was a werewolf. Even in his human form, she'd sniffed out the disease in his blood the moment he'd first walked down the hall.

"Back up," he said now, banging his palm against the bars right by her face. "You're coming with me."

"Ask nicely, mutt," said Atalanta, backing up a few paces.

"I speak with my fists, elf," said the werewolf, pulling a key from around his neck and boring into her with his dark eyes. "Keep quiet or I'll break those bird bones of yours—maybe keep an ear for a trophy. Get back against the wall."

She pressed her back to the wall, but her muscles were taut and ready to spring. She was weak from malnutrition, but her adrenaline was buzzing as the werewolf put the key in the lock. It was the first time the door had ever been open. It was her first and possibly her only chance to escape.

He shut the door behind him, but did not lock it. She kept her eyes on it even as he approached her and unhooked the iron shackles from his belt.

"Keep still," he said, his face inches from hers.

Atalanta gagged as his breath hit her face. It smelled of stale meat and rot.

"Been eating rats, dog? I thought that was a cat's favorite food. Do you change into a kitty when the moon is full?"

With a dog-like snarl, he grabbed hold of her long, auburn hair and yanked her head sideways.

Atalanta ignored the pain and kept her face calm as she said, "Quite a grip, scruffy. I'm very impressed."

With a grunt of rage, he flipped her around by her hair and shoved her against the wall, face first. With one hand still wrapped in her hair, he clamped a shackle around her left hand with the other. He reached for her right, his fingers brushing her wrist, but she raised her arm and jammed her elbow into his nose. He howled in pain and put his free hand to his nose, but did not release her hair. She spun, ignoring the pain as hair ripped from her head, and swung the loose shackle hanging from her wrist into the side of his head. The blow staggered him, and he let go. Summoning her remaining strength, she jumped and gave him a spinning kick to the throat. He fell sideways, and his head smacked the stone wall. He slumped to the floor, his eyelids fluttering as he struggled to stay conscious, and groaned. She snatched the key from around his neck, yanking it free when the chain tangled in his hair, smiling at the sound of hair ripping free from his scalp. She got out the iron door and locked it behind her.

"I wonder how long it will take for them to come looking for you, doggy," said Atalanta, grinning for the first time in a long time.

The werewolf rubbed his head and looked at her with his lip curled in a snarl. She waved at him, and to her surprise, he grinned. Her muscles tensed. How had she not sensed it, heard it, smelled it?

She turned slowly to find herself face to face with a tall, pale man with dark hair and a red mouth. He grabbed her arms and held them tightly to her side before she could make a move. She had not sensed him because he had no heartbeat. She had not heard him because he moved like a ghost. She had not smelled him because she could not distinguish his scent from the rot and decay of the dungeon. She swallowed hard. She had never seen a vampire before.

"Well, well, well, Nathaniel, his Majesty was right. She did get the best of you," the vampire drawled in the dialect of the Southern regions, sounding dreadfully bored.

The werewolf, Nathaniel, growled deep in his throat as he rose to his feet. The vampire smiled, revealing his enlarged canines. It ignited something primal in Atalanta, and she thrashed in the bloodsucker's grasp, but his claw-like fingernails dug into her ivory skin and she could not free her arms from her sides.

"It would be best to cease your struggles, my dear. I am not like this buffoon. I don't bleed," the vampire said, forcing Atalanta's arms behind her back and closing the loose shackle around her right wrist in one fluid motion. He looked over Atalanta's head at Nathaniel and said, "His Majesty will have to hear about this, you know. I've tried to tell him so many times: never send a werewolf to do anything of importance."

Atalanta's mind raced. A vampire and a werewolf together. She had never heard of such a thing. Vampires and werewolves hated each other. Who was their king?

Nathaniel rose from the cell floor, wiping blood from his nose. He ran at the vampire and slammed into the locked door.

"I swear, Thetis, one of these days I'm going to drive a stake through your heart!" he said, reaching through the bars, his hairy arms brushing Atalanta's face as he swiped at the vampire.

Thetis looked coolly at Nathaniel with dark blue eyes. "A cage suits you, dog."

Nathaniel screamed curses, incoherent with rage. Each curse was lost in vicious snarls, growls, and even barks. His brown eyes were crazed. Tonight was the second night of the full moon cycle, and Atalanta feared the man might transform and break out of the cell.

"Now, now Nathaniel," said Thetis, clucking his tongue, "that temper of yours is what gets you in trouble with his Majesty."

Nathaniel backed up from the bars, hands in fists at his sides, panting hard. His whole body shook.

"Are you going to settle down, so I can let you out?" said Thetis with a wicked smirk. "It's probably best that you explain in person how you almost let our lovely guest escape."

"The little harlot caught me off guard!" said Nathaniel, sucking in slow, raspy breaths to calm himself. "Next time, I'll wring her scrawny neck."

"Oh, I can think of much better things to do to a pretty neck like this," said Thetis, tracing a finger along Atalanta's throat.

She shivered and thrashed again, but Thetis grabbed the chain linking the shackles and turned her to face the way he had come. He picked up the key from the floor and freed Nathaniel.

Atalanta held her head high as Thetis shoved her down the passageway, Nathaniel skulking behind them. They came to a steep set of stairs with a large, wooden door at the top. Thetis opened it and shoved her through. She blinked in the sudden light. It wasn't nearly as bright as sunlight and it had a sort of bluish glow, but it was still much brighter than the dungeon she had been inhabiting for the past week. Once her eyes adjusted, she began to take in her surroundings. They had entered a domed fortress made entirely of stone. The bluish glow came from lit torches, enclosed in blue glass, lining the walls. Atalanta looked above her and saw at least five circular levels where monsters bearing the faces of men and women milled about like a pack of lazy dogs on a hot summer's day. Each level had stone railings on the side to prevent someone from falling to their death. She almost laughed at the idea of vampires and werewolves being concerned with safety.

Everyone they passed stared as Thetis pushed her up flights of stairs and through back hallways until she had completely lost her bearings, even though she had been paying very close attention, looking for an exit. There were so many different doors, stairways, and passages all leading in a circular fashion that she began to feel dizzy. The smell of dog and death met her nose at every turn, and she began to feel nauseous.

At last, Thetis stopped abruptly in front of a set of tall, wooden, double doors with gold knockers, and Atalanta had to steady herself on the stone wall.

"Here we are, my dear," crooned Thetis. "You're very lucky. The king wishes to speak to you. It is a high honor. Be sure to kneel."

Atalanta mustered her best scowl in response.

As Thetis reached for a knocker, Nathaniel took a step forward so that he was on the other side of Atalanta and took hold of her arm. Thetis smirked.

"Trying to make it look as if you had something to do with her safe arrival, eh, Nathaniel?" he said.

Nathaniel responded with a throaty growl and started muttering angrily to himself. Thetis held his toothy smile as he grabbed the golden knocker and banged it three times.

"Enter."

The voice made the hairs on the back of Atalanta's neck stand on edge. It was smooth and satiny, but somehow alien and threatening, like the low warning growl of a predator. Her pointed ears twitched like a rabbit sensing danger.

When Thetis opened the door, she firmly planted her feet and prepared to resist, but to no avail. Thetis and Nathaniel wrestled her inside.

It was not often that Atalanta was stripped of her confidence, but the creature—the horror—before her made her weak in the knees. She wanted to scream, to run, but her voice and legs would not obey.

The creature sat in a high-backed chair lined in purple velvet. Thick black hair covered his body, sprouting from between the buttons of his dirty white shirt and out of his collar. It was sparse in some places and thick in others, giving him the look of a mangy dog. Beneath the sparse patches, his skin was sallow and pale gray like a corpse. His face was disfigured by a short, hairless dog snout. The skin of his face was leathery, gray, and mostly hairless, though a dark stubble on his jaw suggested that he shaved. Large vampire fangs came down over his bottom lip. Dog-like ears poked out from the thick, shoulder-length mane of black hair on his head. Beneath almost ludicrously bushy and tangled black eyebrows, his eyes were bright orange with slit-like pupils. They looked cruel ... and hungry. He tapped long, sharp, yellow fingernails on the arm of his chair. Even his hands and fingers were hairy. Hairy, paw-like feet with long silver claws stuck out of his ragged grey trousers.

Over the top of his pauper's ensemble, he wore a purple velvet cape clasped at his throat. Atop his head he wore a crown formed of what looked terribly like the bones of children. He examined Atalanta with his orange eyes and his face contorted in an evil grimace that was meant to be a smile. One side of his muzzle pulled up above his gums like a snarling dog and revealed yellow, canine-like teeth.

"Princess, welcome to the palace of King Tyrannus," he said, and Atalanta tried not to gag as a forked tongue danced along his teeth when he spoke her name. "What do you think of it?"

"I find your cave much too dark, and it smells of mold, putrid blood, and disease."

The monster king chuckled, and she wished she hadn't spoken. It was the sound of claws on stone.

"As fiery as your hair, I see," he said. "Don't care much for fire. I have no need for it. It does nothing to warm me. Blood, though, that's a better analogy, don't you think? Fresh blood warms me to my core." He leaned forward in his chair and licked his jowls. "I desire the blood of your people and the blood of your human cousins, too. The two races that pushed my kind to the brink of extinction. I plan to return the favor, and I'll be far more thorough."

"Your kind?" said Atalanta, her eyebrow raised in mockery to distract from her paling complexion. "What exactly is your kind?"

"I am one of a kind, princess," he said. "A mix of the two greatest species in history: werewolf and vampire."

"It's impossible," said Atalanta, but she could smell the truth.

"Is it?" said Tyrannus. "I desired immortality from the moment I was old enough to understand what it was. The desire is in everyone's hearts. Death is feared by all. Most are simply too cowardly and lazy to go looking for the solution."

"Only fools think they can cheat death," said Atalanta, repeating a favorite adage of her father's.

"I do not wish to cheat it. I wish to conquer it," said Tyrannus. "At the age of twenty-five, I got my wish. Back in those times, the massacres had just begun, and I found a vampire who desired to carry on his kind. He would grant me my wish, but in return for his service, my sire required that I be his servant for a space of five years. I was his ... daily snack, shall we say. He drained me in small amounts daily and in return injected me with small amounts of the venom that would eventually turn me into a vampire.

"The night I was bitten by the werewolf, I was bringing my sire his dinner. Young blonde maidens were his favorite. Apparently, the werewolf had a penchant for them as well. I was bitten in the struggle.

"Had I been a full vampire, the bite would have simply healed and had no effect. If I had been fully human, I would have either died or become a werewolf. Since I was neither, the vampire venom and the werewolf saliva comingled. The transformation may well have killed me had my vampire sire not taken pity on his poor servant and performed a full vampire transformation so that I might heal.

"But, alas, the two species were not meant to mix. The curse of the werewolf was meant for humans, not the undead. And so I earned this monstrous visage. I was once a handsome man, though you may not believe it. But beauty is nothing without power.

"I do not transform at the full moon, for I keep a partial wolf form at all times. At the full moon, I do not lose sense of who I am; I only grow stronger. So, I embraced my misfortune. But power comes with a price. My own mother turned her face from me.

"I had no place amongst humans any longer, but that was all

right with me. Humans are weak. They do not accept those who are not like them, and elves are only a higher species of human who think themselves superior over all other kinds. So, I found my refuge among the shunned and the hunted: werewolves, vampires, ogres, goblins, hags, and other poor creatures who are feared for their faces. They accepted me without qualms. Even admired me. They were more than willing to set aside their differences when I promised them revenge on those who had slaughtered them. So tell me, princess, who are the monsters?"

"What do you want from me?" said Atalanta, her hands in fists behind her back.

"Humans and elves are the true monsters. And monsters must be exterminated. Right, princess?"

"What do you want from me?" said Atalanta through gritted teeth.

Tyrannus sighed. "Are you even listening? Your ears are certainly big enough." When Atalanta said nothing, he leaned back in his chair and said, "Very well, we'll get to the heart of the matter. What I want from you … is your magic."

The laugh burst through her lips unexpectedly. "Magic? You cannot perform elvish magic, fool. Magic is in our blood. Your blood no longer even pumps."

"Hmm, you're far more stupid than I anticipated," said Tyrannus. "I am well aware that I cannot perform magic myself. That is why you will do it for me, as my servant."

Atalanta smirked. "I'm afraid you've captured the wrong elf, your royal manginess," she said with a curtsy. "I am no mage. I have always much preferred the blade to magic. I know very few incantations and have very little practice. Perhaps my lack of desire comes from the fact that magical power improves with age. I am but seventeen — merely a blink in the life of an elf. Even if I wanted to help you, I could not."

"Oh, I think anything can be achieved with the right motivation," said Tyrannus. "You see, I picked just the right elf.

You are Zanthus' only heir. Such a shame about your brothers and sisters. Mortality is a fragile thing. It can be taken by sickness just as easily as a blade.

"I believe your father will do just about anything to have you returned. If you will not complete the tasks I set before you, I will send him a message. Him for you. But I'll have to kill him, of course. An elf as powerful as Zanthus can't be trusted to follow orders. So, which shall it be, princess, your magic or your father's head?"

"My father and my people will crush you and your band of filthy creatures of the night," she said, spitting out her words to mask the shake in her voice.

"I will kill him before your very eyes," said Tyrannus, lunging forward in his chair, teeth bared. "I will hang his head on my door!"

"Your head will roll at my father's feet, you rotting dog!" said Atalanta. "But mark me, if I get a chance of my own, be assured I will drive a silver stake into your blackened heart and laugh in your face as you die and are reunited with the filthy soul that you sold to the devil."

Thetis struck her across the face with a lazy backhand hard enough to cut her cheek against her teeth.

"You will respect your king," he said.

Tryannus laughed, and the awful sound echoed off the stone walls.

"I think she needs a few more days in the dungeon to really think it through, don't you, Thetis?"

A knock at the door spared Atalanta the vampire's response.

"Who dares interrupt the king's council," said Tyrannus.

"A million apologies, my liege."

Atalanta recognized the strange, echoing, raspy voice.

"But I have news of the humans."

"You may enter, Callid."

The door opened and Callid stepped inside.

"You!" Atalanta said in a voice like the yowl of a wild cat ready to pounce, eyes narrowed at the two-headed, hunchbacked cyclops.

With a massive exertion of strength, she wrenched her shackles from Thetis' grasp and launched herself at Callid. He screeched in terror, both mouths open wide, as she kicked him in the chest and knocked him to the ground. She jumped through the loop of her bound arms, pinned the rising cyclops to the ground with her knees, and wrapped the chain connecting her shackles around both his necks.

Choking and sputtering, he looked to Tyrannus and reached out to his king with an imploring hand as Atalanta crossed her wrists to tighten the chain.

But it was Thetis and Nathaniel who came to the little beast's rescue, ripping her off the cyclops by the hair and the back of her dingy silk dress.

"You two had better hope that your prisoner doesn't escape you again, for both of your sakes," said Tyrannus.

"Yes, my lord," said Thetis, "I won't let it happen again. Of course, Nathaniel has already done it once. If I hadn't arrived when I did, the little elfling might already be on her way back home."

"So help me, you leech ..." said Nathaniel. He seemed unable to complete the thought, and instead growled deep in his chest.

"Enough quarrelling!" said Tyrannus. "You will both be dealt with soon enough. Callid, what is your news?"

"Master, King Markus sent out a search party yesterday, with his four children among them, to find the elf princess. Six of your werewolf soldiers sniffed them out and positioned themselves near the camp on the night of the full moon. I stayed out of their way, but when I returned early this morning, I found all four siblings alive. The rest of their party is dead, but so are the wolves. I had my escort fly me back here to report as soon as I saw them. I do not think they know the way back, for they still linger in the forest."

Callid finished his message with a low bow that became a cower at his master's angry scream. His scream was even more terrible than his laugh: a vampire's cry, like breaking glass, and a werewolf's growl together in a hellish symphony. It stopped Atalanta's heart.

"How is it that children are slaying my warriors?" he said. "First, Vladimir at the ball and now a whole platoon of werewolves. You were supposed to watch them, Callid—learn everything about them! You said they had no experience in killing anything other than each other, like all the other humans. You have either lied or you have failed me, and both make me furious! I'll have both your heads on a pike!"

"Please, master, please have mercy," whimpered Callid, cowering supine on the floor. "I would never lie to you, your Grace. I told the truth of their training. There was no change until after Vladimir failed to deliver the eldest princess."

"Mercy must be earned, and all any of you have earned is punishment," said Tyrannus, suddenly eerily calm. "Deliver the princess back to her chambers to consider my offer. Surely with the three of you present, she cannot possibly escape. If she does, I will be sure to kill you all by whatever means applies to your species. When the deed is done, return to me at once."

Thetis, Nathaniel, and Callid all bowed low. Callid's teeth clacked together he was shaking so hard. Even Nathaniel had exchanged his sour expression for a humble look of fear. Only Thetis remained unchanged, not even the threat of deadly punishment seemed able to cure his boredom.

When they led her back to the dungeon, Atalanta didn't even bother to try and memorize the passageways. Her mind was on other things. The humans were searching for her, too? Her father must have contacted them.

And though she'd just learned that a hybrid king planned to decimate the human and elf populations, it was the young human royals her mind kept returning to. Few living beings, human or elvish, had slayed a vampire or werewolf. Their deeds impressed her, and few things did. It seemed the humans had sent their best. Her hope for rescue was suddenly renewed. A small smile crept its way onto her face ... until the clang of the door closing wiped it clean. Trapped again.

Chapter 4

Wanderer

The siblings ate their breakfast in the middle of a graveyard. They moved slowly, stiff from the previous day's work of collecting the remains of their fallen fellows and digging graves in the clearing. The earth was soft, but the work was still hard, and they had not buried the fallen men as deeply as was customary. Still, they had done their best. They'd even fashioned crude crosses from tree branches as grave markers. They had encircled Sir Gregor's grave and hung their heads while Andromeda recited a funeral prayer as best she could from memory. When she finished, the siblings looked to one another in the silence with fear and uncertainty marked across their faces. Their protector was gone.

One of the men who had fled was missing. They had found all of the deserters horses, though, savaged and partially eaten. Their own horses, along with Sir Gregor's were still securely tied to the trees, but they were jumpy. They barely grazed, and at every snapping branch, they stomped their feet and nickered to each other softly.

"So, which way are we headed?" said Andrew, picking at his dried strip of venison.

The question hung in the air, thickening it like a rich stew. Though it had remained unspoken, that very question had been on all their minds since the previous morning. Perhaps it was why they had taken so much time and care with the graves.

"The wise thing would be to head back and regroup with a new search party at the palace," said Michael.

"We'll be days, even weeks, behind all the other parties by then," said Felicity, swatting her frizzing curls off her face. "There would be no point in even coming back. If the elf is not

65

found by then, she is dead."

"So we're supposed to go on alone?" said Michael. "These woods are far more dangerous than we anticipated. That was a whole pack of werewolves. A pack, Felicity. There aren't even supposed to be lone werewolves anymore. What happens if we are attacked again?"

"We'll kill every last one of them like we did this time," said Felicity.

"We are the only Avalon heirs," said Michael. "We may not be so fortunate in the next fight."

"Fortunate?" said Felicity with a scoff. "We survived because we've been trained to survive. To excel."

"Sir Gregor was trained, was he not?" said Michael.

Felicity's haughty expression was wiped from her face.

"Yes, but ..." mumbled Felicity.

"He was battle tested," said Michael, jaw hard. "He had more experience than all of us combined, and yet he now lies in a shallow grave. Continuing the search on our own would be foolhardy. These woods are more dangerous than we realized. If we are killed, our family name and rule dies with us. Are you willing to risk all of that?"

"When did you become a coward, Michael?" said Felicity, blue eyes hard as gems as they bored into her brother.

Michael flushed the color of his hair and slammed his fist into the earth.

"I am not a coward!" he said, jabbing a finger in Felicity's face. "I am the eldest. It is my duty to be the voice of wisdom. It is my duty to protect the three of you."

"We can protect ourselves, Michael, and you know it!" said Felicity, swatting Michael's hand away.

"It's true, Michael," said Andrew, his blue eyes fierce in his angular face. "We killed the moon mutts. Us and Sir Gregor. We stood our ground when others fled. We are as skilled as any knights, despite our age."

"I have not said we aren't skilled," said Michael. "I am saying training is no guarantee of survival. You must all understand that!"

"I ..." Andrew stared at the ground and picked at the fallen pine needles, pulling apart a frond. He took a deep breath and looked Michael in the eye. "I do understand. But there is risk of danger and death in any quest; we have always known that, even as children."

"You and Andromeda are still children," said Michael, "and it is my duty to keep you from harm." He rounded on Felicity. "That does not make me a coward!"

"Mother and Father said we were to listen to Sir Gregor and to turn back at his command," said Andrew. "Well, Sir Gregor is dead. I think that means you're in charge now, and I will follow your orders if you decide that we should return home. But I will also follow your orders in battle if you wish to carry on. I think we can do it."

Michael's breathing steadied, his face regained its normal hue, and he looked at his brother wide-eyed and a little afraid, though he tried to cover it by raising his chin and looking at Andrew down the bridge of his nose.

"Do you mean that? Truly?"

"Yes."

Michael lowered his chin and reached out to clasp his brother's shoulder and give him a rough but loving shake.

"I will follow you, too," said Andromeda, twirling a strand of her long, black hair tight around two fingers, "whatever you decide. But consider this. If we go back and tell this story—that our party was slaughtered on our very first night in the woods— do you think Mother and Father will listen to us the next time we wish to venture out like this? They barely let us go this time. And your age won't matter after this. They will keep us locked up like they did after the night of the ball. They will do it for our safety and for their love for us, but they will do it all the same.

"They are afraid, Michael. I know you saw it. They are terrified. The Diseased Ones are rising under their reign, and princesses are being snatched from their castles. Had we not been there, Felicity would be gone, just like Atalanta. Someone has to stop this, whatever is going on. Why shouldn't it be us?

"Mother and Father will choose defense, fortifying villages and cities behind walls of stone and soldiers. But if we can find Atalanta, maybe she or whatever took her can lead us to what's going on before things get worse. And even if it isn't connected, we would prove to Mother and Father that we can act out our duties to protect Arcamira."

Silence.

Michael searched Andromeda's face. Felicity was slack-jawed and rather unladylike, revealing the remains of her partially chewed bread.

"Here, here," said Andrew, banging his deerskin water bag on the ground like it was a goblet on a dining table.

Michael smiled.

"Ah, to hell with it. Being the voice of wisdom is no fun anyway. We press on."

So they packed up their belongings, used Gregor's horse as a pack mule, and headed off into the woods.

"Do we just keep heading in a straight line north, or should we fan out and search large areas of the wood?" said Andrew.

"Fanning out would have been easier with a larger party," said Michael. "Now we would have to split up, which is unwise, or spend a great deal of time in the same area, which is also unwise when there are werewolves wandering about. We head for the mountains and search there. Then we can take a different route back to try and cover the most ground. Of course, if we find something that might lead to Atalanta, we follow that wherever it leads."

Andrew saluted him by thrusting up his arm and making a fist by his head. "Aye, Sir Michael."

"Quit that," said Michael.

The day eked on in an endless scene of green and tree bark and semi-darkness. The air was stale with decaying foliage and the tightness of the air under the cramped canopy.

"Why is it that in all of the legends, the heroes find the trail one page after they decide to look for it, but we haven't even found a trace of anything but rodents?" said Felicity when they dismounted to stretch their legs and eat a few pieces of their fruit before it went bad.

"When was the last time you actually read a book, Felicity?" said Andromeda with a smirk.

Andrew's short, bark-like laugh earned him a smack to the back of his head.

"Whoa, she said it, not me," said Andrew, hands up.

"This grand adventure is only serving to make me saddle sore," said Felicity, looking to Michael.

"If I recall correctly, you're the one who was so vehement about continuing this quest. If you can't handle a few saddle sores, how are you going to make it the rest of the way?"

"I didn't say I couldn't handle it," said Felicity with a scowl.

"Then quit whining."

Felicity's scowl deepened, but she didn't say anything.

"I'm sure you'll be missing this pace when we reach the mountains," said Andrew, a sly look on his face as he examined his nails, picking dirt and food out from under them with his dagger. "The goblins live in caves all over the mountain range. You'll have to sleep with one eye open with hair like yours."

"Oh really? Why is that?" Felicity crossed her arms, but the flicker of uncertainty on her face did not go unnoticed.

Andrew's lips twitched in a smile that he suppressed by pursing his lips and shrugging his shoulders. "Female goblins envy human beauty. They'll scalp you and wear your hair as a hat."

He reached out and tugged a golden curl. Felicity recoiled,

real fear paling her complexion and making her eyes stand out.

"I've never heard that. That's not true," she said. "Right, Andromeda?"

"Yes and no," said Andromeda, shifting her hair behind her ear. "They do keep hair as trophies, but it's not just the females, and they make it into necklaces and tie it on spears." She shot Felicity a wicked grin. "Don't worry, Felicity. They won't kill you for your hair. They'll find some other reason to kill you, and then just cut off some hair as a trophy. No scalping involved."

"How comforting," said Felicity, wrinkling her nose.

When she turned to remount her horse, Andromeda and Andrew exchanged an amused look.

"It would be more amusing if it wasn't true," Michael whispered as he passed them on the way to his own horse.

They carried on until dusk, coming across nothing of note.

"We'll need to make camp," said Michael. "Should we stop here or press on for a better spot?"

Andromeda opened her mouth to speak, but Michael answered himself.

"We should press on. We won't be able to see anything coming. The trees are too close here."

"Excellent idea," Andromeda mumbled, knowing he would not hear her.

"But what about the dark? The sun's setting fast," said Michael.

Andrew made to answer this time, but he, too, was cut off.

"I'd rather not have to journey in the dark," said Michael, "but I think it will be worth it to find someplace where we can keep better watch through the night."

"Brilliant idea, Michael," said Andrew under his breath.

"Thank you, Michael," said Felicity, deepening her voice as she whispered back. "I came up with it all by myself."

Andromeda dropped her reins to stifle her laughter with both hands.

"The best thing would be to find somewhere with a water source. Don't you think?" Michael asked.

None of his siblings bothered to answer.

"Yes, that would be ideal," he said, "but I'm not sure if it will happen. We should have started looking early in the day. We should try to find a stream tomorrow and follow it to—"

"Michael," Andromeda whispered, no playfulness in her voice this time.

"—the mountain, if possible."

"Michael," she said again as loud as she dared. "Something is coming. Two somethings. Predators of some kind. I'm not sure what they are."

"The moon isn't out," said Michael, reining in his horse and swinging its head around to face Andromeda.

"It's not werewolves. They're two different species. I'm not sure if they're dangerous. They seem to be docile. I don't sense any anger or hunger from them."

Michael drew his sword. His horse whinnied uneasily.

"Which direction?"

Andromeda drew her own sword and pointed it to the right.

"All right. Keep still. Hopefully they'll pass us by."

They waited quietly, barely breathing, with swords drawn. Night began to fall more quickly, the sun dipping too low to shine between the leaves overhead. The rustle of brush made them all squint in the same direction. The crack of a snapping branch made them all raise their swords higher.

"Really, Aquila, watch where you're going," said a voice from the growing darkness. "You'll scare those poor travelers to death."

The siblings looked to each other, their own surprise reflected in each other's eyes. Then three heads swiveled to Andromeda.

"What? I can't sense humans."

"Show yourself," said Michael in a booming voice that made

him sound eerily like Sir Gregor. "There are four in our party, and we are armed."

Three forms appeared around the edge of a thicket. Four swords tipped down toward the neck of the foremost intruder, a tall boy with shoulder length hair who could not have been any older than eighteen. His hands went up by his ears in surrender, and the sleeves of his already too-small, tattered tunic slid back a few more inches on his arms. His brown eyes slanted down at the blades, and he backpedaled two steps, nearly stepping on the cloak that was tied around his neck. With the blades farther from his flesh, he stood straighter and adjusted the large pack on his back before letting his fingers fall casually to the hilts of the two unusually large daggers sheathed at his hips. He clucked his tongue and shook his head.

"Aquila, look what you've done," he said to the creature on his left. "We could have made some friends, and I wouldn't be talking aimlessly to animals all day long."

Even in the dark wood, the Avalons recognized the creature he called Aquila as a griffin, with its eagle head and lion body.

"Perhaps you'll be less likely to run me through if we have some light, yes?" said the stranger, looking up at Michael who was the only one not to have lowered his sword at the sight of the griffin. "Then you can see what a trustworthy face I have. Just give me a moment."

The stranger shook off his pack and pulled out a torch made of a thick branch wrapped with oil-soaked cloth. Then he rummaged in his pocket and pulled out a flint. It only took him a moment to get the torch blazing.

"Ah, that's better."

In the light, the stranger looked younger, more like Andromeda and Andrew's age. His hair was a dark auburn that perhaps would not have been so dark had he not been so thoroughly dirty. His clothes looked as though he'd been wearing them for years—dingy and tattered beyond repair and too small for his lanky form.

The griffin, though, only looked more magnificent in the firelight. The feathers of its head and wings were gold, bronze, and rust colored. The wings sprouted from the lion half's shoulder blades and tucked neatly along the body, ending just behind the rump. Large, piercing, yellow eyes studied them quizzically above its sharp, hooked beak. Its lion's pelt was the same gold as Felicity's hair. The tuft on the end of its tail was copper. From its lion's paws sprouted an eagle's hooked black talons.

"Amazing," Andromeda murmured, sheathing her sword and staring spellbound at the griffin.

The stranger's face split in a smile. "He's really something, isn't he?" he said.

Andromeda pulled her eyes from the griffin and found the stranger's smile. She thought to herself that it was rather lopsided, but her dazzled expression didn't change as she nodded mutely.

"Who are you?" said Michael. "And what is that thing?" He thrust his sword at the ground, at an odd little creature who had thus far been overshadowed by the griffin and its charismatic pal.

It was long and very low to the ground. Grey fur covered its body everywhere except the eyes. There the fur turned black, giving the little beast a shady look. The only handsome thing about it was a long bushy tail much like a fox's. It wove between the stranger's legs on little clawed feet.

"I'm Erro," said the stranger, eyeing Michael's sword with amusement rather than concern. "This funny little fellow's name is Zezil. I wasn't sure what he was at first either, but I asked around, and I'm pretty sure he's something called a vexar. Something like a badger, a raccoon, and a wolf all rolled into one. The wolf comes out when he's upset. It's not a pretty sight. You may want to put that sword away."

"I'm not convinced," said Michael.

"All right, but just know that you're invading my home. You may want to be more polite. And by the way, this is Aquila." He stroked the griffin's feathers. "He doesn't take too kindly to swords being pointed at me."

The griffin clicked its beak and twitched its head to the side. Michael looked at the griffin warily and drew his sword closer to his body.

"We don't want any trouble," said Erro. "In fact, I can help you if you've lost your way. I've lived in these woods since I was eight, and I like to move around. I know just about every inch. It would be nice to have some human company. Who are you, and where is it that you're headed?"

"I'm Andromeda Avalon, daughter of King Markus and Queen Isabelle. These are my siblings: Michael, Andrew, and Felicity. Very pleased to meet you."

Michael ran a hand down his face with a sigh.

"Michael, he has a griffin for a companion," said Andromeda with a roll of her eyes. "A griffin will not ally itself with anything wicked. To win a griffin's loyalty you must have a good soul and be strong of character. Put your sword away."

"Thank you, princess," said Erro with a bow. "I don't believe I've ever been described half so nicely before."

"Are you going to make a habit of telling strangers that we're royalty wandering the woods alone?" said Michael, sheathing his sword.

"Are you going to make a habit of pointing swords at clear allies?" said Andromeda.

"I'm flattered to be championed by someone so beautiful, but I don't mean to cause any discord between relatives," said Erro. "If you don't need my help, I'll be on my way."

"Come now, Michael, he can probably help us find a trail if there's actually one to find," said Felicity.

"Trail of what?" said Erro. He appraised their horses and

weapons. "Are you on a hunting trip or are you looking for someone?"

Michael sighed. "We're looking for the elf princess, Atalanta."

"We don't get many of those running around here," said Erro, scratching his head. His eyes were the only thing that betrayed his interest.

"No, I wouldn't expect so," said Michael. "She was taken by a strange creature. The trail was last spotted by elves on the edge of our northern border, so King Zanthus requested human search parties."

"And you are one of those parties?" said Erro. "Just the four of you? No protection?"

"We began with twelve other men just two days ago, but we were attacked by werewolves."

"I believe you mean werewolf," said Erro.

"I wish," said Andrew. "Our party wouldn't be gone in that case. There were six."

"Six? I've known their numbers were growing for a while now, but I've never seen any sign of packs."

"You already knew there were still werewolves?" said Felicity.

"The people of the northern forest have never believed they were ever really gone, just massacred to the point of near extinction. Vampires, too. Nobody outside the woods wants to believe it, but this is where they retreated. This is where they've hunted ever since they were driven out."

"Told you so," said Andromeda.

Felicity gave her a scathing look.

"An elfin princess captured? I suppose you miss out on a lot when you're living in the woods," said Erro.

Zezil climbed Erro's back, draped himself around his neck, and licked his face. Erro scratched the vexar behind his short grey ears.

"So will you help us?" said Andromeda.

"I am your humble servant, Your Majesty," said Erro with

another bow and lopsided smile. "Just tell me what sort of creature took the princess and I'll find its trail."

"I doubt you've ever tracked anything like it before," said Michael, "no matter how long you've wandered the woods. They say it was a two headed cyclops with a hunched back."

"Until about a month ago, you would have been right," said Erro.

"You mean you've seen it?" said Andrew.

"Yes, and in fact, he was headed west, toward the elf kingdom. He crossed my path as we were headed to one of the few small villages in these woods. I was making a trap, and he just walked through the trees right in front of me, humming to himself out of both heads. He saw me and squealed like a pig. Ran off before I could even make sense of what I was looking at. Aquila and Zezil had been off fishing, but when they came back and smelled him they both got pretty agitated.

"I'll help you find his trail so long as you can find it in you to trust me."

Erro looked at Michael.

Michael stared back, working his jaw.

"Michael, how many times must I tell you we can trust him?" said Andromeda. "The griffin trusts him; I can sense it. That should be good enough for anyone."

"I'm with the griffin," said Andrew.

"If you can find a trail and lead us to a village with a place to wash, I'll let you do just about anything," said Felicity.

Andrew choked in his effort to stifle a laugh.

Felicity blushed fiercely. "Oh you know what I mean."

"I'll lead you to a village as soon as tomorrow morning," said Erro. "As for the trail, I know where to start."

"I suppose we're now a party of five," said Michael.

"I'm honored," said Erro, bowing his head. "I swear to guide you well, Your Highnesses." He raised his head to look at Andromeda. "Might I ask how you know what Aquila thinks of me?"

"Elfin bracelet," said Michael with a dismissive wave. "Now's not the time to explain. We need to find a place to camp."

"There's a clearing not far up ahead. I'll lead you to it, and tomorrow I'll take you to the village so you can freshen up and replenish your supplies," said Erro.

"Is this village out of the way?" said Michael. "We're heading toward the mountains, and I'd rather not waste any days. The princess has already been missing for a long time."

"It just so happens that the village I was thinking of is the closest one to the mountains," said Erro with a smirk. "Never fear, Your Highness."

To the siblings' amazement, he swung a leg over Aquila's back, and the griffin headed off into the woods. Erro motioned for them to follow. Aquila kept a steady pace through the underbrush. Strange little Zezil bounded along beside him as best he could, stopping to sniff trees and just about anything else and then sprinting to catch back up to the group.

"So, you've truly been wandering these woods since you were eight?" said Felicity, breaking the silence.

"Yes."

"Where did you live before?"

"Not far from your palace, actually. A small cottage on a hillside. My parents were farmers."

"Where are your parents now? Did you run away?" said Felicity.

Erro stiffened. Andromeda shot Felicity an accusing glare. Felicity shrugged and gave Andromeda an innocent look.

"I didn't run," said Erro, almost too quietly to be heard over the footsteps of the animals. "They were murdered by a gang of raiders."

Felicity examined her hands clasping her reins. Michael cleared his throat. Andromeda opened her mouth and closed it again.

"It's not much longer," said Erro.

They passed the remaining time in tense silence. The only light in the forest now was Erro's torch and the occasional glint of the moon. It was the third and final full moon of the cycle.

The clearing was almost a meadow. The grass was full with small, flowering weeds, littering it with hints of color that would grow vibrant in the daylight. The trees stood far apart. A small stream trickled through the center. They were finally free from the stuffy air of the enclosed forest, and a cool breeze gently ruffled hair, fur, and feathers.

"Here we are," said Erro. "This is one of my favorite places in the whole forest."

"It's perfect," said Michael a little too cheerily.

The moon's light was no longer hindered by the trees, and it lit the clearing well enough for Erro to put out his torch.

Andromeda started to unload their blankets from the horses. She peeked over the top of the horse's dappled back to secretly watch Erro as he rubbed Zezil's belly. He turned his head, smiling at his strange pet, and looked straight at Andromeda. She quickly ducked back behind her horse.

As she began laying the blankets out on the grass, she made it a point not to look in Erro's direction. She let her black hair fall in curtains in front of her face.

"Aquila and I will go find something to eat, unless you four have something," said Erro.

"We've got bread, some dried venison, and a few figs," said Andrew, taking one of the last loafs out of his saddle pack.

"That's not a meal," said Erro with a disapproving shake of his head. "I'll find something small that won't take long to cook." He looked to the griffin. "Come on, Aquila. Zezil, you stay here. I don't want a repeat of yesterday's incident."

"No, you stay," said Michael. "Andrew and I will go get something. It'll be quicker and easier. He has a crossbow."

"These are just as effective, and you don't have to waste

arrows," said Erro, patting his daggers. "But I'll accept that offer. I'll make a fire. Do you need my torch, or can you hunt in the dark?"

"The trees aren't as thick around here," said Michael. "Fire will scare everything off. We'll manage. If we can't find anything, we'll just eat what we have."

"Fair enough."

Erro and the girls had a fire blazing in record time. Aquila and Zezil watched the whole process with mild interest.

"Feel good on your feathers, Aquila?" said Erro, sitting down next to the griffin.

Aquila ruffled up the feathers on the top of his head.

"You hungry?"

The griffin looked at him.

"Me, too."

"Why do you do that?" said Felicity. "It's not as though he can understand you."

"I don't usually have anyone else to talk to," said Erro.

"Don't be so sure he doesn't understand either," said Andromeda. "Griffins are far more intelligent than most animals."

"Practically human," said Erro. "Zezil's pretty smart, too. In a crafty way."

Zezil, who had been snapping at a moth, looked up and cocked his head at the sound of his name. He bounded to his master's side, panting.

Andromeda started to reach out to touch him, but then hesitated.

"You can pet him if you'd like," said Erro. "He's real friendly as long as you don't catch him when he's angry and transformed."

"He transforms? I thought you just meant he was vicious."

"No, his body changes. He morphs. Sort of like a vampire does, and he's almost as blood thirsty."

"I'd like to see what he looks like when he does that. I've

never heard of such a thing," said Andromeda.

She sat down by Erro and held her hand out to the little creature. He trotted forward and put his head against her hand. She scratched behind his ears. Zezil licked her arm happily and then jumped into her lap. She cuddled him close to her chest, laughing, and he licked her chin.

"He really likes you," said Erro with a smile. "Maybe even more than he likes me."

"I doubt that," said Andromeda. "What did he do yesterday that made you not want to take him hunting?"

"Oh, that," said Erro. "He was being a nuisance to Aquila, biting his ankles and that sort of thing, so Aquila took a snap at him. He lost his temper and transformed. He tried to attack Aquila. They made so much noise while I was trying to keep them from killing each other that they scared everything off."

"Do they usually get along?"

"More or less," he said. "Now I've got a few questions for you. If you don't mind."

Andromeda shook her head, and Erro shifted in the grass so that he could sit cross-legged in front of her with his back resting on Aquila.

"How does that elfin bracelet work?"

"Well, it's sort of hard to explain, but it lets me hear the thoughts and feelings of the animals around me. If I focus on one animal, I can read its mind and sort of … become the animal. Or, I can focus on the emotions of all the animals at my chosen range. It gets harder to handle when I try to reach out too far. And the thoughts never totally go away, but I've learned to control it pretty well."

"That's extraordinary! The elves must have more magic than I would have given them credit for.

"I've only seen elves once. One summer, when I was ten, I saw them here in the forest. I'm still not sure what they were doing. I wasn't all that impressed. I guess they're pretty."

Andromeda chuckled. "I haven't ever seen one. I wouldn't know, but they are supposed to be the most beautiful beings in Arcamira."

"I've seen better."

The way he looked at her made heat rise in her cheeks.

"Could you tell me what Aquila or Zezil is thinking?" he said.

"I'd love to."

"I've always wanted to know what they are thinking. What they think of me."

Andromeda smiled and pushed her hair out her eyes. Erro watched as she focused on Zezil first. He watched her grey eyes begin to glaze over as she looked into Zezil's. He waited patiently until her eyes refocused.

"He has a funny little mind," Andromeda said with a laugh. "He's easily distracted. He feels content and happy here lying between us, but there's a cricket a little ways away that he's keeping a close eye on.

"I can feel something else in him, like a barrier—part of his mind that he's not using right now. I suppose that's the piece that is triggered when he gets angry or scared."

"Amazing," said Erro, shaking his head. "Absolutely amazing."

Andromeda smiled. "I'm pretty fond of it myself. Want me to listen to Aquila now?"

"Yes, please do."

She spent far longer looking into Aquila's yellow eyes.

"His thoughts are even more developed than I thought," she finally said.

"What's he thinking?"

"He's thinking about how much he loves this clearing. He wishes you would stroke his feathers again. He really loves it when you do that."

Erro's hand went straight to Aquila's feathers.

"He feels a great deal of love and loyalty for you. His affection is very much like a human's. But, that loyalty is the nature of all griffins, I suppose. They find a person with a good heart and good intentions, and they stay with them for life. Also, he ..."

Andromeda blushed.

"What?" he asked. "What else was he thinking?"

"He was pondering about me, deciding what he thinks," said Andromeda.

"And what does he think of you?" said Erro, a mischievous grin spreading across his face.

"He seems to think I'm of good heart and good intentions," said Andromeda hesitantly. "He thinks he sees bravery and courage and ... beauty."

"Smart bird."

Andromeda lowered her eyes and smiled, unable to meet Erro's gaze. Perhaps it was his lack of regular human company that made him unafraid to stare unabashedly as he did. His eyes were rather small, but they were a warm, rich brown, and his gaze was soft and kind.

"I'm not so sure I'm needed here," said Felicity, startling Andromeda. "I'm going to get some extra firewood. I'm sick of sitting."

Felicity wore a smirk that made Andromeda blush.

Chapter 5

Hidden Village

Michael and Andrew found Felicity on the edge of the clearing, gathering fallen branches to keep the fire fueled.

"You, working?" said Andrew, rubbing his eyes. "I don't believe it."

A stick bounced off Andrew's forehead. The force of Michael's laugh threw back his own head.

Andrew wiped his brow, looking sour, and sucked the blood from the scratch off his thumb after he examined it.

"Get anything?" said Felicity.

Michael, still trying to get his laughter under control, held up three rabbits, their feet tied together with rope.

"Not much of a meal," said Felicity, her face scrunched up in disappointment.

"We saw a deer, but it got away," said Michael, wiping his eyes. "It's not easy hunting in the dark. Luckily, most of the animals around here don't seem afraid of humans. Two of these fellows hopped right by us."

"Well, fire's good and hot," said Felicity. "We should be able to cook those little things in no time."

"Why are you alone?" said Michael, suddenly stern. "Tonight is the last full moon. You shouldn't be by yourself at all tonight."

"Oh," said Felicity, the right side of her mouth curling up in a smirk, "well, I thought Andromeda and our new friend might want a little privacy."

The boys blinked at their sister, faces temporarily wiped of expression.

"Huh?" said Andrew.

Michael's shoulder bumped Felicity's as he rushed forward and thundered his way into the clearing, crashing through the underbrush like a raging bull.

"Damn," said Felicity. "Hold this."

She shoved the firewood into Andrew's chest.

"Hey!"

Felicity took off after Michael. Andrew threw the wood down and followed.

Andromeda and Erro looked around as Michael crashed into the clearing.

"Lord above, if you were stomping around like that out there, we're going hungry tonight," said Erro.

Michael raised a finger and opened his mouth just as Felicity jogged from the trees and collided into his back.

"Rabbit stew tonight, folks," said Felicity, unusually sunny as she snatched the rabbits from Michael and held them high.

"Pretty good haul," said Erro, "considering the conditions."

Michael adjusted his coat and tried to start again, but Andrew appeared next. Felicity looked him up and down and then smacked him on the shoulder.

"Where's the firewood?"

"Back there where you tried to dump it on me."

"You left it?"

"Uh, yes," said Andrew, arms crossed.

"Why? Why would you do that?" said Felicity, making wild gestures with her arms.

"Why'd you shove it at me? That's not my job. I got the rabbits."

Felicity seemed unable to articulate the feeling that contorted her face. She bent her hands into claws and outstretched them toward Andrew's neck, working her mouth silently.

"Both of you go get the wood," said Michael, a hand to his forehead.

"What?"

Felicity and Andrew glared at each other, each affronted by

the other's mimicry.

"Go get the wood," said Michael, fixing them with the eerily blank, stiff-jawed look that meant he'd had it.

By the time Felicity and Andrew got back with the collected wood, Erro and Michael had the rabbits skinned and Andromeda had their one pot over the fire and filled with stream water nearly at a boil. She'd also collected bits of stray ingredients like wild onions from the clearing and carrots from their food supplies to add to the stew.

The meal was prepared in near silence. Eyelids drooped and heads nodded, only to shoot back up again when chins hit chests. While the humans nodded off and the rabbit stew boiled, Aquila and Zezil slipped off to catch their own dinners.

Aquila returned with blood staining the feathers around his beak. Zezil brought his rat back to the clearing to show it off. He settled next to his master and began crunching away at it.

"I think I may be sick," said Felicity, nose wrinkled.

"Too bad. Dinner's finally ready," said Andromeda, stirring the stew before removing it from the embers.

They dished the stew into wooden bowls and ate with wooden spoons.

"I miss cook," said Felicity after her first sip of the broth.

"Tastes pretty good to me," said Erro. He tipped his bowl back and guzzled, spoon unused in the grass.

"You eat like your pet," said Felicity.

"You eat like a princess."

"I wonder why."

"Me, too."

Andromeda snickered at Felicity's confused look. Felicity bent in toward her younger sister, her blonde ringlets tickling Andromeda's nose and said, "Hey, you owe me. Big time."

Now it was Andromeda who wore the confused look.

"So you're a knife thrower?" Michael asked Erro, staring at

the younger boy a little harder than was necessary for such a casual question.

"Yes," said Erro, his voice muffled by stew.

"Who taught you?" said Andrew.

"I taught myself," said Erro. "It's a lot more practical than a bow and arrow. For me at least. I don't have the money for buying arrows all the time, and making them is hard work. If you don't do it right, they don't fly straight. Knives are just easier."

"So are you actually any good?" said Andrew. "Most knife throwers I've met think throwing halfway straight means they're experts."

Erro smiled. In a single fluid movement, he pulled a dagger from his belt and threw it between Andrew and Michael's heads. The dagger struck a tree behind them.

"I can hit a tree," said Andrew, quickly recovering from the shock of the dagger whizzing past his ear. "I'm unimpressed."

"The tree wasn't the target," said Erro. "Go look."

Andrew raised an eyebrow, but got up all the same.

"By God, I don't believe it," said Andrew when he reached the tree.

His siblings perked up and craned their necks to try and see the dagger's mark in the firelight.

Andrew tugged on the dagger, but the tough bark didn't want to release it. After another good yank, the dagger came free, and Andrew snatched at something that looked like a leaf as it floated to the ground. Andrew searched through the grass for a moment. He brought his prize back to the group and held it out in his palm.

A large moth lay in two pieces in his hand.

"Sorry about throwing at your heads, but it was flying around behind you," said Erro. "Figured it was as good a target as any."

He received awed looks all around.

"That's amazing!" said Andromeda.

"You've got talent," said Michael a little stiffly, as though it was some sort of concession on his part.

"I take everything back," said Andrew, tossing the moth away. He looked to Michael. "Maybe we should recruit him as part of our search party."

"Not sure you can afford me, Your Highness," said Erro.

"Then do it for honor and duty to your kingdom, dear lad," said Andrew, rolling back his shoulders and deepening his voice.

"Never really considered myself part of any kingdom," said Erro with a small grin. "Though I suppose these woods are like a kingdom of their own."

"You've really lived out here all alone since you were a child?" said Felicity.

"Not entirely alone for most of it," said Erro. "Aquila found me not long after I lost my parents." He hung his head and suddenly became interested in a blade of grass he ripped from the ground. "Found Zezil a few years ago. I stop by the villages, too, when I'm running low on supplies or need new clothes."

"You need new clothes now," said Felicity, staring pointedly at the frayed cuffs of Erro's brown breeches, which brushed his knees rather than his ankles.

"Felicity," said Andromeda in a low hiss.

Erro laughed. "No, she's right. I suppose it's good fortune that you need an escort to a village."

"How long will it take to get to the village?" said Michael.

"It shouldn't take very long on horseback," said Erro. "If we leave fairly early, we should arrive around midafternoon."

"We'd best get some rest then," said Michael, surveying the sky. "I'll take first watch."

Thick clouds had moved to cover the stars. They tried to cover the moon, but it shone through, a blurred, shimmering orb. The siblings curled up in their blankets, using their lighter furs as pillows. Michael propped himself up on a boulder by the little stream and wrapped himself in blankets and furs. Erro wrapped himself in his rough green cloak and cushioned his head on Aquila's warm, feathered side. Zezil curled in the crook of his arm.

Michael let the fire dwindle down to a small stack of ash and a few sticks, not wanting to give up the heat, but not wanting to attract unwanted attention. But about the time that Andrew began to make a whistling snore, Michael's head began to droop. He snapped it back up twice, but on the third time, it stayed nestled against his chest.

But two sets of eyes stayed open. One watched the fire, the other the stars, neither quite brave enough to look the other's way, though they lay only a few feet apart.

Andromeda shifted in her blankets.

"Are you still awake?" said Erro, just barely audible.

"Yes." She concealed a smile within her blanket.

"Am I bothering you?"

"No."

"Can you see an animal's dreams?"

Andromeda closed her eyes.

"No, sorry. But I can sense their emotion. Zezil is having a happy dream. Aquila ... I'm not getting anything from him, really."

"Oh." There was a moment's pause before he said, "Thank you. I don't mean to be a pest."

"You can ask me to do that any time. I understand."

Andromeda chewed lightly on her lower lip in the silence that followed. "Erro," she said into the still night.

"Yes."

"Why did you never stay in a village? Why live by yourself in the woods?"

He was silent for so long that she nearly apologized for asking.

"I didn't want to be pitied. When I went into a village, I was the orphan boy. When I stayed in the woods, I was whatever I wanted to be. I grew up as a farmer and a herder. Living on the land has never been hard for me. Besides, the villagers here are poor folk who work hard for what they have. They can't afford to adopt a child when they can barely feed their own. A few people offered." He paused. "I nearly accepted one."

"Why didn't you?"

"I didn't want to be a burden. And ... I had unfinished business. I still do. Something I need to do on my own."

"Why should you have to do it on your own?"

"I just do."

Andromeda hugged her blankets closer, unsure of what to say.

"I suppose I'm just not used to doing things on my own," she said finally. "I have three siblings who are always around. Andrew and I are especially close. We were never apart as children. When we were very young, we would cry if the other was taken away for even a few minutes. Our nursemaid always said that was the way of twins."

"I've never met twins before," said Erro. "I've heard there are some who look so alike you cannot tell who is who."

"It's true, I have met a pair of girls that way—daughters of an eastern nobleman."

Once again, Andrew's whistling snore, the fire's dull crackle, and the chatter of wildlife were the only sounds. But neither closed their eyes. Instead, both waited with stilled breath and thumping hearts for the other to speak.

"I don't know what I would have done if I'd had to face that pack of werewolves alone. Or that vampire."

"You fought a vampire, too?" said Erro, pushing himself up on one elbow. "In the woods?"

His movement disturbed Zezil, and the vexar grunted and rolled over on its back.

"No. He came to one of our mother's balls. She's always coming up with an excuse to throw a ball."

"It just walked right in the door?"

"Yes. It was in the evening. He was dressed like a nobleman. He put Felicity into a trance."

"Seems like a dangerous risk to take for a meal when he could have snatched a peasant from the woods or the hills."

"I'm not sure he just wanted a meal. We think it may be connected to what happened to Atalanta. We think maybe he was trying to take Felicity for some other reason."

"Like what? And what does a vampire have to do with that odd cyclops creature that took the elf princess?"

"I'm not sure," said Andromeda with a sigh, "but it seems too much of a coincidence. Two princesses attacked within a fortnight of each other."

"Has there been a ransom arranged for the elf princess?"

"No. Not that I know of."

"Then it doesn't make any sense."

"Not in the slightest, but that's why we're out here. To find Atalanta and try to figure it out."

"So what happened with the vampire?"

"Michael tried to fight it off, but he didn't have the right weapons. We had never been trained to fight vampires … or werewolves. We didn't have any stakes. So I made one out of a table leg."

"A what?"

"A table leg. But that's not the point. We managed to kill it, but I don't think it would have worked without all of us."

"Why do I feel as if you're trying to tell me something?"

Andromeda laughed softly. "Because I am. I'm just trying to say that maybe you should ask yourself why you think you need to be alone for this … thing … you need to do. I mean, you've said yourself that you aren't really alone already. You have Aquila and Zezil. So why force yourself to be away from other people?"

"I'm not so sure anymore. I suppose now it's just my way of life."

"Fair enough," said Andromeda, "but people's lives change all the time."

Erro grunted and put his hands behind his head.

"So which one of us is going to wake up your brother?"

"No one. He needs to rest. He's been keeping watch twice as long as anyone else every night. I'll do it." Her last few words were distorted by a yawn.

"Aquila will do it," said Erro, ruffling the griffin's head feathers. "Won't you, boy?"

Aquila made a high, undulating sound in his throat and raised his head, his large eyes fully alert.

"He's a better lookout than any of us anyway," said Erro. "Really, he doesn't even have to be awake to keep watch. Nothing has ever snuck up on me in the night with him around."

Andromeda didn't respond. Her soft, rhythmic breaths were her only answer. Erro snuggled down into Aquila's feathers with a smile on his face.

* * *

Zezil, though rather heavy, was a warm stole around Andromeda's shoulders as she rode. He had blanketed himself with her hair, and every time she reached up to scratch him behind the ears, an odd chattering coo vibrated his belly against the back of her neck.

"I told you he liked you better than me," said Erro, after one such coo. He had to turn his torso around to look at her from where he rode astride Aquila, leading the pack.

"He enjoys the feel of my hair," said Andromeda.

"So can Aquila hold two people when he's flying?" said Andrew.

He'd been drilling Erro all morning, ever since Erro let it slip that he had flown atop the griffin's back on many occasions to scout out the forest. He wanted to know what it felt like, how many times he'd done it, if the griffin could do any tricks in the air. Though the others never pressed, they listened with rapt attention. Erro didn't seem bothered by the barrage of questions.

"I don't know. I've never given anyone a ride."

"Oh," said Andrew, his head drooping a little.

"Except Zezil. Once. I won't be making that mistake again if I can help it. Nearly got us all killed."

"Did he transform?" said Andromeda.

"As soon as we left the trees," said Erro with a shake of his head. "Frightened him, I guess. Aquila has a scar on his wing joint."

Erro rubbed a hand over the afflicted area, where a pattern of white teeth marks stood out bald against his lion's pelt and the start of his wing. Andromeda rode up closer and leaned as far over on her horse as she dared to get a better look.

"Those marks look much larger than Zezil's teeth," she said.

"They grow too, just like everything else."

"Is it terrible that I'm hoping something will happen that makes him transform?"

Erro laughed. "You may regret your enthusiasm when it happens. He takes out his aggression on whatever's in front of him when he transforms. It's very handy if we run into a bear or a wolf. Not so much when you're the one in his line of sight. I've got a few scars myself."

"I'll be sure to step out of the way," said Andromeda.

Erro smiled, his eyes locking with hers easily, naturally. Aquila was nearly as tall as her horse. The top of his plumed head hit at about her mare's neck, and Erro was tall enough that he hardly had to raise his chin to look at her.

"Would you ever give someone a ride?" said Andrew, careful and deliberate with each word.

"That would be up to Aquila, not me. Ask him."

"Uh, ask him?"

"Sure."

"Now?"

"Why not?"

Andrew clucked his horse up beside Aquila. He leaned over his stallion's neck to look the griffin in the eye.

"Uh, Aquila, would it be all right if … well, would you object to … what I mean to say is, would you take me flying?"

Aquila twitched his head around to look at Andrew and clucked his beak. Andrew looked to Andromeda.

"Any idea what that means?"

Andromeda's eyebrows were turned down in puzzlement. "Odd. I almost got something very clear from him. Almost like a true thought, like words. But it vanished before I could make it out."

"So? What is that supposed to mean?"

Andromeda shrugged, and Andrew huffed and let his horse fall back.

With Andrew discouraged, the party fell into silence for a while. But as they rode on through the day, they began chatting idly and telling stories. Erro asked about the vampire who'd crashed their ball and about the werewolf pack which had decimated their search party. The Avalons asked about Erro's life in the woods. He told them about seeing elves in the forest, as it seemed appropriate under the circumstances. He talked about trapping and hunting, and misadventures with his furry, feathered companions.

"So Zezil chomps down on the bee, gets himself stung right on the tongue, and I know we're in for it," said Erro as the noon sun began its western course toward the horizon. "He starts breathing heavy and shaking. All signs he's about to lose it. So I start to run to him, because sometimes I can calm him down by petting him and talking to him, but on the way, I stepped right in the trap. I forgot all about it. So I go flying up in the air by my ankle." He paused to enjoy the laughter. "Luckily, Zezil thought that was pretty amusing. He started running circles around me, yipping right in my ear."

Zezil was walking beside Aquila, looking up at his master each time his name was spoken, unaware that the laughter was all about him.

"We're almost there," said Erro, sitting up a little straighter and surveying the area. "We won't be able to see it until we're right on it. The villagers like their privacy. They go to great lengths to hide it to keep out unwanted wildlife, people, and anything in between."

The Avalons began looking around, peering through the trees to catch a glimpse of a home or any sign of human life.

"It's through that cluster of pines over there," said Erro, pointing.

The pines in question had taken root uncharacteristically close together, and the ground was uneven with mounds of earth pushed up by roots. Some of the larger roots burst through the ground and intertwined with each other in ankle-breaking configurations. The riders dismounted and led their horses carefully through the sticky branches.

After they pulled back the last of the resilient foliage, the siblings stopped to take in the peculiar but impressive sight. A large wall, made of tree trunks halved and set side by side protected the village. Moss and vines made a home on the wall, and limbs full of fresh leaves were leaned against it, camouflaging it from predators. The only entrance was a small, rectangular opening just tall enough for a horse to walk through. A rider would have to dismount for fear of head injury. The opening was not wide enough to see much of anything besides a dirt road.

"Impressive," said Michael, craning his neck to take in the full height of the wall. "Is it like this all the way around the village?"

"Yes," said Erro, sliding off Aquila's back. "They have another entrance on the other side, but they keep that one covered unless there's an emergency."

Erro made to lead the way, but stopped with his foot suspended in the air. He set it down slowly, sidestepping to avoid something in the dirt.

"That's odd," he said, eyes on the ground.

"What?" said Michael, coming in for a closer look.

"Tracks. Lots of them. Horses and people," said Erro, a hand on his chin. "The villagers rarely leave. They have everything they need inside the wall. There shouldn't be this many fresh tracks."

Now everyone observed the ground. Boots and horse shoes stamped the dirt all the way to the entrance. Prints on top of prints. Erro's hand shot from his chin to his dagger hilt, his eyes nearly as big as Aquila's, his face rapidly losing color.

"Not here," he said, his voice hoarse. "Please, not here."

Aquila's feathers ruffled into a mane as he gnashed his beak. Andromeda could feel his wrath, hot and consuming like a white-hot flame. It invaded her own feelings, clenching her fists and grinding her teeth. She went to one knee, head in her hands, fighting to regain control of her own head.

Erro sprinted for the entrance, and Aquila sprang after him, launching himself on the tightly coiled muscles of his lion haunches.

Andrew was at his twin's side almost as quickly, but she was already rising when he put his hand on her shoulder.

"What's going on?" said Michael, looking to Andromeda.

"I'm not sure."

She grabbed up her horse's reins and led it off at a trot through the entrance. Her siblings followed. They all pulled up their horses and stared in horrified awe at the destruction.

Houses lined either side of the dirt path, made of wood and mud and what used to be thatch. Many were burned to the ground, nothing more than black, smoking planks of wood. Those left standing were crippled by large smoking holes in ceilings and walls. In the far distance, at the end of the road, were what was left of the villager's crops. More black than green and yellow. Still smoldering. Worse than the char and the smoke were the crimson stains splashed in the dirt and on still standing doorways. Pools of it leached into the earth. The owners of the blood pools had been removed from the road, but the stench of dead flesh proved their resting place was not far off, behind the houses or behind closed doors.

There were no screams of terror, though surely the air had rung with them in the night. Now there were cries of anguish and wails of lament echoing from half-burned houses. Through the opening left by a devastated wall, a woman was pulling at her long blonde hair, the body of a man laid on a bed in front of her. Three children with soot-blackened faces streaked with tears huddled in front of a decimated house. They pressed closer together at the sight of strangers, but then the eldest girl stood.

"Erro?" she said.

Erro was on his hands and knees, his fingers tracing the shape of a patch of blood-soaked dirt. He looked up, dazed, and searched for the sound of the voice with murky eyes.

"Lora," he said, rising unsteadily.

The child ran to him, and he rushed toward her, meeting her halfway and hugging her tight.

"Lora, where's your mother?"

Lora looked up at him, her chin resting on his chest, and burst into tears. Erro's own eyes brimmed with tears, and he chewed his cheek to keep from freeing them. He hushed the girl gently, stroking her brown braids.

"What about your father?" said Erro, the fear of her answer clear in his eyes.

"He's taking care of the hurt people," said Lora.

"All right. That's good," said Erro, crouching down to the girl's height and holding her hands. "You go back to watching your sisters and wait for him, all right? I have to go see Jeremiah and Fiona. Are they all right?"

"I don't know," said Lora, wiping at her tears.

Erro led the girl back to her sisters, and then set off at a jog down the road, passing the Avalons without a glance. Michael caught him by the arm.

"Erro, whoever did this is going to pay," he said.

"I know."

The venom and the surety in his voice raised Michael's eyebrow.

"Do you already know who's responsible?"

Erro pulled his arm free and made off for a house farther down the lane, Aquila and Zezil matching his pace. The Avalons led their horses along behind, whispering to each other.

"I think he knows who did this," said Michael.

"Then he ought to tell us," said Andrew. "Whoever did this should be hanged."

"Beheaded and left for the birds," said Felicity.

"Shh," said Andromeda.

Erro had stopped in front of a flame-licked door, his fist raised and hovering. Half of the roof had collapsed, and the western wall looked like it might do the same at the slightest provocation. Erro looked at his feet and exhaled long and slow, his cheeks puffing up with the air before he let it out. He knocked on the door just as the siblings pulled up behind him. The hitching post in front of the house was broken in half, but they did their best to tie their horses to the foundation while they waited for an answer to the knock.

Erro's breathing became quick and shallow as he waited, hearing no sound. He knocked again, more urgently. He opened his mouth to call, but shut it again.

This time there were murmurs from within the home. Rustling and grunts of effort drew closer to the door. A short, stocky woman with wild, curly, bright red hair opened it. She had a nearly perfectly circular face with bright rosy cheeks washed clean of soot by the tears from her swollen, pale-blue eyes. The corners of her full, pink lips and the few lines of her face pulled down at the corners with grief.

"Erro, love!" she said, reaching up on her tiptoes to grab his face in her hands. "I haven't seen you in two moons. What are you doing here?"

Erro gently grabbed her wrists and gave her a small smile.

"Never mind me, Fiona. What happened here? Are you and Jeremiah and the kids all right?"

Fiona's eyes filled with tears. "They came in the dead of night. Nobody was ready. We—"

Her eyes found the Avalons in their slick black leather armor and fine furs, and she dropped her hands from Erro's face.

"Who are your noble friends?" she said with a stiff curtsy, pulling at the folds of her sackcloth dress.

"The Avalon children. Our princes and princesses," said Erro. Fiona's eyes widened, and her second curtsy was deeper, bowing her head.

"Pardon me, Your Highnesses. Had I but known, I ..." She blushed. "Forgive my rude behavior."

"There's no need for apologies, dear lady," said Michael. "Please, stand."

He took her hand in his and gently pulled her up from her curtsy.

"Thank you, Your Highness," said Fiona. "You honor me."

"Who did this?" said Andrew. "They shall feel the wrath of the crown."

"A group of raiders, Your Highness. There are many such parties in these woods, but this was a large one. Their leader wears a wolf skin cloak."

"What of his hair?" said Erro through gritted teeth. "Is it long and free to his shoulder blades? The color of a common rat?"

"Yes." Fiona's mouth opened in an 'o', and she looked to Erro. "It's your raider, isn't it?"

Erro's face curled in a snarl as he nodded his head. "Brock."

He spat the word, his face contorted as if he'd tasted something vile.

"Your raider?" said Andromeda, barely above a whisper. "You don't mean the—"

"How many were with him?" said Erro, grabbing Fiona's shoulders.

"At least thirty."

"His numbers have grown since I last ran into him."

"That wasn't the worst of it. Nor the burning and the stealing. They had a wolf with them, Erro. A moon mutt. Biggest beast I ever saw, walking upright like a man. I haven't seen one since I was a girl, just a glimpse. This one was far bigger."

"They had a werewolf?" said Felicity, incredulous. "It didn't harm them?"

"No, princess," said Fiona. "Not that I saw. Only picked off villagers. Savaged them. We had to ... we had to kill some of our own, so they wouldn't change. Did you know they change right there? Right there in the light of the moon they're bitten under? Takes a little while, but they do."

Fiona shivered.

"But you and yours are all right?" said Erro, as the Avalons exchanged looks of horror.

A sob slipped between Fiona's lips.

"Who?" said Erro, shaking her.

"Katrina."

Erro's hands fell away from Fiona, and he choked out a surprised moan, as if he'd been punched in the gut.

"She's alive," said Fiona, her tears falling and her words shaky, "but I don't know for how long."

Erro sidestepped Fiona and pushed the damaged door so hard it fell off its hinges, disappearing into the blackened depths of the home.

Chapter 6

Erro's Blood Oath

Atalanta's bruised knees hit the stone, and she wobbled, head rocking backward, about to pass out. Thetis released her hair and dabbed at the blood in the corner of his thin mouth with his thumb. He stuck his thumb in his mouth between his top two elongated canines and winked at Atalanta as he sucked the blood.

"Don't enjoy yourself too much, Thetis," said Tyrannus, though he looked unconcerned as he fiddled with his velvet cloak, rubbing at a dark stain on it.

"I cannot help it, Your Majesty," said Thetis, his deep, ocean-blue eyes more alive than Atalanta had ever seen them. "Elf blood is so much … cleaner than human. Sweet like honeysuckle. I haven't had it since my days as a fledgling."

"If you fully transform and take off her head, I'll have yours on a spit."

"I haven't been a fledgling for nearly two centuries," said Thetis, suddenly dull and eternally bored once again. "I won't lose control."

"How do you expect me …?" Atalanta swallowed hard, head swaying forward now. "Expect me to do magic in this state?"

"I don't need your magic at this very moment, my dear," said Tyrannus. "What I need is your compliance."

"Then I suppose you should just kill me," said Atalanta, licking at her cracking lips.

Tyrannus pushed himself out of his chair in the time Atalanta needed to blink. His orange eyes glowed as he approached. Atalanta rocked back with wide eyes to look up at him. Slouching and lounging in his chair, he seemed not much taller than an elf. In truth, he was massive, both in height and in muscular girth.

Eight feet tall and built like a wolf, he curled his hairless snout in a slobbery snarl.

"If you do not comply, it will be your father who dies, not you," he said. "Don't forget that."

"He won't trade himself. The council won't let him," said Atalanta, fighting off dizziness as she got to her feet.

"I think you know your father will do whatever he pleases without thought for consequences, just as all elves do. He will do anything to get you back, and you know it."

Atalanta's eyes flitted momentarily to the ground, though she tried to keep her gaze steady. Tyrannus smiled.

"Of course, I would much prefer your company to his," said Tyrannus. "I do not underestimate your father. He will not break or comply with my wishes. He will die, and you will take his place on the throne, and though I will have a lesser adversary, I still will not have magic at my disposal."

Atalanta was too weak to expend her rage. She clenched her fists and tried to stay upright.

"That is why we are playing this game," said Tyrannus. "You will break. If you withstand the bloodletting, we will try real torture. If you withstand both, I'll have Thetis do more than drain you."

Atalanta stood as a stone, eyes fixed on the end of Tyrannus' snout, fighting the fear trying to creep onto her face.

"Are you too much of a babe to know what happens when an elf is fledged?"

Atalanta's eyes went wide and she sucked in a sharp breath. She turned her face from Tyrannus only to find Thetis's cheeky grin.

It was old lore, passed down as fairytales—frightening stories young elves told one another of elves with gemstone eyes and faces so lovely it hurt your heart. They ripped other elves in half and licked their blood from the ground. But it was more than a fairytale. It was why for nearly a century, any elf bitten by vampire or werewolf was killed by companions or family members without question, even before they'd begun to transform. The threat of a diseased elf was far too terrible to entertain, even for loved ones.

"That's right, my dear. If you keep up this admirable but foolish resistance, Thetis will envenomate you a little more each day as you are drained, replacing your blood with our venom. Don't fret, though. I'm not so foolish as to make you such a powerful creature when you hate me so. I might risk coming out on the wrong end of that fight. Still, partial transformation is rather painful, and you will have ... urges that weren't there before. I will make you unable to recognize yourself."

Tyrannus gripped her chin, pricking her cheek with his yellow nails, and tilted up her head.

"Think about it. What's a little magic, really? You either give me magic or your soul."

He bent his head and licked the trickle of sticky blood still on her neck, and she shuddered. And though she tried to hold it back, a whimper escaped her lips and a tear rolled down her cheek.

* * *

The walls of Fiona's entry room were entirely black, and there were puddles of water and piles of the sawdust used to extinguish the fire covering the floor. The breeze blew freely through the massive hole in the roof, stirring up the scent of smoke and char. The only thing still standing amongst the wreckage of ceiling beams and wooden furniture was the simple stone fireplace.

Zezil tried to follow Andromeda inside, clambering over a crumbling, blackened beam.

"No, Zezil," said Andromeda, pointing at him and shaking a finger, unsure how to command him. "Stay outside."

Zezil just kicked his back legs, looking for purchase as he

dangled a little above the ground. Andromeda sighed. Aquila's paw reached in the door and urged the vexar off the beam. Aquila then put his head in and nudged Zezil out with his beak.

Andromeda watched the griffin, a ponderous look on her face, until Andrew tugged her forward. The whole house shuddered as they walked through it.

"Fiona," said Felicity, eyeing the walls with distrust, "we can stay outside. Please don't feel obligated to invite us in."

"Truth is," said Fiona, her voice timid and shaky, "I think it might do Katrina good to see you. She always talks about being a princess. She knows all of your names, and she sometimes puts you all in her little games. But she doesn't know what you look like. I think it would be nice for her to know that."

Felicity put a hand to her chest and played with the silver cross resting there. "How old is Katrina?" she said, her own voice nearly as weak as Fiona's now.

"She's four," said Fiona, stifling a sob. "She's to be five next month."

Fiona turned away and led them down the one narrow hallway in the home. The flames had only partially reached inside it, and the black marks on the wall only extended a short way inside.

Fiona went in the first room of the three rooms branching from the hallway. The Avalons crowded around the doorway, as there was no more room for them in the small bedroom.

A man with deep brown hair and a small beard sat on one side of a child-sized bed that took up most of the room. His expression was hard, the skin of his neck and jaw taut, but his eyes were weary and tear-filled. On the other edge of the bed sat a young boy no more than thirteen. He had the same brown hair as his father, but his had been allowed to grow out long enough to curl as it brushed his earlobes. He had a few angry red patches on his exposed skin, and his clothes were covered in tiny soot-rimmed holes.

Erro was on his knees, holding the hand of the round-faced

little girl who lay shaking on the bed. Felicity's hand tightened on her cross, and Andromeda's eyes stung with tears. Andrew looked at the floor, distress in the crease of his brow. Michael rubbed a hand across his jaw, fury and grief warring for dominance on his face.

Katrina had the red curls of her mother, but much of it was singed black or missing. She lay on the bed in nothing but a diaper cloth, clothes being too painful. The burns covering her body rivaled the color of her hair. Much of the skin of her arms and chest was peeled away by flame, leaving raw sores and blisters full of infection. The skin still intact over the rest of her body was bright red with the fever that had driven her into a deep, fitful sleep. With every ragged breath, her small body shook and twitched.

Erro's back rose and fell with quick, haggard breaths, and he lay his face on the bed to muffle his crying. At his tears, Andromeda's poured down her face, and with one look at her sister, Felicity's came too.

"Someone shall pay for this," said Michael. His voice sounded odd as it was forced around the lump in his throat.

"Aye, someone shall," said the man on the bed, turning his hollow face to Michael. "Who might you be, nobleman?"

"Jeremiah, these are the Avalon children," said Fiona.

Jeremiah's eyebrows raised. "In truth?"

"Yes, my good man," said Michael, with a tilt of his head.

Jeremiah moved to get up from the bed and bow, but Michael's upheld hand made him sink back down onto the blankets.

"Tell me who has done this, and they shall feel my royal wrath."

"I know no names," said Jeremiah. "There is a group of raiders that have terrorized these woods for many decades now. Here in our walls, we don't see much of them. In the past, when they tried to get in and pillage our livestock and crops, we cut them off at the entrance. We had the advantage, as they can only get in one-by-one on horse that way. There were usually no more than fifteen at a time, normally less, and they always made enough racket to let us know they were there well before they made their assault.

"This time they came in the dead of night, and they were more than thirty strong. You may not believe me, Your Highness, but they had a werewolf with them."

"I've no reason to doubt you," said Michael.

Jeremiah nodded once and said, "They took what they wanted—sheep, pigs, corn, barley, women, and half our men's lives—and then burned the rest. I fought with the other men, and Brent worked with the other boys to put out the fires." Jeremiah pointed to his smaller mirror image on the other end of the bed. "I got a few of the bastards, but I couldn't ever get close to the leader. The werewolf was always nearby. I fought until I heard Fiona screaming. One of them was dragging her out by the hair and the house was ablaze. He was a big fellow, took a lot to take him down. While I was fighting him off, Brent ran in the house after Katrina, but he couldn't get her out in time. The roof collapsed."

"I was so close," said Brent, shaking his head and rubbing his eye. "She was right there in front of me, running to me. Then a beam fell right on top of her. Would have crushed her, but it lodged. She screamed so loud." The young boy's lip quivered. "I pulled her out, but her clothes were on fire. I carried her out and rolled her on the ground until they went out, but I didn't do it fast enough."

"Wasn't your fault, son," said Jeremiah.

"It was Brock's," said Erro. He gripped Katrina's hand as he looked out the window. "I'll kill him this time. I swear it. Werewolf pet or not." Erro reached out for Brent and tipped the boy's chin up so that their eyes met. "I'm going to track him down again and kill him for Katrina."

"We'll help," said Andrew, hand in a fist on the doorway.

"Erro, how do you know this Brock?" said Michael.

Erro turned dark eyes on Michael, his face a solemn scowl. "He's the man who slaughtered my parents."

* * *

Katrina died just as night fell.

Aquila had joined the vigil, looking in the single window above the bed, his head slightly bowed to look at the little girl, never moving an inch. Fiona was on the bed with her husband and son, Katrina's head pulled into her lap so she could drip water into the child's burning mouth. Katrina's body shuddered and convulsed in her mother's arms, and she nearly sat up, back rigid and arched in the effort to pull in another breath. None came.

The room flew into chaos, everyone yelling orders and trying to help at once. Despite her many would-be rescuers flocking her bed, Katrina slipped away, her body relaxing finally as she lay back in Fiona's arms, utterly still and no longer in pain.

Fiona's wail made the Avalons look away, feeling unwelcome in such a private moment of grief. Aquila chirped out his own cry of morning—a trilling sound of such melancholy that Zezil began to whine beneath the sill. Jeremiah held his wife and soaked up his tears in her hair, but Fiona's wails only turned to screams. Brent curled up on the end of the bed to cry in silence.

Erro rose from his place by the bed and shoved roughly past the Avalons without a sound.

"I think we'd best leave them to mourn in private," said Michael, turning from his siblings when they looked to him, wiping at the tears on his face.

Outside, the siblings huddled around their horses, unsure of what to do or what to say. Aquila and Zezil were no longer by the window. Erro and his animal companions had vanished. Felicity took a shaking Andromeda in her arms, and the sisters wept into each other's hair, gold and pitch comingling around their heads. As much as they had trained for battle, the young royals had very little experience with death. The death of their search party companions had shaken them, but the loss of one so young in such violent fashion was unimagined and they were utterly unprepared.

A yell of rage and loss cut the quiet of the budding night.

"Erro," said Andromeda. "We have to find him before he does something rash."

"I'm inclined to join him," said Andrew.

"Andromeda's right," said Michael, casting a scolding look at Andrew. "Come on."

Once again at the helm, Michael stood straighter and his eyes regained their usual fervor. They found Erro on the far edge of the village where burned crops and broken sheep corrals scattered the landscape. The few sheep that had not been stolen or slaughtered huddled together a good distance from Erro, eyeing him warily. Erro sat with his back to a massive tree that in the daytime managed to keep two of the corrals in complete shade. His hands were pressed to his face, his fingers twisting in his hair. His sobs reached the Avalons from a long way off. Aquila lay next to him, a wing outstretched to curl around him as the griffin nudged his face gently with his beak. Zezil was curled in his lap, his eyes upturned to his master, whining. A quick peek into his brain told Andromeda the vexar knew of his master's pain, and his own distress came from not knowing what he needed to attack in order to fix it.

"Erro?" said Andromeda, approaching first.

A quick, surprised inhale cut off his sobs, and his hands fell from his face.

"Erro, I'm sorry. It isn't enough, but I don't know what else to say. Except maybe ... you're not going anywhere tonight, are you?"

"Not tonight. I'll leave in the morning." He looked at his

hands as he talked.

Andromeda knelt on the ground in front of him, making her face level with his, and at last he met her eyes.

"Won't you see her buried?"

"I'd rather see Brock buried."

"Erro, you shouldn't go alone," said Michael. "Help us complete our search for Atalanta, and then we will go with you to bring Brock and his men to justice."

"Why shouldn't we just go with him on the morrow?" said Andrew.

"Because," said Michael, meeting his brother's defiant look with sternness, "we must complete our quest. Atalanta could very well be alive. She must remain our priority until we have exhausted our search area, located her, or found evidence of her death. Little Katrina is gone. She will be avenged, but Atalanta needs our help now."

"Do as your brother says, Andrew," said Erro. "He's right. The elfin princess needs your help. I can kill Brock on my own."

"I'll do what I like," said Andrew, earning himself a miniscule smile from Erro before Michael shoved the younger boy behind him none too gently with a muttered, "We'll see about that."

"So you won't come with us? You won't let us help you?" Michael asked Erro.

"My business with Brock is long overdue."

Aquila gnashed his beak and pulled his wing away from Erro.

"Don't talk to me that way," said Erro, glaring at the griffin. "I'm going after him whether you approve or not, as you well know."

Aquila clicked away again, feathers ruffling.

"Fine. You don't have to come, but if I die you'll feel rather awful, now won't you? I need the both of you."

Aquila shook his whole body and then lay his head in the grass between his paws, averting his eyes from Erro.

"Please don't do it, Erro," said Andromeda. Her reaching

hand pulled back when his eyes found it, but she chewed her lip and extended it again, wrapping his hand in hers. "There are too many. They have a werewolf who does their bidding. It's a fight you cannot win alone, no matter how true your knives fly. And if you die then I … well, I shall be very sad."

Erro stared at her hand on his. He swallowed hard before meeting her eyes.

"You don't understand, Andromeda," he said. His eyes were wide with a frightening memory, and he gripped her hand too tightly. "I heard them die. I heard her screaming. The blood dripped through the floor."

Andromeda's throat closed, but she could not tear her eyes away. Michael moved forward, but Felicity threw out a hand to block his way.

"I remember her like an angel," said Erro. "With hair like a chestnut mare and the loveliest voice in all the world. She was singing me to sleep like always when they came. I heard the shouts and the horses. Father came in with his daggers—the ones I carry—and I got scared. 'Raiders, Elizabeth,' he said. 'They want the cattle. Take Erro to the cellar.' The cellar was in the floor underneath the kitchen. It was so dark, but it smelled like my mother's preserves. I couldn't hear anything until they started laughing. That's when Father yelled and Mother gripped me so tight I could hardly breathe. They sounded like monsters when they came inside, stomping and breaking things, grunting and whooping. Mother shoved me behind the shelves of preserves and the grain crates. 'Don't move,' she said. 'Don't make a sound until they go away. Promise me, Erro. Promise your mother.' And I never should have made that promise."

None of the Avalons moved a muscle. They hardly even breathed. And Erro kept his eyes on Andromeda's face, even as fresh tears began to spill down her cheeks.

"It didn't take them long to find the door," said Erro. "Brock came down the stairs himself when he saw her in there. And she stood tall and strong, and she didn't scream when he yanked her out by her braid. She screamed later, though, when he threw her on the floor." Erro's eyes brimmed with tears and his voice barely made it past his lips when he said, "She screamed for a very long time.

"I covered my ears and prayed for her to just stop screaming. The cellar door was still open, but I couldn't see her. I saw him take out his knife, though. And when she stopped screaming, I prayed for her to start again. To make any sort of sound.

"I kept my promise, though. And then when they were gone with our herd and I saw her lying there and Father in the yard, I made another one. To myself. That I would find that man and kill him and anybody else who got in my way. It took me some time, but I found out that he lived in these woods, and so I live in them, too. And I'll live in them until he's gone."

Chapter 7

The Cyclops' Lament

The uneasy bleating of sheep carried on the wind. The Avalons struggled to find words with which to extend comfort and came up wanting. When Erro released her hand, looking down at the grass, Andromeda held on. He raised his head slowly, moving to her hand first and then her face. She met his eyes with tears shimmering in her own.

"Erro, the extent of your loss is something I can't imagine, but the image of what may happen to you if you go after those men alone is clear and terrible behind my eyes. If you go, I will not be able to banish it, and it will haunt me mercilessly until I know you are safe. I beg you, please, let us help you. Stay with us. You have waited all these years, why can you not wait a little while longer to guarantee a better chance of success?"

Now not even the sheep made a sound. Andrew opened his mouth, stepping forward, and then closed it, his eyes moving between Erro and his twin.

"If my princess desires my company, who am I to refuse?" said Erro.

Andromeda blinked back her tears and allowed a smile to brighten her eyes.

"We'll be happy to have you as part of our company," said Michael.

"On one condition," said Andrew.

Erro looked at him with a cocked brow.

"Convince your large, beaked friend there to take me flying."

"What say you, Aquila?" said Erro. "Seems a small favor to exchange for my eternal soul and all that."

Aquila made a soft cooing sound, twitching his head ever so slightly as he gazed at Erro.

"I'd say that's a yes," said Erro. "Of course, we can just ask Andromeda."

"He didn't say yes in so many words," said Andromeda, sparing her and Erro's intertwined fingers one more glance before releasing her grip, "but he is feeling ... relieved."

"I guess we won't know for certain until he throws you off his back," said Erro.

Their laughter broke through the last of the careful, unspoken horror and pity hanging between them.

"Might I request one thing?" said Erro when the merry sounds died away.

"Name it?" said Michael.

"I would like to stay for Katrina's burial and help with the repairs as much as I can before we set off."

"Of course," said Michael, lowering his head. "Though, I don't think we should stay more than a day."

"That should be sufficient. I wasn't far from Everly when I ran across the cyclops beast. Though I doubt there is any trail, it will still give us a starting point, and we can set off at first light morning after next."

"Everly?" said Felicity.

"It's the name the villagers gave this place, after the evergreens that keep them safe ... or did."

* * *

The Avalons were hardly able to assist the residents of Everly with repairs. Instead, they spent most of the next day digging graves and performing burial rites.

The Herons buried Katrina under the ancient tree where Erro had confessed his dark past.

"She told me she saw fairies living in that tree," said Brent as he walked beside Erro, behind his parents who were carrying the little coffin. "She played there every day. She was always asking me to join her games. I should have said yes more often."

Brent wiped at his nose with the sleeve of his tunic, and Erro put a hand on the boy's shoulder and squeezed it somewhat roughly.

"Are you going to find those men, Erro?"

"Yes."

"Are you going to kill them?" Brent forced the question through gritted teeth.

Erro looked down at the boy. "Yes, Brent. I'm going to kill them all."

Brent slowed his pace, causing the Avalons to slow behind them and allowing his parents to get out of earshot.

"Take me with you."

"You're too young, Brent," said Erro, shaking his head as he looked down at Zezil snaking around his ankles.

"That's a load of dung and you know it," said Brent. "You were only ten the first time you killed one of them. I'm thirteen."

The Avalons exchanged wide-eyed looks. Erro stiffened. Aquila clicked his beak.

"You don't want to be like me, Brent. You don't know what it's like to spill blood, to take life. You don't want to know. Right now you're angry, and you think you do, but you don't. I won't take you. That's final. Turn your mind to fond memories of your sister."

Brent shook Erro's hand from his shoulder.

"I'm sorry, Brent."

Brent looked up at the older boy, and suddenly his face crumpled and he looked away, wiping at his eyes.

The funeral was an excruciating affair. All of the villagers came to pay their respects to their youngest fallen neighbor. Fiona's tears fell in a constant stream as the dirt was replaced, bouncing off the tiny coffin with a horribly hollow sound. The villagers filed by, dropping flowers and handmade dolls and hand-carved wooden trinkets beside the stone that served as a marker.

Lora, the girl who had lost her mother to the werewolf, approached the grave with her sisters. Her face was now washed of soot and her blonde hair was plaited down her back. She bent to kiss the marker.

"Goodbye, Katrina," she whispered. "I'll miss you. You made up the best games."

Lora's little sisters nodded in solemn agreement. Fiona's knees hit the dirt, and her scream made the sisters jump back with guilt on their faces. The youngest began to cry, mixing her frightened whimpers with Fiona's wails of agony. Jeremiah scooped his wife in his arms as best he could and murmured in her ear. The crowd parted respectfully, leaving the Herons to grieve in private.

Erro moved with the crowd, but after a few paces he began to run. The Avalons watched him crash through the blackened crops. Zezil raced after his master, yipping excitedly at the unexpected game of chase. Andromeda looked to Aquila. The griffin watched Erro out of one large, amber eye but did not move to follow. Instead, he lay down by Fiona, wrapping his body around the headstone, head up high like a vigilant watchman.

"Should we go after him?" said Andromeda.

"He's not headed for the wood. I think it would be best to let him be," said Michael.

With their palms red and raw from shoveling graves, the Avalons began to help the villagers clear the charred wreckage from the buildings. They dragged the blackened wood and destroyed possessions to the outskirts of the village.

"At this pace, we won't have time to help cut any fresh planks or begin restorations," said Michael, trudging through the remains of a decimated home as the sun began to dip toward the horizon.

"At this pace, we won't even be able to get everything cleared," said Andrew with a grunt as he tried to lift a fallen beam from what used to be the doorway.

Erro materialized at his side.

"When do you plan to head out tomorrow?" Erro asked Michael as he moved to hoist the other end of Andrew's beam.

"First thing."

"Good. The sooner we find the elf, the sooner we can go after Brock."

* * *

"Truly, we cannot carry one more thing," said Michael, holding up his hands to the old woman thrusting the parchment-wrapped package at him.

The villagers had stuffed their horses' packs to bursting. The late Sir Gregor's horse was covered withers to tail with blankets and bulging packs of food, flints, oil, and common arrows so that Andrew could spare the silver-tipped ones reserved for the hearts of moon mutts. Most of the villagers had returned to work clearing wreckage and cutting new wood after delivering their gifts, but a small ring of well-wishers surrounded the royals, the Herons among them.

"Please, we would much rather you share it with the village. We have more than enough," said Felicity, gently lowering the woman's outstretched arms. "Give it to the children."

The old woman smiled at the idea. She didn't seem able to speak, or perhaps she just did not like the way her voice sounded with so few teeth in her mouth. Instead, she nodded and tottered to the cluster of children watching the departure of the royals. She unwrapped the parchment and let the children pinch off pieces of the warm cornbread loaf, smiling her toothless smile.

"You shouldn't have done all of this," said Andromeda, taking Fiona by the hands. "You have lost so much. You should be receiving goods, not giving them away."

"You're going to hunt down the raiders," said Jeremiah.

"Brent told us," said Fiona.

"Yes, as soon as we have completed our search for the elf princess," said Andromeda. "She may still be alive."

"Make sure they don't come back to hurt us or anyone else again, and you will have helped us more than any goods could," said Fiona.

A murmur of assent rippled through the crowd.

"You have our word," said Michael. "They will fall beneath our blades. Their moon mutt as well."

The first cheer came from a man in the center of the crowd, his head wrapped in a bloody bandage. The Avalons mounted their horses with humble smiles, having never truly felt the admiration of their subjects before. It was a feeling they would not soon forget. Erro kissed Fiona's cheek, embraced Brent, and exchanged a meaningful nod with Jeremiah before climbing atop Aquila, his mouth a thin line, his eyes turned to the woods rather than the crowd.

The small party set out with a throng of cheering onlookers trailing behind their mounts. Zezil ran ahead, already chasing after the barrage of scents the woods provided. They passed single file out of Everly, looking back to wave and thank their gracious hosts one last time. The crowd quickly disappeared as the pine needles concealing the village entrance swallowed the party in a sticky, prickly curtain.

"Lead the way, Erro," said Michael when they had fought their way through the natural barricade.

"It's not far from here."

Andromeda studied Erro's face with side glances through the shield of her hair as they rode. He seemed unsure of what expression to wear. Mostly he stared straight ahead, his face blank, perhaps a little thoughtful. Every now and then she caught a small smile at something the others had said as they chatted. More often, she caught a glimpse of a row of three thin lines between his eyes.

"We should have brought cook along," said Andrew. "I feel as though I haven't had a decent meal in ages."

"I would like to try what a prince calls a decent meal," said Erro, turning to Andrew.

"Oh, you'll find out. After all of our business is done in these woods, you're coming back to the palace with us. No more need to wander when the raiders are gone. You can stay at the palace."

Erro turned his eyes to the heavens, pondering the thought. A true smile lit his face for the first time since they had entered Everly. "What shall I do at the palace?"

"You can be my squire," said Andrew with an impish grin.

Erro's laugh was a short, loud bark. "A squire is not supposed to be better than his liege."

"Better at what, pray tell?"

"I'm not sure your pride could handle the answer," said Erro.

Zezil threw his head back in a wild, excited howl. Erro perked up like a hunting dog on point. Aquila froze. Andrew's horse pulled up just behind him, hooves sliding in the dirt, snorting with disapproval.

"He smells something. Perhaps we can get some fresh meat to go with all of our fruit and cheese."

"It's not prey," said Andromeda, her nose wrinkled in concentration, her fingers to her temples. "He recognizes it, but he doesn't want to eat it. Wait, Aquila is thinking something." Four pairs of eyes watched her impatiently as she closed her own and concentrated. "Aquila doesn't ... smell it exactly. He ... senses it. Its aura. Just as he can sense those who are good of heart and pure of soul, he can sense those with wicked intentions. He doesn't like whatever it is, but he recognizes it, too." Suddenly, she gasped.

"What?" said Felicity.

"It ... it was an image. In my head. A memory, I think. I've never seen anything like that from an animal before. I think it was Aquila's. I saw the cyclops with two heads."

"Is the bracelet meant to do that?" said Andrew.

"I don't know," said Andromeda, shaking her head. "Aquila isn't like other animals. He's more intelligent. I get complete thoughts from him, not just feelings. Sometimes, I even think I get whispers of real words."

"It was the cyclops, truly?" said Michael. "Was it as they described?"

"Yes, two necks on one torso, and each head had only one eye. It's a hunchback as well, and utterly hairless."

"I told you as much," said Erro. "Did you not believe me?"

"It's smaller than I had imagined," said Andromeda. "Just a deformed man, really. A rather short one. Even more so because he's so stooped. But his muscles were larger than an ordinary man."

"He was here? How recently?" said Felicity.

"It would have to be only a day or two, or even Zezil wouldn't be able to get a scent," said Erro.

"How close are we to the place you saw him before?" Michael asked Erro.

"Not all that far, just another mile or two."

"Perhaps it lives around here," said Michael, looking around as if he expected to see it running through the underbrush.

"Where exactly does a two-headed cyclops live?" said Andrew. "Does he build a cabin or live in cave?"

"What difference does it make?" said Felicity.

"Maybe he lives in trees," said Andrew.

Felicity rolled her eyes.

"He could live underwater for all we know of him," said Michael. "It would help to know where to look."

All heads turned to Andromeda. She sighed. "I don't know everything."

"Quick, where's pen and parchment?" said Felicity, rummaging through her saddlebag. "I must get it down in writing or no one will ever believe me. Andromeda doesn't know everything."

Andromeda rolled her eyes.

"If he didn't wade through a stream or swing through the trees, Zezil can lead us right to his door, no matter where that might be," said Erro.

"Then let's make haste. He could be just ahead," said Andrew.

"Andromeda, does Zezil smell anyone else?" said Michael, face solemn.

Andromeda's eyebrows lifted in understanding, and she frowned. "No. He doesn't smell Atalanta at all. Although, I'm not sure he knows what an elf smells like." Her head twitched towards Aquila, as if he had whispered and she was trying to catch the words. She looked at him curiously. "Aquila doesn't sense her."

Felicity bit her lip. "That doesn't necessarily mean she's dead, right? The cyclops could be holding her prisoner."

The teenagers exchanged concerned, unbelieving looks.

"We press on," said Michael, putting his heel to his horse's side. "We need to know either way."

* * *

Callid's vampire escort had arrived at Tyrannus' palace just before dawn broke over the horizon. Callid had remained outside to watch the pink and purple clouds drift overhead as the sun rose over the mountains. He enjoyed the sunrise, but the true reason for his lingering in the cool Northern breeze was the choking fear of delivering unsavory news to the hybrid king. Had he not been sure that his master knew of his arrival and was awaiting his report, he would have lingered until the sun had fully risen and his master was asleep.

With each level of stone he traversed in the massive, spiraling fortress, his steps grew stunted, his legs shaking more and more until his knees knocked together. The dungeon was cold and dank, and the musty smell of old hay and urine always made him sneeze. He walked past the cells, all empty. Most prisoners didn't stay long with so many hungry mouths walking above. The elf was different. His Majesty wanted something from the elfling, so she was allowed to live.

Her screams met him halfway down the hall, wild and high. A strong scream. It would be different in a few days. If she made it that long.

Callid grunted with the effort of reaching for the iron handle on the torture chamber door. His back ached with the strain on his curved spine, but pulling open the heavy door posed no trouble for his corded muscles.

Atalanta was on the rack, her arms secured above her head. Her silver dress was ripping at the shoulders from the strain the rack placed on her arms as Thetis cranked the wheel that moved the wooden boards and pulled her arms and legs in opposite directions. The breast of the dirty, tattered garment was splattered with blood from a nasty cut on her dirt-caked lip. She was paler than when she'd first arrived. Dark purple circles rimmed her lower lids. Her fingernails cut into her palms as she clenched her fists against the pain, her tongue vibrating with a vibrato scream.

Tyrannus' orange eyes never left her, tracing her body. To the hybrid king, true beauty was only found in pain, and he looked at the screaming elf with lust. He did not look over when Callid came through the door, for which the cyclops was grateful. Atalanta's eyes were closed tight, but Thetis turned lifeless blue eyes on Callid for just a moment.

"What news do you bring of the Avalons?" said Tyrannus, his eyes never moving from the elf. "Have they fled back to their palace yet?"

"I don't believe so, my king," Callid's heads said together.

Tyrannus' head turned slowly. Thetis released the crank, his eyes coming to life with malicious glee.

"You don't believe so?" said Tyrannus. "You don't know?"

"N–no, Your Majesty. Not with absolute certainty."

"Explain." The word was drawn and emphasized; the harsh ex turned into a hiss.

"I had my escort leave me in the clearing where they buried their dead, but their horses' trail didn't lead toward their palace. They went deeper in the woods. I followed as far as I could. They seem to have banded with a woodsman. I found the place their paths met and followed them to a new clearing. The woodsman … I believe he may have the company of a … a griffin. The paw prints and feathers I found would indicate as much. It was no stray beast, for from the prints … I believe he rides it."

Tyrannus' muzzle curled on one side.

"I … I cannot be sure. I never saw the woodsman nor the griffin. By the time I reached the clearing, they had moved on. I l–lost the trail not long after. The ground there was hard and not good for prints. I searched until my escort came back last night. I doubled back. I did everything in my power, Your Majesty, truly. I don't know where they went."

The elf began to laugh, tears glistening in the corners of her closed eyes.

"Perhaps they are better trackers than your pet," she said. "Perhaps they are making their way here. They may already be at your door."

Tyrannus snapped his clawed fingers. Thetis grabbed the wheel with both hands and spun it a full turn with a simple flick of his wrists. The pop of the elf's dislocated shoulders was drowned by her wails. Her eyes flew open with the shock, green as emeralds.

"You disappoint me, Callid," said Tyrannus, adjusting his crown.

He took two steps toward the trembling Callid, one of his pointed dog ears turned back to fully enjoy the gasping cries of the elf.

"I'm sorry, m–master, Y–Your Majesty."

"You are a brave little imp to come back with such disappointing news. Did you wish to gall me?"

"No! No, master!" Callid bowed with hands and knees on the filthy, bloodstained floor.

"So you are a fool then?"

"That is no new discovery, your grace," said Thetis.

Tyrannus' muzzle wrinkled in a hellish grin. "No, I suppose you're right, Thetis. Perhaps I should show mercy on the little fool. Failure is to be expected from one such as he."

"I'm unsure, Your Majesty," said Thetis. "The rack may do his twisted back some good."

Callid whimpered, and had he not been practically kissing the dirty stone, he might have seen the look of pity that flashed in the wet, green eyes of the elf.

"P–please, Your Majesty. I will go back. I will find them. I shall not return until I do."

"You'll only waste time," said Tyrannus, with a wave of his hairy, corpse-colored arm. "Thetis, you will go. Tonight. Take your best soldiers. Make sure the Avalons are outnumbered. I've underestimated them. I won't make the same mistake again. Do not come back unless you've had your fill of royal blood."

"Children are always sweeter," said Thetis. "I wonder if royal children are the sweetest."

"Get up, Callid," said Tyrannus. "Leave us. I don't want to look at you any longer."

"Yes, Your Majesty. My humblest apologies," said Callid, rising on the balls of his feet, unable to contain the soaring feeling of relief.

Tyrannus' claws raked Callid's right head from behind the ear to the tip of the chin in a blow hard enough to knock him off his feet. The hot blood poured down his neck as both heads shrieked and both hands clutched at the wound.

"You ought to thank me for being so merciful," said Tyrannus.

"Don't be ungracious."

"Th–thank you, master," said Callid through his whimpers. He pushed himself off the ground with one hand and backed toward the door, cradling the wound with his other hand. "You are most m–merciful."

Callid shut the door behind him. Tyrannus grinned at the sound of the cyclops' bare feet slapping against stone as he ran.

"Now, Atalanta," he said, his eyes roving her body once more. "I apologize for the rude interruption. Though, you were rather rude yourself. I'm willing to forgive, so long as you give me what I want."

Atalanta turned her head as far away from him as she could, staring at the iron-spike covered chair shoved against the west wall, thinking of the home that lay beyond it.

Tyrannus sighed, and the sound that came from his muzzle was almost a whistle. He snapped again. Thetis turned the wheel. At first, Atalanta could not catch the breath needed to scream. Her whole body shook, the veins in her neck bulging. At last, the agony was released in a scream that made Tyrannus flinch with discomfort, his ears flicking. Thetis' top canines elongated.

"Stop," said Tyrannus.

Thetis let go with a frown. Atalanta's breaths heaved from her lungs hard enough to make her parched throat ache. She gulped.

"I c—" Her vocal chords faltered. She sucked in a harsh breath. "I cannot do magic in here. Elvish magic is tied to nature."

"I'm well aware," said Tyrannus, his head cocked to the side. "Does that mean you will cooperate?"

"It means I'll show you just how poor at magic I really am. You might as well just kill me."

"We'll see. It isn't out of the question. Take her down, Thetis. And fix her shoulders."

Thetis pulled a lever, and the rack fell back flat like a table. Atalanta didn't move when Thetis undid the bindings. Thetis scooped her up and set her on her feet. Her legs buckled as her arms dangled awkwardly at her sides, making her cry out in pain. Thetis caught her and steadied her until she stood on her own.

"Here, my dear, bite down on this," said Tyrannus, shoving a frayed bit of thick rope in her mouth.

Atalanta gagged, her tongue fighting to spit out the foreign object, but when Thetis wrenched her right shoulder back into place, her teeth sank deep into the braided cords. The tears flowed freely as he did the same to the other.

"Better?" said Tyrannus.

Atalanta's lids fluttered, and her eyes rolled back into her skull. Thetis snatched her up like a babe as she swooned, her auburn hair a rich waterfall dangling over his arm.

"No matter," said Tyrannus. "I'd just as rather not have to venture out into the sunlight. Take her back to her cell. Make sure she has water, and fetch her something decent to eat when she wakes. Good behavior must be rewarded."

"Of course."

"Choose your soldiers as soon as you're done. Shake them from their roosts if you must. You will leave at sundown."

"Yes, Your Majesty," said Thetis with a bow of his head.

He switched Atalanta to one arm so that he could open the heavy door, and she murmured against his shoulder.

"Thetis," said Tyrannus.

"Yes, my king?"

"Fail me, and the next time you find yourself in this room, you will not be the one at the wheel. Never fear, though, I'm sure we can find plenty of other things for you to do. Vampires are so resilient. So long as no stakes are involved, they just keep on healing. A new canvas all over again."

"I will not fail, my lord."

* * *

Erro and the Avalons rode side by side as best they could amongst the crowded trees. Zezil scurried up ahead with his pointed, black nose to the ground, following the trail.

"If the creature's trail keeps cutting a straight path to the mountains like this, we'll reach the base of the central peak in about two more days," said Erro.

The forest was already beginning to darken as the sun dipped toward the western horizon, no longer high enough for its beams to cut through the top of the canopy.

"I knew heading to the mountains would be the best course," said Michael. "Didn't I say so?"

"Hmm, I don't recall," said Felicity, fingertips to her bottom lip.

"I thought I said it," said Andrew. "What about you, Andromeda?"

"It's not coming to me," said Andromeda, not quite able to contain her grin. "It sounds familiar, though. I thought Felicity said it."

"Heaven strike all three of you," said Michael. "I said it and you know it."

Erro's chuckle was barely audible, but it made Michael's cheeks twitch.

"Thank heaven that we have Zezil," said Andromeda. "If not for his nose, there would be no way to track this creature. I haven't seen a single print, and there's no sign of him stopping to rest or eat."

"There were a few prints about a mile back in a place where the underbrush was not so dense, but not full indentations," said Erro. "I've caught a few signs of broken branches where something tried to squeeze through a tight cluster of foliage. But there would be no way to tell that those were the creature had I not seen Zezil sniff at them. Could have just as easily been a wildcat or a wolf." He caught the Avalons looking at him. "What? I track and trap for my daily meal, and when I need money for clothing or trapping supplies, I collect pelts to sell. It's my livelihood. I wouldn't be alive if I wasn't skilled at it."

They had ridden without stopping since Zezil had found the trail that morning, choosing to eat on horseback. The excitement was palpable, everyone wondering if the next tree or bush would hide the creature they sought. They'd only paused momentarily to let the horses drink from a stream.

Zezil had no problem with the pace. If his tail wasn't wagging, he was bounding from one bush to the other, whining in anticipation. But suddenly, as they talked, his whining became melancholy, and he turned back toward them, sniffing in a loop.

"Did he lose it?" said Andrew.

"Give him a minute," said Erro, halting the party with a raised finger. "He may pick it up again."

Zezil made three loops, taking the time to thoroughly sniff anything and everything in his path. Then he sat in front of Aquila and looked up at his master with one final, trembling whine.

"Damn," said Michael.

"What do we do?" said Andromeda, looking from Michael to Erro.

"We keep pressing on in the same direction," said Erro. "The path never wavered until now. It was always steady toward the mountain. It would be no surprise to me if the creature lives there. Though, that would raise the question of why he's ventured so close to Everly at least twice; it's a long journey from the mountain."

"Perhaps if we press on, Zezil will find the scent again," said Michael.

"It's entirely possible," said Erro, looking hard at a rather large branch laid across their path. He then turned his eyes to the canopy. "Hmm, odd."

Four other heads leaned back to observe the sky. All were surprised they could see it so clearly. A large hole had been broken through the close branches, evidenced by the exposed, pointed edges of the snapped limbs.

"Something came through the top of the trees," said Andromeda.

"It looks the same way when Aquila can't find a clear space to land," said Erro.

"So what does that mean?" said Andrew.

"Not sure," said Erro. "That thing can't fly. Of that I'm absolutely sure."

"We need to keep moving," said Michael. "I want to try to regain the trail before we make camp."

"Agreed," said Erro. "Still ... odd."

Though dusk was still a few hours away, as they pressed on for another half mile, the sky darkened rapidly. In the excitement of the chase, none of them gave it much thought until they began to have trouble seeing Zezil move among the black trees. Andromeda looked up just in time for the first raindrop to find its mark on the tip of her nose.

"Oh, lovely," said Felicity, swiping at the fresh raindrop on her cheek.

Like an uproarious call to arms, the rumble and crack of thunder summoned an instant downpour that tore through the canopy, shaking the leaves until the trees became swaying, dancing maidens. Felicity's grumbled cry of frustration was nearly lost in the torrent.

"Oh, loosen your corset," said Erro, almost shouting. "I know a place not far from here where we can make a shelter."

"Exactly how far is this magical place?" said Felicity.

"If we keep a steady pace, it shouldn't take more than an hour."

"We'll be soaked through by then!"

"We're going to be soaked no matter what we do," said Erro.

"We build a shelter right here," said Felicity, reining in her horse and crossing her arms. Aquila stopped, and Erro crossed his own arms and glared at Felicity, whose ringlets were already straightening and sticking to her face like a second skin.

"There's no arguing with her when she gets that look about her, Erro," said Michael. "We take shelter here."

* * *

A strange flock took flight from the jagged crests of the mountains, taking advantage of the early night brought on by the storm. Still, the vampires dipped low, brushing the canopy with their leathery black wings, ready to dive for cover if the thick clouds should clear before the sun was fully set. The heartbeats of the creatures below pounded in their ears, and not even the rain could dilute the scent of blood rising off the teeming life below. The flock paid them no mind. They sought beats with a unique cadence, a scent sweeter than the blood of animals. Human blood called out to them in song, and they kept their ears toward the earth as they flew, waiting for the first note.

Chapter 8

Blood, Mud, and Ashes

The smell of wet fur kept Felicity's nose permanently wrinkled.

"I hope this doesn't ruin them," said Andromeda, looking up at the makeshift tent of furs they'd strung between two trees for shelter from the raging storm. "We're going to need them later. It'll be cold on the mountains."

"It shouldn't, so long as we let them dry properly," said Erro.

He was mashed between Andrew and Andromeda, all of them still damp, but he didn't seem to mind in the slightest.

Erro had had the foresight to salvage some wood before everything got completely drenched, and they'd made a tiny fire in the middle of their shelter that kept them all pressed together on the outskirts of the tent, not wanting to get a face full of the smoke that was leaking out of the tent through the small opening in the side. Without the fire, they would have been unable to see each other at all. Though dusk had only just fallen, the forest was fully dark, shrouded by the thick rain clouds above, and the inside of their tent was black as pitch without the glow of the flames. Andrew shifted further from the opening so that the rain would not soak his shoulder.

There was a whine from outside the tent.

"Come on, let's let him in," said Andromeda, pouting at Felicity.

"No! He'll stink worse than the furs," said Felicity, her fingers frozen in the act of braiding her hair. "There isn't any room anyway."

"He's fine," said Erro, nudging Andromeda's shoulder with his own. "He's just a trickster. He knows how pitiful he sounds when he does that. He's probably got himself snuggled up under Aquila's wing, dry as a bone. He just wants someone to scratch behind his ears."

"This storm is going to ruin our chances of finding the trail again," said Michael, brushing his nearly dried hair back from his face.

"Something tells me we wouldn't have found it anyway," said Erro. "We'll just have to hope we can find a new trail once we reach the mountains."

Lightening cracked through the sky, and the horses whinnied and pulled at the bonds tying them to the trees. A strong gust of wind smacked against the fur tent like a battering ram, pulling two of the bindings loose so that one of the flaps flew up toward the sky. The companions cried out as a torrent of cold water doused the fire that was their one source of warmth.

* * *

Thetis pumped his wings hard against the howling wind. He let a gust spin him in a barrel roll, and the rush made his upper canines elongate in excitement. His eyes had no trouble deciphering the land below and the group of vampire soldiers around him. The humans would be nearly blind. It would be a massacre. He would feast on royal blood and please his king in the bargain.

"Thetis, I smell blood," said Nessie. Her high-pitched giggle grated against his overly sensitive eardrums. "Human blood."

Nessie's wet, light-brown hair flew behind her. As Thetis watched, all of her teeth began to morph into fangs, disfiguring her round, youthful face. Only a maiden of sixteen when she was fledged, she would be a decrepit old woman had she stayed mortal. Thetis was of the opinion that sixteen was too young to be fledged. He found that they were wilder, more unpredictable, no matter how ancient they became. Still, Nessie was a formidable warrior. She fought like a cat, ripping apart her quarries in a wild flurry of attacks. She liked to eat messy, lapping from the ground and off her own skin.

"I smell it, too," said Drazzela, a forked tongue slipping through her teeth as she cooed the words in her rather deep voice.

"Get yourselves under control," said Thetis. "You'll have your fill soon enough."

"But, Thetis, we outnumber them," said Nessie, retracting her teeth so that she could pout in his direction. "It's not enough to go around."

"Then you'd better pray that one of us doesn't survive," said Thetis.

"Here's hoping that it's Nessie," said Caleb. Of the seven vampires Thetis had brought along, Caleb was by far the largest, and the ugliest. Though his skin was smooth and free of blemish, as all vampires, the perfecting effects of the venom could not erase his overly large forehead, bushy brows, and hooked nose.

Nessie curled her lip back and snarled at him.

"Would you like to decide who dies right now, Caleb?"

"Silence! Or I shall maim the both of you," said Thetis, diving in between them.

Ariel moaned through heart-shaped lips, tugging at a strand of the blonde hair whipping around her face. "It's getting stronger," she said, shivering with anticipation. "I can hardly stand it."

"I smell something else," said Tristan, the nostrils of his long, thin nose flaring. "What is that? I don't like it."

Thetis closed his eyes and inhaled, and a hiss escaped through his teeth. "It's the griffin. I told you they might have one."

"And who's going to battle the griffin?" said Sage, swooping in closer to glare at Thetis through his strawberry lashes.

"Caleb, Celine," said Thetis, "that's your task. Keep it at bay. Kill it if you can."

"Only if I get to share your kill, Thetis," said Celine. "I don't have a taste for griffin blood."

"Everyone will get their fill. Now keep quiet and slow down. Land as lightly as you can."

* * *

"Get the corner," said Michael, on his knees holding down one end of the unanchored shelter.

"I'm trying."

"Try harder."

Andrew jumped for the billowing fur coat again and caught it.

"Hold it down!" said Erro, yelling over the thunder as he tried to secure the dripping fur with rope again.

"Ouch! Get this crazy thing off me!"

Zezil scrambled over Andrew's bent back whining and barking as he tried to reach his master.

"Something's wrong," said Andromeda, just as Aquila screeched and looked to the sky.

"Everything's wrong," said Felicity, throwing up her hands and scowling through the rain.

"If you would lend a hand rather than complain—" said Michael.

"I'm serious!" said Andromeda.

Zezil was practically climbing Erro.

"Be quiet and listen to her," said Erro, fighting off the frantic vexar. "I've never seen Zezil act this way."

"He's trying not to change," said Andromeda. "He's trying to warn us before he does."

Erro's eyes widened and he hugged Zezil to his chest, stroking his back and murmuring gently to him.

"Forget the shelter; grab your weapons!" said Andromeda. "Vampires. Lots of them. And they're almost here."

Aquila screeched and scratched a paw in the dirt, his head twitching back and forth, his amber eyes searching the trees. The

Avalons ran to their horses.

"Here, Andrew," said Andromeda, unsheathing one of the thin rapiers hooked to her horse's saddle and handing it to her twin.

Andrew held it in his left hand and withdrew the retractable silver stake from his boot with his right. Fighting with both sword and stake was one of the new tactics Archimedes had taught them before their departure. The sword kept the vampires at bay and could injure them long enough to land an easy blow with the stake. Michael, however, stuck to his broadsword and loaded a stake into the machine on his wrist.

Felicity was the first to pull her cross necklace out from beneath her undergarments, not wanting to become entranced again, and the others followed suit.

"Zezil can't hold on much longer," said Erro, appearing at Andromeda's side with his dual daggers clutched in his fists. "Make sure you aren't in front of him when he transforms. I hope he's able to keep it under control until the vampires show their faces; that way we could aim him directly at them."

Three sets of eyes looked to where Zezil stood amongst the trees, sides heaving with labored breaths, but Andromeda's fixed on Erro's daggers.

"You can't fight vampires with those," she said. "You'll be savaged."

"I don't have any other weapons," said Erro with an uneasy shrug. "I've never fought vampires before."

"Here take my stake," said Michael, pulling the silver cylinder from his boot and pressing the buttons to send the stake zinging from its casing.

Erro jumped and then gave the older boy a nervous grin as he took the weapon. "Thanks."

"Take this as well," said Andromeda, rummaging in her bag for the small sheepskin water bag she had kept with her since the first vampire attack. "It's holy water. Get it on their skin and it burns them. Get it inside them and it kills."

Erro hung the bag across his torso by its leather strap.

"Felicity, give him your other rapier," said Andrew.

Felicity's hands shook slightly as she obeyed her younger brother without a word of protest. Andrew stared at her in amazement.

"Exactly how many are coming?" said Felicity.

Andromeda closed her eyes. "I can't be sure. The animals have no real sense of numbers, and I can't sense the vampires. Neither can Aquila. Zezil can only smell them."

Aquila's high call of warning made them look around just in time to see a dark shape barreling toward them through the trees. A clawed hand snatched Andromeda's braid as she ducked, yanking her off her feet and into the air. Erro slashed the hand with his rapier, taking off two fingers. Andromeda landed in a crouch, and the small party instinctively pressed their backs together, but it was short-lived. The horses snorted and reared at the strange scent of the living dead, and their flying hooves forced the group to scatter.

Drazzela, who'd grabbed for Andromeda, perched on a tree limb, her deathly pale skin and her white garment making her slightly more visible to their dark-adjusted eyes. She watched with mild interest as her fingers regrew from their severed stumps.

The shaking of limbs and leaves signaled the arrival of her fellow vampires, and Erro and the Avalons grouped together again, surrounded on all sides, their eyes darting from tree to tree. The female vampires wore little more than undergarments, their clawed toes gripping the bark of the limbs for purchase. The males wore only breeches, giving their wings full range of movement. Able to regenerate, they needed no armor. Tooth and nail were the only weapons they required.

A girlish giggle tinkled through the rain. "Oh, they're pretty," said Nessie. "My favorite."

Zezil whirled in circles, locking onto each threat with eyes made for night stalking. His sides heaved with ragged breaths that turned into a low, rumbling growl that rivaled that of a werewolf with its ferocity. It was a wild sound, hellish, and it only grew louder as Zezil's very bones began to expand and reform, crunching and cracking. The pain only fueled Zezil's rage, and he snapped and snarled, biting at the air as his shoulders broadened, his limbs lengthened, and his fangs elongated into a wolfish maw. By the end of the transformation, he was a foot taller and taut muscle shifted under his hackles when he moved, the hellish offspring of a wolf and wolverine with banded eyes that burned yellow.

"What in the name of all the lords of hell is that?" said Sage, running a distressed hand through fiery hair.

"That's your reckoning, leech," said Erro as Zezil fixed his eyes on the vampire, drool and foam dripping from his fangs. "Come and have a go at him if you dare."

"You said nothing about a devil, Thetis."

"It's no devil, you coward," said Thetis, though he was eyeing Zezil a little warily himself.

"Sage is scared of a little beasty," said Nessie.

Sage hissed. Nessie bared her fangs just as Erro's dagger pierced her left eye, rocking back her head and sending her crashing to the ground, wings crumpling under her.

Andrew had just enough time to laugh before the vampires roared in unison, transforming to their fullest. Their nails became talons and their mouths could hardly contain rows of long, razor sharp fangs. Black leathery wings expanded as far as the crowded trees would allow, and the vampires attacked in a swarm.

Aquila sprang to meet Caleb midair. His beak clamped down on a leathery wing, and with a single pump of his own wings, he spun the huge vampire in a half circle and slammed him into a tree hard enough to break his spine with a crack like a snapping tree branch. Aquila pounced on Caleb, digging his claws into his shoulder blades, and bit at his neck in an attempt to tear off the one feature that could not be completely regenerated, the head. But Celine, wild curls flattened against her face and neck by rain, jumped on his back tearing at his delicate wings with her claws. Grabbing him at the wing joints, she flipped him on his side and bent to bite his jugular. Andromeda's stake poked through the left side of Celine's chest, staining her billowy blue nightdress with black blood.

"Is Aquila all—?"

Andromeda turned as Erro was knocked off his feet by the enraged Nessie. Both Andromeda and Aquila moved to help him, but Caleb rose to his feet, spine popping, and wrapped Aquila in a fierce bear hug.

Andromeda kept moving. Nessie slammed Erro into the ground, sending dirt and rotting leaves and pine needles spraying in every direction.

Andromeda nearly ran into Michael as he reeled backward into her path, losing his footing. Drazzela's wing knocked Andromeda down as she swooped at Michael, only able to glide on the storm wind with her wings half-extended. A large gash on her shoulder was knitting itself as she ducked Michael's sword and swiped at his chest with her talons. Unprepared for the strength of his unassuming armor, Drazzela managed to get partway through the leather, but the dwarf-made chainmail ripped three of her nails from their beds. Her surprised cry of pain was cut short as Michael punched his fist into her chest and shot the stake from his armband clean through her heart.

Andromeda ran through the cloud of Drazzela's ashes, her eyes set on Erro.

Only a few feet away, her twin and Sage were circling each other like cats. Sage sprang first, hovering just above the ground and swiping wildly with both hands and feet in a flurry of attacks that

Andrew couldn't keep track of. He parried a kicking foot with a slice to the ankle and jumped to the side to avoid a clawed hand only to meet the other with his right arm. He nearly dropped his sword from the pain of the three nasty gashes on his forearm, but gritted his teeth and resumed his defensive position.

Sage's nostrils flared and his eyes found the blood, watching it fall to the ground. He took a wild swing at Andrew's throat, but Andrew's sword was already arcing through the air, and it took off the vampire's arm just below the shoulder. No blood spilled from the wound, but the vampire threw his head back in a cry of pain. Andrew was just about to put his stake into Sage's chest, when a furry shape in his peripheral made him duck.

Zezil jumped onto Andrew's bent back and used him as a launching pad to reach Thetis who was flying overhead. Thetis' arm was so badly mauled it was barely attached to his shoulder and dangling limply as he flew, but it was healing fast. Zezil sought to remedy that and latched on to the dangling wrist mid jump, yanking Thetis to the ground.

Andrew was unable to see anymore as Sage rose higher off the ground with a pump of his wings and snatched Andrew up with the talons on his toes like a giant bird of prey. Andrew's feet left the ground. He tried to call for help, but his breath hitched up near his Adam's apple as Sage swung his legs back in a pendulum and flung Andrew through the air.

Andrew screamed and dropped his weapons as he flipped end over end toward the ground, and then Aquila appeared, leaping up to enclose Andrew in a furry, feathery embrace, shielding him with his lion's paws and wings as the two of them hit the rain-flooded forest floor. Aquila skidded through the mud on his back and released Andrew only when he stopped.

Disoriented, Andrew lay on the ground a moment, eyes searching for his weapons. Mud-smeared, clawed feet hit the earth just in front of his face, but a black boot took the vampire's legs out from under him, and he hit the wet ground with a thump, splattering mud into Andrew's open mouth.

Felicity pinned Sage's remaining hand to the ground with her sword. The other arm was still just a stump, leaving the vampire's chest open, and making it easy for Felicity to drive the stake into it. Sage's skin cracked and turned gray as he screamed. His ashes drifted away in hundreds of tiny, rain-made streams.

Felicity pulled Andrew to his feet and grinned.

"Now you owe me—" Her head snapped back as the petite blonde vampire, Ariel, yanked on her curls, exposing her neck.

Andrew snatched up Felicity's sword—still upright in the ground— and knocked Felicity aside just as a mouth full of fangs was encircling her neck, and ran Ariel through the stomach. She snapped at him, impaled on the sword at arm's length, and Andrew kicked her back as he withdrew the blade. Ariel advanced, undeterred, but Felicity met her in a deadly embrace, ramming the stake through her chest.

"I owe you what?" said Andrew with a grin of his own.

She scoffed.

"Really, if it wasn't for Aquila, we'd both ... Hey, where is he?" said Andrew.

Erro gasped for breath, all his air dispelled when his back hit the ground. His lungs ached in their futile effort to scream. Nessie's talons were still digging into his lower back and the pain was so intense that for a moment he only saw swirling dark colors mixed with the sparkles of the raindrops.

His vision returned just in time to see Nessie's forked tongue reach out to trace his jaw.

"Ready to play, pretty boy?" she crooned.

Her breath was putrid with the scent of old blood and rotted flesh. Erro gagged and tried to free his arms, but they were pinned beneath the vampire. He'd lost the sword, but the stake was still clenched in his right hand and one of his daggers was still in his belt.

"Erro!"

His eyes found Andromeda, running through the rain, her black hair flying behind her, no longer in its pristine braid. Tristan landed in front of her, and Erro heard the clang of her sword as she blocked the swipe of his claws.

"Which limb shall we take first?" said Nessie with another giggle. "Or shall I just rip you in half?" She flexed her fingers, still embedded in his flesh, and his eyes rolled back in his head.

The vampire giggled again, but it was a different sound that brought him back from the edge of unconsciousness. Andromeda. She was hurt.

His eyes flew open and found her. She was cradling her left hand to her chest, her stake on the ground. She blocked another blow from Tristan, but nearly lost her sword in the process.

Erro bucked, sending another wave of agony through his back, but surprising Nessie enough to free his left arm. He punched her hard enough to dislocate her jaw. She reeled back, her claws ripping free of his skin. He bit back his cry of agony and splashed holy water from the bag around his neck onto her face. She leapt off of him, her hands pressed to her burning face. He rose unsteadily to his feet.

Nessie lowered her hands. One of her eyes was blinded, and she didn't see him coming until it was too late.

"Ready to play?" he said.

Her one good eye widened and her lips curled back in a snarl just before he ended her with the stake.

He turned to help Andromeda, but Aquila was already there. The griffin shredded Tristan with his forepaws and tore into his neck with his hooked beak. He held the shrieking bloodsucker in place while Andromeda staked him.

"Everybody, help Zezil!" came Michael's call.

Andromeda had to squint through the dark rainy night to make out the black shapes of Zezil and the final vampire grappling on the ground. She raced past Andrew—who was pulling his stake from Caleb's chest for good measure, since the decapitated vampire had turned into a rotting corpse instead of ash—and Felicity, and reached her elder brother's side just as Thetis kicked Zezil off and took flight.

Zezil had little concept of how to kill a vampire, and the maddened vexar had savaged Thetis over and over, undeterred by his healing powers. The vampire's flight was stunted at first, his wings repairing themselves of countless rips. A foot was completely missing and both arms were twisted and nearly unrecognizable.

Zezil, not without his own share of wounds, jumped into the air, snapping at the heels of the fleeing vampire.

"Andrew, get your crossbow," said Michael, loading a stake into the mechanism on his arm.

Andrew rushed for his saddlebag and tried to calm his frantic horse as Michael took aim and fired. The flying stake breached the canopy at nearly the same time Thetis did. Thetis's cry of pain as the stake pierced his side made Michael smile, but Thetis kept flying.

"I doubt he'll be coming back anytime soon," said Michael.

At the sound of Michael's voice, Zezil whirled around, eyes burning and teeth bared.

Michael backpedaled so fast he slipped in the mud and landed on his butt with a soft "oof."

"Easy, Zezil," said Andromeda, stepping in front of Michael and holding out her uninjured hand. "It's all right. Easy, boy. There isn't any danger."

Zezil cocked his head toward the sound of Andromeda's soothing voice, and his breathing slowed. He whined as his rage cooled, his heartbeat slowed, and his skeleton reformed.

"Good boy," said Andromeda, bending down to scratch his head and making his tongue loll lazily out of his mouth with delight.

Michael cleared his throat as he got to his feet.

"Is everyone all right?" he said, brushing futilely at the seat of his trousers.

A soft chorus of yesses came from the Avalon children, though they each bore their fair share of injuries. Felicity limped up beside Michael, nursing a cut to her inner thigh. The back of Michael's head was bleeding from a collision with a tree. The horses neighed in a chorus of their own, long and panicked, like screaming, but they were untouched.

"My wrist is broken," said Andromeda, holding it out gingerly.

"Let me see," said Andrew, reaching out with the arm that wasn't sliced open. His fingers moved lightly over her already purpling wrist. "We'll have to set it."

"What happened?" said Felicity, coming in for a closer look.

"I was trying to get to ... Erro!"

He was on his knees in the mud, swaying like the trees all around him. Aquila hovered over him like a worried mother, pawing the ground and clicking his beak.

Andromeda reached him just as he swooned, skidding on her knees in the mud to catch him against her chest, ignoring the pain in her wrist as she held him close. She called his name and gently patted his cheeks, but he only groaned. Tears ran down her cheeks, indistinguishable from the rain still pouring down on her.

"What happened to him?" said Michael, getting down on his knees beside her.

"It's his back," said Andromeda. "He didn't have any armor and she ..." She bit her lip.

"Andrew, Felicity, get that shelter back in order," said Michael. "We'll need to keep his bandages dry. Andromeda, help me stop the bleeding."

* * *

Ancient elvish felt odd on Atalanta's tongue, and she stumbled over some of the harder pronunciations. The rain wasn't helping her concentration. She resisted the urge to lean back her head and allow the cool water to trickle down her throat. The very scent of the air demanded her attention. She hadn't been outside in so long. Her heart fluttered, and her brain screamed at her to run, run until her legs gave, laughing the whole way. But Tyrannus leaned over her as she pressed her hand to the earth, speaking the old elvish spell.

The flower that sprouted from the ground, called up by the words, was a rather lackluster yellow and drooped on its stem.

"Would you like to braid it into your fur, your unholiness?" said Atalanta, unable to help herself. She felt alive again.

The hard kick to her side took her breath away.

"You think I want flowers?" said Tyrannus, pulling her up by the jaw, his claws biting into her cheeks. "Create a firestorm! Make the trees walk on their roots! This is all elvish magic, is it not?"

"Yes, but there isn't a single elf my age who can do those things. That's what I've been telling you all this time! You think you're so clever with your feeble little scheme of ransom and coercion, but you've failed to understand the simple concept that only an elder elf can do the things you desire! You think you know of elves and—" He cut off her air with a hand to her throat.

"You will learn or your father dies!" he said as he flung her to the ground.

She laughed, rolling onto her back with her eyes closed, enjoying the feel of the rain on her skin.

"Even if my father exchanges himself for me, I should like to see you try and kill him."

He was on top of her in an instant, his weight crushing her slight frame.

"I will have a flock of my vampires all grab a piece of him and pull in different directions," he snarled, his lips moving against her jaw, his wet canine nose breathing in her ear.

She squirmed beneath him, her breath coming in frantic sobs, her skin crawling to have him so near. He laughed as he pushed himself up, dragging her up with him by her hair.

"Try again. Do something else." He was more revolting than ever as he stared her down with his patchy black hair matted to his gray flesh by the rain.

"The only other thing I know how to do is create a fire, but it won't work in a downpour like this; I don't have enough magic to keep it burning."

"You're the king's daughter," he said, pacing around her like an animal circling before the kill. "You know more than you're saying. Do something else or I'll put you back on the rack."

"I told you, I don't know anything else," she said, planting her feet and holding her chin aloft. "I never had any interest in learning magic. It's boring, tiresome work full of endless concentration and memorization, and I'm too young to be of much good at it anyway. You need a mage—someone who has completed the Trial of the Elements—and I know of no mage younger than a century. You have picked the wrong elf."

He turned on her with a wolfish growl, his short muzzle curling back to show his yellow teeth, his orange eyes so intensely fixed on her that she took a step back to distance herself from their gaze.

"You'll learn or you'll die, and I won't make it quick."

Though her heart was pounding hard enough to make her ears feel stuffed with cotton, she held his gaze, her green eyes defiant. To her surprise, his snarl widened into a grin. Her strong expression wavered, and he chuckled.

"You just need to be stronger, my dear," he said.

"Then perhaps you shouldn't starve me or let me waste away in a dark dungeon," said Atalanta, narrowing her eyes in suspicion.

"Well, that part is up to you and whether you are willing

to work on your ... How did you put it? Concentration and memorization."

"Seems a vicious circle to me," said Atalanta.

"Don't worry. Your waning strength is nothing a little vampire venom won't remedy."

Chapter 9

A Wandering Spirit

By the time the rain stopped, they'd managed to dress each other's cuts with bandages made by cutting two of their blankets into strips and administering the salve from the pack they had salvaged from the dead medic after the werewolf attack. Erro's wounds had required the most care, and in the few hours it took the storm to end, they changed his bandages three times, washing the old strips in the rainwater and applying dry ones.

Michael had done his best to realign the bones in Andromeda's wrist before holding it in place with a makeshift splint of sticks and bandages, but his inexperience meant more pain for her, as it took him three tries to get it right. Each time, Andromeda screamed in agony and bit down on the stick in her mouth that kept her from biting through her lip, and each time, Erro stiffened and groaned in his sleep.

The horses pawed the earth and conversed in nervous nickers and whinnies outside. In their terror, Andrew's mount had become entangled with Felicity's, hooked together both by the stirrups straps and by the leads of their halters so that they were stuck together at the middle and at the mouth. Michael had nearly received a broken rib from a flying hoof while he untangled the two horses, their eyes bulging in wild terror, frothing at the mouth and unable to see Michael as he approached. Andromeda's mare had snapped her chin strap and nearly pulled free of her halter. But not much attention had been given to the poor steeds, as they were free of injury while their riders were not.

Everyone breathed deep when they were finally able to toss the shelter of wet furs aside. Zezil, his right foreleg wrapped tightly with bandages, greeted them with yips and kisses to the face before catching sight of his wounded master. He froze, a soft whine whistling through his nose. Erro babbled softly in his sleep as the vexar curled up beside him.

"We need to close up the wounds," said Andromeda. "We're going through the bandages too quickly."

"I could try to stitch him up," said Felicity. "But the only thing I've ever sown is a hemline."

"There's a few needles in the medic's bag, but no thread," said Michael with a frown.

"That's probably because he saw no need to haul it along when he could just use horse hair," said Felicity.

Her siblings stared at her.

"What? Do you think me a complete idiot? I know things," she said, crossing her arms.

"Of course, you do," said Andrew. "Now, uh, you go fetch the horse hair, since it was your brilliant idea."

Felicity studied the jittery horses from the corner of her eye, but snorted derisively at Andrew nonetheless and marched over to the horses, arms still crossed.

Michael and Sir Gregor's stallions had faired the best in the chaos, and it was from their tails that Felicity retrieved a number of long tail hairs to thread through the medic's needles.

Andromeda and Michael unwrapped the gashes on Erro's lower back one by one and gave them a final thorough cleaning with water from their canteens and one of the bars of soap gifted to them by Everly's villagers.

Then Felicity set to work on the wounds. Erro never fully came out of his fevered sleep, though his eyes shot open a few times and he squeezed Andromeda's good hand so hard he nearly broke a few of her fingers. That was not what brought her tears. It was the cries for his mother that sent them rolling down her cheeks. She had to turn her head aside so as not to catch sight of Felicity's needle knitting the jagged wounds together. The very thought turned her stomach. Andrew and Michael held Erro in place as he bucked and shook in confused, semiconscious pain. Andrew seemed unable to look away from Felicity's handiwork, his mouth open and pulled back in a wide grimace that would have been comical had it not reflected everyone's own feelings.

When it was finally over, they applied another layer of salve and bandages, depleting their dangerously low supply of both.

"Andromeda, now you have to stitch me," said Felicity, holding out a fresh needle and the final horse hair.

"What?" Andromeda recoiled.

"Don't be a child. I won't risk infection just because you have a sensitive stomach. My thigh needs to be stitched up. Now take it." She wiggled the needle and thread in Andromeda's face.

"I can't. I only have one good hand." Andromeda held up her splinted wrist, summoning the most pitiful look she could muster. "Someone else will have to do it."

"Like who, them?" she said, snapping her head in the direction of the boys. "They've never held a needle in their life. They'll botch it so bad I'll lose my leg. You can do it one handed. I can't do it myself."

"Why not?"

"It's rather hard to hold a needle steady when you're in considerable pain. What happens if I swoon?"

"Do it, Andromeda," said Michael.

After one pleading look toward her older brother, Andromeda conceded and the deed was done without too much incident, though it was a slow process one-handed and Andromeda had to stop once to control a gagging fit.

Finally, a few hours before dawn, they all lay down to get some much needed sleep, the furs laid out to dry around them. Aquila and Zezil served as their watchmen.

* * *

Thetis' flinch at his master's enraged roar was minimal, a mere twitch of the eye. Tyrannus slashed the stone wall of his throne room with a swipe powerful enough to send a puff of rock dust into the air, and Callid squealed and conked his heads together in a wild attempt to cover all four ears.

"You've lost seven warriors to children!" said Tyrannus, stalking toward Thetis with runners of drool hanging from his jowls, yellow fangs bared. "You dare show your face here, standing proud and tall before your king?"

"I told my flock not to underestimate them," said Thetis, lazily raising his oceanic eyes to meet Tyrannus' orange ones. "It seems they paid me no heed. And it wasn't only children, Your Majesty. They did indeed have a griffin; Callid was correct about that. However, he failed to mention the strange, fury little demon that guards them as well. I've never seen such a beast. We had intended to outnumber them, just as you requested, but the hellhound threw things back into balance." Thetis's head swung like a heavy door on a freshly oiled hinge to glare at Callid. "Had I been better informed, I can assure you the outcome would have been different."

Callid let out a weak, tittering laugh and shrank deeper into the corner.

"A million apologizes, master," he said with a bow, "but I assure you that when I was following their trail, I found no signs of a terrible beast such as Thetis describes, and I was correct about the griffin prints. It is possible that Thetis is making the hellhound up."

"Listen, vermin," said Thetis bearing down on Callid like white rapids in a flooding stream. "Suggest such things again, and I will rip out both of your tongues."

Callid squeaked and covered his heads, and then Thetis was sailing across the room, hurled by the nape of his tunic by Tyrannus' powerful arms. Thetis struck the wall and slumped to the floor, dazed. Tyrannus pulled him back up the wall with one hand, his fingers clamped around Thetis' throat, strangling him.

"I told you to outnumber them, so you brought one extra warrior?" said Tyrannus, his teeth snapping together centimeters from Thetis' face. "Hubris such as that must be earned, and just what have you done with your eternal life to make you think so highly of yourself?"

Thetis' mouth gaped as he struggled for the air he didn't actually need, his lungs burning.

"I warned you of the consequences of failure, did I not?" said Tyrannus, his ugly maw parting in a grin. "Callid, would you care to witness your accuser's punishment?"

"You're too kind, master," said Callid.

"Come along, then. We're headed to the dungeons." Tyrannus cocked his head and clucked his tongue. "Most unfortunate that Nathaniel isn't here; he really doesn't care for you, you know. Especially not since the debacle with our elf princess. You'll have to recount it for him, Callid."

"With pleasure, master," said Callid, both heads split in a wide, dog-like grin.

* * *

The screams triggered Atalanta's adrenaline, and she paced her cell, rubbing her thumbs along the tips of her tingling fingers. Her heart pounded and her breath came in pants, as if she were running.

The hideous sounds of Thetis having his limbs ripped from his body might once have given her some sick sort of joy (she could still remember his sneer when he caught her after she'd managed to escape), but ever since Tyrannus and Callid had marched him past her cell, she'd felt nothing but terror.

Thetis was being punished, but not killed. And as per Tyrannus' promise the night before, if Thetis was back, she would receive her first dose of vampire venom that night.

* * *

"Almost there," said Erro, hunched over on Aquila's neck. "We should reach it well before nightfall."

"Good. We'll need to hunt," said Michael. The others couldn't help but notice that he was sitting straighter on his horse, his wolf furs whipping in the wind on his shoulders.

They were running low on the fresh food supplies from the villagers. They had slept most of the day after the attack, and with the stitches holding firm, Erro had awoken from his fever dreams. Still, they hadn't traveled the next day either, as Erro was still too weak to ride. Even today they'd created a sort of belt for him out of rope to keep him astride Aquila.

The lost time and the reduced pace agonized Michael, but he did his best to keep it hidden, meaning all of his siblings cast him sideways glances, waiting for the outburst. Michael's gaze kept shifting to Zezil at the head of the pack, willing the vexar with his eyes to once again find the trail of the cyclops.

So when Zezil began to scratch at the ground and jitter with excitement, tipping and wagging his bushy tail, Michael whooped so loudly he scared his stallion.

"It's not the cyclops, Michael," said Andromeda quietly.

Michael, shushing his horse, didn't hear.

"I want to follow the trail until nightfall. I won't lose it again," Michael said. "We can make supper from what we have left, hunt tomorrow."

"Michael," said Andromeda, wincing, for she had attempted to turn her horse about with her left hand, momentarily forgetting about her injury, "it's not the cyclops."

Michael ran a hand through the flyaway strands of fiery hair that had escaped his leather tie. "What is it then?"

Andromeda looked to Erro and then at the ground, where a jumble of horse hooves, boot prints, and wheel ruts marked the dirt. "It's a scent he's very familiar with."

Erro put a hand on Aquila's neck to push himself up straighter. "It's Brock, isn't it?"

"Erro, you can't," said Andromeda, pulling at her hair with two fingers. "Remember the plan. We'll find him after we find Atalanta, when you're strong again."

Erro sucked in a breath and stared at Andromeda a long while, holding it in all the while. When he let it out again, he said, "Let's press on, then."

Zezil whined, circling between Aquila's paws, his nose twitching up at Erro.

"Come, Zezil," he said as Aquila began to move on, "leave it."

Zezil cocked his head before returning to the trail. Erro looked straight ahead, saying nothing when Zezil began to veer to the east. The Avalons looked to each other. Michael spurred his horse, a frown sculpted deep in his face. Andromeda clucked her tongue at Zezil, bringing up the rear of the party. He looked back at her, tongue lolling and head cocked. He looked one last time into the thick of the woods to the east and then bounded back to trot alongside her horse.

Though the sun beat down through the slowly thinning trees, the air had bite close to the mountains. Felicity fussed with her furs, grunting and sighing as she pulled them on, then off again, chilled by the wind without them but sweaty within them. Andrew's solution was to wear his draped across himself like a sash, leaving his arms free, but his chest protected, and making it easy to pull the furs up to block his face from nasty rushes of wind.

Andromeda gave him a brow-raised look that silently proclaimed her admiration for his ingenuity and moved to do the same with her own furs, no small feat one-handed atop a horse.

"I'm going after Brock," said Erro, bringing Aquila to a sudden halt with a not-so-gentle tug on his feathers.

Andromeda's fur coat fell off her shoulders and sent up a small cloud of dirt and dead leaves from the forest floor. Erro found her eyes.

"I'm sorry; I can't just head in the opposite direction when he's so close. You don't need me anymore anyway. You couldn't miss the mountains if you tried, so long as you keep heading straight. You'll be there in a few hours. I ... I hope I'll see you — you all — again someday. Come on, Aquila."

Aquila's feathers stood up and he clicked his beak angrily as Erro urged him to turn around with both hands and feet.

Andromeda put her horse in his path. Her grey eyes were steel blades, her mouth a thin dagger.

"And just how do you plan to clash blades with a band of raiders in your condition? Without dying, that is."

Erro leaned back, head tilted warily as her anger struck him full force. "I don't plan to clash any blades until I've recovered. I'll follow them at a distance, but I have to move now, while the trail is fresh, or I'll lose them again."

"You're going to get Aquila and Zezil slaughtered, too. Do you understand that?" said Andromeda. "They will die because of your pig-headedness."

"You're not listening," said Erro, color coming to his cheeks, his own voice rising.

"Oh, I'm listening," said Andromeda, her eyes widening with holy fury. "I'm listening to the ramblings of a hurt boy who can convince himself of anything to further his blind search for revenge."

"What would you know of hurt, princess?" said Erro, his jaw set like stone.

Andromeda bit her cheek and looked away, and Michael almost asked Erro just what he thought that expression on her face might be, but he held his tongue. It was Felicity who swung her horse around beside Andromeda, violently shaking her golden ringlets back from her face, like a stallion about to charge.

"She's only trying to protect you," said Felicity in the slow, measured way she reserved for those she found particularly dim-witted. "Can't you see she—?" Felicity gave the air a back-handed swat. "Oh, never mind. Go then! Get yourself killed and squander your chance at revenge or justice or whatever you call it in your little fantasies. Just go!"

"Gladly, if you both would get out of my way," said Erro, doing his best to keep himself straight in his seat.

Felicity obliged with a scoff and another toss of her thick mane.

"Michael, you can't let him leave," said Andromeda, the tears she'd not yet released from her eyes evident in her voice.

Something flashed across Erro's face, softening it for the smallest of moments, and then he urged Aquila around Andromeda's horse.

"Do something!" said Andromeda, looking up to her brother with supplication. "He'll die. You know he'll die."

For the first time, Michael looked dismayed at being asked to take charge, but even Erro paused to hear what he would say.

"I may be his prince, but I am not his commander," said Michael. "He has helped us willingly. He is his own man, not our servant. If he wishes to go, I cannot stop him. But Erro," he turned to the other boy, "I do wish you would stay. We will find the trail again, together."

"I thank you for letting me come along with you, and for the help you gave in Everly, but I simply don't have it in me to let him get away when he is so close. Best of luck finding your elf princess."

Andromeda put her heels to her horse and raced ahead through the forest without a word.

"Damn," said Felicity under her breath. She looked at the three boys, all looking after Andromeda with bewildered expressions, and gave them a look of disdain fierce enough to cut flesh before urging her horse to follow after her sister.

"Uh," said Michael, scratching at the new beard growth on his chin and jaw, trying to bring his focus back to Erro. "Well … thank you for your assistance, and I do hope you meant it when you said you would wait for your strength."

"I did. Good-bye, Michael. I hope to see you again."

Michael nodded and turned his horse.

Andrew lingered. "You know we meant it when we said we would fight with you?" he said, a sad, ponderous expression dulling his usually lively face.

"I do."

Andrew looked down the path that would lead him to his twin. "You are a bit of a fool, aren't you?"

Erro blinked, his brow knitted. "I'm unsure how to respond."

"Don't worry, we all play the fool from time-to-time," said Andrew with a soft smile. "You only run into trouble when you make a habit of it."

Erro tilted his head and a corner of his lip twitched.

"Good-bye, Andrew. I shall miss your company."

"Probably," said Andrew with a grin, "but it isn't my company you'll come back for."

He clucked to his horse and trotted off after his siblings, their furs bobbing in the distance.

"Oh yes?" Erro called after him. "And just what does that mean?"

Andrew turned in his saddle. "That I shall see you again sooner than you think," he yelled back, "and if I don't, then you truly are a fool."

Erro narrowed his eyes and curled his mouth in a closed-lipped grin, shaking his head slightly. He watched the shapes of the Avalons disappear among the trees, and then sighed.

"Just us again, boys," he said, looking down at Aquila and Zezil.

Aquila screeched loud enough to make Erro shake a finger in his ear, wincing.

"Temper, temper," he said, tutting. "Come on, you know where to go, and you know there's no stopping me. If you toss me off, I'll only crawl the rest of the way if I have to."

Aquila gave a raptor hiss, but traipsed on back the way they'd come. It took a moment for Erro to realize that Zezil was not following. The vexar was rooted to the earth where Andromeda's horse had stood not long before, staring after her.

"Come, Zezil."

Zezil looked back and whined, a heady sound that carried to Erro's ears like a melancholy whisper, faint and drawn out.

"Come now, Zezil. We're going to do some hunting."

It was one of the few words the little beast seemed to recognize, and he turned from the Avalons' trail without another glance, bounding off into the forest after his master, ready for the chase.

Chapter 10

Night on the Mountain

"Don't be foolish, Andrew," said Michael, his arm extended down to his brother from atop his horse. "It will take twice the time with you walking along behind."

"I'd just as soon not get that well acquainted with you," said Andrew. "Why can't I ride with the goat?"

"Because the goat already weighs twice as much as you do. I told you we should have brought Gregor's horse."

"I didn't expect to be lugging back a goat the size of a pony. Next time, we bring the pack horse and you lead the damned thing."

"All right, so long as it keeps you from whining," said Michael, beckoning with the fingers of his extended hand.

Andrew gave the massive, horned carcass of the mountain goat draped across his saddle a look of disdain, though only a few moments before he had pulled his silver arrow from its hide with a look of glee. He grabbed Michael's arm with a groan and used it to hoist himself up onto the very back of the saddle. The curved shape made him slide into Michael, no matter how he adjusted. Michael had adopted Sir Gregor's bearskin to ward off the biting winds that were inescapable high in the mountains, and the teeth of the animal rammed into Andrew's cheek.

"Move forward," said Andrew, impatiently flipping the bear's head so that it served as Michael's hood.

"I'll be sitting on the poor beast's neck if I do that."

With another groan, Andrew scooted himself back so that he sat on the horse's haunches instead of the saddle. It was a position he didn't keep for long. Michael's steed, already growing impatient at the new, shifting weight of a second rider, bucked, and Andrew hit the rocky dirt of the mountain path.

"I'm riding with the goat," said Andrew, his grumbled words hardly audible over Michael's loud guffaws.

By the time the boys rode up to the elevated cave, Andrew reluctantly bouncing and swaying in the unsteady seat on the back edge of Michael's saddle, there was already a fire burning inside. The cave had served as their camp for the past two days. It was Michael's favorite so far during their week on the mountain, because of its security. At first his siblings had hated it, as a precarious climb up a sheer rock face was required to reach it. But once they'd realized they could use Felicity's odd hook-shooting crossbow to reel themselves to the top, coming and going from the cave had become a sort of game.

Felicity's head appeared over the lip.

"Lord above! My hook won't hold that massive thing and you! Just how do you expect to get that up here without breaking your neck?"

"Piece by piece," said Michael as Andrew slid off the horse behind him. "We'll skin and prepare it down here."

"Find anything other than supper?" said Andromeda, her dark head materializing next to Felicity's gold one.

"Some more of those tracks," said Michael.

"Us, too," said Andromeda, "but they were still too muddled to make anything out of."

"We followed some to a hole in the rock. Could lead to a larger cave, but we couldn't fit inside."

"Do you think one of us could?" said Felicity.

"No. Only a child would have a chance of squeezing in there," said Michael.

"It has to be goblins," said Andromeda. "Nothing else makes sense."

"You don't know that for sure," said Michael. "Erro said the cyclops was short, the size of a child. There could be a whole village of them up here in these caves."

The strange, four-toed, child-sized footprints had appeared

on the second day of scaling the mountainside, but they had grown more and more frequent as the party reached the middle, and tapered off again as they neared the peaks. For a week now, the Avalons had been staying in caves at night and splitting up to search the paths made by the dwarves by day for some sign that the cyclops or Atalanta had made their way over or into the mountains.

Though none of them said anything, they were all beginning to think they were chasing a corpse. Atalanta was surely dead. The truth could be found in their lack of speech rather than what they said. When they'd first started the mountain search, they'd been enthusiastic, always expecting the next cave to hold a burned out fire or sign of inhabitation. They'd speculated whether King Zanthus had received a letter demanding ransom at last. Now they set out each morning in near silence, saddling up and setting off with the dull, tired, and somewhat cranky looks of people headed out to complete a familiar menial task.

"I bet Erro could have made sense of those tracks," said Andrew. "We should have paid more attention when he was tracking, asked questions."

"We thought he would be coming with us," said Andromeda with a weak, stilted smile before disappearing into the cave.

Andrew's apologetic wince came too late. Felicity shook her head and retreated into the cave, too.

Andrew flinched at the loud thud of the goat carcass smacking the earth. He turned to find Michael with his hunting knife already unsheathed. Andrew, grateful not to receive another reproach, moved to help.

The brothers managed to finish their task just as night was falling, and the smell of roasting meat escaped into the unseasonably chilly air along with the smoke that billowed from the cave mouth.

Supper proceeded in weary silence, until Michael surprised the others by setting his haunch of meat aside and saying,

"Perhaps it's time we started making our way back down."

For a while there was only the sound of the crackling fire.

"And then back home?" said Felicity.

"Then we find Erro," said Andromeda.

"No, we go back to the last place we found the trail and start over in a new direction," said Michael.

"There won't be any trail left to find," said Andrew.

"Not if it lives around there."

"Before, you were sure it lived in the mountains."

"Well maybe I was wrong," said Michael, each word slow and stiff as it shoved its way out from between his lips. "If those tracks do turn out to be goblins, we'll know for sure. I wish we could find one."

"If we're going back we need to find Erro. Make sure he's all right," said Andromeda.

"We need to find Atalanta. That's what we've been tasked to do," said Michael.

"How do we know somebody else hasn't already found her?" said Andromeda, heat rising in her cheeks.

"How do we know she isn't dead?" said Felicity. "If she hasn't been ransomed or rescued, she's carrion by now."

* * *

Atalanta retreated into her own head. She was on the training field, the orchard in the distance, the gold and white palace at her back as she spun in the dance of swordplay with Mikael and Breanna, her closest friends. If she concentrated hard enough, she could conjure their voices, recreate their smiles. She lost herself in the moving images to forget. To forget the cold, clammy feeling of Thetis' long-dead flesh on her cheek and shoulder, forget the chains encircling her wrists, forget the sharp pain of fangs piercing her skin and the burn of the venom in her veins.

A small dose would not turn her. For that, she would first

have to die, her drained blood replaced with a full dose of venom. The knowledge hardly made the bite more pleasant.

When it was over, she opened her eyes to a sharpened world. She could see every pore in her skin, every hair on Thetis' head, every crack in Tyrannus' long, yellow nails with precise clarity. She smelled all of the blood, sweat, and urine in the dungeon threefold. She could smell the old, black blood in Thetis' still heart and the lycanthropy virus-tainted blood under Tyrannus' skin. Her heart fluttered and thumped in turns, trying its best to filter out the alien substance in her blood. Her hands flew up to snatch at Thetis' face as he withdrew, licking blood from the corner of his mouth, and the chains nearly ripped free of the dungeon floor, stopping her nails centimeters from his face. The hiss of a jungle cat bubbled up from her throat, and the urge to bite and tear and taste the coppery tang of blood on her tongue overwhelmed her. Thetis laughed.

"We'll return when you've calmed down a bit, hmm?" said Tyrannus. "Tonight you summon more than a campfire for me."

Atalanta hardly heard him. She had slunk down the wall, eyes closed, chest heaving as she tried to get control over her own head. The urges would pass. They always did. But it took longer each time, and she was beginning to worry that very soon they would linger as long as the heightened senses and added strength ... or perhaps they wouldn't leave at all.

"I think we'd best keep the chains on her tonight," said Tyrannus, flicking the train of his cloak behind him as he reached for the door of her cell. "Bring her when she's ready."

Thetis gave a small bow. Both he and Tyrannus missed the smile that played at Atalanta's lips for only a moment. They were turning her into a monster in a quest to make her stronger, more like them. But she wasn't like them. She was an elf, and the monster they were creating was stronger than they thought. Soon, it would bite back.

* * *

Andrew's eyes flew open on the pitch-black canvas of the cave. His heart raced from what he thought perhaps had been an instantly forgotten dream. Then he heard the shuffling of feet and the crunch of pebbles on the cave floor. Someone stood right behind his head. Another was moving around the mouth of the cave. Andrew began to inch his hand down and bend his knee so that he could grab the dagger from his boot. The intruder behind him made a series of odd clicking and gurgling noises, and Andrew froze. The second intruder responded with a similar soft call. Andrew heard the one behind him move toward the second. He pulled his dagger from the sheath strapped to his boot and slowly raised his head just in time to see two dark, silhouetted heads disappear below the lip of the cave.

Andrew tapped on Michael's head with the toe of his boot. Michael grunted awake, snatching at his belt for the sword that was propped up against the cave wall.

"Michael, somebody was just in here. Two of them. Could have been cyclopes."

Michael became entangled in the bearskin he used as a blanket in his rush to get to his feet.

"Felicity, Andromeda, get up," he said, tripping over himself and then tossing the skin aside in a huff.

"Hmm?" Andromeda rubbed at her eyes.

"I may have to kill you," said Felicity, when Michael rousted her with his boot.

"Cyclopes," said Michael. "Andrew said they were just in here."

"I said they could have been cyclopes," said Andrew.

"Get up, we're going after them. Grab the torches."

Each night they saved a few pieces of firewood and wrapped them in small strips of cloth from their singular remaining blanket, keeping the ones they didn't use in a pack. The girls scrambled to their feet and grabbed up that night's small batch from a corner of the cave. Michael was already on his knees beside them, his flint at the ready.

With four torches blazing, they lowered themselves from the cave one by one with Felicity's hook. Felicity started reeling in the hook, but Michael grabbed her wrist and pulled her away.

"No time," he said. "Andrew, get down. We can't risk taking the horses."

"Why not?" said Andrew, sliding down from his horse's bare back.

"You want to risk them laming themselves in the dark?"

"Michael!" said Andromeda, pointing to a group of small, bristly shrubs growing in the scant soil between the rocks. "I saw something move over there."

Torch held high, Michael took off at a jog—the fastest he dared go on the rugged terrain of the mountain in the dark. His siblings went after him, four torches bobbing in the night. Michael crashed right through the shrubs, crunching their brittle branches under his boots.

"Damn," he said, the flame of his torch whooshing as he spun this way and that.

"There," whispered Felicity.

The others looked up the slope just in time to see what appeared to be a child pull itself up over a boulder and out of sight. They raced to catch it, but on the other side of the boulder there was nothing but more mountainside.

Clicks and gurgles echoed from inside an alcove cut into a rock face.

"You think it's calling for help?" said Andrew.

Michael looked to Andromeda.

"Whatever it is, it isn't an animal," she said with a shrug.

Michael put a finger to his mouth and motioned for his siblings to follow him as he tiptoed toward the alcove. They surrounded the little niche in the stone, swords drawn, and Michael shoved the torch inside with a triumphant look.

Nothing was inside. He frowned and shoved the torch farther in, walking into the alcove himself.

"There's an opening back here," he said, sheathing his sword. "It looks like there's some sort of light coming from inside. We'll have to crawl."

Keeping his torch held out at eye level, Michael got to his knees and carefully scooted the torch through the opening first. He crawled in after it, head ducked and eyes fixed on the ground. His shoulders almost didn't fit, but he forced his way through. When he lifted his head, he was met by a sea of little faces grinning at him with tiny, needle-like teeth. Before he could open his mouth, a club struck him on the head, making his vision blacken and swirl. Small hands pulled him away from the entrance on his back, and through his clouded vision, he saw Andrew's head appear through the opening. The brothers' eyes locked. Andrew backpedaled, but a noose flew over his head and tightened around his neck. Clubs made from stalagmites beat at his shoulders, and hands pulled at his leather armor, pulling him inside. Andrew's eyes bulged as he tried to pull back, tightening the noose around his neck.

"Andrew?" said Andromeda, concerned by her twin's flailing feet on the other side of the opening.

"Andromeda, Felicity, run!" said Michael, earning himself another whack with a club. This time, the darkness stayed and enveloped him.

At the command of their brother, both girls looked to each other and redrew their swords. Andrew was inside the opening up to his ankles. Andromeda made a grab for his feet, but they slipped through her fingers. A small head full of bluish grey hair poked out in their place. The creature's pallid skin held a greenish tinge, and the eyes set deep into the face were a murky blue. It grinned at her and gnashed its pointed teeth.

Andromeda cried out and stumbled back as the creature

slashed at her with a knife made of sharpened bone. She countered with a swipe of her own blade that nearly cut the three-foot creature in two. Two more rushed out of the entrance to take its place, their ragged goatskin clothes hanging off their childish bodies.

"Goblins!" said Felicity, moving beside her sister, sword raised.

"Where there's three, there's probably three hundred not far behind," said Andromeda, backing up from the two goblins that were now growling and snapping at them.

Goblins began to swarm from the entrance, forcing the sisters back with swipes at their shins and hips. Andromeda decapitated three with a single swing, and Felicity ran two of them through at a time, skewering them on her rapier like kabobs. But more only stepped forward to take their place.

"Andromeda?" said Felicity, a slight shake in her voice. "Know any tricks for fighting goblins?"

"Run!"

Torches and swords in hand, the girls turned tail and sprinted, Felicity wincing against the pain of a popped stitch in her partially healed thigh.

The goblins took chase with a unified war cry. Andromeda's ankles snapped together, tangled in a rope weighted by two bones thrown by a skilled hand so that they whipped around to encircle her legs. She hit the ground awkwardly, trying to save her broken wrist from further damage. Felicity stopped running at her sister's cry of pain and doubled back to free her. With a quick flick of her sword, she cut the ropes, but more flew at them from all directions as the goblins bore down on them in a wave. Lassos grabbed their limbs and necks, forcing them to the ground, and clubs beat them into submission as they were hauled back to the alcove and shoved bodily through the entrance, their legs bound together and their arms bound to their sides.

"Michael!" Felicity tried to reach for her brother, unconscious on the cold stone beside her with blood trickling down his forehead, but she was bound too tightly and received a kick in the ribs for speaking.

Andrew's whooping, painful coughs mixed with the chatter of the goblins. A large, purple welt encircled his throat like a necklace. Andromeda tried to be as still as possible, not wanting to inflict any strain on her bound, broken wrist, which was already throbbing from the rough, unceremonious journey inside the alcove.

But it wasn't just an alcove. They were in a large cavern lit by torches on the walls. The stone was black, not grey, and held a purple, metallic tint that rippled in the firelight. The stalagmites and stalactites had a purple hue as well. And beyond the cavern was a tunnel carved into the stone. Just from the light of the torches, two different passageways could be seen branching off in the distance. It was an intricate cave system, a goblin palace. Andromeda guessed it might have been crafted by the dwarves.

The sea of green-skinned goblins parted and blue-topped heads bowed as a goblin slightly taller than all the rest made his way to the Avalons. He wore a crown of sorts, crafted from the purplish rock and the bones of small animals. Two, large, blue-green feathers poked up like rabbit ears on either side of it.

"Your Majesty, I presume," said Andrew, his chuckle ragged as it forced its way from his damaged throat.

He hissed in pain as a bone knife slashed at his forearm, accompanied by the angered chatter of a nearby goblin.

The goblin king appraised the siblings, statue-still but for his murky eyes. Then he raised his hands and gurgled to his people. A cheer rose up from an unknown number of voices. Leather blindfolds that smelled as though they'd recently been used for loincloths were secured over the siblings' eyes, even Michael's. Dozens of hands gripped the siblings and hoisted them up.

The siblings grunted and cried out when their noses or foreheads occasionally bumped and scraped against the low ceilings on their winding, blind journey through the system of caves. Michael awoke with a groan when his shoulder was slammed into a wall on a particularly tight turn.

Disoriented and in serious discomfort, the Avalons could not have said how long they traveled, carried on small shoulders, before they were tossed to the ground and had their blindfolds removed.

This cave was domed, sanded smooth so that no loose stone could be used for a weapon. It was a prison. The goblin king stood in the circular entrance, grinning, his tribe behind him, crammed into the passages, all eager to hear the king's verdict for their captives.

The king raised his hands again, this time looking to the ceiling in worship.

"Olga!"

The unified cries of "Olga!" reverberated loud enough to make the Avalons wince.

The goblin king stepped backward, out of the cave, his grin never slipping. A number of his subjects rushed to his side and began to roll a large boulder over the entrance, grunting and clicking their tongues with the effort. It slid into the circular opening with a thunk that seemed dangerously final.

"What's Olga?" said Andrew.

"It sounds familiar," said Michael. "And the memories aren't all that pleasant."

"That's because it's a name that's in all the goblins' lore," said Andromeda. "It's their god."

"I don't suppose it's a nice god," said Felicity.

"Sure, so long as she gets her blood sacrifice. Humans make her particularly happy."

Chapter 11

Blood Sacrifice

Still bound from shoulders to ankles and stripped of all their weapons in the struggle, the Avalons lay prostrate on the stone floor. They rolled about and tried to prop themselves up against each other or the smooth, rounded cave wall, wiggling like giant, hooked worms and cursing like hardened seamen or battle-weary soldiers.

Andrew let out a theatrical sigh of relief when he and Andromeda managed to inch their way into a semi-sitting position with their backs pressed together.

"Can you untie each other's ropes from that position?" said Michael, panting on the floor.

The twins scrunched their brows and bit their tongues in identical looks of concentration as they tried to reach the knots of each other's bonds. With hands bound at their sides instead of their backs, though, they were only able to brush fingertips.

"What if I came over to you?" said Michael. "Could you reach mine?"

"Powers above! Just try it," said Felicity, who was just now managing to inch her back up the curved side of the cave wall, her chin pressed into her chest as she wriggled upward, listing slightly to the left.

Michael writhed like a wounded snake, inching himself toward the twins. When Andrew started laughing, Michael groaned in frustration and rocked his body hard enough to send him rolling toward the twins at full speed, his chin knocking into the stone on each roll.

"Whoa, whoa, whoa!" said Andrew.

Michael collided with the twins and sent them teetering to the side. With no way to hold themselves up, they crashed to the stone.

"Brilliant idea, Michael, truly brilliant," said Andrew.

Michael moaned, seeing black spots. Rolling hadn't done his goblin-clubbed head much good.

Andromeda let out a sort of exasperated giggle. "If we weren't about to be sacrificed, boiled, and eaten, this might be rather funny."

"Ah ha!" said Felicity triumphantly.

"Just what about being boiled and eaten has made you so giddy?" said Andrew, unable to see his older sister from his prostrate position facing the boulder that blocked the domed cave's exit.

"Excellent, Felicity!" said Michael. "Now hop over here and let me try to untie your feet."

"Hop?" said Andrew.

Felicity had managed to inch her way into a standing position, using the cave wall for support. She bit her lip and braced herself for the precarious journey to the middle of the cave floor. The first hop sent her tilting forward, and to compensate, she hopped like a mad rabbit, trying to keep her footing. But each hop only made her forward lean more pronounced, and she crashed on top of her three siblings. Her chin drove the air from Andrew's lungs in a whoosh, and as he coughed and sucked in ragged, desperate breaths and Michael and Andromeda groaned in pain, one of the torches on the purple mineral-flecked black walls fizzled out.

"Oh, wonderful," said Felicity, spitting out the words through gritted teeth. "Soon we won't be able to see anything. Just what are we supposed to do?"

Andrew made an odd sound underneath her.

"What?"

"Get ... off," he wheezed.

With a scoff from deep within her throat and a pronounced eye roll, Felicity rolled herself off, crushing the twins' heads underneath her as she went.

By the time a band of goblins rolled aside the boulder again, all of the torches had burned through their oil and the Avalons had been in total darkness for hours, only managing restless and fleeting fits of sleep. Andrew had dreamed of food piled high in the grand dining hall; Michael, of finding the elf princess ... a mere pile of bones; Felicity, of hot baths and beautiful gowns. Andromeda's sleep had been plagued with visions of Erro wounded and alone; Erro calling to her for help, Aquila's bloody feathers scattered around him; Erro crawling away from a tall, man-like shadow that bore down on him with taloned hands.

She was almost happy to see the goblin's grinning faces. The king was nowhere to be found, only a small hoard of his subjects. There was a bounce in their steps. They gestured to each other excitedly, and each step grew more like a hop or a skip. Their animated chatter was punctuated with multiple mentions of "Olga" as they encircled the siblings.

Felicity's breathing became hard and wild; color rushed to her face as her chest heaved with barely contained sobs. Her childhood nightmares flashed behind her eyes.

"You're not eating me, you ugly little bastards!"

Felicity's voice was shrill, unfamiliar. The sound of her older sister's fear brought frightened tears to Andromeda's eyes and planted panic deep in her chest.

Felicity lashed out with her bound feet, swiping two goblins' legs out from under them. She screamed as they regained their feet and fell on her with their clubs and fists. Andromeda clenched her eyes and screamed with her sister, struggling against the little hands that were attempting to hoist her from the ground. A sharp tug at her hair ripped the roots from her scalp and sent her tear-filled eyes shooting open to lock with Michael's.

Michael's face twisted with righteous fury, and he let out a bellowing roar as he flexed his muscles against his bonds, a bear caught in a net. A few of the goblins squeaked with terror at the sound of snapping rope fibers. The goblins abandoned the other three siblings to jump on Michael, clubs and knives at the ready.

"Get off him! Get off!" Andromeda's voice was a childish wail, but she threw powerful kicks at the goblins with her bound legs, sending a few flying.

Andrew and Felicity maneuvered themselves around Michael, too, helping Andromeda kick the hoard off of him. But more goblins piled into the cave, subduing the siblings with their numbers.

Felicity wiggled herself to face Michael as the goblins withdrew from his chest to try and hoist him up on their shoulders. She gasped at his battered, bloody face and buried her head against his shoulder, her tears flowing over his leather armor.

"It's okay," he whispered to her through cracked lips, one eye swollen shut. "It's okay."

Goblins pulled her from him by her ankles, and her screams rang off the walls. They dragged her past Andromeda, and the two girls tried desperately to reach one another with their bound hands.

"Michael?" said Andrew, licking his lips in a nervous gesture to stave off his own terror as he looked from his screaming sisters to his beaten brother. "Michael, what do I do? Just tell me what to do."

"Keep them calm," said Michael, his one open eye dull as he was lifted into the air.

Andrew's breaths turned shallow as he stared at Michael, wide-eyed. "O–okay."

Pointy little shoulders bit into Andrew's back as they lifted him up and carried him into the tunnels. He heard his sisters crying up ahead and sucked in a shuddering breath.

"Hey, Felicity," he said in a lighthearted tone. He heard the girls' sobs catch and turn to sniffles as they strained to hear him. "You don't have to worry, you know. Once I explain to them how crusty and tough and generally unladylike you are, they won't want to eat you, I'm sure of it."

It wasn't his best, not by a long shot, but he smiled a little when he heard Andromeda's watery, if somewhat hysterical laugh.

"Andrew, you are such an ass," Felicity called back to him, but there was love rather than anger buried inside the words. After a few moments, she said, "I guess that means you're safe, too. No one wants to eat a scrawny thing like you."

"Now you've gone and mortally wounded my pride. How shall I ever recover?" He smiled as he said it, but the grin felt hollow.

He heard Felicity gasp.

"F—" His call of concern was cut off as his goblin escorts carried him into a huge stone chamber, dancing with light from at least a hundred fires blazing in circular alcoves carved into the walls, as well as the sunlight filtering through the small, chimney-like hole in the chamber ceiling. It was filled from wall to wall with goblins dancing to wild, screechy music. The musicians, scraping bone saws together and strumming harp-like instruments with blue-tinted strings that could only have come from the goblins' own hair, danced in two rings: one around the large stone basin raised above an overly-large cooking fire that was sending curls of smoke up through the hole in the ceiling, and one around a man-sized statue in the very center of the room.

Though it was crudely cut from black stone, the resemblance to a goblin was unmistakable, though whether it was male or female was not completely clear. Despite its resemblance to the dancing hoards around it, it was not an ordinary goblin. Wings sprouted from its back, and six arms held out clawed hands over the crowd. Around the statue's base, the Avalons' weapons gleamed in the firelight, an added offering of violence to the bloodthirsty goddess.

The goblins passed the siblings hand over hand so that they glided over a moving green and blue sea of bodies until they reached the stone altar beside the statue of Olga. The goblin king stood by it, waiting for them, a bone sword as long as he was clutched in his hand. The siblings were tossed unceremoniously onto the hard ground as the goblin king stepped onto the altar to address his subjects. When he raised his hands, the music and the dancing ceased. His voice was too loud and powerful for his childish body as he raised it in a strange song of chants that his subjects echoed back to him. With one last ringing cry of "Olga!" the music started up again and the goblins began to dance so fast their limbs seemed to vibrate.

Despite the ventilation in the ceiling, the cooking fire beneath the human-sized stone basin made the air stifling, and sweat poured down the Avalon's faces, stinging their eyes. Andromeda wriggled her wrists in her bonds, hoping the sweat dripping down her arms might serve as lubrication.

The goblin king slowly lowered the sword so that the tip pointed right at Michael's chest. Goblins swept forward to cut the ropes at his ankles. Michael stumbled to his feet with the help of little hands.

"Run, Michael, run!" said Felicity.

A goblin kicked her in the face for her trouble.

"Don't touch her!" said Michael charging at the goblin, but hands grabbed at the ropes binding him and pulled him back. Clubs battered him from all sides, bouncing off his armor and leaving small bruises underneath.

With one last look at his siblings, Michael turned away and allowed himself to be led to the altar and forced to his knees without a fight.

Felicity screamed and thrashed at her bonds no matter how many times she was pinched, kicked, or smacked. Andromeda tried to shush her, but her own tears were doing little to calm Felicity. Andrew was pale as milk, his mouth a thin line as he watched Michael, hardly breathing, as if willing Michael to do something. To save them.

When Michael turned his head, Andrew's face lit up. His mouth became an expectant O.

"I'm sorry I failed you," said Michael, tears glistening in his red lashes. "I never meant—"

A goblin forced his head around and shoved it down on the altar. Felicity screamed her brother's name and thrashed so fiercely that three goblins had to sit atop her to keep her in place.

The goblin king looked at her with a malicious grin and gripped the sword tighter.

An eagle's cry pierced through the chanting and the grating music, and all eyes turned skyward as a streak of gold and red shot through the chamber entrance. The griffin's claws scraped the stone goddess' head, and a silver dagger flew from the sky, embedding in the goblin king's chest. A crimson blossom bloomed on his skin, and he crumpled backward, the bone sword slipping from his fingers before he'd even raised it.

The goblins' shrieks of outrage at the slaughter of their king under the very eyes of their goddess became screams of terror. Across the chamber, goblins were parting in a wave, tossed into the air with bits and pieces missing. A furry back crested the surface of the blue-green sea of bodies, and from the hoard, the fully morphed Zezil leapt atop Olga's likeness, gnawing at her stone head as she toppled to the ground. Michael only just scrambled out of the way before the idol crashed into the stone altar, cracking it in two. As goblins rushed out of the way, shrieking in terror and surprise, Michael hurried to the pile of weapons and gingerly embraced his broadsword in order to cut the bonds around his arms.

Aquila swooped low, and Erro slid off his back, tumbling into a roll that brought him face to face with Andromeda.

"Hello, princess," he said, his smile slightly off kilter as he searched her eyes.

"Erro," she said through a soggy laugh as he cut her bonds.

A goblin jumped on his back. Andromeda punched it square in the jaw before its blade could pierce his neck. Another took its place, but this time Erro was ready and slammed his back into the ground. The goblin's bones crunched beneath his weight.

"Hurry, hurry! Cut us loose," said Felicity, squirming on the ground.

"Well, that's the plan," said Erro in a choked voice, wrenching tiny arms from around his neck.

Andromeda kicked a goblin in the jaw as it stabbed at her armored hips, snapping its head sideways.

Michael appeared and shoved a rapier in her hand. A grin split her face, and she swung it wildly at the oncoming hoard while Michael made short work of Felicity's and Andrew's bonds.

"Where's our swords?" said Andrew.

"I can only carry so many. You'll have to get them yourselves."

"Look out!" said Felicity.

Michael whirled to face the oncoming goblins just as Aquila swooped down and scattered them with his wings, swiping any stray ones with his claws. He snatched one up in his beak and tossed it into the chamber wall. Now with a clear path to their weapons, Felicity and Andrew sprinted to the desecrated statue together.

"We have to get out of here fast or they're just going to overwhelm us again," said Andromeda.

Zezil streaked past her, leaving a bloody spray on her trouser leg and taking at least four goblins with him.

"I have an idea," said Erro. "Make your way to the exit." And with that, he was gone.

He used a goblin's head as a spring board and landed next to the fallen king. He wrenched his dagger from the goblin's chest and put his fingers to his lips. The whistle wasn't even complete before Aquila appeared above him. Erro leapt atop the griffin's back as he flew past.

The Avalons regrouped with their backs together, fighting as a unit toward the exit, each swipe of their swords backed with fury, revenge, and the memory of the taste of terror still fresh in their mouths. Aquila dove into the goblins whenever it looked like the siblings might be overwhelmed, clearing them a path. When they'd reached the exit, they all looked up to search for Erro and Aquila and found them circling the giant basin full of boiling water.

Erro was gesturing wildly to the griffin, and his commands were barely audible over the din of the goblins' cries of war, pain, and terror.

"Does he really think Aquila understands him?" said Felicity, her nose wrinkled in exasperation.

"He does," said Andromeda, a smile playing at her mouth as she unarmed a goblin with a clean swipe of her sword and then looked up at the griffin. "He understands more than even Erro thinks he does."

Aquila circled the basin one last time before tucking his wings and diving at it with all four paws outstretched. He collided with the stone from the back end, and it rocked precariously forward. Aquila pumped his wings as Erro cheered him on, and boiling water splashed over the lip, scalding the goblins nearest it. But the basin began to tip back into place, and Aquila's wing beats grew labored. A black and grey wrecking ball slammed into the basin at the base, and the smell of singed fur reached the Avalons' noses from across the room. Zezil backed off, sneezing and whining and rubbing at his muzzle, but no more effort was needed from him. The basin toppled, sending boiling water rushing out at the remaining members of the goblin hoard. Those in the far corners of the room only suffered scalded feet, but it was enough to send them clambering over one another, running for the jagged stone walls which they tried their best to climb. The Avalons ran back into the tunnel system as the water came for them.

Back in the chamber, Zezil's skeletal structure was reforming. The burns on his paws and muzzle had discouraged him rather than enraged him, like a babe struck suddenly on the hand for an unintended misdeed, and he whined like a pup when Erro leaned over Aquila's back to scoop him up and carry him safely over the boiling river he'd created. Erro slid off of Aquila's back just before he landed in the tight tunnel entrance, holding Zezil like a swaddled child.

"Go, go!" said Erro, blocked from the Avalons' view by Aquila's bulk.

The griffin had to keep his wings tucked tight to his body to move through the tunnels, ducking his head like the humans behind and before him.

Erro shouted directions, leading the Avalons out the way he'd come in. He looked over his shoulder every few paces, but it seemed the goblins were either unable to pursue or had lost all desire to continue the battle they'd lost so sorely.

Still, when they all squeezed back out of the alcove, Erro jumped astride Aquila's back again. "Mount up," he told the Avalons, gesturing to the horses grazing lazily on the dew-soaked grass in the early morning light.

"Our horses," said Andromeda. "How did you ...?"

"I found them before I found you. I'd been tracking their prints all over the mountain. Wasn't easy with all of the backtracking you did, moving from cave to cave every few days. No, go on." He looked over his shoulder at the unsuspecting groove in the rock face. "Let's get as far away as we can before they decide to avenge their king."

They rode their horses as fast as they dared on the slanted and sometimes dangerously rocky terrain of the mountainside. They moved sideways rather than down or up to keep the pace even, rather than precariously fast or labored and slow. Erro soared over their heads, Aquila's shadow spanning out before them like a compass needle. Zezil ran alongside Andromeda's horse.

Michael was the first to rein in his stallion, clutching at his head, leaning as if he might fall from the saddle. The others helped him down, and Felicity undid the ties of his armor, stripping him to his undergarments. His armor, mistaken by the goblins as common leather and thus left untouched, had protected his chest and the tops of his limbs from serious injury even through countless beatings, but he was black and blue just about everywhere else, and his head had taken quite a walloping.

Andromeda tried to help Felicity in her examination, but Zezil had taken it upon himself to lick every inch of her, and he kept knocking her to the ground, tickling her with his tongue. Erro tried to rescue her, but it was no use; the vexar wriggled free of his arms every time.

"Here, have some of this," said Erro, holding out his water skin to Michael.

Felicity snatched it and helped Michael drink. Michael had to turn his head to see Erro with his one open eye.

"Thank you. We owe you our lives."

"Yes, thank you," said Felicity, sparing a soft smile.

Andrew clapped Erro on the back, and Erro grunted. "Still not fully healed back there," he said through tight lips.

"Oh, right, sorry," said Andrew with an apologetic grimace.

"It's all right. I think I may have overdone it in there, though," said Erro, jerking his head back the way they had come. "I think one of the wounds is seeping."

"Let me look," said Andromeda, moving forward. Then she pulled back, color high on her cheekbones, and said, "If I may."

Erro looked away, somewhat bashful as he reached back to pull up his tunic. Andromeda sucked air through her teeth.

"The stitches have come loose in one place," she said, her fingers hovering over the marred skin of his back, never quite touching it. "Hold on."

She rummaged through her horse's saddlebag and pulled out the last of the medic's salve.

"We're truly in your debt," she said as she sat cross-legged behind him and began applying the salve gingerly with two fingers. "We will repay you. I promise."

"I know. You're going to help me bring Brock and his raiders to justice ... after we find your elf princess, of course."

Andromeda smiled.

"Unless, you've already found her," said Erro.

"Not a trace of her," said Andrew. "You didn't find Brock? Did Zezil lose the scent?"

"No. We only spent about a day on his trail. The rest of the time has been spent finding you."

"Really?" said Andrew, a playfully malicious grin stealing onto his face.

"Well, I figured I couldn't let four highborn youths bumble around on the mountain by themselves," said Erro, mirroring Andrew's expression. "Sounded like a disaster in the making to me. Guess it turns out I was right."

"You were a bit late," said Andrew. "I thought your tracking skills were insurmountable?"

"I wasn't exactly in fighting shape, now was I?" said Erro. He turned his head around to see Andromeda as best he could. "I suppose that's what you'd been trying to tell me all along, right, princess?"

"I'm done," said Andromeda quietly. "You can let your tunic down now."

She took the salve over to Michael, and Erro watched her go, a sad pull at the corners of his mouth.

"The first few days were slow going," he said, not looking at Andrew as he spoke to him. "You got a good distance ahead of me. If you hadn't stayed in the same place every now and then, I would have been too late. I almost sat and waited with your horses. Thought you'd gone to the stream or something. But then I saw the goblin prints. Didn't know what they were until I found the cave. When I realized something was wrong, I gathered up your furs and a few other things and brought the horses with me. Oh, by the way, Felicity, I believe this is yours."

From his pack he withdrew her grappling hook, left behind during their mad chase of the goblins, and handed it over.

"Thank you," she said, only sparing it a glance before turning back to Michael, salve thick on her fingers.

They patched each other's cuts, but when it was done, they'd used all of the salve. When Michael's dizziness subsided and he was able to mount his horse, they found a new cave to make camp in and made a meal of the rest of the goat meat, cooked the night before and preserved in one of the saddlebags.

Michael was the first to fall asleep, curled up by the dying fire, the bearskin cloak draped carefully over him by Felicity. From the look on her face as she propped herself against the cave wall with her eyes fixed on his sleeping form, it seemed she meant to watch him through the night, but she fell asleep with her chin on her chest shortly after. Andromeda eased her into a more comfortable position and made sure her furs were wrapped all the way around her. Andrew dozed off next, laid out on his back with his arms crossed on his chest.

"Why do you keep looking at me like that?" said Erro, leaning forward from his cozy position tucked into Aquila's wing.

"Like what?" said Andromeda, her eyes averted as she scratched Zezil's ears.

"I don't know … like you want to say something."

"Shh, you'll wake them."

"Come outside with me, then."

Andromeda raised her eyes to his. "Why?"

"Because I haven't given you a proper apology, and I'd like to. And I'd like to hear what it is you want to say."

"I don't want to say anything."

"Then will you come outside and listen to what I have to say?"

She studied him for a moment, her face hard but her eyes malleable and searching. She stood up without a word, displacing Zezil gently, and walked out into the falling night, not looking back as she headed to the stream babbling nearby.

"Should I be worried?" Erro whispered to Aquila.

The griffin didn't answer, but as Erro stood up, Andrew's whisper made him fall still.

"Hey, Erro."

At first Erro thought he'd imagined it. Andrew's eyes were still closed. Then one blue iris peeked out of a half-opened lid.

"Yes?"

"I supposed this means you aren't a fool."

Erro smiled. "I guess it does."

"It also means I was right."

"Don't grow accustomed to it."

Andromeda had her boots off and her toes dipped in the stream when Erro reached her.

"I saw you dead in my dreams," she said when she heard his footfalls in the grass that grew lush beside the stream bed. "I thought of how I might have better swayed you."

Erro stayed perfectly still, rooted into the soil.

"In the days since you abandoned us on your foolhardy quest I've hated you and feared for you." She stopped and ran her hands over her face and through her hair. Her voice, which had been so fierce at the start, had broken just at the end. He almost went to her, but she spoke again. "Most of all I've missed you. It's a terrible ache deep in my chest, and it's plagued me from the moment you turned your back. And from the moment I saw your face again, it's vanished and been replaced by furious elation and … and an uncertainty that's somehow pleasant each time you look at me or speak to me. And I want to hate it and curse it, and curse you for so easily swaying my emotions, because though I can't feel it, I can still remember that ache you left behind. And I never wish to feel it again. But I can't hate you or curse you … not when you're here. Not even when I can't see you, only feel you at my back."

Erro's steps, usually sure and nimble, were hesitant and clumsy as he approached her. He held out his hand to her, sure she wouldn't take it, but she squeezed it tight as she pulled herself up to stand and face him. Her smoky eyes shimmered with tears, but she forced them to meet his.

"I never meant to cause you pain. I hope someday you can forgive me."

Her laugh was almost angry. "Weren't you listening? You were forgiven the moment you came back. Perhaps the moment you left."

"I won't ever cause you such pain again, princess. The only time you'll see my back again is when you send me away when you inevitably see your mistake and grow tired of my face. You have my solemn vow."

This time the laugh was soft and sweet, and she wiped away a tear that was rolling down her cheek. "Please don't call me princess. You call Felicity by her name."

"If I call you by your name, it will only tease me."

"Why?" said Andromeda, one eyebrow saluting him.

"Because it belies an intimacy that I cannot have with you … no matter how strongly I wish it."

She looked down only for a second, a smile too large to contain playing at her mouth. When she looked at him again, her face was playfully stern.

"And why can't you have it?"

Erro's eyebrows rose in surprise, and he dropped her hand to rub nervously at his neck.

"Well, because it simply isn't done."

"There's no law against it."

"Perhaps not, but it's an unspoken law of the kingdom nonetheless."

"So far as I'm concerned, I left my kingdom and entered yours from the moment I took the first step into the Northern Wood," she said, taking his other hand.

His smile was sure, but his breath shook. "Perhaps, but we aren't in the Northern Wood anymore. The mountains were the dwarves' kingdom. Now I suppose they are the goblins'."

"Ah," said Andromeda, moving closer so that her body pressed into his. "But you slew the goblin king. And to the slayer goes the victory and the land."

When his mouth met hers, a small sigh escaped through her lips, and the memory of not only the recent ache, but all pain, fled with it.

Chapter 12

The Palace Under the Mountain

Rocks and miniature dirt slides raced the Avalons down the mountainside. They gave their horses their heads to pick the best path down, but it was still slow going. Michael rode in back of the procession, ignoring the looks his siblings threw over their shoulders. It wasn't the purpling bruises disfiguring his handsome face that made them stare, but his silence.

He had accepted their return to the forest without protest. When they laid plans to hunt Brock and his raiders rather than continue the fruitless search for Atalanta, he'd only gazed into the fire. Only after his siblings had gawked at him, casting nervous glances at one another, did he speak.

"We should keep heading east for a while before we go down," he had said to the flames. "That way at least we can cover new ground on the way."

They had done as he'd suggested without complaint. They'd traveled east along the face of the mountain for nearly two days, going far beyond their previous search radius.

Now, heading down, they weren't making much progress, and dusk was falling. Despite following Michael's request to cover new ground, no one was really looking for a sign of the lost elf princess. The Avalon's eyes were glued to the sloping terrain ahead (except when they chanced a jealous glance up at Erro, soaring overhead on Aquila's back), all hands white-knuckled around the reins. When Zezil threw back his head in a triumphant howl, Felicity, who was in front, reined in her horse too quickly in fright. The mare reared, and then brayed in terror as its front hooves slipped on the loose ground when they returned to their rightful place.

"Damn devil dog!" said Felicity, struggling to keep her seat as she tried to soothe her mare with soft strokes on its neck.

Aquila's paws met the earth next to Zezil in near silence, his wings folding easily to his sides.

"He's found something," said Erro.

Zezil's haunches shook with excitement and pent-up energy.

Andromeda's eyes closed for a moment. "I don't believe it! It's the cyclops. He's found a trail!"

"Good boy, Zezil, good boy," said Erro jumping down and scooping up the vexar so that he could scratch his belly. Zezil squirmed in his arms, eager to get back on the ground and chase the scent.

"Go find him," said Erro, pointing in no direction in particular after he let the vexar jump from his arms. "Search, Zezil."

Zezil took off at a precarious diagonal angle up the mountain and to the east, jumping onto boulders and over shrubs like a regular mountain goat.

A familiar light was back in Michael's eyes, bruised and swollen as they were, and his horse charged after Zezil at the urging of his heels. Aquila and Erro took to the air, and the remaining Avalon siblings took off after their brother, whooping and laughing.

The enthusiasm was short-lived, at least for everyone but Michael and Zezil. The horses, already hard-pressed by the day's travel began to flag, foamy sweat staining their coats. Aquila wheeled above them on gusts of wind, circling like a vulture.

Andrew took up a habit of yelling, "See anything yet, Erro?"

He must have asked three dozen times as night drew closer and closer. Around the end of the first dozen, Erro's calls of, "Not yet," became more drawn out and groan-like. And all the while, Zezil kept up a steady jog, his nose twitching just above the ground. Michael was forced to fall behind a bit because of his horse's fatigue, but he kept his eyes trained on the little beast up ahead, fully erect in the saddle.

His siblings, however, began to droop forward, supporting

themselves on their horse's necks.

"Anything?" called Andrew half-heartedly. His request had steadily begun to lose words over time.

No response. Andrew looked up. Erro was no longer directly above them. He searched the sky to see the griffin headed back their way from farther up the mountain.

"Could be something up ahead," said Erro as Aquila dipped closer to earth. "Hard to make out. It's getting too dark. Could be a cave."

"Can we make it?" said Andromeda.

"I think so."

"Keep up the pace!" called Michael, sparing them a glance from up ahead.

It was a cave, much larger than any they'd taken up camp in. It was a gaping whale's maw cut into the side of the rock. The light was fading fast as they pulled up their horses in front. Zezil was poking his head into the pitch black hole, whining. Michael dismounted first and approached the cave mouth.

"Steady, Michael," said Andrew. "No more charging into strange caves."

Michael stood on tiptoe, reaching up to trace his fingers along the perfectly arched mouth.

"There are carvings here," he said.

The others squinted through the growing dark as they approached him.

"That's dwarvish," said Andromeda, walking from one end of the cave opening to the other, her eyes following the boxy words carved into the arc with artful, almost mathematical precision.

"Is this the word for king?" said Michael, tracing his fingers over markings near the top.

"I think so," said Andromeda, coming to stand by him. She traced her fingers along another word not far away, allowing her touch to substitute for her failing vision. "And this looks like 'palace.'"

Light flared behind Michael and Andromeda's heads as Andrew lit a torch.

"Can you read any more of it?" he asked, bringing the torch so close he almost singed Andromeda's hair.

"These two are names," said Andromeda after a moment. "King Gwythyr. The other is Nerthol. I think … it's the name of the palace. I can't read the first bit, but the last bit says, King Gwythyr, conqueror and … uh … bedfellow of Mother Earth, ruler of Nerthol, the palace under the mountain."

Andrew wrinkled his nose. "Bedfellow? Are you sure you translated that right?"

Michael drew his sword. "Follow me."

Felicity snatched him by the collar of his armor and yanked him back. "No," she said, putting herself between him and the cave, a motherly, scolding finger waggling in his face. "No way."

Zezil whined, his legs fidgeting as he forced himself to stay in a sitting position.

"It's in there, Felicity," said Michael, suddenly lowering his voice to a whisper. "Right now."

"You don't know what else is in there. For all you know, goblins ate the cyclops, and they're in there waiting to do the same to us."

Erro shoved an arm into the blackness.

"There's cool air coming from in there, Michael," said Erro. "That thing goes back far. It could even go down. The inscription says the palace under the mountain. This is an old place. Who knows what's been living in there since the dwarves."

"Perfect place for vampires … a palace under a mountain," said Andrew, mostly to himself.

They all looked at him, blood running cold.

"You don't think," said Andromeda, looking to Erro.

"They did come from the direction of the mountain."

"That cyclops is dead for sure," said Felicity. "The elf, too."

"Zezil only found one scent," said Andromeda, looking sadly

to Michael. "Atalanta wasn't here."

"The break in the trees!" said Erro, eyes going wide.

"What?"

"When Zezil first lost the scent," said Erro. "The first time it vanished. There were broken branches everywhere and a hole in the canopy, like something crashed through the trees. I said it reminded me of when Aquila can't find a clear place to land. What if it was a vampire?"

"So what?" said Felicity. "What does a vampire have to do with the cyclops?"

"I'm not sure," said Erro, brow furrowing, "but don't you think it's odd that he would be in two different places where he may have crossed paths with a vampire? I mean, you just said yourself that he's probably been eaten by now. But if his path crossed with a vampire's in the woods, why wasn't he eaten then?"

"Maybe cyclopes aren't very appetizing," said Andrew with a cheeky grin.

"I'm serious," said Erro. "There's something strange going on … I'm just not sure what."

"Well if there's a brood of vampires in there, we're definitely not traipsing inside," said Felicity in a low hiss. "In fact, we ought to get as far away from here as possible. It's time for them to wake up."

"If it was you who'd been captured, would you want us to back down?" said Michael, thrusting his sword at the cave depths. "What if she's in there? What if this is where that cyclops thing has been keeping her all this time? What if it was you, trapped in there? Imagine having someone come this close and then give up on you."

The scolding frown on Felicity's face fell into a pitying, somewhat ashamed one. "Michael, I'm not saying we shouldn't go in. I'm saying we should back off and wait until morning."

"I wouldn't wait if it was you trapped in there," said Michael, his eyes boring into Felicity's face. "Would you wait if it was me? If it was Andrew or Andromeda?"

"No," said Felicity, her shoulders slumping. "But ..."

"What? This is different? She's not your blood?" said Michael, forgetting to whisper. "She's somebody's blood. Why should it be any different?"

Felicity hung her head like a reprimanded child, studying the toes of her boots. "It shouldn't," she mumbled.

The high, singing ring of silver-coated steel leaving scabbards made Felicity look up. Andrew and Andromeda had drawn their swords, both looking a bit timid. Erro sighed and pulled out his daggers, twirling them in his fingers. Felicity straightened up, fixed Michael with a defiant look, and drew her rapiers.

"She'd better be worth dying for," she said.

Michael smiled. "Andrew, give me that torch. I'll go first."

Andrew handed it over, glad to grip his sword with both hands, and Michael held the flame out ahead of him, his broadsword balanced expertly in one hand. They crept through the cave, Michael swishing the flame back and forth, but only lighting up an empty chamber with a floor scattered with small animal bones and dung. Still, they pressed against one another, forming a misshapen circle, with Zezil wrapped around Erro's neck like a stole and Aquila creeping silently along in back.

At the very back of the cave was a narrow staircase cut into the stone. It hardly sloped at all, cutting straight down into the heart of the mountain. The flame of the torch could only penetrate deep enough to illuminate five steps.

"Everyone who thinks it's a terrible idea to climb down a stairway into the depths of hell in the middle of the night, say aye," said Andrew.

Four "ayes" made Michael groan. "I'm going down there with or without you," he said.

"I hate it when he does that," said Andrew to Andromeda, who nodded.

"Does what?" whispered Erro.

"Comes up with a terrible plan and then prods us into going along with him by making it seem as though it'll be our fault if he maims himself," said Felicity.

"He does this often?" said Erro.

He was answered with three affirmative grunts.

"Never anything this dangerous before, though," said Andrew.

"If you're done talking about me as if I'm not here, let's get going, shall we?" said Michael. He raised an eyebrow. "Unless you aren't coming."

"Yes, damn you, we're coming," said Andrew.

"If he wasn't already beaten bloody ..." said Felicity through gritted teeth.

They filed down the narrow steps one at a time. Michael, then Felicity, then Andrew, then Andromeda, and Erro bringing up the rear. But Erro had only put one foot on the first step when Zezil started shaking on his neck.

"Hold on, we may have an issue," said Erro.

"What?" said Michael in a harsh, rather annoyed whisper.

"Zezil's frightened," said Andromeda.

"I think he may transform if I make him go down there."

"Leave him, then," said Michael. "And hurry up about it."

"Sorry, boy," said Erro, gently lowering Zezil to the ground. He snapped his fingers and pointed out into the fresh night air. "Go on."

Zezil eagerly ran out of the cave, but then turned back and whined.

"Stay, Zezil. Good boy."

Zezil lay down with his head on his paws.

"Come on, Aquila," said Erro, rushing down the first two stairs to try and stay in the torch's faint light.

Aquila made a low, frustrated noise and ruffled his feathers.

His wing joints stuck fast against the sides of the stairway, barring his entrance. Erro cursed.

"What now?" said Michael, now truly exasperated.

"Aquila doesn't fit," said Erro.

"That decides it then," said Andrew cheerfully. "Back up we go."

"Don't even try it," said Michael.

"We're going to go down there without the griffin?" said Andrew. "Are you mad?"

In answer, Michael moved down the staircase, taking the light of the torch with him. The others grabbed for each other in the sudden dark and rushed after him.

"I'll be back, Aquila," Erro called up into the darkness. "Don't worry. Watch Zezil."

The stairway seemed to go on forever, and the air grew colder every few feet. It held a bitter mineral smell that emanated from the stone above, below, and beside them. At last, a new light mingled with Michael's torch, but instead of golden yellow, this one was a hazy blue. Michael slowed, holding a hand back toward the others to make them do the same.

Gruff, sleepy words of greeting from just out of view made Michael rush back up the stairs a few paces, shoving the others in front of him, shushing them as silently as he could. Then he tamped out the torch with his boot and pressed his back to the wall. The others did the same, not sure what else to do.

The band of five held their breaths and listened. Heavy footfalls passed on in opposite directions. Then there was an unmistakable swishing sound—the downward beats of sinewy wings. Lots of them by the sound of it. More footfalls approached, two sets together.

"I hate it when they do that," said a man's voice.

"You can smell the whole lot of them at once," said a woman. "Like meat gone bad just over two centuries ago."

The voices faded away as the man started complaining about close quarters with leeches.

"Humans with vampires?" whispered Andrew after he was sure it was safe to speak.

"Michael, this isn't a cyclops' hiding place," said Andromeda. "We need to go back. There's too many of them out there."

But even as she spoke, the sound of wings began to abate.

"We need to figure out what the hell is going on," said Michael. "The cyclops came in here. There's humans here, too. Don't you see that's the perfect opportunity?"

"Opportunity for what?" said Felicity, her half-crazed whisper dangerously loud.

"We can blend in. We're just a few more human ... servants ... or soldiers, or whatever the humans are here."

"Maybe they protect the vampires while they sleep," said Erro. "But why?"

"Perhaps Michael's onto something," said Andromeda. "People used to enslave themselves to vampires in exchange for being turned into one."

"Why would anyone do something so insanely foolish?" said Erro.

"Immortality," said Felicity. "Our history tutor said it used to be a real problem. Humans would lure other humans for their vampire master's meal."

"That's all beside the point," said Michael with a quick shake of his head that the others couldn't see in the dark. "We can put away our weapons and walk right out, and the vampires won't be the wiser."

"You really are mad," said Andrew. "What will we ever tell Mother?"

Erro snickered, but Andromeda elbowed him in the ribs.

"Michael, that truly is madness," she said.

"She's here, Andromeda," said Michael, and even in the dark, his siblings could imagine his face—his eyes wild and sparkling while his mouth lay in a firm, determined line that meant no one was talking him out of anything. "I can feel it. Even if she isn't—

and she is—we can't just walk away from this. This bodes ill for all of Arcamira. We have to scope it out if we can and report it back to Mother and Father. I'm going." They heard him sheath his sword. "You can wait for me here or back with Aquila and Zezil if you like."

A stunned Felicity tried to grab at him as he crept down the stairs, but he shook her off. Felicity made a snarling noise deep in her throat.

"He's a dead man," she muttered.

"He is if we don't go with him," said Andrew with a sigh.

"No, I mean I'm going to kill him myself," said Felicity, sheathing her rapiers.

"I'll hold him down," said Andrew, doing the same with his broadsword.

"Look at them, working together," said Andromeda, putting away her weapons.

"Do Avalons have a history of madness in the bloodline?" said Erro.

"Perhaps," said Andromeda, "but we also have a long list of victories. Let's hope this is one of them."

"Good of you all to come along," said Michael, grinning back at them from the last step.

When he turned around, Felicity held out her hands toward his neck in a mime of strangulation. The sound of wings had stopped. It seemed the roosting vampires had all gotten to wherever they wanted to be for the night. Michael peered his head around the staircase opening, and with the coast clear, he strode into the adjoining passageway with easy confidence. The others took a moment to steel themselves and take a few calming breaths before following him.

The blue light came from iron torches encased at the top in blue glass and ending in sharp points at the bottom. They lined the walls, nestled in sconces shaped like crowns. The passageway backed into a solid stone wall on the left-hand side and a railing dropping off into open space on the other. Erro and the Avalons approached the railing and looked up and down. They were in the middle of five spiraling levels. The very bottom was a stone atrium where a few people milled around on their way to other places.

"This way," said Michael, waving them after him toward a staircase in the distance. There were doors spaced unevenly along the left-hand side of the passageway, but Michael never paused at any of them. Just as they were almost to the staircase, a slight man who looked in a hurry, shuffling his feet over the stone so fast he almost tripped when he looked back over his shoulder, appeared from it and came toward them. Trying their best not to stiffen up, the small party walked with purpose, hardly sparing him a glance. He returned the favor, rushing past in that same nervous fashion.

Michael stopped when they reached the stairs, pondering. The others let out the breaths they'd been holding in since the other man's appearance.

"If she's here, she'll be in the dungeons," said Michael just above a whisper. "Which means we head down."

The staircase cut through the levels of the underground palace in a tight spiral.With Michael in the lead, they sped down the loops in a disorienting swirl of blue and grey. When Michael crashed into someone going the other way, it caused a catastrophic collision that knocked Felicity on her butt and nearly sent Andromeda over the railing. Michael grumbled a meek apology as he stepped back from a man with biceps like boulders and a dark braid down his back. The giant of a man scowled down at Michael with his nose curled as if he'd smelled something foul.

"Bloomin' 'ell!" said the tall, rather stocky woman behind the man. "Watch where you're goin'." She shook her head in distaste; matted blond curls bounced against her cheeks.

"Sorry, didn't see you there," said Michael.

The woman scoffed, but the man sucked a deep breath through his nose, raising one nostril.

"Something don't smell right about these ones, Gretta," he said, an odd, aggressive smile forming on his face.

The woman leaned forward and wrinkled her nose as she sniffed, and her eyes widened.

"Humans?" she cried with a snarl. "Humans, here?"

The man grabbed Michael around the throat and lifted his feet off the steps in a crushing grip. Erro's silver dagger stuck into the man's forehead with a dense thunk.

The woman screamed as the man sank to his knees—a high, enraged note that was cut off by Michael's broadsword ramming through her chest.

"Someone will have heard that," said Andromeda, her ivory skin pale as a vampire's.

Indeed, the sound of running footsteps and curious exclamations echoed both above and below them.

"Put away your weapons," said Michael, already moving down the steps again. "We'll act like we're investigating as well."

"And what if we're smelled again?" said Andrew.

"Keep moving!" said Michael.

There was no choice for the others but to obey. When the stairway ended, they found themselves in the vast, unprotected atrium. Two women chatted at the far end of it, not sparing them a look. Michael silently gestured for the others to follow him into a cold corridor branching off from the atrium, where the torches were no longer encased in blue glass in order to better light the extreme darkness. There was only one door—a thick wooden monstrosity with iron hinges — at the end of the hall.

"Nothing that way but the dungeons, dears."

They all whirled around to see the two women from the atrium blocking the corridor entrance. Their skin was white and creamy as milk. The taller of the two, the speaker, grinned as her fangs grew out.

"A couple of mice trapped in a hole," said the second.

* * *

"It's been a while since I smelled you," said Atalanta, sensing Nathanial from the moment he opened the door at the top of the dungeon stairs. "Where do you go when you aren't entertaining me with your fine feasts, pungent odor, and stump-like wits?"

She moved closer to the barred door of her cell.

"Shut it or I'll bloody it," said the werewolf from the end of the hall.

"He doesn't trust you with me, does he? Ever since I got the best of you. He sends Thetis or that scrawny nervous mutt instead. The little dog's not half as interesting as you, but those darty eyes of his are always looking out for trouble."

She'd only seen the scruffy, heavily bearded Nathaniel twice since the day she'd met Tyrannus, including today.

"Gave him the day off," said Nathaniel, appearing behind the bars. "Shut up and eat this fast. His Majesty is right eager to see you. Says you're getting close … whatever that means."

She could see the varying shades of yellow filth on each tooth as he spoke, smell every rotten cavity. She was to have another enforced magic lesson tonight, and Thetis had pumped her full of more venom the night before. The whole world was in sharper focus than ever before.

"Trying to prove yourself?" she said, just the right amount of taunting pity behind the curious remark.

"Don't need to prove anything," said Nathaniel. "Keeping away from you is no punishment. I've been sent out on His Majesty's business of late."

"Running errands, then?"

Nathaniel threw her water cup through the bars with a growl. The pottery smashed against the far wall and the liquid dribbled down into the dirt and filth. Atalanta didn't move or look at it.

Her eyes were fixed on Nathaniel's arms, waiting. Nathaniel's chuckle hissed through his teeth as he tossed her bread and fruit onto the ground instead of setting it carefully on the plate just inside the door like the other werewolf usually did. Atalanta's hands clenched at her sides in silent fury and disappointment.

There was a boom from down the hall, as if a body had slammed into the door. A death scream followed shortly after—a desperate wail of agony that assaulted Atalanta's sensitive ears.

"What the—?"

Atalanta sprang forward faster than any cat, shot her hands through the bars, and yanked Nathaniel forward by his tunic, violently slamming his head against the bars.

As he groaned, she yanked the chain off his neck. She slammed him against the metal again before he could recover, and then let him fall as she unlocked the door. He was clambering to his feet, murder in his eyes and blood on his face, as she stepped out of her cell. She smiled at him, and for a moment, he looked afraid. She wound back her fist and shattered his cheekbone with a blow mightier than any ordinary elf could have managed. She felt and heard the bones of his face crack under her knuckles. Blind with pain, he threw back his head and screamed helplessly on the ground, his face terribly misshapen. He might heal faster than the human he once was, but it would not be instantaneous, as with a vampire. The thought made her smile. She ached to kill him, but she didn't have any silver, and she couldn't waste more time hurting him. Instead, she gave him a solid kick to the temple that would have killed a human, but instead knocked him out cold.

She sprinted down the familiar corridor. This time, no vampire would stand in her way. This time, she knew how to escape. She'd been outside many times now, chained and beaten, to perform magic.

She raced up the stairs, yanked open the dungeon door, and froze. Humans. Five of them.

A vampire was crumbling to ash as Andromeda pulled a stake from its chest. Another vampire lay dead at Michael's feet.

This was not what stopped her. It was the smell. The smell of their blood. She salivated, her heart beating faster at the sound of theirs. She wanted to bite them, but she had no fangs.

"My God," said Michael. "Princess Atalanta?"

Arcamira

Chapter 13

Atalanta

The sound of her name quelled the sudden murderous bloodlust inside Atalanta. Conversations that seemed ages past echoed in her head. I did everything in my power, Your Majesty, truly. I don't know where they went.

Michael's voice startled her. "Princess Atalanta, my name is Michael Avalon, prince and first heir of —"

"You are the humans come to save me, yes?" said Atalanta. "You survived Thetis and his vampire horde."

"Uh," stammered Michael, momentarily thrown, and then a proud grin spread on his face. "Yes, in fact, we are. We've come at the behest of your father. There are many search parties looking for you."

"Well, you've found me; let's get out of here," said Atalanta, the quick dismissal in her voice making Michael's face fall slightly.

"With pleasure," said Andrew.

Atalanta rushed past all five of the humans down the narrow passageway.

"Come," she called back, "I know the way out."

Just as Atalanta was about to run into the atrium, three figures blocked her path: two vampires and a werewolf.

The humans called out a needless warning behind her, but Atalanta never stopped running. She snatched two of the torches off the walls and leapt onto the surprised vampire in the middle like a lion pouncing prey. She rammed the tapered, pointed end of the torch into his chest before he even hit the ground. She felt and heard the air from the female vampire's swinging, clawed hand, ducked and then sprang to her feet, swinging her arm in a backward arch to slam the second torch into the vampire's

198

throat. She pulled it free, blocked another blow, punched the leech's widening mouth closed with an uppercut, and then stuck her in the chest, moving faster than she'd ever moved in her life.

She whirled to face the werewolf only to find that Andromeda had dispatched him with her thin silver-dipped sword. Atalanta's eyes were drawn to the makeshift splint on Andromeda's left wrist.

"What's your name?" Atalanta asked her.

"Andromeda."

"You're fast."

"You're faster."

"We need to hurry," said Atalanta, running again, listening to the humans' galloping hearts and heavy breathing behind her and pacing herself as she flew across the massive atrium so that she could keep close to them. "Those three didn't get to sound an alarm, but this place is crawling with vampires. If any of them pass close enough, they'll smell us."

Atalanta drew up short at the far stone wall. Erro nearly ran into her.

"Umm," said Felicity, looking at Atalanta in a way that obviously said she thought Atalanta had lost her mind, held captive in a dark dungeon for too long.

Atalanta ignored her and felt along the rock face. She felt the grooves, wrapped her fingernails around them and pulled out. A cylindrical stone slid partially from the wall. Atalanta twisted it a quarter turn to the right and then shoved it back in with a click. The wall in front of them began to shift to the right on a hidden mechanism. The humans murmured and gasped.

But it moved far too slowly. Atalanta bounced on the balls of her feet, her ears attuned to every miniscule sound. She could hear footsteps approaching. They were heavy footfalls, a tad clumsy, not the fluid movement of a vampire ... at least she thought. She prayed she was right. If a vampire walked into the atrium, they would be discovered, and a horde large enough to block out the moon would follow them out of the door. Her escape would be short-lived. If it was a werewolf, even if he came into the atrium, he wouldn't automatically know that the five people slipping outside weren't meant to be there.

She slipped through the door sideways as soon as it was wide enough and beckoned the humans to follow. The footsteps grew closer as the five humans rushed through the widening door. Atalanta gestured wildly to them to get out of sight of the opening. They obeyed quickly enough, and she performed an identical process with a cylindrical stone on the outside of the mountain. The door shuddered to a halt and then began to inch its way closed just as the footsteps entered the atrium.

It was a werewolf. She could smell him now. All he would see was a nearly closed door that, for all he knew, another werewolf or two had just slipped out of to get some fresh air. Atalanta pressed her back to the mountainside and sucked in a deep breath full of relief and delight. She could smell the forest, the fresh night air. She felt like an elf again, not the monster she'd been battling inside herself for far too long now. Her skin tingled with joy.

"The Northern Wood?" said Erro. "Can we truly be at the base of the mountain?"

"The dwarves who once lived here carved out the entire mountain to make a castle," said Atalanta. "We just exited the bottom floor."

"Our horses," said Felicity, craning her neck up the mountainside, "they're still near the summit where we came in."

"Aquila and Zezil are up there, too," said Erro.

"Who?" said Atalanta.

"A griffin and a vexar. They're waiting for us."

Atalanta felt her face go lax in disbelief. "Did you say a griffin?"

Erro nodded and said, "We have to go get them."

"We ought to head into the forest for cover," said Atalanta.

"The werewolf guard I attacked to free myself will be waking up any minute, and he'll sound the alarm."

"That's exactly why we should head back up the mountain," said Andromeda, fixing Atalanta with smoky eyes. "We won't get very far no matter which way we choose, and back up the mountain is the direction they'll least expect."

Atalanta debated for only a breath before racing up the slope and saying, "Come on then!"

She zigzagged over the rough terrain, finding the best footholds by instinct alone, though she could see perfectly well in the moonlight. She was just propelling herself up a steep rock face as a shortcut with the agility of a mountain goat, when she realized the humans sounded very far away. She swung herself up on a ledge and turned to find them. They were huffing along fifty yards back. To their credit, they were moving rather quickly for humans, but they were no match for her elvish speed combined with the effects of the vampire venom so recently injected into her blood. They were also squinting in the dark, and some of their steps were uncertain.

It took serious effort to make her sit still and wait for them. Each second was precious, but even though they hadn't actually saved her, they'd come all this way for her, and their fight in the passageway had allowed the distraction she'd needed to free herself. It would be wrong to leave them behind—ungrateful. But still it pained her. She wanted to run free, to feel the wind on her face.

Her stomach rumbled. Perhaps it was good the humans were slowing her pace. She oughtn't to overexert herself in her malnourished state.

"What are you waiting around for?" said Andrew when they all reached her. "I thought we were in a hurry."

He trekked up the mountain without looking back. Atalanta looked to the others, bemused.

"Don't mind Andrew," said Michael. "He thinks he's far

funnier than he actually is."

Atalanta began to smile, but then snapped to attention, her pointed ears twitching like a deer's.

"Hide," she whispered.

Michael's eyes went wide. "Andrew," he called in an urgent whisper. "Take cover."

Andrew looked back, nodded, and obeyed without hesitation, sliding a bit down the mountain to crouch behind a large boulder. The others hid behind a nearby jutting outcropping with Atalanta.

"What is it?" said Felicity softly.

"The wall is opening," said Atalanta. "They're coming."

A rush of wings and angry shouts answered her words.

"We aren't far enough," said Felicity. "The vampires will smell us."

"The wind is blowing in our favor," said Atalanta. "So long as we stay quiet, we should be all right. Sounds like they're already heading in the wrong direction. You were right, Andromeda."

They huddled together until the sound of flapping wings had long since passed.

"We should move on before they begin to head back," said Michael.

Atalanta nodded and then headed back up the mountain without a word, jogging rather than running this time. They picked up Andrew along the way. Everyone kept looking back over their shoulders as the night lengthened, looking for signs that they'd been spotted, trying to catch a glimpse of the returning vampires.

The going was treacherous at first. When the night was at its deepest, the Avalons and Erro could hardly see their hands in front of their faces. Atalanta, imbued with superior night vision, pushed them on until Andromeda chose a poor handhold for her injured wrist while scaling a steep rock face and nearly tumbled to her death. Atalanta and Erro each caught one of her arms and hauled her to safety. The party rested until the distant rays of the unseen sun began to lighten the sky, and then the trek began anew.

Atalanta spotted the returning vampires in the far distance just before dawn, and they hid amongst spare foliage and rocks until the sun had peeked over the horizon.

"All right, let's keep going. How far are your horses and your griffin friend?" said Atalanta.

"Sorry, princess," said Michael, leaning back on the scraggy grass, "but we need to rest. We've haven't slept in a day and two nights. No vampires can find us from the sky in the daylight, and it will take even werewolves hours to get close to us. We must sleep."

Atalanta pursed her lips, but nodded. Her own limbs were fatigued more than she cared to admit. The vampire venom was slowly burning out of her system, and her once flawless physique was diminished by poor nutrition and torture.

They slept on the ground, in the warmth of the sun, a cool northern breeze blowing over their skin. They slept well, and by the time Atalanta woke, sunset was approaching. She roused the humans gently, and they looked up at her with sleepy eyes as she said, "We need to keep moving. The faster we reach your mounts, the sooner we can turn our sights homeward."

"Exactly whose home are we heading toward first?" said Felicity as she got to her feet.

"Mine," said Erro.

Atalanta had learned that he was the companion of the griffin, and she eyed him curiously, wondering what spark of heroic character this lanky boy in peasants' garb carried deep within himself to earn a griffin's loyalty.

"And if we come across Brock's trail, we take the time to follow it. I can't justify letting him pillage and destroy the villages of the wood. With that werewolf in tow, he can finally rule the forest with an iron fist ... or perhaps iron jaws would be more fitting."

"Who is this Brock and why does a werewolf do his bidding?" said Atalanta as they began their ever-upward journey.

"He's a coward and a monster," said Erro with a snarl.

"He is but a human?" said Atalanta.

"Hardly," said Erro.

"Hmm, that's most unusual ... although after what I've seen during my captivity, I should not be surprised by oddities any longer," said Atalanta. "You have history with this man?"

"He killed my parents and a dear friend of mine. A child."

Atalanta's eyes went wide. "I am sorry for your loss. If we find him along the way, I will be happy to help you dispatch such a man, but I don't want too much delay in returning home. If we must wander days from our path, I would request that you wait to deal with him at a later time. I've been gone from my people far too long."

She spoke as she would in a council meeting, in the formal way attached to royal duties, still not feeling at home with this gaggle of humans, even if most of them were royalty like herself.

Erro bowed his head toward her. "That's a fair deal."

"My father is probably becoming most desperate. We need to get word to him. Tyrannus will no doubt act as if he still has me under his control, and I fear my father may surrender himself if Tyrannus gets another demand to him."

"The last news we heard before setting out to find you was that your father had received no demands for your return," said Michael.

Atalanta's brow furrowed. "That bastard! I should have known he was lying. How could I have been so foolish?"

"He could have received a demand after we left," said Michael. "We've had no contact with anyone for nearly a month."

"Who's Tyrannus?" said Andrew.

"My captor," said Atalanta, her steps faltering for a moment.

"Who is he? What did he want in capturing you?" said

Andromeda.

"He's a beast unlike any other, half vampire and half werewolf."

"Impossible," said Erro. "The two species don't mix."

"I would have said the same if asked before I saw him for myself," said Atalanta.

She told them Tyrannus' story of how he'd come to be and his plans to eradicate Arcamira of the two species he saw as monsters, the ones who'd shunned bloodthirsty beings such as himself: humans and elves. By the time she'd finished, the whole party had come to a stop, the humans ogling her in horror and disbelief.

"And he actually had an army?" said Felicity.

"I'm unsure how the vampires and werewolves actually work together," said Atalanta. "I often heard his two righthands, Nathaniel and Thetis, arguing with each other. The two species still despise one another, but Tyrannus, being like both of them, has rallied them to his side. They live under one roof and do his bidding. He also has that slimy little cyclops under his thumb, Callid."

"He's the one who captured you?" said Michael.

"Yes, I'm sad to admit. The only one of his kind that I saw. He's very strong, and he surprised me in the palace orchard."

"You mustn't blame yourself," said Michael. "I've seen your fighting skill. You were ambushed."

"Yes, you mustn't beat yourself up," said Andrew.

Atalanta tried to ignore the moony way they were both looking at her, but she saw Andromeda snigger behind her hand out of the corner of her eye.

"He's nothing if not stealthy," said Atalanta, not betraying her inner smile. "I can't believe he managed to get into the orchard undetected. He's been following you, you know. He set a pack of werewolves on your search party, and followed you as far as he could. After he lost your trail, Tyrannus sent Thetis and his horde after you. I thought you dead for certain, until I heard him being tortured for his failure. You're very resilient for humans."

"What's that supposed to mean?" said Felicity.

"Normally humans are ... breakable," said Atalanta with a shrug.

Felicity harrumphed, but Atalanta made no apologies.

"How could he report back so quickly?" said Michael. "We were attacked by the werewolf pack at the edge of the forest, at least a week's journey from the mountain. The vampires came after us much faster than that."

"He often talked of an escort," said Atalanta.

"A vampire escort," said Erro. "I was right!"

"We have to warn Mother and Father of this threat," said Michael. "Vampires and werewolves in large numbers, with a hybrid king rallying them for war? Arcamira won't have seen battle like this since the time of extermination."

"I have to warn my father as well," said Atalanta.

"Our realm is much closer to the threat than yours," said Felicity. "We ought to go back home first before heading west."

"That will be an extra fortnight's journey at least at a human pace," said Atalanta. "I've told you, I can't wait that long; my father may do something rash."

"We can send a message home," said Michael, cutting off Felicity and shouldering her behind him so that he could walk side-by-side with Atalanta. "Do they have messenger birds in Everly, Erro?"

"Yes, but the only routes they know are between the woodland villages. You'd do better to hire a messenger. I'm sure after your help with the rebuilding you'll get plenty of volunteers."

"Excellent, problem solved," said Michael throwing an uncharacteristically goofy smile Atalanta's way. "Mother and Father will get the news and we can still escort you back to your palace. I could even ask Father to send a garrison to meet us to ensure safe passage."

Felicity gave the back of Michael's head a disgusted look.

"If this Tyrannus truly never sent a ransom demand to your father, what did he want from you, Atalanta?" said Andromeda.

"The one thing his army and his mutated blood can't provide him: magic."

"I've always wanted to see elvish magic in action," said Andrew eagerly. "Can you really turn the trees into warriors?"

"No, that's what I tried to tell that stinking beast," said Atalanta hotly. "Magic like that can only be performed by fully matured elves, and even then it takes years of learning and mastery to become a true mage. I'm only seventeen; I've only lived a fraction of the average elvish life—a blink. The most I could do was grow a little flower or start a small campfire, at least until he started ..." She shook her head and stretched her long legs to march ahead of the others.

It didn't take nearly as long to scale the mountain as it had when they'd first headed up, taking their time to search for signs of the cyclops. A little over three days later, they crested a steep slope onto a partially level plain, shielding their eyes from the savage summer sun directly above them. Andromeda suddenly said, "We're close. The horses are scattered, though. We'll have to round them up."

"How did you ...?" said Atalanta.

"Aquila's anxious ... oh wait ... he just sensed us. He's flying this way."

Atalanta's eyes found the bracelet pushed up on Andromeda's bicep. She grabbed the other girl's arm suddenly in an iron grip, like a big cat swiping prey into its paw.

"Where did you get this?" she said, scrutinizing it and Andromeda with a mixture of awe and rebuke. "This is elf made. It allows you to sense the thoughts of animals, yes? Very rare, never meant for human use."

Felicity scoffed, squinting one eye in a grimace of disgust.

"And why not?"

"Humans slaughter animals heedlessly, for sport. Elves are close to nature. We feel the movings of the earth in our bones; we carry the spirits of nature in our blood. This device was created to help us get closer."

"It was in our treasury," said Andromeda, blushing but holding eye contact.

"Stolen during times of war," said Atalanta, turning Andromeda's arm this way and that to get a better look at the silver and gold band.

"Or given as a gift in times of peace," said Andromeda, freeing her arm with a tug.

Atalanta humphed, but appraised Andromeda with a look of mixed scrutiny and respect.

"Use it well."

"I do."

The whoosh of wings made them all look skyward. Rays of sunlight caught Aquila's gold and tawny feathers as he circled above them, spiraling down to earth.

Atalanta muttered an awed exclamation in the elfin tongue the others couldn't understand as Aquila landed in front of her.

To the humans' surprise, she stepped back with her right foot and dipped into a graceful bow, her hands out to her sides and slightly back. The siblings cast amused looks at each other until Aquila folded in his wings, lifted a large paw, and bowed in return.

"Don't expect me to start bowing to you," said Erro, grinning, with his arms crossed.

Aquila cooed softly and moved to nuzzle his feathered head into Erro's chest. Erro embraced the griffin, rubbing his head against Aquila's and stroking his feathers.

"Hello, old friend," he said.

Atalanta stared at Erro, slack-jawed. He didn't seem to notice. He kept his attention on Aquila and said, "Now where's—"

The odd little fur ball with banded eyes, after whom he'd been inquiring, leapt from an elevated ledge and slammed into his back, smothering his ears in kisses and ripping at his rough, green, traveling cloak with his little claws in an attempt to hold on.

After an odd, monkey-like dance, Erro managed to grab Zezil and extract him from his back, cuddling him like a baby in his arms as happy whines escaped from his muzzle.

"Interesting travel companions indeed," said Atalanta. "I wasn't even sure vexars were real."

"A real laugh is what they are," said Erro. "And a real pain in the backside."

Aquila moved to Andromeda and nipped gently at her hand with his beak. She scratched him at the wing joints and he cooed. Atalanta's eyes went once again to the magical bracelet, but this time with curiosity rather than disdain.

"Come on, let's go round up the horses," said Michael. "Andromeda, you lead the way. Once that's done, I say we head west along the mountainside as far as we can before going down, so we don't end up anywhere near the entrance to Tyrannus' ... cave. After that, we head to Everly, hire a messenger, and then take the straightest path to the elf palace."

Chapter 14

Night Raids

Nathaniel howled like the wolf caged inside his blood. The poker blazed blinding white at the very tip, fading to yellow and then angry orange. The pain was excruciating no matter which part touched his bare skin. He writhed against the bonds holding his limbs outstretched like a grotesque star. His scruffy hair and beard were matted with sweat and blood. The scalded lines of flesh would take hours to heal. The shattered bones in his face would take longer, and it was the elf wench he cursed in his head as the iron baked a fresh line down his chest.

The beast he called king wielded the poker. The grey flesh of Tyrannus' biceps bulged as he brought it down again and again without mercy. The coarse patches of black fur stood on end along his shoulders and at the back of his neck. Long runners of drool flew from his deformed muzzle as he roared.

"You let her escape!" he said. "You imbecilic, worthless, lump of fur!"—the poker came down harder with each insult—"I ought to gut you on this filthy floor!"

Callid danced behind his master, clapping his hands together in delight at the very thought, hissing like a cat through both sets of teeth in what was meant to be a laugh.

"I ought to bring that mangy bitch you call a wife in here and make her take your blows while you watch!" said Tyrannus, ceasing the blows to point the white hot poker at his Adam's apple.

Nathaniel's eyes, shut against the pain, flew open. His pleas came out ragged and raw. "Mercy, Your Majesty, mercy. This is no fault of Brenna's. I shall bear whatever else you have in store."

Thetis, leaning against the chamber door, smirked, his usually dull oceanic eyes sparkling.

"There it is," said Tyrannus, edging the poker close enough to singe Nathaniel's beard. His orange eyes widened and his forked tongue licked his jowls. "There's the fear. We've finally found it. Think on that. Think on this feeling long and hard when you take up your next task."

"M–my king?"

"That's right, Nathaniel. I'm still in need of you. The raider trusts you now. I will bestow mercy this last time, for let it never be said that I am not a loyal king to my subjects. We have all suffered far too much at the hands of the human worms and elf snakes. I do not like inflicting pain on my own." He smiled just long enough to see Nathaniel breathe easier, and then flipped it into a snarl. "But should you fail again, I fear it's your wife who'll bear the brunt of my wrath."

"Thank you, Your Majesty. You are truly a merciful king. I shall accomplish whatever task you set before me."

"Thanks to you, the elf and human kings will soon know of our plans to march against them. Our army is not strong enough yet. So few of us left, I'm afraid. Thankfully, the power in our veins can be shared. You and Thetis will go back to the raider tonight and let him know it's time for him to hold up his end of the bargain. Take a garrison with you to help make the changes swift. Once you've made every available soul in the wood part of our horde, make your way west. I will bring the rest of the army to meet you in the Black Forest. The both of you,"—he looked back at Thetis with a stern warning in his burning orange eyes—"remember I want the numbers of each species equal; I'm sick of all the bickering over numbers and favoritism."

Thetis bowed his head and said, "We shall build you an army like none other in the history of Arcamira, my king."

"That's exactly what I expect," said Tyrannus in a tempered voice, fixing Thetis with a meaningful look. Then he turned his attention back to the strung-up werewolf. "Nathaniel, the raider only knows the villages of the forest, correct?"

"Brock and his men sometimes venture out to the farmlands around the forest, but he knows the Northern Wood best."

"Once he has worn out his usefulness, dispose of him and his fellows," said Tyrannus, his muzzle curling in mild disgust. "I have no use for traitors in my army."

* * *

"Campion."

"What?" Michael snapped to attention, turning to see Atalanta peering over his shoulder at the place on the parchment where his quill had been hovering, threatening to drop a blot of ink onto the page.

"Tell your father to send his reply to Campion. It's the first elvish city we'll pass through on the way to my palace."

"Oh, uh, thanks," said Michael, color rising to his cheeks as he hunched over the parchment.

"Certainly," Atalanta said, turning to leave.

His shoulders relaxed, and he dabbed at his brow with the heel of his hand.

"By the way," she said with the hint of a smile in her voice, "my eyes are more like emeralds than jade."

He bit down hard on his lip, scrunched up his eyes, and threw a protective arm over the letter, not daring to turn back and look at her. At last the door shut behind her.

"Stupid," he muttered.

When he at last emerged from Fiona and Jeremiah's newly rebuilt home, the others were playing a heated game of tag with the children of Everly.

"That little blighter's fast," said Andrew, stopping in front of Michael, his cheeks puffing out as he caught his breath and pointed accusingly at a scrawny boy who couldn't have been older than nine or ten.

The child in question stopped and turned around long enough to stick out his tongue at Andrew before shooting off behind a nearby home. Erro laughed so hard he had to support himself on the window sill of the home across the street. Andrew's eyes narrowed, and he took off in Erro's direction rather than chasing the boy. Erro cursed and shot off toward the sheep paddock, clutching at a stitch in his side, Andrew in hot pursuit.

"Is that it?" said Andromeda, appearing at Michael's side just as Andrew made a spectacular leap and wrapped his arms around Erro's legs, bringing them both crashing to the ground.

"Yes," said Michael, holding up the rolled parchment on his index finger and spinning it around, "ready to be sent off to Mother and Father."

"Erro's it!" yelled Andrew, running down the center street away from Erro, who was scrambling to his feet.

A chorus of "Erro's it!" echoed through the whole village, half of the speaker's remaining unseen while others darted in and out of the spaces between houses passing on the message.

"Can I read it?" said Andromeda.

"Why, who've you been talking to?" said Michael, drawing the letter close to his chest.

Andromeda gave him a curious once-over. "Uh, no one."

A girl of about seven squealed with delight as she ducked under Erro's reaching hand. Her butt hit the dirt, and she skidded on her skirts into an open cellar to escape him.

"Aw, come on Georgina," said Erro, peering into the black hole, "you know I'm scared of snakes. I can't come down there; it must be crawling with them."

Georgina squealed again, but she didn't sound frightened.

"I'm disappointed, Erro," said Andromeda, clucking her tongue. "I thought you weren't afraid of anything."

"Oh yeah?" said Erro, his lips curling in a playful grin, his eyes dancing with a wicked glee as he took two stealthy steps toward her.

"Yeah," said Andromeda, crossing her arms over her chest and staring him down.

Michael watched in amused silence as the two squared off for a few solid seconds. Andromeda turned first, her boot heels kicking up a cloud of dust as she took off, running at full speed. Erro sprang after her, and Michael smiled as he walked down the lane and heard Andromeda's excited shrieks and laughs fading into the distance, so very like the delighted squeals of little Georgina.

The messenger waited at the concealed entrance to Everly, mounted on a black steed that the villagers had assured Michael was the fastest for miles around. The man atop the steed was a young man just a few years older than Michael.

"I've given instructions to the king and queen in my letter that you are to be paid handsomely for your efforts, enough to bring back and spread among the whole village as a thanks for all of your aid."

"Thank you, Your Highness," said the messenger, bowing on his horse as he took the letter with great care and placed it in his saddlebag. "I shall deliver it as swiftly as possible."

"I have no doubt. Take extra care through the wood," said Michael. "It's no longer safe."

"Twas never safe, sire," said the messenger, tipping his hat to Michael and setting his heels to his horse.

* * *

Night had only just fallen on the little woodland town of Glenn.

"Tilly, darling, time for bed," said Melanie Borsten to her four-year-old daughter, playing with her rag doll at her father's feet.

Tilly pouted her bottom, rose-colored lip. "Aw, Momma, but I'm a big girl now. I'm dunna be a big sister."

The baby in Melanie's belly was Tilly's new favorite excuse

as to why she ought to be allowed to do things. Joseph stifled a smile as he leaned back in the rocking chair by the burning hearth. The look Melanie shot him as she bent down and picked up the still pouting Tilly was only half-reprimanding.

"Big sisters must get their rest, too," said Melanie, brushing back a chocolate curl from Tilly's face.

"Goodnight, Tilly," said Joseph, getting up from his chair to kiss Tilly's cheek.

"Nighty-night, Papa," said Tilly, reaching out with her small hands to cup her father's face as she kissed his nose.

Melanie carried Tilly to the cottage's single bedroom and laid her down on the smaller of the two cots. Tilly clasped her soft little hands and bowed her head so that her rich brown curls, identical to her mother's, fell over her face. She closed the powder blue eyes also inherited from her mother and said her prayers, then wiggled down under her blanket.

"Nighty-night, Momma."

"Goodnight, Tilly," said Melanie, tucking the dolly in beside Tilly and kissing them both. Tilly would not have allowed the doll to be forgotten.

"Nighty-night, baby," said Tilly, resting a hand on her mother's stomach.

Melanie smiled at the feathery touch. She kissed Tilly once more before leaving the room. Tilly snuggled her doll and was asleep almost instantly.

Glenn stood on the far eastern side of the Northern Wood, on the very outskirts, so that half the town peeked out from the depths of the surrounding trees and into the fields beyond. Raiders didn't usually come out to this far side of the wood for fear of running into a royal brigade on patrol, but on this night the moon had hardly made its appearance before a dark force turned its ugly face toward the little town.

Little Tilly Borsten awoke with a start, and instinctively cried out for her mother. Screams carried through the unlatched window of her bedroom. Melanie rushed through the door, ripped the blankets off Tilly, and clutched her to her chest.

"Melanie," said Joseph, framed by the doorway and wielding an axe, "take Tilly out the back. Hide behind the barn until you have a clear path, and then head for the nearest village. Away from the forest."

"What's happening? Is it raiders?"

"I can think of nothing else. Hurry, you must go."

"I'll not leave without you," said Melanie, her eyes wide but her mouth set.

"Go! Protect Tilly and the baby," Joseph said, his dark eyes ablaze under his midnight hair. "I'll hold them off, and then I'll be right behind. Now go!"

"Momma?" said Tilly, clutching at her mother's dress, her head buried in her breasts.

Melanie looked down at the toddler in her arms, nodded to Joseph, and then ran down the hall to the back door. Joseph followed protectively behind her, his axe poised to strike. The window by the back door exploded inward, making Melanie and Tilly scream. Melanie covered Tilly's face with her arm, but broken glass pricked at her own cheek.

A taloned hand grabbed at Melanie's dress, and her scream caught in her throat at the sight of the fanged mouth grinning at her. It was Tilly who screamed, shrill and piercing. Joseph brought the axe down on the vampire's arm, chopping it off at the elbow. He swung it in an upward arch, ready to slice the male vampire's head clean off, but it ducked the blow.

Melanie ran for the front door, the back exit now blocked. She had her hand on the handle when she froze. Joseph. She looked down the hall. Joseph was backing up slowly, axe raised. The vampire was smiling as it bore down on him. Joseph swung for its neck again, but this time it caught the handle. With a tug on the axe, it pulled Joseph to it and snatched him by the throat. It slammed his head against the wall and dropped him limp to the floor.

"Joseph!"

The vampire flicked its eyes to hers. Her heart skipped a beat, and she yanked the door open, only to meet the grinning face of a tall, filthy man with long, scraggly hair and a number of blackened teeth. There were no fangs in his mouth, but his grin was more predatory than the vampire's. She recognized him from his depiction on notices pinned up in the marketplace. He was the leader of the most deadly raider gang in the Northern Wood. The notices called him Brock—no last name given.

"At last, a pretty one," Brock said.

Melanie turned to run, though there was nowhere to go. Brock grabbed her hair in a fist and pulled her to him. He put his long, thin nose to her neck and sniffed deeply.

Melanie shifted Tilly to her left arm and threw her right elbow back into Brock's jaw. He released her hair to clutch at his face, but his boot collided with her back and sent her sprawling. She only just managed to twist and fall on her shoulder, protecting Tilly and her womb from smacking the floor. Tilly was wailing now, clutching desperately at Melanie's dress and hair. Her little body trembled as Brock stomped toward them, spewing all sorts of disgusting names at Melanie.

Melanie tried to shush Tilly, but all of the air had left her lungs in the fall.

"Don't forget yourself, mortal," said the vampire.

The vampire's hair and eyes were as pale as his bloodless skin, and he had his head cocked in an expression of bored disapproval as he appraised Brock. Melanie, though, was looking at her husband, draped over the vampire's shoulders as if he weighed nothing. A steady trickle of blood dripped from his head onto the living room rug, but he was breathing.

"We aren't to seriously harm them," said the vampire. "King Tyrannus has a larger purpose in store. They aren't to be touched until their conversion."

Brock gave the unconscious Joseph a pointed look.

"This was necessary," said the vampire. "Do you really need to beat a woman to subdue her? If you can't handle her, I can take them all myself."

"I'll handle her," said Brock under his breath.

Melanie shrank back as he approached, bracing for the blow with her eyes half-shut. He snatched Tilly from her arms in an instant.

"No! Don't touch her!"

"Momma! Momma!" Tilly's cries were rough with the sobs that wracked her body.

She wriggled in his arms, bending her whole body backward to try and reach her mother, small arms outstretched to their full extent. Melanie rose from the floor slowly, hampered by her belly and the pain of her fall and the strong kick to her back.

Brock grabbed Tilly by the hair and yanked her back toward him.

"Stop that," he thundered, spraying spit in her face, his fingers still entangled in her hair.

Tilly's eyes went wide with pain and terror, and the shock of it all stopped her cries.

Blind with rage, Melanie grabbed the iron candlestick from the table and raised it above her head screaming, "Let go of her or I'll—"

Brock whipped a dagger from his belt and pointed it at Tilly. Melanie froze, heavy candlestick raised and chest heaving.

"Come along quietly, and the little girl keeps her pretty face."

Shaking, Melanie dropped the candlestick.

"Good lass."

"Humans and their theatrics," said the vampire with a sniff before carrying Joseph out the back door.

Melanie kept her eyes on Tilly, who had begun to wail again.

"It's okay, Tilly. Hush, now, baby. Momma's all right. We're going to go with this man for a little while. Yes?"

Tilly's wails quieted to sniffles, and she nodded and rubbed her eyes.

Melanie walked behind Brock out of the house with her head hung and tears streaming down her face. As she walked down the familiar lane, she tried not to look at the destruction. Houses were ablaze, and villagers were being herded out like sheep. Some were slung unconscious over their captor's shoulders, and some were pulled along by strong ropes bound around their wrists. Most of the screams had turned to sobs. She saw two men walk out of the butcher's home, carrying a small trunk containing valuables. They busted it open with a hatchet and bickered over a battered silver cup. They appeared entirely human, but it made no sense. Why had men allied themselves with vampires?

Tilly's pale, tear-streaked face rose up over Brock's shoulders. Her head bounced slightly as violent sniffles and hiccups jolted her small frame.

"Momma," she said quietly, "where's Papa?" Tears swelled in her eyes, and she let out a small sob.

Melanie wiped at her own tears and tried to smile.

"Shh, Tilly, it's all right," whispered Melanie, a hand reaching out, longing to hold Tilly and wipe away her tears. "We're going where Papa's going."

"Momma, hold me," said Tilly, stretching out her arms over the raider's shoulder. "Don't want this bad man."

Melanie glowered at the back of Brock's head, but he showed no reaction at all.

"I can't right now, angel," said Melanie, fighting to keep her voice light. "Soon."

"Please, Momma." Tears fell down her chubby cheeks, and she stretched out with her fingers splayed and reaching as far as she could make them.

With another look of hatred at the tangled mass of Brock's hair, she reached out a finger and let Tilly grasp it, silently daring the man to say anything. He twirled the dagger in his hand and made sure she saw it over his shoulder, but he said nothing.

"Soon, Tilly, soon."

Melanie followed Brock up the steep hillside beyond the forest that lay just to the south of the village. At the top, all of Glenn were being shackled together in two long lines. Men on horses and vampires with bat wings circled the captives.

"Let her go, pig!"

It was Joseph, chained behind the butcher, his eyes wild with fury at the sight of his daughter in a strange man's arms. He made to charge Brock, but he pulled everyone else in the line after him, tipping over elderly Bertha who lived two houses down. A vampire flew by and swatted him across the face. The crack was awful, and Joseph fell straight on his butt, dazed.

"Brock," said a large man with a matted brown beard, riding up on horseback, "put the girl with the other children. If they're old enough to walk, they're to stay separate from the rest."

He pointed to a ring of children cowering together in manacles, guarded by three sword-wielding men.

"What of the woman?" said Brock with something of a whine. "I've got a thing or two to teach her."

"You'll do as I say," said the scruffy man. "I'll take the woman."

He reached down from his horse and grabbed the nape of her dress in a wad to steer her with.

"Don't forget our deal, Nathaniel," said Brock. "I know this forest. You've been locked up in your caves. You can't do any of this without me."

"That remains to be seen. Besides, we promised you valuables and livestock. The prisoners are not to be harmed."

"What the hell are they for anyway?"

"That's none of your concern. Now go."

Brock sneered but turned toward the ring of children.

"Momma!" said Tilly, squirming in the raider's arms, fear

widening her eyes.

"No! No! Don't take her! You promised!" Melanie tugged hard against the man's restraining grip, and she heard the seams of her dress pop.

"Be still, woman! You'll be chained with the rest and behave, or your daughter gets the punishment."

He exchanged his grip on her dress for a fistful of her hair and dragged her to the line. She bit her lip against the pain, but she heard Joseph raving with fury, screaming curses and threats until he was silenced again with another blow that made Melanie wince.

She was chained behind Clancy, the farmer whose fine herd of cattle was being guarded closely by hooting men on horses. Joseph was three people ahead of her in the line, but he craned his head around to see her. Blood flowed freely down his face, and a nasty bruise already marred the left side.

"Melanie, are you all right?" Joseph said.

"Yes, but they took Tilly," said Melanie, panicky sobs hurting her chest as they fought their way out.

"We're going to get her back. We're going to get out of here," he said, but his smile faltered and his eyes said he was lying. "I'll find a way."

"I know," she said, but it only came out as a whisper.

Chapter 15

Drained

Melanie's feet ached as she walked along in the darkness. Her dress was torn and covered with sap from the reaching fingers of the trees. The night air was cool, but rather than feeling good on her sweaty skin, it made her feel clammy and chilled.

For three days they'd walked in their line of chains. The two lines had grown longer each night. Their captors forced them to halt outside every village they passed and endure the sounds of the ransacking. The grotesquely deformed cyclops would be sent out ahead during the day to watch the towns and look for weaknesses. He would report back once the town was silent, practically dancing a jig with glee as he conveyed his ill-gotten information out of both mouths at once. First, it was Green Way, then tiny Dally. The morning following a raid, Brock would send three of his men off with the livestock—to sell them or corral them somewhere, Melanie didn't know, but the men always caught back up in time for the next raid. She was starting to feel like livestock herself.

Last night, they'd raided Everly. The cyclops had been especially proud of himself for slipping inside the town's well-hidden entrance unseen. Melanie had known the town as soon as she'd seen it, marched past it once the raiding was through. She'd never actually been there, but Tara, her next-door neighbor, had lived there before she'd married her husband. Tara's description of the perfectly hidden town with its splendid wall of carefully cut trees had not been an exaggeration. But now the thought of it would be forever marred by the screams of the captured villagers now towing the line behind her. Some of them were still weeping. No one from Glenn wept; all their tears had dried out with exhaustion and despair.

Melanie's eyes drooped. They were forced to walk at night under guard of the vampires. Melanie still could not get proper sleep during the day, even with the thick canopy dulling the shine of the sun's rays. The vampires left each day just before dawn to hide themselves from the fatal light of the sun, but the raiders and the werewolves stayed to guard the prisoners, keeping watches of a dozen men at a time. When she'd first heard the vampires calling some of the men mutts, she'd just assumed it was an insult, but she'd picked up on enough conversation to know that a good number of her captors were moon mutts.

Melanie craned her head around to try and find Tilly in the large ring of children herded behind the procession. There were new faces—boys and girls from Everly with disheveled hair and tear-stained cheeks. Only very young children were kept separate from the adults. There were a number of teenagers scattered between the two lines, shackled to those before and behind them with iron manacles and chains.

A teenager from Everly had been shackled behind Melanie, wedged into the line farther up to separate him from his parents as punishment for his father's courageous and nearly successful attempt to strangle the long-haired raider, Brock, who had attacked Melanie in her home. Brent was the boy's name; he'd introduced himself as they'd lain down awkwardly to try and sleep in their chains that morning.

"Are you all right?" he said now, noticing that Melanie's pace had become stunted and that Clancy, the man ahead of her, was involuntarily pulling her along half of the way. "I'll make them give you some more water. You oughtn't be made to trudge on like this in your condition."

"No, no, Brent," said Melanie. "I'm fine. They'll only punish you for asking."

They were given water only at meal times, right before they stopped to rest for the day and when they got up to move again at night. The stale bread and scraps of fat from their captors' meals only made Melanie thirstier rather than truly easing her hunger pains.

Brent let out a huff of frustration, and Melanie heard him grind his teeth.

"When my brother hears about this ..." He made a low, guttural growling sound instead of finishing the thought.

"Your brother wasn't captured in the raid?"

"No ... and, well, he's not really my brother. He's an orphan, but he's the closest thing I have to a brother. When he hears about this, raider throats will spill blood, I guarantee it. He's done it before. If he'd only been able to get Brock last time ..."

"You knew of Brock before this?"

"Yes, he killed Erro's parents and he killed my little sister."

"So that's why your father tried to kill him."

"Yes, if it weren't for the bloodsuckers he would have done it, too."

"What did you say, boy?" said a ghostly-pale woman with ice-blonde hair walking beside the prisoners.

"Nothing," said Brent, averting his dark eyes but clenching his hands into fists.

"That's what I thought."

"Who's Erro?" said Melanie, trying to keep Brent's attention so that he didn't do something foolish.

"My brother ... my sort of brother. The one I was talking about. He may already be trailing us, waiting for the right time."

"He's only one boy; if he is following us, he'd better stay hidden."

"He's not alone," said Brent. "He left Everly just a few days ago with the Avalons."

"Avalons?" said Melanie in an urgent whisper. "The royal Avalons?"

"Yes, the princes and princesses; Erro helped them track down the missing elf princess, Atalanta. She was with them, too. They were heading to the elf palace, but Erro promised he would keep an eye out for any sign of Brock on the way."

Melanie didn't ask how Erro could possibly know of the misfortune of Everly if he'd left it in the opposite direction days ago, for she saw no harm in letting the boy keep his hopes alive of his adoptive brother charging in to save them all with the Avalons and an elf princess. Foolhardy as the notion might be.

Brent fell silent, and Melanie hoped he was lost in his daydreams of rescue, wishing she had something to distract her from her rumbling stomach and her aching legs. Even in the northern climate of the woods, the midsummer sun produced a beating heat at the height of the day. Strands of Melanie's brown waves stuck to the sweat on her neck. The underbrush grew dense in places, but still the prisoners were forced to walk a straight line through the maze of trees and occasional thickets.

After another hour of continuous walking, Melanie began to feel woozy. Her back was aching fiercely under the burden of her belly, so much so that it was making her feel sick.

"Brent," she said, her tongue feeling like cotton, "Brent, I think I might ... I think I need ..."

Melanie's vision clouded, and she felt herself fall backward. Brent's lean but surprisingly strong arms caught her under the armpits.

"Melanie? Somebody help!" Brent's voice—too loud in her ears as he lowered her to the ground.

"Melanie?" Joseph's voice, loud and urgent.

Melanie managed to open her eyes just in time to see Joseph hauling the line of prisoners along with him as he ran for her. He crouched at her side and propped her up on his lap gently.

"Get back in formation!" said the female vampire who'd scolded Brent earlier.

"She's pregnant," said Joseph, baring his teeth at the vampire. "She can't keep walking like this with hardly any food and water."

"Then we'll make better use of her," said the vampire sweetly.

"We're starting to get hungry, and the useless will be the first to go."

"You won't touch her."

"Oh? And how are you going to stop me, mortal?"

"What's the hold up here?" said a male, black-bearded werewolf who Melanie had grown familiar with. He wore a nasty whip on his belt next to his sword and had no qualms in using it on the more strong-willed of the prisoners. He'd used it on Brent's father before the lead vampire—the one they called Thetis—had stopped him, reminding him of their orders not to harm prisoners.

"The pregnant woman and her husband are messing up the line."

The whole procession had been forced to a stop, and everyone was watching Melanie and Joseph. The leaders of the grisly pack, Nathaniel and Thetis were turning around in the front to find the source of the delay—Nathaniel on horseback, Thetis hovering a few feet above the ground, powered by his leathery wings.

"Get up, bitch," said the werewolf, advancing on Melanie and Joseph. "Carrying a whelp doesn't let you slack off in line."

Melanie felt Joseph tense, and he gently laid her on the ground. He remained in his crouch, staring stoically at the ground until the werewolf bent down to grab at Melanie's arm.

Joseph grabbed the werewolf's wrist and snapped his arm around at an awkward angle, tossing a punch into his jaw at the same time. The werewolf staggered back, and Joseph snatched his sword from its sheath. The vampire woman leapt forward, but Joseph met her with the tip of the blade, embedding it in her chest. Her scream mingled with Brent's cheers. Joseph attempted to remove the blade, but the werewolf had unleashed his whip. With a crack, the cruel metal pieces tied into the end of the leather slashed through Joseph's tunic, bringing crimson stains to the surface that quickly spread over the soft, beige material.

Joseph's knees hit the ground and he gasped in pain, unable

to free the scream that choked off his breath. Melanie screamed for him.

"Stop it! Please! Have mercy!"

But the whip kept falling, and the female vampire, pulling the sword from her bosom, cheered on the werewolf.

Melanie, nearly blinded with tears and growing hoarse from screaming, threw herself on top of Joseph, trying to shield him from the blows.

"Please, stop!" she cried, but the whip cracked again.

It ripped through Melanie's dress and cut into her shoulder. The searing pain made her scream and whimper. Joseph roared beneath her, pushing her off him as he rose to his feet. The man raised the whip again, a crazed look on his gnarled face, but as he brought it down Joseph caught it just behind the metal pieces.

He twisted the length of the whip around his wrist and yanked it from the man's hands. He took hold of the handle and slashed the werewolf across the face with it once before the female vampire lifted him off his feet by the throat.

"Put him down," said a sharp voice, startling them all.

It was Thetis, his leather wings folding into his back as his feet touched the ground. He glared at the female vampire, who had tightened her grip on Joseph's throat, turning his face purple. The whip fell from his limp hand. With a snarl, the vampire tossed him roughly aside.

Joseph lay bleeding and choking on the ground, and Melanie saw the vampires closing ranks, drawn to the smell. Her heart raced so fast she feared she might faint again. Thetis looked around at the stalking vampires, too, and sighed.

"I had meant to wait another day, but since the mongrel has spilled so much blood, it would be cruel to let it go to waste."

Many of the vampires grinned, revealing elongated canines. The icy-haired female slid her tongue across her fangs and along her lower lip.

"Only a few at a time," said Nathaniel, his lip turned up in mild disgust. "If your whole lot has their fill, we'll lose half the captives."

"Yes, I remember the king's words just as well as you, Nathaniel," said Thetis with a smirk. "No need to parrot them back at me."

The cyclops chuckled behind Thetis' leg, his eyes peering out at Nathaniel from opposite sides of Thetis' trousers. Thetis' deep blue eyes moved lazily over his fellow vampires. He called out a dozen names, pointing to the vampires who had the least amount of color and were beginning to look skeletal. They stepped to the front of the ring surrounding Thetis, Nathanial, and Joseph. The icy-blonde vampire skulked away, muttering to herself.

"You'll have to share," said Thetis. "We're building an army. Each worthless life here can serve a greater purpose and must not be wasted. We'll take three from each line. This one is the first."

He pointed at Joseph, and Melanie rocked in her kneeling position. Brent's hand steadied her.

The prisoners shrank back and closed ranks. Family members reached up and down the lines for one another. Brent, with his hand still on Melanie's shoulder, looked back toward his parents, his face bloodless.

"Please, I'll do anything," said Melanie. "Please, not him." But her voice was weak and her mouth dry, her tongue sticking to the roof of her mouth as she tried to speak, and no one seemed to hear.

Thetis walked alongside the two lines, rubbing at his chin. "This one is a liability, much too slow." He pointed one long, pale finger at an old woman across from Melanie. At his words, two of the chosen vampires grabbed for her. They didn't bother with asking for the key to her manacles. Instead, they pulled together and ripped them open with a terrible screeching noise.

"Don't destroy the restraints, fools!" said Thetis, throwing up a hand in exasperation. "We'll need them later."

"Papa?"

Melanie's eyes darted to the pack of guarded children at the end of the lines. Tilly's face was peeking around a raider's leg, her blue eyes wide as two vampires forced Joseph to his feet and fumbled over a key that Nathaniel handed over.

"Tilly, don't look!" cried Melanie, her breath rapid and shallow. "Somebody, please, don't let her look."

A girl of about ten with ashen-colored pigtail braids who was already clutching her own younger sister pulled Tilly into the embrace, turning Tilly's head against her shoulder so that she couldn't watch. Melanie's gratitude came out as a shuddering sob and a pained smile at the older girl.

Joseph's shackles clanked on the ground just as the old woman made a run for it. She hardly got one wobbly step forward before the slighter of the two male vampires pounced on her back and sank his fangs into her neck. The other roared and ripped him off, trying to get his own share.

A middle-aged woman not three feet from the gruesome squabble began screaming for her dying mother, eyes as wide as dinner plates and fingers shoved in her mouth like a panicked child.

Joseph kept his dark eyes on Melanie's blue ones as the female vampire on his right tilted back his head, her clawed hands wrapped in his black hair. Melanie watched silent and open-mouthed, the tears streaming down her face the only sign that she understood what was happening.

"I love you, Melanie," he said.

"I love—" But her sobbed, choked words turned to wild screams as both vampires sank their fangs into opposite sides of his neck.

Brent grabbed her around the middle, holding her back as best he could while she threw herself toward Joseph. She heard the high, crazed screams, but they hardly felt like her own. The cyclops shrank away from her behind the crowd of vampires, trying to cover his four ears and cringing against the noise. Melanie was conscious of little else but the color quickly draining from Joseph's skin. She didn't stop screaming when they dropped him, lifeless, to the ground.

"Melanie? Melanie, please, it's okay. Please stop, they'll hurt you next," said Brent in her ear. Her screams only turned into shuddering sobs. "Mother? Mother, what do I do?"

Brent was looking down the line to a woman with wild red curls.

"Just hold her, dear; you're doing fine."

Thetis seemed oblivious to the commotion around him. He continued strolling up and down the lines until he'd selected three more people: a young woman whose whooping cough had grown more serious each day they'd travelled and who could hardly stand, an old man with a twisted back, and a man with a wooden leg.

The wood rang with hellish sounds of death and grief, but Thetis only scoured for the last blood meal.

"What about this one?" said Nathaniel, pointing at Melanie. "She's the reason this all got started. She fainted. With that belly, she won't be able to go on like this much longer."

Melanie's wails became loud sniffles as she ogled Nathaniel, trying to process what he'd said.

"She just needs a little more food and water," said Brent, jaw clenched as he positioned himself in front of her.

"The boy's right," said Thetis, coming to a halt in front of Melanie and brushing Brent aside with a sweeping motion of his arm. His head tilted slightly to the left as he appraised the soft brown waves caressing her rounded, girlish cheeks and framing her red-rimmed powder-blue eyes. "Her condition must be taken into consideration. She's much too fine a specimen to lose. You"—he thrust a finger at the nearest werewolf—"fetch her water."

With a look of loathing, the werewolf turned slowly toward

the packhorses. Thetis, with one last look at Melanie's rosy lips, turned back to his search.

"What about that one?" said Brock, pointing to Brent's father. "Tried to kill me."

"No!" Brent shouted, and this time it was Melanie who had to hold him back as he thrashed against her, fingers reaching for the raider's neck. "I swear to God I'll kill you! You hear me, I'll kill you, you yellow-bellied son of a whore!"

"Easy, boy," said Thetis with the hint of a smile. "No one blames your father for trying to kill that one." Brock turned red and glowered at Thetis but kept his mouth clenched shut. "Besides, he's perfectly healthy. He'll make a strapping werewolf."

Brent's screams of rage cut off at once.

"A ... a what?"

"Take that one and be done with it," said Thetis, ignoring Brent and pointing at feeble older man who had once been a vegetable farmer in Glenn before arthritis had crippled his hands.

Melanie's heart turned to ice in her chest. She'd heard their captors talk of conversion and making an army many times already, but she hadn't wanted to believe her sneaking suspicions. There was no denying it now. Those who were not sacrificed to the vampire's bloodlust would be turned into monsters. She would become a vampire or a werewolf. What of the children? Would they be changed too? She looked to Tilly, still shielded from the horrors of the night by the unknown older girl who was weeping into her sister's hair.

The werewolf appeared with the water bag as the vampires set into the old man. He thrust it in her face, but she only looked up at him with a glazed expression. Brent took it in his shaking hands and helped her drink, but the glorious sensation of cool water trickling down her throat was deadened by the screams and pleas of the old neighbor's loved ones and the sight of her beloved Joseph in a tattered, broken heap nestled in a bloody bed of brown pine needles.

Chapter 16

Out of Time

The ever-growing lines of prisoners stumbled to the westernmost edge of the Northern Woods a few hours before dawn. Melanie cradled her rounded stomach as it growled and cramped with hunger. Her eyes burned from the endless stream of tears that plagued her, thoughts of Joseph always playing out in her mind: the touch of his callused fingers on her face, the smell of fresh earth on his clothes, the sound of his whispered adorations, the sight of him running through the forest with Tilly laughing on his shoulders.

When Thetis called the party to a halt, Melanie lowered herself to the ground with a sigh and some assistance from Brent, giving her aching feet a much needed rest.

As the number of prisoners increased, so had the number of captors. More and more vampires had appeared for the past two nights. The new werewolves had come on horseback during the day. Where were they coming from? Surely the forest couldn't house so many without detection. Still, they did not quite match the numbers of the prisoners, who were now just a little under two hundred strong.

"Brock," said Nathaniel suddenly. "Come."

Brock trotted up on his horse, scowling at being commanded like a common dog.

"Why've we stopped? Daylight isn't for another hour at least," said Brock.

"You're being dismissed," said Nathaniel.

The way Nathaniel cocked his head as he smiled made Melanie shift her attention away from her aching feet.

"Why?" said Brock, tugging at the reins as his horse shied away from the werewolf.

"This is the end of your domain, is it not? You keep to these woods, yes?"

"Mostly," said Brock slowly, as if testing the word and its consequences. Melanie watched his Adam's apple bob the length of his neck. "Does this mean my men and I are free to go?"

Thetis landed gently on the back of Brock's saddle, wings still unfurled, and spoke in his ear like a lover. "It means you've outrun your usefulness."

Brock's horse reared, and Thetis slid off to hover nearby, grinning while his fangs grew over his lip. Brock's eyes were nearly as wide as his mount's as he wrangled it back under control.

"Wait! Wait! Please! I used to raid outside of the forest before the king sent an extra guard to the lords of the North," he said, tripping over his tongue, his eyes darting from Nathaniel to Thetis. "I know the villages to the west. I can make sure you don't miss a single one from here to the elvish border. That's where you're headed, right? Into elf country? You ... you need me."

Thetis' bare feet nestled soundlessly in the grass and pine needles.

"What of your companions?" he said, his eyes boring into Brock. "Do we need them?"

Brock's knuckles turned white as he gripped the reins. He stared back at Thetis, his mouth an almost invisible line. A bulging vein in his neck betrayed his racing pulse.

"Do what you will with them," said Brock just above a whisper.

"Good man," said Thetis. He pointed to a group of about two dozen weakened vampires who had expectant looks on their faces. "You lot, drink your fill."

Fangs slid over lips and wings unfurled with soft flutters of wind. Brock's men had watched their leader curiously from the end of the procession, most of them gathered around the children and unable to hear. When the vampires' hungry eyes slid over them, they stood frozen for a moment, all eyes swiveling to their leader. The vampires leapt into the air, streaking toward them on leathery wings. The raiders set their heels to their horses, but the vampires snatched them from their saddles.

"Good riddance," said Brent, most of his face buried in his knees.

Melanie couldn't say she disagreed.

* * *

"There it is!" said Atalanta, pointing from atop Sir Gregor's horse.

"Just in time, too," said Michael. "The next full moon is in just two days."

Cradled in the valley below and surrounded on all sides by large, sloping hills stood Campion.

"It looks ... green," said Andrew.

Atalanta laughed, and Andrew's eyes slid out of focus, drowned in the ethereal sound. "I suppose it does."

From a distance, the buildings of Campion looked like little mole mounds: rounded structures of earthy grays, greens, and browns. As the companions rode closer, the oddities of the homes grew more pronounced. There were no sharp edges, only smooth curves. The wood used to build them was rough and unsanded, with the bark still fully intact. Vines, leaves, and flowers grew out of the very walls.

"What are they made of?" said Andrew.

"Trees," said Atalanta, "just like your homes."

"I've never seen wood like this."

"Well, of course not," said Atalanta with another small laugh. "They're made from living trees. An elf must never harm any natural living thing unless it is a danger; it is our law. We sing the trees into those shapes."

The humans took second looks, their mouths hanging open. The homes were, in fact, rooted to the ground. Whole trunks bent into domed and cylindrical shapes, their branches and leaves making unique patterns, designs, and doorways.

"Amazing!" said Andromeda, leaning over in her saddle to rub her hand along the living wall of the nearest home.

"Does all elfin magic involve singing?" said Michael.

"Only spells that must coax nature to take on new shapes," said Atalanta. "It takes a bit more persuasion."

"Princess Atalanta?" a male voice asked in hushed tones.

A small crowd was forming in the middle of the main road. Faces of breathtaking beauty peered up the lane and out of windows. The elf who had spoken was a head taller than Atalanta with blonde hair braided down his back and long, oval-shaped blue eyes. All the elves had high, sharp cheekbones, flawless complexions, and slender, willowy builds. They had eyes only for Atalanta.

"The princess has returned!" came a voice from the crowd, and suddenly the elves rushed around them, bowing low at Atalanta's feet.

Atalanta observed them with a bright smile and beckoned them to rise.

"The king must be told," said the blonde elf who had first spoken.

"Aye, he must. I'll need a swift bird," said Atalanta.

"It shall be given," said the blonde elf, snapping his fingers at a young elf boy who scampered off with one last look at the princess. "You can retire to my home while you wait."

"Many thanks. What is your name?"

"Gelwyn, Your Highness," said the elf, bowing again. "This is my wife, Mendaline." He wrapped an arm around a striking black-haired elf with emerald eyes much like Atalanta's. "She will make sure you and your ... companions are made comfortable."

Luminous eyes turned to the humans as if only just seeing

them, with curiosity and a hint of worry.

"They are no ordinary companions," said Atalanta. "They are my friends and our allies, the Avalons."

Erro cleared his throat and muttered something that ended with, "not an Avalon."

"And a very talented tracker and woodsman," said Atalanta with a flick of her hand.

The elves hardly spared Erro a glance, but there were many murmurs about the griffin standing at his back and the vexar sitting between his feet. When Aquila turned an amber eye on Gelwyn, the elf bowed to the creature, who returned the gesture, just as he had done to Atalanta.

"You will treat them all with the same respect you show me," said Atalanta, raising her voice slightly so the whole gathered village was sure to hear, "no matter their parentage or the shape of their ears."

"Or the deformity of their faces," muttered a young female elf with hair like fresh honey.

A low chorus of tinkling chuckles spread through the crowd. Andromeda looked hurt, Andrew startled and affronted. Felicity looked about to commit murder.

Atalanta's face turned cold, and those surrounding the young elf took a step away as Atalanta fixed her with a hard stare.

"These humans came to my aid when no elf seemed able to find me. What have you done for your princess or your people? Look pretty? You don't look so special to me."

The elf blushed crimson and studied her feet. "Forgive me, Your Highness," she said.

Atalanta merely looked away, her eyes scanning the other elves. "My friends are expecting a message from King Markus Avalon. I want to be notified of its arrival immediately. Is that understood?"

"Yes, Your Highness," said Gelwyn. "Please, come inside, all of you, and rest yourselves."

"Aquila," said Erro, stroking a finger down the length of the griffin's beak, "take Zezil and enjoy some time to yourselves, hmm?"

Aquila chirped and blinked his large eyes. When Erro and the others followed Mendaline and Gelwyn into their birch tree home, Aquila corralled Zezil off in the other direction, thrusting out a large paw to gently bat the vexar away when he tried to follow his master.

Come, you stubborn thing. The deep, scolding voice echoed in Andromeda's head, startling her, just as Aquila squawked impatiently at Zezil. She whirled around to eye the griffin, a look of great shock on her face that made Andrew pause beside her.

"Something the matter?" he asked.

Andromeda gave her head a sharp shake. "No, nothing."

She held her gaze on Aquila all the same, but the griffin did not return her look, having at last persuaded the vexar to follow him into the surrounding valley. Andrew, now at the doorway, looked back to his twin, who slowly followed him inside.

The elves' home smelled of fresh earth, flowers, and wood. The furniture in the home was made from roots that rose out of the ground to create the shapes of tables, chairs, and dressers before digging back beneath the earth. A young elf stood in a corner of the far wall watering a bed of herbs growing out of the floor, pretending not to have just been peeking out the window before they arrived.

"My daughter, Bree," said Gelwyn.

Bree turned a bit too quickly and curtsied in the same movement. She had her father's blonde hair, though it was a slightly darker shade, but her eyes were a rich brown that matched the small beauty mark at the corner of her left eye.

"Pleased to meet you, Your Highnesses," she said.

"Very pleased to meet you," said Andrew before anyone else could respond. He stepped forward as he spoke, partially blocking Michael from view (though he couldn't sufficiently conceal his older brother's bulk), and adjusted his furs.

"Perhaps you'd like to sit down," said Gelwyn pointedly.

"Can I take your coat?" said Bree, rushing forward to help Andrew slip off the heavy furs.

Andrew wiggled his eyebrows in Erro's direction.

The young elvish boy returned with parchment, quill, and ink in hand and a handsome falcon perched on his shoulder.

Atalanta received all of this with a hurried thanks and asked Gelwyn where she might find a quiet place to write her letter. He directed her up the smooth birch stairs to the study above.

"Can I do anything to make you more comfortable?" said Mendaline. "Are you in need of food, water, fresh clothes?"

"It would be nice to get out of this armor and take a warm bath," said Felicity eagerly.

"Certainly," said Mendaline with a gracious smile. "Follow me, Your Highness."

Michael struck up a conversation about elvish magic with Gelwyn, and Andrew took advantage of the elf's distraction to settle into a chair next to where Bree continued to tend the herb garden ... or at least keep up the pretense of tending it.

Andromeda looked around for Erro just in time to see him slip out of the home. With soft, hurried steps, she followed him around the back of the house, which looked out onto a pasture filled with a few dozen squat, shaggy-haired cows. But Erro wasn't looking at the cows; his eyes were turned to the east, staring intently, as though if he concentrated hard enough the Northern Wood might materialize on the horizon.

Andromeda watched him silently, guilt making her bite at her lip. Leaving the forest without first finding the raider, Brock, had been hard for him. She'd seen the way he'd hesitated at the edge of the wood, hand wrapped tightly around the rough bark of a pine, teeth gritted with the determination to not look back.

After a few moments, she wrapped two fingers around his wrist. He looked sideways at her, smiling slightly as he intertwined his fingers with hers.

"Thank you, for coming with us," she said.

He nodded slowly, eyes back on the horizon. "There are bigger enemies to worry about now. I'll find him someday, when this is all over."

"That could be a long time," said Andromeda.

Erro shrugged, but Andromeda saw the pain in the set of his mouth. She held onto his hand in silence, watching him watch what wasn't there.

"For a very long time, all I had was him," said Erro suddenly. "The drive to find him, to hurt him. Everything else was just a distraction. It's an empty way to live."

Andromeda squeezed his hand, listening, waiting for him to go on.

"Fiona and Jeremiah gave me a sort of home, but they had their own children to care for, and I didn't want to be a burden. But now ..." He scuffed his boot through the dirt. "Now I feel I have a home again, with you, with your family ... even the elf's not so bad."

Andromeda laughed softly.

"And it doesn't make any sense," said Erro, talking faster now, "because I'm nothing like any of you. I'm an orphan. I'm not royal. I'm no one, but for some reason you've taken me in, and somehow I feel like I belong. I haven't felt that way around people for a very long time. So thank you. Coming here with you wasn't a sacrifice. I'd be a fool to let you go for the likes of Brock ... again."

He hadn't looked at her once as he spoke, but he turned to her now, the fingers of his free hand tentatively tracing her cheek. His eyes searched hers, almost pleading.

"What are you waiting for?" said Andromeda. "Permission?"

His lips met hers with pleasant force, setting her blood aflame.

Erro and Andromeda returned inside just as Atalanta came down the stairs without the falcon or her letter.

"It's done," she said with a small sigh. "My father will no doubt send an envoy for us. I've explained everything as briefly as I could and suggested that he start assembling the army."

Gelwyn and his family exchanged frightened looks, but said nothing.

"Our father should have received my letter by now," said Michael. "It will take time for his messenger to reach us, though, so far west."

"So now we wait," said Andromeda, crossing her arms with a look of disappointment, blowing a stray strand of black hair from her eye.

"That's perfectly all right with me," said Felicity, coming down the stairs with her blonde curls slightly tamed, damp with water, and wearing a finely made powder-blue, cotton dress cinched at the waist with silver-dyed cord.

"I'm sure Andrew agrees with you," said Michael in an undertone.

"Andrew agrees with what?" said Andrew, his eyes never fully leaving Bree as he turned his head toward Michael.

* * *

On the day of the full moon, the werewolves didn't sleep. They appeared agitated, pacing along the line of prisoners. They lashed out at the humans with irrational rage. Without the vampires to keep them in check, they'd nearly ripped out the throat of one man who'd briefly held up his line to relieve himself.

The vampires returned with the graying of dusk, much earlier than usual. The sun's rays were barely visible on the horizon and muted by the heavy overhang of clouds, but the vampires kept their leathery wings wrapped around their bodies, hissing with discomfort.

Only Thetis braved the painful half-light, soaring a few feet above the crowd and speaking at the top of his voice.

"Tonight is a very special occasion, humans," he said. "Tonight you leave the chains of mortality behind. You will shed your feeble bodies and be reborn in King Tyrannus' image."

The crowd of prisoners murmured uneasily, some in high-pitched, quavering tones of terror, others in confusion.

"Who's King Tyrannus?" said Brent.

"I don't know, but if he rules this lot, I don't want to meet him," said Melanie. She felt the feeling leave her fingers and toes, and she heard herself speak to Brent from far away. It was going to happen tonight.

"The hybrid king is a noble being, and the first of his kind. Half werewolf, half vampire, and he has chosen you to be his newest children. He loves all creatures of the night equally, and no matter which you become tonight you will be treated with kindness so long as you show your fealty."

"We will never become one of you!" rang a voice from the crowd.

Melanie looked around for the speaker, but could not distinguish him from the rest. Thetis did not bother to look; he continued his lazy sweeping motion over the length of the two lines.

"Oh, but you shall, and you shall fight under your king's command against the human and elf armies."

Calls of dissent rang through the meadow.

"You'll have no choice!" said Thetis sharply. "Those of you who become werewolves will bow to your alpha's wishes,"— he thrust a finger at Nathaniel—"and those of you who become vampires won't be able to resist your newfound hunger for blood. In exchange for your immortality, power, and eternal youth, you are a slave to the great thirst. If you try to return to your homes, to your fellow humans, you will spill blood in your wake. Your loved ones will fall beneath your fangs. Should you decide to dissent, your children's blood shall be spilled—it only takes a few drops to summon the thirst in a fledgling. You'll tear your own offspring apart. Those of you without children … well, you shall find out just how much suffering a vampire can withstand.

"Still, some of you may fight your way free, it's true." Thetis' voice was pleasant now, as if conversing with old friends. "Vampires are resilient, after all. But let me ask you, where will you go? You will be hunted down by your own kind. Without the strength of the coven, you will be slaughtered. You will die soulless and rejected by those you once called brothers. That is the way of humans!

"Join the true king's army and you shall receive power beyond your wildest imagination. You will be accepted, loved. You will live forever with your friends, neighbors, and spouses at your side. Together we will reshape Arcamira into a unified kingdom ruled by gods!"

The crowd was alive with wails of dismay and cries of outrage. From the midst of the chaos, one voice rose louder than the rest. This time Melanie recognized it as Brent's father, Jeremiah.

"You cannot have me or my family, devil!"

"Oh?" said Thetis, loud enough to be heard over the growing din as the sun at last sank fully behind the horizon, making way for the moon to light up the clouds with its pale, murky blue glow. "And just how do you plan to stop us?"

Chapter 17

Venomous Heart

The werewolves began to look sick — shaking and doubling over with strained grimaces. Thetis turned his attention to them and his fellow vampires.

"The children must not be converted. They are of better use to us as mortals, and fledglings turned too young are far too dangerous." As he spoke, he swept over the lines. He began pointing to some of the older children chained up with their parents. "That one's still too young. Put her with the little ones. That one, too. And him."

He pointed at Brent. Melanie heard his mother give out a relieved sob. The smallest of smiles curled her own mouth, not just for Brent, but because Tilly would remain unharmed ... for now. But Melanie's body had begun to shake with dread. Which would she be? Vampire or werewolf?

Brent was unshackled and tossed into the circle of younger children guarded by two vampires who'd been freshly fed by Brock's men. Brock himself was at the back of the group of children, as though distancing himself as much as possible from the inhuman creatures he'd allied himself with. Brent didn't put up any resistance. He just kept looking back to his parents and Melanie, his face almost translucent he'd gone so pale.

"This line is for the mutts," said Thetis, pointing to Melanie's line. "This one is ours." A girl in the vampire line screamed and pulled at her face in despair, her nails raking dull pink lines in her pale skin.

Perhaps a werewolf would be better, Melanie thought. At least she would be herself most of the time, only hungry for blood at the full moon.

But the werewolves were grunting and moaning in pain. The

full moon had emerged, tinted orange by the retreated sun, as though dipped in hellfire.

"Nathaniel!" said Thetis, the faintest hint of panic in his voice. "Get your pack in the proper positions."

Nathaniel, bowed over in pain, straightened up with a grunt of effort and barked at his pack to form a line, each wolf standing next to a human. A gangly, hairy man who looked only a few years older than Melanie took his place beside her. When Melanie turned away from his hungry gaze, she realized all the werewolves were becoming unnaturally hairy, even the women. The female to her left had sprouted a fine, thick beard that trailed down to her bosom.

"Wait," said Thetis.

Melanie jumped. Thetis had spoken just behind her, alighting in the grass without a sound. Instinctively, she fixed her eyes on him, wanting to keep track of his every move. The way he looked at her made her shiver. It was lust. She'd seen it in men's eyes before. She'd seen it in Joseph's, but there it was alluring and coupled with love. In Thetis' eyes it was unfiltered—hot and violent, like flames licking at her body.

"This one is too frail, in her present condition, to become a werewolf," said Thetis. "The transformation is more violent and painful. She must be traded for another."

Thetis moved so deftly that Melanie was unshackled and caught tight in his arms before the werewolf could even think to form a protest. Melanie, taken utterly by surprise, snapped to attention and moved to kick Thetis, but before she could command her body to carry out the deed, she was shackled again, this time in the vampire line. A young, handsome man was shoved quickly into her former place. The werewolf snarled, and it was the sound of a dog.

The werewolf made an aggressive move toward Thetis, but suddenly his spine snapped backward with a force so terrible it seemed to break him in two, with a crack like a felled tree. Then his torso snapped forward and threw him onto his knees, where his body heaved and shuddered. All around him, the other werewolves underwent the same gruesome transformation. Their skin ripped in bloody lines, sprouting hair and newly formed, bulging muscles from the wounds. Their bones cracked and lengthened and reshaped. Claws shoved through their fingernails. Their teeth tore free of their gums and scattered on the ground to make way for drool-coated fangs. Their faces elongated into snouts. Perhaps the most horrible of all was the eyes—slitted and yellow, utterly devoid of anything but wild rage and hunger. Most began to stand upright, but a few seemed to prefer an animalistic crouch. Melanie smelled urine. It dripped from the trousers of the young man who'd taken her place.

Nathaniel was the largest wolf of all. At least ten feet at his full, upright height. His fur was longer than most, and curled into a matted, bushy mess. He flung back his head and howled, and his pack joined in.

Thetis was gone from Melanie's side in an instant, and reappeared at Nathaniel's shoulder just as he turned his yellow eyes on the slender blonde woman in front of him. The vampires swarmed the werewolves as the mutts swarmed the closest line of prisoners. Melanie was yanked backward by those in her own line as they attempted to get as far away from the brutal attack as possible. It was not far enough. The chains had been secured with thick wooden braces pounded into the ground at even intervals to keep the line from moving.

The werewolves lunged for the exposed flesh of the humans without discrimination in a mad frenzy. Vampires dug their nails into the werewolves' backs or wrapped their stony arms around the wolves' necks to keep them from biting off limbs and heads. Cries of agony pounded in Melanie's ears until she was sure she would go mad. Flesh was ripped from bones in savage bites, and hellish sounds escaped the vampires and werewolves as they grappled. Thetis was having the hardest time. Nathaniel bucked, bit, and slashed, dealing Thetis what should have been multiple fatal blows—one that nearly severed his head. But no matter the injury, Thetis kept the claws of his hands and feet embedded in the massive wolf, yanking him off his back paws and biting into the soft flesh of his neck when necessary.

Blood soaked everything: clothes, faces, trees, the earth, and the muzzles of the wolves. Melanie tried to keep her eyes on the children, but fighting bodies kept blocking her view. Brent held Tilly this time; the girl who'd held her when Joseph was slaughtered had a whole mess of clinging, screaming children to comfort this time. Brent kept Tilly's eyes buried in his tunic and placed his hands over her ears, but his own eyes were fixed on his mother and father. His mother had been bitten across the face, and blood stained her orange hair deep crimson, almost black. His father clutched at the gaping wound on his neck and shoulder, his other hand groping for his wife. Brent's cries were lost in the din.

An eternity passed, but the end came too soon. Brent's parents, Fiona and Jeremiah, began to shake so hard their teeth gnashed, their heads whipping back and forth. The cracks and crunches echoed once more into the night. The other werewolves quieted, sniffing at the writhing humans, their ears perked forward and heads cocked to the side.

Fiona's face grew fresh, pink skin before Melanie's eyes, then sprouted strawberry fur. Jeremiah grew claws and tore at his clothes. A new wolf pack slowly rose on unsteady paws and turned their yellow eyes to the moon. Their howls, comingled with the old pack, reverberated in Melanie's head, and she shoved her palms against her ears. Iron screeched as they tore free of their shackles.

The vampires shifted their positions, forming a solid barrier between the humans and the enlarged pack. Thetis bared his fangs and hissed at Nathaniel like an ill-tempered feline, his clawed hands braced in an offensive position at his sides. The other vampires hissed and snarled at the werewolves, puffing up their chests or arching their backs to look larger, their fangs fully elongated, wings forming a black wall. The wolves snarled back, yipping and growling, but all their eyes turned to their alpha. Nathaniel snorted gruffly through his muzzle and bared his fangs in an agitated grin, but he took a step backward. With a shortened, more muted howl, he turned heel and put all four paws on the ground. The other werewolves howled back and took off after him, across the meadows outside the forest to hunt.

The vampires slowly turned back to face the prisoners, forked tongues licking at fangs and groans of desire and hunger passing over lips. Melanie pressed herself harder against her fellows, wrapping her arms protectively around her stomach. Her legs vibrated uncontrollably, threatening to collapse. The pounding of her blood made her ears feel stuffed with cotton.

Thetis had his eyes fixated on her. Other vampires moved out of his way as he approached. Melanie's breath came in shallow gasps. The baby lurched inside her, distressed by the changes. Her eyes flicked down to her rounded womb, and hot rage bubbled up into her chest.

"Don't worry, my lovely, it won't hurt for long," said Thetis, extending a hand toward her, his eyes boring into hers.

She began to feel light-headed. Her rage ebbed, and her muscles began to relax. Thetis used one grey, clawed fingernail to pop open her shackles. Melanie swayed, feeling on the edge of dreaming, unable to look away from his entrancing eyes. The babe squirmed again, and Melanie threw a wild punch at Thetis, her own yell reverberating in her ears and clearing her head. Thetis caught her wrist and laughed softly. She kicked frantically at his shins, but he didn't even wince. He pinned her arms behind her back and encircled her wrists in one hand, holding her tighter than the shackles ever had. With his other hand he brushed back her rich, brown waves, exposing her neck.

"I tried to let you sleep, to float on cotton clouds while the change took place," said Thetis. "But you refuse to cooperate; it just won't do. I suppose you'll just have to endure it."

Melanie squirmed and kicked, and yanked her body forward so hard she feared she would dislocate her shoulders, but to no avail. His fangs pierced her flesh like hot needles, and a gasp pushed through her clenched lips. She soon began to feel weak. She could here him sucking, swallowing gulps of her blood. Her eyes slid out of focus.

A scream ripped from her throat. Searing pain, like a white hot iron, as vampire venom filled her emptying veins. The burning travelled along with the venom, and she tracked its progress with mounting terror. After it had filled her head and neck, it flowed down her arms to her fingertips, and into her chest. Her heart galloped, beating a painful rhythm.

"No! No, please!" Her tears burned in her eyes as the venom reached its tendrils toward her stomach.

The pain was like a flaming sword, and the baby twitched and kicked. Melanie's anguished scream was cut off abruptly by the final, thumping pain of her heart's last beat. She looked up into the dark sky, and the blackness branched out and became absolute.

Melanie awoke with tears on her cheeks. One was planted against the pine-covered grass. Her hand groped for her stomach. It was diminished—the vampire venom already working to make it slim and perfect. No movement. Her wail was high and terrible, but no one came to comfort her.

Then a scent hit her nostrils with such strength it filled up her brain and fuzzed out all other thought. Warm, sticky blood on her cheek, on the grass all around her. Insatiable desire washed over her, and two cold, hard fangs pricked her bottom lip. The disgust she felt as she slid a finger over them quickly dissipated. The blood overtook it. The blood alone mattered.

She pushed herself up onto her hands and knees, and bent to lap it from the ground with her long, forked tongue. It glistened like rubies. She could see every blade of grass, watch herself lick the blood from each pine frond. Her sigh of satisfaction mingled with hundreds of others. She could hear her fellows' tongues against the grass and the pine.

Her wing joint twitched as a pine frond fell from the trees and tickled it. For the first time, she became aware of the thin, leathery wings tucked so tightly into her body they were like a second skin. She unfurled them slowly, standing up as she did so. She stretched them wide and flapped them once, sending pine needles drifting over the grass.

A man (if he could be called that any longer) near her observed her actions and copied them. The breeze from his wings wafted a new scent up Melanie's nose. Fresh blood. Living, pumping blood. She began to salivate as she looked around for the source of the smell, and she was not the only one. Her gaze fell on the huddle of children. She could see the smooth, fresh perfection of their skin. Every pigment in the eyes, hair, and skin tones popped out at her. But her eyes focused on their veins and the blood flowing within.

They stared back with petrified, open-mouthed horror. She would have them all. Needed them all. Then blue eyes, formerly tucked into the tunic of a boy she vaguely recognized, peeked around to lock with hers. Curls brushed the girl's red, puffy, tear-stained cheeks.

Tilly.

The name filled her up, dashing away desire. Her fangs retreated into her gums. She took a stride forward and then froze, hands clenched in fists. Coppery blood made her head buzz again, crushing her hopes of snatching up her daughter, stretching her new wings, and flying off into the night.

The elder vampires were forming a larger ring around the children. Melanie looked to her fellow fledglings. A good number had retracted their fangs as well, but not all. Those without a parental bond to dissuade them gazed upon the children, bending their legs into poised crouches, ready to fly at any open gaps in the ring of vampires.

"Thetis, dawn will be here in a few hours, and they must have a meal before we find shelter," said a pale-haired male vampire. "Perhaps we ought to let them have the children."

The low, venomous hiss that issued from Melanie's throat startled even her, but still she crouched low, fangs and claws bared. A particularly large fledgling male nearby uttered a ferocious growl and came to stand by Melanie's side, blocking the pale-haired vampire from the children.

"I feel that would be an unwise decision, don't you, Ricken?" said Thetis with a half-smile.

Ricken, who had taken more than one step back, nodded quickly.

"Besides," said Thetis, "until they've shown they're willing to cooperate, their meals will remain most unsatisfactory. The children will also be under constant heavy guard. Do you hear that?" Thetis turned from side to side, catching the eyes of all the fledglings. "If you wish to unlock the full potential of your new powers, you'll have to prove yourself loyal. Until then you will receive only enough blood to keep upright. In a weakened state, your children will look most appetizing. You think the desire is strong now; you think you've beaten it? Wait until their sweet, soft skin is pricked. If you try to starve yourself instead of flee, and squander the glorious gift you have been given, your child's blood will be generously spilled before you to save you from your own stupidity. Is all of this understood?"

A few more hisses jumped through the crowd of fledglings, but heads nodded in assent all around.

"Now come, my new little children, and you shall have your first blood meal!"

Thetis spread his wings and hovered a few feet above the fledglings as they tested their own. As they began to take flight, headed toward a scattering of farmhouses in the distance, Thetis glided close to Melanie.

"You, my lovely, shall fly by my side. We'll share your first meal together."

Chapter 18

A New Course

"Your escort grows impatient, Your Highness," said Gelwyn.

"Let them shuffle their feet and grumble under their breath all they like. I won't be moved," said Atalanta. "We will wait for King Marcus' reply. He was told to send his letter here, so here we must remain."

"I think they fear your father's wrath. He is no doubt anxious to have you back."

Atalanta stifled the urge to ask, "Then why didn't he come himself?" She knew it was a childish thing to think. She knew why he had not come; with her news of Tyrannus' impending threat, he had begun to gather the lords and their armies. Still, she had swiftly searched the escort of elf soldiers as they had approached three days before, looking for his crown amongst the golden helms. They had brought no letter either. The only word she received had been through the mouth of the leader of the party, who'd told her, in the dutiful but emotionless tone of a soldier, that her father was overjoyed to hear of her safe deliverance.

"They need fear nothing," she said to Gelwyn now. She sneered at the green and gold clad soldiers gathered outside the stables in the distance. "I will make sure Father knows of their incessant nagging to be gone."

"Perhaps you should tell them that … though not in exactly that way," said Gelwyn with a small smile.

She was growing quite fond of him. Though he was a commoner, he held himself with the grace and dignity of a noble, and he spoke wise council. His suggestions were just that, suggestion, never spoken in a way that implied she would be a foolish little elf child not to follow them, as the lords on the royal council always spoke to her.

"I shall, so long as they leave me in peace for the rest of this day," said Atalanta, returning his smile.

Gelwyn's face suddenly soured, and Atalanta followed his gaze to watch Andrew emerge in the main square, leading Bree along by the hand. The young prince was properly bathed, and he had adopted elfin garb to replace his leather armor. He wore soft, dark-green breeches and a tan tunic that revealed the V of his throat and a bit of his collar bone. A thin white scar marred his skin just at the collar of the shirt. His hair, though clean and shiny, was still rather rumpled, sticking out at odd ends in a wild, black halo about his head. His top lip was a bit too thin to match his bottom, and his right eye was just slightly smaller than his left—an almost imperceptible difference, but still blatantly obvious to her keen elvish eye. Bree didn't seem to mind any of his imperfections. Her cheeks blushed with color and her fingers remained wrapped firmly around his. Atalanta herself was beginning to see the appeal of humans' imperfect beauty. Each of them was so unique, with their asymmetrical faces, mismatched heights, and drastically different body shapes. Even within the same family, their differences were far more than just varying tones of hair, eye, and skin color. Michael, for instance, was much broader than his younger brother, though Andrew was threatening to outdo him in height. Michael was sturdier, with rounded shoulders and thick limbs that kept him planted firmly to the ground, while Andrew seemed to skip slightly with every few steps, light as a bird on its toes just before flight. Though they had the same eye color, Michael's eyes were wider, more rounded, and they held a calm assuredness, a warmth, that nearly put her in a trance when he fixed them on her.

Shouts from the eastern side of the village caused Atalanta to shake her head and come back to herself. Just as she realized the shouts were announcing the arrival of a man on horseback,

Michael flew from Gelwyn's house just behind her and raced toward the noise. Andromeda stuck her head out the window, her washed hair draping over the bark in a perfectly straight, unbroken sheet as she watched him run. She, too, had adopted elfin clothing, borrowing a dark-blue, cotton dress, embroidered with white flowers on the bodice from Bree. Andromeda's body type suited the slim, plain cut of elvish dresses far better than Felicity's. Felicity had been grumbling for a week about the lack of corsets and the tight fit of Mendaline's dresses, which strained so hard over her bosom they threatened to split down the middle. Her curly blonde head appeared next to her sister's.

"Lord be praised," Felicity said, tracking Michael's progress out of the village and into the surrounding meadow. "I'll go fetch my armor."

Michael met the horseman a few yards from the outskirts of the village. He recognized the man by the crest (two black stallions rampant on a field of blue) on his saddle blanket even before he removed his helm. Marcus had deemed to send a knight rather than an ordinary messenger. He had taken Michael's warnings seriously, then. Michael inwardly swelled with pride.

"Sir Boris Cavalry," said Michael with a respectful bow of the head, "you've come quite a ways. I thank you for being so swift."

Sir Boris saluted by pressing his right fist above his heart and bowing as best he could while ahorse.

"The king advised me of the urgency. Is it really true, Your Highness? Vampires and werewolves rising again."

"It would take nothing less to snatch Sir Gregor from this world," said Michael. "I know the two of you were as brothers. It should come as no surprise to you that he died with incredible honor, the only man to stand and protect me and my siblings."

"Aye, that was Gregor. Thank you, Your Highness, for your kind words, but it seems that Avalon children need very little protecting. The four of you have become something of legends back home. First, you slay the vampire at the ball, and now your father has told everyone of your rescue of the elf princess."

"She is another who doesn't need much saving," said Michael.

"To have survived so long in such malicious hands, I have no doubt. Still, you and your brother and sisters are being heralded as the heroes of this new war. Your names are spoken with awe amongst the commoners."

"Father has told the people of Tyrannus and his army?"

"Against the council of a good number of his wise men. He said to conceal it would only work to betray their trust. If this Tyrannus monster plans to act on his threats, they will be sure to find out eventually. He saw no reason to deceive them. I and most of his knights agreed. He is a man of sound leadership, your father."

"Yes, most assuredly. I hope he's sent instructions. I could use his leadership now."

Sir Boris withdrew a scroll from his cloak and held it out to Michael. "I have another for the elf king, if you'll let me ride with you to the palace."

"We would be honored," said Michael, holding the letter tightly, rubbing a thumb over his father's signet ring seal. "Follow me into the village and cool your mount. Our hosts have been most accommodating. I will see to it you are shown the same courtesies."

"I have never seen elves up close," said Boris as he rode at an even walk beside Michael. "The only time I've ever caught a glimpse was when that messenger showed up after the vampire attack."

"They're all quite easy to look at," said Michael, "though you shouldn't expect them to look at you with the same curiosity."

Boris went slack-jawed at the sight of so many beautiful beings and their magnificent houses.

"Are those ...?"

"Living trees? Yes. Incredible aren't they?" said Michael.

Boris only nodded, eyes wide.

"Excellent," said Atalanta, approaching with a soft smile, "now I won't have to suffer the whining of my father's men any longer."

"Boris, this is Princess Atalanta," said Michael.

"Your Highness," said Boris, sliding from his horse and moving gracefully down onto bended knee, "I am glad you have been found alive and well. My prince has spoken of your bravery and resilience."

"Please rise, dear knight," said Atalanta, gesturing him upward with a hand. "You are a knight, yes? That is the nature of your colorings?"

"Yes, Sir Boris Cavalry, Your Highness," said the knight, rising slowly. "I bear a second message from my king to your father. Will you allow me to ride with you and deliver it by hand so that I might extend my king's courtesies?"

"So long as you do not incessantly nag me as that lot has done," — she jabbed a thumb in the direction of a closely knit party of tall, male elves in green and gold— "I'll be happy to have you ride right at my side, Sir Boris."

Boris held himself higher as he chanced a look at the elf escort and said, "To ride at your side, I would speak of any subject or remain utterly silent for as long as Your Highness wished."

Atalanta assessed him top to bottom, a hand on her hip, and finding the flattery genuine, granted him a bright, shimmering smile of those impossibly white teeth.

Michael hid a grin at the expression on Sir Boris' face and ducked into Gelwyn's home, carrying the message from his father. He rushed up the stairs and into the now-familiar study with its view of the wheat fields on the south side of the village. He sat at the chair growing from the floor and unrolled the scroll on the fat, bowed limb that served as a desk.

Dearest Michael,

Your letter has delivered an odd mix of emotions. I am relieved to hear that you and your brother and sisters are safe. When I didn't receive any word of your whereabouts, as planned, I sent a scouting party for you, and what they found has left your mother sick of heart for nearly a fortnight. At last the color has returned to her face. I myself have had many a sleepless night, but with no sign of my darlings in the gruesome scene, I held onto the hope of you powering onward, determined to complete your goal. And so you have. The four of you have made your father a proud man, and you have brought glory to your house and your kingdom.

But it seems all of our hardships are far from over. The people do not wish to believe that vampires and werewolves survived the Extermination, and to hear that they have taken up a common banner has caused some of my counsel to stomp their feet like the stubborn old men they are and insist that my children's young minds have exaggerated the terrors they've faced. They point to the fact that you have not seen the beast who's dubbed himself Tyrannus with your own eyes. They say you've been swayed by the deceit of an elf. But the blustering of old men has seldom swayed me, and their insult has been duly noted and brought to their attention. I think it's time for fresh faces around me.

Know, my son, that though it chills me to my very bones, I believe your every word. I have already taken steps to prepare the kingdom. Barion is being fortified as I sit to write this. As soon as the ink has dried on this parchment, I shall write summons to all of my lords, so that we might prepare for battle. I'm sending a letter for King Zanthus Galechaser along with Sir Boris as well, to let him know that should Tyrannus move on the elves first, as he's already taken the step to kidnap Atalanta, my army shall join him on his soil.

I've also noted that I hope he will make the same promise to me. I have no doubt that, thanks to you and your siblings, he will not hesitate. I have sent a large garrison to the Northern Wood to take care of the raiding party you spoke of. At a time like this, I cannot have our people plagued by soulless humans alongside Diseased Ones, especially not those so deplorably morally destitute as to ally themselves with the beasts. I have given explicit instruction that the one named Brock is to be kept alive for your wanderer friend, Erro. Please convey my deepest thanks to the boy for his heroics in the goblin tunnels. I've no doubt the lad will find his name in storybooks should this war end fairly.

Though your mother will attempt to have my head when she finds out I've said it, I would have you stay your course and journey all the way to Alatreon. If the elf princess is half as fair as you've described, I'm sure you'll have no complaints.

Tell Andrew to keep shooting true. Tell Felicity to keep her cool and trust in her own strength. Tell Andromeda to keep her wits, but trust her heart. And you, Michael, lead them well and keep them safe. I am proud of all of you and love you dearly. We shall fight this to the end.

With deepest love,
Your Father

"Just how fair did you describe me?"

Michael jumped so violently he nearly fell off the chair. Atalanta took a light step back from where she'd been looking over the top of his head. He looked back at her, his mouth open in surprise and his forehead creased with embarrassed irritation. She smiled coyly at him, arms crossed easily under her chest.

"Do you make a habit of lurking over people's shoulders? Or do you just have a particular interest in me?" he said, letting go of the scroll so that it snapped back into a loose roll.

Atalanta leaned her head to one side, and the coy expression slid off into a neutral one. "I don't mean to pry, but you humans' hearing is just so poor. You never hear me come in, and well, then it's just too tempting."

"If that was meant to be an apology, you really ought to practice more," said Michael, spinning around on the chair to fix his annoyance directly on her.

"You are very lucky to have a father like that," she said, staring unabashedly back at him.

Michael blinked, taken aback. "What?"

"See what I mean about human hearing?" said Atalanta with an upward roll of her eyes. "I said, you are very lucky to have a father like that. One with so much faith in you and your abilities that he would defy his council. One who trusts you to leave the palace and have your own experiences, to make your own way."

Michael's expression turned quizzical, but he tried to hide it with a smile. "It took a good deal of persuasion for him and our mother to allow us to join the search party meant to find you."

"Still, he let you go. Did he not?"

Michael nodded.

"And he cares for you all a great deal."

"Do not all fathers care for their children?"

"Perhaps, but not all of them know how to show it. Not all speak such tender words so freely." She broke eye contact with him, her eyes flicking down to the rough floor, and the question on Michael's face deepened. After a deep breath, she looked back at him. "As I said, you are lucky."

"Yes, I suppose so."

"Most of the day is gone. We might do well just to stay here another night, but I doubt I'll be able to hold the escort off any longer now that your father's letter has arrived."

"The sooner we make it to your palace the better, is my thought," said Michael. "From there we can actually begin working on a plan of action to stop Tyrannus."

"I'll let the escort know," said Atalanta. "They'll be most pleased." She didn't sound as though that particular fact pleased her.

* * *

The cave above the small cove was packed so tightly with hard, cold bodies that Melanie could touch someone else by half-extending her arm in any direction. It was a relief to shove her way to the lip of the cave and shake her wings free. She took off into the brand new night, still a shimmering grey with clouds clearly visible. But though the cool night breeze blew her hair around her as she flew, she couldn't feel its touch on her face. The momentary pleasure of stretching her joints was short lived. Thetis appeared at her side, his oceanic eyes soaking her in as always. He was always there, adding to her constant torture. It was not enough that he'd taken her life and her soul and made her into a monster; not enough that on that first night he'd forced her to make the kill that would feed her, but then drank half the meal before allowing her to partake, keeping her belly groaning with hunger; but he also had to follow her around like a stalking cat, circling her with eyes filled with a hunger of a different kind, reaching out his hand to touch her, laughing and hurting her every time she flinched away from it.

She ignored him, but her thoughts didn't turn to happier things. Her hands found her stomach, no longer round and full of life, but perfectly flat and toned. It had shrunk rapidly, the vampire venom eating away at any imperfections, injuries, and dead tissues. She sank into the familiar sorrow and wallowed in it. At least there she could think back on what her life had been. She could remember Joseph. She could remember that she'd been sure the new baby was a boy, and had thought perhaps they would name him after his father. She could remember Tilly happy and innocent—when only beautiful thoughts took up space in her head. Thoughts of Tilly hurt most. She was still alive, still needed her mother, but Melanie could not touch her or hold her close. She would never do those things again.

If not for Tilly, Melanie would have attempted suicide. She wouldn't really be killing herself, would she? She was already dead, and by destroying the shell she now lived in, she could save the lives of others. But if she was gone, Thetis and the others would have no need for Tilly. The thought was moot anyway. Constantly surrounded by the flock, the lengths it took to kill a vampire were too great to achieve undetected. A man had been caught just two days ago trying to fashion a stake for himself. They had ripped apart everything but his chest, and kept only his head still attached. It had taken him a very long time to regrow what was lost. Thetis had explained to the other fledglings that this was because he hadn't been properly fed, and he assured them the same thing would happen to any of them should they attempt to squander the gift they'd been given.

Still, a small group of childless fledglings had made a break for freedom the very next night. The werewolves had surrounded the children to keep the others from getting any ideas, while the elder vampires swarmed the escapees. The sounds of vampire battle were like mountains and oceans clashing, sending rubble hurtling to the ground and tearing the very earth asunder. The thundering and the tearing and the shrieking didn't last long, though. The weakened fledglings had stood little chance. Their lesson had been taught with the agony of severed limbs, and Melanie guessed such a thing would not be attempted again any time soon. She herself saw no point in running. As Thetis had said just before he'd taken her humanity, where could she go? What could she do?

What could she do even now, as they flew toward an unsuspecting village? She had tried to stop her hunger that first night, had tried to turn and fly away when Thetis held out the screaming woman toward her in one hand. He'd shaken her lightly, like a doll, in Melanie's face, taunting her. She'd looked into the woman's eyes and seen the terror there. Had seen her own reflection in the brown irises. With her mouth a spiny maw of massive teeth and her eyes wild, she was a bloodthirsty beast, and the woman had screamed to the very end, when the animalistic urge took over and Melanie had sunk her fangs into the soft neck.

Tonight would be no different. Although, perhaps tonight she could fight Thetis off and drink her fill. At least then the life would not go to waste. She might be strong enough to free herself just long enough to fashion a stake. But what of Tilly? Yes, what of Tilly. Even if she was strong enough to fight off the horde of werewolves and vampires and escape with her daughter, what was to keep her from sucking her own daughter dry? True, she'd retracted her fangs that first night, but she hadn't actually had Tilly in her arms then.

Another small flock approached from their daytime hiding place to join the main group, gliding on an air current. Melanie could see the group of werewolves standing in a loose formation a few miles up ahead, right where they had left them that morning. Beyond that, if Melanie narrowed her eyes, she could easily make out the shapes of a village. But the houses looked odd somehow. It was hard to tell from this distance.

"Tonight is a very special occasion," Thetis said loudly so that as many as possible could hear and pass on the news. "For both the young and old among us. From tonight onward, my friends, we dine on elves."

* * *

As the sun sank, the cool breeze that had just an hour ago been refreshing and pleasant became mildly uncomfortable. It was nothing compared to Atalanta's frigid stare. She waved her arms about as she shouted, "That is the most foolish thing I've ever heard. You cannot order me to do any such thing. Just who do you think you are?"

"I've told Your Highness many times, I am Galen, son of Dolan Highcliff, Lord of Hellena," said the leader of the royal escort, his lips pouted in a sour, almost petulant expression. "I am of noble blood, sent to your father for service in my youth, now elevated head of Alatreon's guard and entrusted with overseeing your father's most delicate and important matters."

To Andromeda, the fair-haired elf seemed much too young to hold such a lofty title as Head Guard, but age was hard to tell with elves. Mendaline looked as though she could be Bree's sister, not her mother.

"Yes, I've heard you drone on about your bloodline and your servitude and your titles enough," said Atalanta. "Would you like me to spout mine? I am Princess Atalanta Galechaser, daughter of High King Zanthus Galechaser and Her Late Beloved Majesty Queen Iovanna Galechaser, heir to the throne of Alatreon, the head of the elvish realm. I think perhaps I outrank you, dear Galen. Don't let my age fool you. I will not follow you blindly because you are a brave, important soldier. You are a fool if you think heading off into the night instead of waiting until morning is going to grant us any headway or save us any time in reaching the palace. When a horse twists its ankle in an unseen hole or wolves or some other predator begin to stalk our party, would you then at last admit your flawed judgment? Something tells me you would not, and I'm not going to let it get that far. We rest here one more night and start fresh in the morning, by my order. Understood, little soldier?"

Galen's nod was tight and his expression stiff. "Understood, Highness."

"At last! He speaks sense!"

Galen and his fellow guardsmen had finally looked a bit lively when Atalanta told them the letter from King Marcus had arrived and that they could try to press on toward the palace for the few hours they had until dusk. However, getting the party together had taken a good deal longer than expected. First, everyone had to be rounded up. Andrew was nowhere to be found. Neither was Bree. Felicity was out on a horseback ride by the stream a few miles away. Aquila and Zezil were off enjoying the countryside as well, and Erro had no way of calling them back. When at last everyone was gathered, properly dressed, and sufficiently packed, dusk was less than an hour away, and then Atalanta discovered that the escort, though so eager to get moving, hadn't gathered up their supplies. They'd used the food and water they'd brought and hadn't bothered to stock their bags with more. Her berating of their competence had only made them sullen and harder pressed to get moving, but they'd only just gathered their things and the sun was only a crescent hovering above the horizon line.

"Head of the City Guard, pah!" said Atalanta shaking her head so that her hair danced about her shoulders. "There's only one reason my father would make a dolt like that head of the guard. Politics! Always politics. Dolan Highcliff rules one of the largest provinces. My father probably owed him some sort of favor as well. At least he didn't make him head of the Royal Guard, or I should fear for his life with that blundering idiot in charge of his safety."

"Easy there, heir of Alatreon," said Erro. "Don't hurt yourself. He got the point. We're leaving tomorrow. No harm done."

Atalanta wrinkled her nose in a childish expression of annoyance, and for a moment Erro was sure she'd stick her tongue out at him, but she didn't. Instead, she shook out her arms, wiggling her fingertips, and sucked in a slow breath that pulled in her thin nostrils.

"Finding your inner peace?" said Erro.

She fixed him with half-lidded eyes. "Yes, and you would be wise not to interrupt me until I do."

"What did Father say, Michael?" said Felicity. "In all the

chaos, I forgot to even ask."

Michael pulled out the scroll, and they all huddled around him to read it.

"Just how fair did you say she was?" said Felicity with a smirk.

Michael only sighed.

"Little did the lot of you know you were travelling with a storybook hero," said Erro, straightening his back and bouncing on the balls of his feet as he gave Andromeda his best comically sultry look.

"He said nothing about you being the hero of the book," said Andrew, shoving Erro with his shoulder.

Night fell suddenly, from a dreary gray into darkness, as the sun dipped below a far hill, and the companions retreated into Gelwyn's home in light spirits. Andrew and Erro played a game of marbles while Andromeda read from a book of elvish lore close by. Felicity helped Bree and Mendaline make supper, though she had very little experience in matters of the kitchen and mostly served as a taste-tester. Michael and Atalanta talked easily with Gelwyn about farming and fighting and any subject that came to mind.

"That was a spectacular display of cheating," said Andrew, as Erro knocked the last of his marbles from the ring, winning the game.

"Why thank you, good sir!" said Erro, jumping up from the floor to take a bow.

"Best I've seen in all my years, good fellow. I mean it," said Andrew, rising to shake Erro's hand.

"It's an art, I find," said Erro, straightening the sleeves of his tunic.

Andromeda's book hit the floor, and an instant later, Aquila barreled into the house, screeching, knocking over a potted plant with the tip of his wing.

"Aquila! Where are your manners?" said Erro.

Zezil wriggled out from between Aquila's front paws and barked urgently.

"Get your weapons!" said Andromeda.

"What is it?" said Michael.

"He doesn't know exactly. He only senses evil intent. But I'll give you two guesses."

"Gelwyn, is there a safe place in the village, somewhere fortified that everyone can hide?" said Atalanta.

"I'm afraid not, Your Highness," said Gelwyn. "What's going on? The griffin has sensed something? Something coming here?"

"Somethings," said Andromeda. "We have to warn everyone. We're going to have to fight."

"I'll alert the village."

Aquila stepped aside to let Gelwyn past him and knocked into a dresser.

"Get out of here, you great feathery thing," said Erro, rubbing Aquila on the head even as he pushed him toward the door. "You've given your message. We'll be ready for them."

The Avalons rushed up the stairs to retrieve their weapons from the bedroom they'd all crammed into each night. Erro, whose daggers never left his belt, and Atalanta, who had no weapons, stayed in the foyer with Mendaline and Bree. Mendaline wrung her hands and stared at the doorway where her husband had just vanished. Bree hovered around the window, looking for the approaching danger.

Andrew was the first back down the steps.

"Any sign of them yet?" he asked.

Bree whipped around with a degree of relief on her face at his return in full battle gear. Then a clawed arm shattered the window behind her and snatched at her hair. At her scream, Andrew leapt over the last three stairs and released his silver stake from its cylindrical holder. Bree met him in the middle of the foyer and pushed him back with her small hands on his chest.

"Get back to the stairwell," she said. "Everyone!"

Aquila screeched again, but he sounded far away.

"Bree, we've fought vampires before," said Andrew. "You and your mother get upstairs."

Andrew's siblings were thundering down the stairs behind him, weapons raised, but Bree flung up a hand, her face set in a hard, commanding expression.

A heavy shoulder was beating against the door, and the vampire poked its head through the small window, assessing the room.

"Get back!" The force of her command made Andrew take an automatic step backward. "Stay there!" she said.

Erro and Atalanta pressed themselves into the back wall, careful not to disturb the herb garden planted there.

Bree pushed past her mother, ignoring her protests, and held out her hand to the cooking fire.

The door fell forward on its hinges and one man, one woman, and one male vampire swarmed the home.

"Ignis displodere!" she said.

The hot embers exploded into a roaring blaze that shot out of the hearth and toward the intruders, directed by Bree's hand. Andrew felt the heat wave given off by the monstrous blaze and feared for Bree, but the fire did not touch her or any part of the house. It swirled around her, leaving her in a circle untouched by flame. It leapt over the window frame, and never touched the walls or floor. But the oncoming enemies were engulfed, and their horrendous screams were the first to pierce the night.

Chapter 19

The Fall of Campion

The heat of the flame brought bright red apples into Andrew's cheeks, and he stepped further back into the stairwell. Two of the intruders—clothes, hair, and skin ablaze—stumbled from the home in a wild bid to douse the flames, but the vampire kept coming, and Bree was out of fire. She was panting hard, hands on her knees, unable to move. The vampire, skin melting and reforming, forced his feet forward one after the other. Michael's arm brushed Andrew's head as he thrust it forward, the device on his arm aimed at the vampire's chest. He made a fist to let the stake fly, and it found its home. With a final cry, the vampire fell face down. The flames continued to crackle over the corpse.

"By the Great Mothers," said Atalanta, "just how old are you, Bree?"

"Twenty."

"That cannot be."

"She is very gifted," said Mendaline. "She could perform magic at birth. She completed the Trial of the Elements at twelve."

Atalanta moved toward Bree, scanning her up and down. She shook her head, bemused, and said, "Tyrannus picked the wrong elf."

"Sorry, but I don't understand," said Bree, righting herself but still breathing heavily.

"Nothing."

The screams started coming through the window, just as Aquila shoved his head through it.

"We have to go help," said Erro, running out the door.

He jumped on Aquila's back and looked to Andromeda before rising into the sky to hover just above the houses. Andromeda followed him with her eyes, and her jaw went slack. "My God," she murmured.

The village was lit by torches on the sides of doorways and sitting in windows. Black shapes flickered in and out of their orange glow. Black, beating wings. Figures alighted on rooftops. Other wingless figures ran through the streets. A black shape slammed into Aquila, and he and Erro nearly crashed into Gelwyn's roof. Aquila righted himself as Erro's dagger slashed through a wing. With his claws, Aquila gripped the other wing and swung the vampire into the ground.

"Aquila, we can't fight up here," said Erro, as Andromeda staked the vampire below him.

Aquila's paws hadn't reached the ground when three werewolves in human form charged the small party with weapons raised. One had a sword, one had a small dagger, and the last had only a makeshift knife made of a piece of jagged iron. A figure in chainmail charged into the sword-wielding foe like a silver shimmering bull.

"You must get to safety, Your Highnesses," said Sir Boris, swinging his sword down in a killing blow, only to be blocked by the fallen man's sword. "The whole village is swarming with them."

"We cannot flee," said Michael, slashing his sword down into the shoulder of the dagger-wielding man. "We must help the elves."

Across the street, a small elf girl shrieked as a vampire took off into the night with her. Andromeda and Atalanta looked over as one. The mother clawed at the face of the man holding her roughly by the hair.

"Erro, the child!" said Andromeda.

"Already on it." Aquila's wing brushed Andromeda's cheek as he took off.

"Wait! Take this!" Andromeda tossed her stake into the air, where it met Erro's outstretched hand. "Be careful!" But he was already just a gold streak in a sea of black.

Atalanta was already across the street when Andromeda tore her eyes from Erro. She had the man in an unforgiving headlock while the elf woman kicked at his torso. A battered and bloodied elf ran from the home and sank a scythe into the man's chest, but it was not silver. Andromeda finished the job just as Atalanta's escort surrounded them.

"Give me a weapon, and then protect the villagers," Atalanta yelled at Galen.

Galen moved into the protective circle and handed Atalanta a sword. She looked at it in disbelief.

"This is not silver!" she said. "Did my father heed none of my warnings?"

"He sent us to you immediately, Your Highness. There was no time for forging new weapons."

"How are you to fight werewolves with this?"

"Werewolves do not regrow like vampires, princess," said the elf who was now clutching his sobbing wife close. "There is little they can do without a head … or legs."

Atalanta stared hard at the bloody blade of his scythe.

"Fair point. But do you have stakes? How will you fight the vampires?"

"Yes, how?" said a voice from above. The female vampire chuckled and snatched up a royal soldier by his mail, her claws sinking into his neck. He screamed as she flew off with him into the night.

"We must get you out of here, princess," said Galen, his face ashen.

"And leave my people to die?" said Atalanta, her enraged face inches from Galen's.

"We will all die if we do not flee."

Aquila crashed to the ground outside the ring of soldiers, and Erro rolled off into the dirt road, something clutched to his chest. Aquila's front paw was injured, and he rose unsteadily.

Erro was bleeding from the shoulder, but he had a smile on his face. The elf girl was cradled in his arms. Her mother shoved her way past the soldiers.

"Thank you, bless you," she said as Erro handed over the child.

Aquila jumped in front of a charging vampire that flew in with her claws outstretched toward Erro. Andromeda looked to Atalanta as the two creatures grappled.

"Atalanta," she said, her eyes displaying her hatred of her own words, "I think he's right this time. There are too many of them. We must do what we can, but we must go. There is a bigger battle to come."

Atalanta tilted back her head and surveyed the other girl as a range of emotions crossed her face: rage, denial, sadness, and finally defeat.

"We fight for as long as we can, and we take whomever we can with us when we go. Start gathering the others, and then we'll head for the western end of the village."

* * *

If beauty had a taste, Melanie thought as she soared above the destruction of Campion with a female elf wrapped in a deadly lover's embrace, it would be this. The elf's blood was ambrosial. It held a subtle flowery scent; it tasted cleaner, and the sharp coppery tang was muted. It was over too quickly. Thetis had sucked the elf mostly dry before handing her over. Around her, she could see other fledglings feeding, carefully watched and protected from any attack by an elder vampire. Most had to share the kill with the elder vampire and another fledgling. Thetis wanted to capture as many elves as possible instead of slaying them. But he did not make Melanie share with anyone but himself.

Melanie carefully laid the elf woman down on the street, a

tightness in her throat. "I'm sorry," she whispered.

Thetis' claws raked her cheek. "Such weakness," he said with a soft hiss. "I'll tolerate it no longer."

Melanie's muscles tensed like springs, but she kept still.

"Come, stick close to my side. Some of these elves will surely be skilled with magic. They are already putting up a more resilient fight than the humans."

Melanie looked up and down the lane as she pumped her wings twice, vaulting herself into the air after Thetis. A few dead werewolves were slumped against homes and face down in the street. Most had been dismembered, their heads severed. No silver needed. It was not the full moon, and their powers were weakened. In the next street over, a vampire lay dead with a crudely and quickly fashioned wooden stake pounded through his heart. Ashes blew in the breeze a few houses down.

Melanie saw an elf running through the streets with a sharpened tree branch in his hand. She considered swooping down and baring her fangs at him before Thetis could stop her. The elf would drive the crude stake home and end the misery.

But she couldn't do that. Because of Tilly. Besides, she was beginning to realize that the dull continuous ache in her belly was mostly assuaged. She felt almost … good. Her muscles felt tighter, stronger. The elf blood was more potent. Since she'd been changed, she had been able to think of little else but her hunger and her pain. Not anymore. But just what good would it do her?

* * *

Gelwyn nearly mowed Atalanta down as she ran down the street in front of her trailing escort, her eyes scanning for Michael, Felicity, and Andrew, with Andromeda at her side and Erro hovering just above her atop Aquila.

"Gelwyn, get your family," said Atalanta, grabbing the elf's upper arm to steady him and command his focus. "We must make our way to Alatreon. We must leave here. And you must come with us."

Sadness carved lines in the elf's flawless face. "I ... I know, Your Highness. But I don't know where they are."

"We'll find them, and then we head west under cover of darkness and don't look back," said Atalanta. "Stick close. We mustn't get separated."

The royal escort moved into a semi-circle around the two princesses and Gelwyn as a werewolf and vampire came charging in from the left. The werewolf crashed into the golden shields and met three different blades, but the vampire spiraled overhead and swooped back in from the right. Erro met her with Andromeda's stake. As she crumbled into ash in midair, Erro put his fingers to his lips and whistled.

"Zezil! Zezil, come!" Erro looked down at Andromeda, worried. "He doesn't respond to me when he's transformed. We have to find him."

"Maybe he wasn't in the village. Maybe he was out in the meadow," said Andromeda. She closed her eyes for a brief moment. "Aquila is searching for him."

Aquila rose higher, threatening to collide with a swooping vampire, but his head twitched to the north, and he dipped his right wing to veer in that direction.

"Meet us at the western border of the village!" Andromeda called after him.

"There's Andrew!" said Atalanta. "And Bree."

Andromeda turned to look, only to find herself staring at a raised blade and the crazed face of a bearded werewolf. She ducked to the left, and moved to counter with her sword, but a silver-tipped arrow embedded itself in his back with a dull thunk.

Andrew was crouched on the roof of Bree's home, expertly sending arrows into the chaos, his arm moving in a steady rhythm—up and back to his sheath, forward to string the bow, and back again to draw it. His quiver was nearly out, but the bodies of werewolves littered the street. Bree stood behind him on the roof, beckoning the wind to do her bidding with her hands. Each time a vampire flew toward them, she sent it spinning backward end over end with a powerful gust of air.

"Andrew," said Andromeda, cupping her hands near her mouth as she yelled over the din, "come down!"

He put the arrow he held back in his quiver, beckoned Bree to follow him, and disappeared on the other side of the roof. He and Bree ran out of the doorway a few moments later with Mendaline in between them. Gelwyn caught Mendaline in an embrace, but looked to his daughter as he spoke.

"We must flee to Alatreon," he said. "Campion is lost."

A vampire grabbed a royal guard by his thin, gold chest plate and soared off with him into the night. Bree turned away from the screaming, twisting elf who was trying to hack at the vampire with his sword, and fixed frightened eyes on her father.

"We cannot leave the others defenseless," she said.

"We cannot stay," said Gelwyn, reaching out a hand to touch his fingers to her cheek.

"Let me give them one last defense, and then I will go. Not before."

Gelwyn nodded, but Atalanta stepped forward. "Bree, you mustn't draw too much attention to yourself. The creature that commands these beasts is looking for an elf that he can force to perform magic, and your abilities surpass that of most elder elves."

"I need only say a few words, Your Highness," said Bree, "but it will drain me. I may need assistance in fleeing."

"You'll have it," said Andrew, touching her hand.

"Do it," said Atalanta.

Bree fell to her knees in the dirt and raised her hands above her head, palms up, as if in supplication. She tilted back her head and beseeched the sky.

"Venire vivus! Venire vivus!" she said, a smile lighting her face as she chanted.

The others turned from side to side, looking for the effect of the spell. It did not take long. The houses lining the street began to move. The branches framing the roofs and windows creaked and detached themselves and rose high into the air, waving in greeting. Bree continued her call until every house in sight was swaying in her direction. Then she shoved her arms out at her sides, palms facing the homes, and her chant became a battle cry.

"Oppugno! Oppugno!"

Willow branches cracked like whips and looped around the ankles and necks of werewolves and vampires, pulling them to the ground. Massive oak branches slammed the earth, crushing skulls beneath them. Even rosebushes planted in the front gardens sprang to life, snatching at the ankles of werewolves with their thorns. Massive roots broke through the ground, tripping their adversaries, and then rising up and clamping down on them, pinning them to the ground. As the others gasped and gaped at the glorious mayhem, Bree swayed on her knees. Andrew caught her before she hit the ground and picked her up, her legs dangling over his arm.

"Their homes will protect them now," she said, staring up at the sky with the smile still strong on her face.

* * *

It can't be. Melanie looked again, just barely turning her head, praying that Thetis wouldn't notice. There they were, just like their images on the small silver coins Melanie had once used to buy bread and cloth and seeds for her garden. Just like the images on the beautiful tapestries and portraits sold by travelling caravans. Prince Michael and Princess Felicity, fighting with their backs turned on each other as they maneuvered the lanes between the houses that connected the main roads. The prince had a device on his arm that shot stakes into the air above him, downing any vampire that ventured too close. They fell, screaming, onto roofs and into the streets. Some changed to ash, others aged, and some stayed the same as they died. The princess was cutting her way through werewolves with two thin swords that danced around her like flashes of starlight. Any doubt of their royalty was assuaged by the knight clad in full armor following at their heels, throwing himself in front of oncoming enemies like a loyal attack dog guarding their flank.

Melanie turned her head back to face Thetis, who was hovering lazily over the village, inspecting the progress of the capture. There were very few elves left running freely through the streets. Most were either trapped by mobs of werewolves or clamped in the iron grips of vampires, being dragged or flown from the village. Others lay face down in the road, milky white, drained of blood. But that meant the number of werewolves and vampires was diminishing, too. Soon, it would be harder for the Avalons to hide from Thetis' scouting eye in the crowd. She did not want to think of what he might do with such prize catches. Then again, perhaps they would manage to kill him. He would undoubtedly send others to do the deed anyway. She had to keep him distracted.

An idea was beginning to blossom in her recently cleared head. But for it to work, she would have to both keep Thetis from seeing or harming the royals and somehow get free of him herself. Even with the help of the elf blood, she couldn't see a way.

The magnolia branch hit Melanie first and propelled her into Thetis. Her fangs burst from her gums as she hissed at the pain in her crushed thigh bone. Her wings flapped frantically as she tried to right herself.

"What the devil is—?" Three willow branches encircled Thetis' neck as Melanie watched in disbelief. They yanked him by his neck toward the roof of the magnolia, and the fat branch slammed into his temple just as he cut away the willow branches with his claws. A root rose from the ground to pin him where he lay moaning, but healing, on the ground.

The odd tree houses were alive! She hardly gave a moment's thought to it. She did not care how. It was just what she needed. With a strong downward flap of her wings, she rose out of reach of even the longest of the willow whips. The laugh came out before she even felt it building in her throat. She pumped her wings once, then tucked them to her sides, spinning in a tight spiral back the way she had come. When she opened them again, she felt them catch an air current, and the laugh shook her belly as she propelled herself like a bullet through the slipstream.

Just how she was going to get Tilly free without anyone noticing, she didn't quite know, but she was going to try all the same.

* * *

The stables were deafening. Horses reared and stomped and kicked at their stalls, telling each other of their terror in ear-splitting brays and almost-human screams. Both stable boys were missing. Blood was sprayed against the living wood of a stall door.

"Stop!" said Atalanta, throwing out a hand to pull back one of Galen's soldiers from opening a stall. "We'll have to wait for the others before we mount. It'll be a miracle if they don't throw us off, and there's no way we'll be able to keep them still once we let them out. We don't mount until we're all ready to go."

"The steeds we brought are elvish war horses, Your Highness," said Galen, "they will not throw us. They are trained to stay steady in battle."

"Do they look steady to you?" said Atalanta, flinging a hand toward the nearest white steed that was tearing at its stall door with its teeth, its eyes bulging from both sides of its skull.

"They feel confined. They will steady in battle with their riders atop them."

"Have they been trained in battle against vampires?" said Atalanta, her voice a frustrated screech, both arms gesticulating above her head. "Have you any idea what affect the presence of vampires has on horses?"

Galen stared back at her in stony silence.

"Hush now, Lillian," said Andromeda to her horse.

The young princess had her hand outstretched toward her dappled mare, whose front hooves were beating the air above her stall door as she reared. At the sound of her rider's voice, the mare settled back into her stall, but she tossed her head, nickering nervously, dancing side to side on the hay-lined ground. Andromeda rubbed the mare's nose, crooning to her. The dancing stopped, but the nickers didn't.

Atalanta made an amused sound through her nose and crossed her arms as she leaned back and looked at Andromeda.

"If you can get your precious war horses to do that, I'll eat my shoe," she told Galen.

Andrew was trying to calm his stallion, but the great black beast was thumping its hoof against the stall and tossing its head.

"Control your mounts," Galen barked at his soldiers. He turned back to Atalanta with a sour look and said, "You'd best gather the rest of your friends, Your Highness. When the horses are ready, we move. My duty is to deliver you, no one else, and I will not linger in danger's path any longer than necessary."

Atalanta shook her head in slow-burning fury. "We'll see if you keep your title after tonight," she said under her breath before running out of the stables to look for the others.

Andromeda appeared at her side. The stables were on the far end of the village, closer to the pastures. From its doorway, the two princesses could watch the battle in the village from a slight distance. The invaders had little interest in the stables any longer. The houses were keeping them busy. The home-shaped trees swayed on their roots, branches dancing under the stars—some of them in agony. Smoke billowed up from the roofs. The demons were setting the homes ablaze.

Andromeda searched the sky for Aquila and Erro, but it was not them she saw first. Zezil leapt from a rooftop and collided with a vampire in flight. The two fell to the ground in a stunted glide, the vampire fighting to stay aloft as Zezil shredded its wings.

"There!" said Andromeda, pointing.

The golden griffin appeared between two houses, flying low, Erro on his back, his belly laid flat on the lion pelt. Aquila shoved Zezil off the vampire, but the vexar pounced the floundering leech once more. With nips of his beak and swats of his massive paws, the griffin began to coax the vexar toward the stables. Zezil snapped at Aquila's wings and legs in annoyance, but the bites seemed almost playful.

Andromeda called Zezil's name again, and the vexar stopped in his tracks and fixed his eyes on her. Then he charged full speed at her, his skeleton shrinking as he came.

"There's Michael and Felicity, and your knight," said Atalanta. "Erro must have found them."

Michael and Felicity ran with their arms pumping at their sides, their eyes on the stables. Boris ran behind them, slowed by his mail, his broadsword still raised defensively as he cast glances over his shoulder, ready to fend off any vampire that should try to swoop down on his prince and princess.

Zezil collided with Andromeda, almost knocking her down. She trapped him in her arms, where he wriggled and whined, his tongue darting out to lick her face. Aquila landed in front of them, and Erro slid off.

"Michael and Felicity are right behind me," he said.

"Literally," said Felicity, slapping Erro on the shoulder. Her nostrils flared as she sucked in gulps of air. Michael's face was red and drenched in sweat, and his expression was grave.

"I don't like it," he said. "We shouldn't just leave. They're taking them somewhere, alive. We should follow."

"I don't like it either. In fact, I hate it," said Atalanta, "but I'm sure you noticed just how many of them there are. We're far too outnumbered, and my esteemed saviors here don't even have the proper weapons."

Galen ground his teeth, but his elves were still unable to calm their horses, so he held his peace.

"You know I'm right," said Atalanta when Michael looked about to protest.

"I still don't like it," he said.

"You don't have to like it, but it has to be done."

"J—Jeremiah?" said Erro.

"What?" said Andrew.

Erro was already running back into the main street. "Jeremiah!"

The tall, dark-haired man turned with a startled expression.

"It is you!" said Erro. "What the hell are you doing here?"

Erro rushed forward with his arms out to embrace the older man, but Jeremiah thrust up a hand, and that was when Erro realized he was carrying a bloody knife.

"Don't! Please don't, boy!" he said. His face was creased in either pain or concentration. Erro could not tell which.

"Jeremiah, what's happened? Did they take you, too? Where are Fiona and Brent?" Erro came closer, and Jeremiah jumped back.

"Don't, I said! I'm under orders. I ... I can't disobey. The alpha ..." Jeremiah clenched his teeth and shut his eyes tight. "Run, Erro, run! Forget me! Don't follow me!"

Jeremiah turned on his heel and sprinted in the opposite direction.

"It really was him," said Andrew at his back, making Erro jump.

"Yes," said Erro, frowning. "Something's wrong. Very

wrong."

"Erro! Andrew!" called Andromeda's voice. "We have to go."

"Aren't we going to go get him?" said Andrew.

Tears stung Erro's eyes. "No. He's … he's one of them now."

Chapter 20

Unchained

Melanie circled the shifting crowd below. Captive elves were shunted left and right between vampires and werewolves, slowly crafting two lines. The mass of bodies seemed to breathe and take life of its own. Melanie could hear the clink and rattle of the iron shackles closing. High screeches of metal made Melanie flinch. Shackles that had been broken in her own conversion were bent back into place by brute force, and the metal screamed its displeasure. Though her eyes were attuned to the large group of captives and captors, her eyes were locked on the small circle a few yards away. She found the top of Tilly's head, the brown curls matted and wild. A smile warmed Melanie's expression when she saw her daughter's small hand wrapped around Brent's. Melanie counted only four guards on the children—all werewolves. Easy enough to overpower, but what she needed was stealth. She analyzed as she circled, but she needed to get out of the air soon. Thetis wouldn't be detained in the village forever.

Callid was dancing around the edges of the crowd. The malformed creature seemed drawn to chaos, but he rarely partook. Instead, his two mouths pulled wide in imbecilic grins, and his four eyes darted around the chaos, touching all they could and soaking it in. He'd returned the day before, always the harbinger of death. Thetis sent him out as a scout to confirm there were actually villages where Brock said there were.

Brock, too, was on the outskirts of the action, sitting atop a stolen horse, but he was not reveling. With his hands overlapped on the pommel, reins dangling loose, he cast contemplative looks at the valley around him and the small dotting of trees that hardly counted as forests in the distance on all sides. It seemed every time Melanie looked at him now, he was on the cusp of running, but he never did. Running had been proven a foolish idea. He'd seen the captives try to run. But his estimations on the location of the elf village had seemed unsure to Melanie. He used to deliver information to Thetis with his hand cocked on his hip, a thumb tucked into his breeches, raising himself up to full height as he looked the vampire directly in the eye, as if to prove to everyone he wasn't afraid. The last time, though, he'd studied the ground and stuttered over his words, only looking at Thetis when he was done, saying, "At least, it was there a few years ago." She doubted he'd ever been much farther. He was just about dry of useful information, and soon Thetis would suck him dry, just like his men. Thetis knew it. Brock knew it, but fear seemed to hold him back. Melanie wondered with only mild curiosity if he would brave it now, while his "allies" were preoccupied. She vaguely hoped that he would; it could only help her own cause.

A crackle like the sound of a fast-approaching lightning storm pulled Melanie's eyes from the children. A vampire was ablaze, wings sending up tendrils of smoke. The elf who had cast the spell was wrestled to the ground by another vampire, who clamped his hand over the elf's mouth. Melanie heard the snap of the elf's jaw. He would speak no more spells. But the others still might.

Melanie glided to the earth, landing silently next to a line of elves who were already chained. An elf with silvery blonde hair near the end of the line sensed Melanie beside her. Her head whipped around, and she staggered backward at the sight of Melanie. The elves before and behind her found Melanie with a swarm of eyes, some widened in terror and others narrowed in such fierce hate that Melanie feared magic would pour from their eyes and burn her to ash floating on the wind. But it was the fear that compressed her heart; she felt enough hate for herself already that the elves' hatred hardly mattered.

Perhaps they would hate her a little less in a moment, but it was doubtful. Nonetheless, she struck out with her hand like a viper and snatched up the chain. The silver-blonde elf opened her mouth to scream, but Melanie grabbed the chain in both hands and twisted them in opposite directions, her muscles straining in one violent, fluid movement. Before the elf could suck in enough air to unleash her scream, the chain snapped in two beneath Melanie's hands, and the elf's mouth snapped shut in surprise. The elf ogled the chain when Melanie dropped it in front of her.

"Go," said Melanie in an urgent whisper. "This is the best chance I can give you."

Melanie didn't wait to see if the elf or the five others behind her would make a bid for freedom. She slunk back into the crowd of vampires and werewolves and averted her attention from them entirely.

"Hey! Stop them!" It was a man's cry, but it was soon taken up by numerous voices.

Melanie didn't look back. Slowly, she pushed through the crowd in the opposite direction, her eyes on the ring of werewolf guards around the children. She looked back only once, when the screaming started. A vampire was ablaze. A wall of thorns had sprung from the ground and was tearing into two werewolves who tried to hack it down with swords.

Emboldened, the captive elves' battle for freedom was renewed. Those who could do magic began shouting their spells to the sky. Those who could not threw themselves in front of the spell casters, shielding them from the horde. Melanie stood aside to let the children's guards into the fray, and then she sprinted for the little ring. She pulled up short a few feet away, turning her head from the smell with her eyes closed in concentration. She held her breath and approached slowly.

"Momma?" Tilly wiggled out from between the legs of the other children.

Tilly drank in Melanie's pallid, pained face — the lips too red against the creamy, flawless, ivory flesh, free of even a blue vein. Tilly grinned. The drained face was still her mother's. Melanie kept her eyes on her daughter as she took the last few steps, still holding her breath. Her lungs were already protesting, but it hardly mattered. She could suffocate for a thousand years and never die.

The other children shrank back as Melanie crouched down and held out her arms to Tilly, and the chains around their ankles rattled. All except Brent, who hovered behind Tilly with the fingers of one hand splayed toward her like the stems of flowers reaching for the sun. He searched Melanie's face with distrust in his eyes but sorrow in the pull of his mouth.

Tilly, left unchained because no shackle fit, walked straight into Melanie's arms and entwined her fingers in her hair. Melanie clutched her to her chest, and she could hear her pulse in her neck, feel the thump of her heart against her breast. For a moment her eyes went wide and wild, and Brent's outstretched hand became a fist.

Her lungs were screaming now, but she ignored them and bit down hard on her lip, concentrating on Tilly's warmth, the tickle of her hair, not the blood in her veins. Her stomach didn't moan or rumble, and she said a silent prayer of thanks.

"My sweet Tilly," she breathed into her baby's hair, and Brent's fist uncurled.

"Where you been, Momma?" said Tilly, and Melanie felt the wet warmth of tears against her neck.

"Never far, baby," said Melanie, her throat tight. She looked to the boy she'd grown to love in just a few, short, hellish weeks. "Brent, I don't have long. You have to take Tilly and get help. The Avalons are in a village a few miles south of here."

"Is Erro with them?" Brent's face came alive with hope, and Melanie wished she had a better answer.

"Your friend? I don't know, but you have to take Tilly and

find them, Brent. Be careful. The horde is attacking the village. It won't last much longer. Wait at a safe distance and look for them. If they've come into elf territory, they'll most likely head west to Alatreon if they get the chance to flee. Tell them what's happening here. They're the best chance Arcamira has. They'll keep the both of you safe."

Brent nodded, setting his disheveled, overlong hair to bouncing on his forehead. Melanie gently extracted Tilly from her neck.

"Tilly, do you remember the stories I told you about the Avalons? How they were trained to grow up strong and brave to protect us all?" Melanie asked, a catch in her throat as she stared into Tilly's large, blue, red-rimmed eyes.

"Oh yes, Momma, I like those stories," said Tilly nodding her head vigorously.

"Brent's going to take you to see them, baby. Won't that be fun?"

Tilly wiped at a tear and smiled just a little. "Yes," she said. "I like Brent."

"That's good, baby. I like him, too. You stick close to him and obey what he says."

Melanie focused on the sounds behind her, gauging her time. There was still shouting, but the crackle of spells in the air was growing few and far between. The elves were losing, overpowered by foes who could not die. She could hear the crunch of bones as vampires crushed fingers and jaws to cripple the spell casters.

"Okay, Momma, but can't you come see the princes and princesses, too?" asked Tilly, hugging Melanie's middle.

"No, Tilly, Momma can't come this time. I'm sorry," said Melanie, her eyes stinging, no longer able to produce the tears that would be rolling down her cheeks. "You'll have to be a big girl and go without me."

Tilly hugged Melanie tighter and began to cry anew. "I'm

tired of being a big girl."

"Oh, but, Tilly, big girl's get to have big adventures," said Brent, and Melanie, who could not speak for the ball of grief lodged in her throat, looked at him gratefully. "We'll have fun."

Tilly turned her head to look at Brent, and the boy drew a step closer, his hands held out. Melanie, who had forgotten not to breathe, sucked in a gasp, and a hand flew to her mouth. "Stop, Brent!"

Brent froze, and Melanie fought to draw the fangs back into her gums, shielding the sight of them from Tilly.

"Momma?" Tilly's voice was scared and high, too high. Melanie hushed her, feeling the fangs slide backward.

"You have to go now," said Melanie.

Brent's shackles were fastened so tight around his ankles that they bit into his skin. Melanie held her breath and beckoned Brent to her.

Brent moved as slow as he dared, his eyes on the chaos behind Melanie. With two mighty tugs, she mangled the shackles enough that he could step free of them. Beneath, his skin was raw and bloody. She turned away with a low hiss, and Brent yanked down his tattered pants legs as far as they would go before stepping back.

Melanie hugged Tilly and focused on her familiar weight in her arms, calming herself. She bent with care and kissed both rosy cheeks.

"I love you, Tilly."

"I love you, too, Momma."

"Go with Brent now. You two will have lots of fun, hmm?"

She gently pushed Tilly toward Brent, who picked her up and propped her expertly on one hip.

"Goodbye, Melanie," said Brent.

She could see in his eyes that he knew the truth. She would probably never hold her daughter again. When the Avalons came with their armies, they would slay her, too, and that was for the best.

"I won't ever forget you. I'll keep her safe, I promise."

"Thank you, Brent," said Melanie, wishing she could hug him, too. "Go, hurry!"

Brent didn't hesitate. He ran without turning back, Tilly bouncing on his hip, held securely against his body as he headed for the nearest rise in the valley so that he could disappear behind it. Melanie stood transfixed by Tilly's eyes peering over Brent's shoulder. One little hand stretched out behind him, and the fingers opened and closed in a wave. Melanie waved goodbye, her chest shaking with unvoiced sobs.

"Miss?"

Melanie took three quick steps back as the girl took one toward her.

"What about us?" She couldn't be more than ten. A slightly older girl stepped out of the ring and snatched her back.

Melanie shook her head and unfurled her wings. There was no way. It would be a miracle if she didn't harm one of them, and someone was bound to notice rather quickly if the whole group disappeared. No, it was better for Tilly if the others stayed put.

"I'm sorry," she said, and launched herself into the sky to keep an eye on Tilly and Brent for as long as she dared.

* * *

The smell of hay and manure was cloying as the heat of gathered bodies warmed the stables. Erro leaned into Andromeda's comforting touch as he recounted his interaction with Jeremiah.

"He's one of them. A werewolf, I think," he said.

"You can't be sure of that," said Andromeda, but she chewed at her bottom lip.

"What else makes sense?" said Erro. "He was armed. He'd hurt someone. He wouldn't come with me. And he said something about ... the alpha, or something strange like that."

A line of worry appeared between Andromeda's brows. "The alpha?"

"Your Highnesses, we must leave now!" said Galen. "We are all accounted for, yes?"

"Unfortunately, he's right," said Atalanta. She put a hand on Erro's forearm. "I'm sorry. Jeremiah was a good man."

"Prepare to mount, whether you've saddled or not!" said Galen, relief easing the sharp lines of frustration on his face.

The horses were quieting in the presence of friendly voices and gentle touches, and all were saddled, if somewhat shoddily. As Andromeda ran through the stables to Lillian, she saw a loosely knotted girth strap and thought the elf would be lucky to stay upright for more than a few paces. No time to fix it. When the village was cleared of elves, the werewolves at least would most likely come looking for the horses.

Andrew lifted Bree into the saddle first while the stall door was still closed She still looked unnaturally pale, but her eyes were open and aware, and she gripped the stallion's mane when Andrew released the latch on the stall door. The taste of freedom was too much for the horse, and it tried to bolt. Andrew planted his heels and tried to hold it back, pulling the horses' head sideways as he yanked on the left rein, but his boots slid across the hay strewn floor. Shifting his momentum, he ran at the horse instead of pulling against it, gripping the pommel and hoisting himself up before the stallion could pick up too much speed. Settled behind Bree, he let the stallion have its head, leading the herd.

The others didn't have any more luck with their steeds—all save Andromeda who had the unfair advantage of being able to read her horse's moods and predict its actions. Still, when Andrew made his headcount they were all there, riding low against their horses' necks, cloaks pulled up and heads bent, trying to hide from the malignant eyes in the sky.

* * *

Run, darlings, run. Just a little bit further.

Brent had been forced to set Tilly down halfway to the nearest knot of trees. The boy was weak from hunger and endless days of walking. They were two specks in the darkness, but if Melanie focused in on them, something in her eyes shifted and made the distance as clear as looking through an only slightly dingy mirror. If she did the same thing a few miles southwest, she could see Thetis. He was farther, and his form was less distinct, but she could still make out his silhouette. She was growing accustomed to the way he moved, the shape his wings took in the air around him. She knew he had other things on his mind, but all the same, her chest tightened. If he caught a glimpse of them out of the corner of his eye … If he decided to take a closer look …

Brent picked Tilly up again. They were only a few more paces from the cover of the trees. A terrible thought nearly knocked Melanie from the sky, and she descended at once. What if he had been looking at her? He usually was. What if he had been searching for her, wondering where she'd flown off to when he was in need of aid? What if he had seen her looking toward the trees?

She paced the grass, the blades tickling her between the toes. The tattered hem of the dress she'd stolen from her first victim swirling around her ankles. Her own dress, the soft blue that she'd sewn herself, had been decimated during her conversion. This one was hardly better off, with the sleeves and much of the back cut out in jagged lines made by Thetis' talons so that she could move her wings freely. Blood stains turned the color of the green material black.

A sniffle, a frightened moan, a nasty cough. The children. She was standing close by them, too close, practically admitting what she'd just done. Their werewolf guard was returning. One, a tall woman with auburn hair tied in a braid, had already taken up her post again, and she eyed Melanie curiously.

Melanie rushed into the subdued mottle of elves. Those she had freed were back in new chains, fingers bent at odd angles, a few with jaws swollen and slack, their shrieks of anguish reduced to shakes and low, tremulous moans. A werewolf was struggling to wrangle two elves into shackles at once, a mother and son … or perhaps a husband and wife—age seemed insignificant for elves. They were locked together in a frantic embrace, each refusing to relinquish their hold no matter how the werewolf slapped or punched or kicked them. Melanie could hear the wing beats of the approaching flock, Thetis among them. She forced her arms between the two struggling elves and wrenched them apart. She knew she hadn't harmed them, but the female screamed as though she'd been whipped. Now Melanie was sure they were mother and son. A numbness settled in her chest while she forced the elf's wrists into the iron rings and latched them shut. She grew talons from her fingers and slipped one into the lock, turning until the mechanism clicked. Nathaniel brushed her back with his arm as he made his continual rounds up and down the line of chains, his key in hand, checking the locks on every elf. She knew him by his atrocious smell—sweat, blood, rotten meat, and his own special musk worthy of a flea-bitten hound—and the almost imperceptible (even to her ears) sound of his beard rubbing against the collar of his tunic. Sometimes she was certain she could hear the lice moving about in it.

"Where did you go, my sweet?" The words came slow from behind her, like he hardly cared if he got them out at all, but Melanie had quickly come to learn that Thetis was most deadly when he sounded dreadfully bored.

She almost smiled when she turned around, but decided against it at the last moment. She'd never smiled at him before; he would find her out in an instant. Instead she took on an indignant wrath.

"Here! Just where else would I have gone? What else was I

supposed to do? The homes came alive!"

"Yes, I'm well aware. I happen to recall being trapped underneath one while I watched you fly away."

"You expected me to fight it off of you, did you? To help you?" she said with a scoff. "You'll pardon me, Thetis, if I didn't think you needed much helping, especially not from a half-starved fledgling."

Thetis' abyssal eyes narrowed as they searched her body. He ran a finger along the length of her jaw.

"You were frightened," he said.

Smiling inside, Melanie cast her eyes demurely to the ground and said nothing.

"Why didn't you just say so, pet?" He ran his hand over her hair, starting from the top and following a loose curling wave down to her shoulder. When the hair ran out, his hand kept moving down her arm. Halfway down, his caressing hand became a vice, and he yanked her into him. "I thought perhaps you had something else on your mind. Something most displeasing. But that wasn't it. Was it, pet?"

"No."

He released her with a smile. "You're learning."

"We're ready, Thetis," said Nathaniel. He nudged Melanie aside, giving her a familiar disapproving look as he did. The look, she had come to realize, was not really for her; it was for Thetis, for the way he favored her.

"That last batch you brought wasn't too lively," Nathaniel said, "but we've had some ... excitement. We need to turn these fast; they're more trouble than the humans. Full moon's a while away, but you could at least turn your half. It would mean less to deal with."

"Oh, how little you know, my bedraggled friend," said Thetis. "We won't be turning the elves until the king is present and the battle is fully underway."

"You mean we're supposed to lug this magic-spewing lot all

the way to Alatreon? The more of 'em we get, the more trouble they'll be."

"That's why we'll only be making a few stops. A handful of elves is worth a battalion of humans. You think they're trouble now, wait until their conversion."

"How the hell do you know all this, anyway?" said Nathaniel with a scowl.

"Sad, really, how little his Majesty tells you." Thetis looked at Nathaniel with feigned pity, complete with a pouting lip, but the smile was hidden in his voice. "Come, round up your dogs. My flock and I will fly with you as long as we can and see to it that the elflings understand the rules. Don't want them getting away from you like the dear princess did, do we?"

Nathaniel's hand twitched toward his sword hilt, but he dropped it and said, "Or how the Avalons got away from you."

"Four armed adversaries and their friends is hardly comparative to a starving, caged elf," said Thetis.

"One elf is worth a few humans, though. Right, Thetis?"

Melanie concealed her smirk by turning back to the children. All four werewolves were back in place, but none seemed to realize two of their charges were missing.

"I said move, dog!" said Thetis. "I would be loath to tell his Majesty how you disobeyed me when he made it quite clear I am in charge in his absence."

Nathaniel spared Thetis one last dirty look before cupping his hands to his mouth and shouting orders. The company was in motion again, the vampires taking to the skies while the werewolves closed ranks around the new prisoners. Thetis remained on the ground, so Melanie did as well.

"Where's the imp? I need him."

"I try not to look at him, much less keep track of his movements," said Melanie.

Thetis chuckled and then leapt into the sky, calling for Callid.

Callid came waddling out of the crowd, both heads upturned

to Thetis,. saying, "Here, here, your grace, your mightiness, your ..."

"Hold your tongues. I have orders," said Thetis, swooping lower to hover just above the hunched cyclops.

Callid bowed his heads, but Melanie heard him grumbling under his breath.

"The raider says there's another village ten miles northwest. I want to know if it's large. I only want to stop once more before we reach the Black Forest."

"I'll find it, your bloodlessness."

Thetis rolled his eyes. "Make no delays, go now."

"Yes, my liege."

Callid bent at the waist—he didn't have very far to go—and put his hands on the ground in fists, like an ape. He set off at a run that way, like a wild animal, his overly large muscles powering him forward as fast as a sprinting dog.

He passed the line of horses that pulled the captives forward, each with a werewolf on top, Nathaniel among them. The company moved slowly again, only able to go as fast as the new captives could walk.

Melanie circled above with Thetis. She had given up on trying to shake him. It only caused pain. They had only been moving a few minutes when a voice called out, "Escape! One of the children's escaped!"

Melanie's heart plummeted into her stomach. One of the werewolf guards around the children was holding a pair of leg shackles in his hands. She cursed herself for being so foolish. Thetis' claws were buried in her head an instant later.

"So that's where you really went, is it?" he snarled in her ear as he pulled her to the ground by her head. "Thought maybe I'd be killed by the elves' magic tricks in the bargain, too."

He tossed her to the ground, picked her up by the neck, and then tossed her down again. When she pushed herself up onto her knees, his claws raked her face. Then his fist crushed her nose.

"It wasn't me! It wasn't even my child in those shackles!" said Melanie, knowing that if she couldn't convince him, or at least calm him, the torture would be long and arduous. "My child was too small for shackles."

Thetis paused with his hand raised and claws bared.

"Where's her child? The blue-eyed child with hair like hers?" he shouted at the werewolf guard.

He scanned the children along with the werewolves.

"That one's gone, and so is the one that was always with her. The boy," said the werewolf still holding the shackles. "These is his." He shook them. "They was all in on it. They was all trying to hide the shackles while they walked. They know who done it."

"So do I," said the auburn haired werewolf. She pointed at Melanie. "She was hovering around the kids when I came back to my post. She did it."

"And just why," said Thetis, "were you not at your post?"

The werewolf woman shrank back under Thetis' fury. "There was an escape," she said. "A bunch of elves got loose. They were tossing spells all over the place. Started a riot; the whole lot almost got away. We had to help."

Thetis looked from Melanie to the werewolves, his eyes narrow. "I'll deal with you later. And you!" Thetis snatched Melanie up by her wing, bending it mercilessly until she cried out. "You just wait here." He looked up at the group of ogling vampires drawing closer for the show. "Make sure she stays here."

Melanie watched as Thetis flew off at full speed after Callid. The cyclops had already made it a good distance, and it was a while before Thetis caught him. The conversation was brief, but Callid shifted his course back toward the company. Melanie watched Thetis return with growing understanding and dread. He would sic that ugly, hunchbacked hound, Callid, on Tilly and Brent. If the beast caught them, it would all be for naught.

Thetis went straight for her as soon as he returned, encircling her throat with his hand and squeezing until she heard something crunch. She bit her tongue against the pain, silently suffocating (if it could actually be called that anymore) until he deigned to toss her aside again and let her throat heal.

"So, I suppose the next step was to fly off into the sunset tomorrow and join them, was it?" he said, towering over her.

"No," she said, letting all of the hate pour out in her words, no longer disguising it on her face. "I'm not that foolish. There's no life left for me. Just this half-life before damnation. But I wanted her to live. To be free."

"Callid is going to fetch her and her little friend. He's good for little, but tracking is his only real strength. He'll find your little girl, and when he delivers her to me I'm going to make sure she's no longer a distraction to you."

Melanie's chest rose and fell in rapid panic. "No! Please! She's just a child. You have me! I'm not going anywhere. I have nowhere to go. You can do what you will with me, just let her be. She's no harm to you."

"Perhaps not, but you can't be allowed such insubordination. Your daughter would have been released eventually. All the little babes would have been. But now, your daughter will be made an example of, to make sure all the mommies and daddies keep their toes in line. You really made it much worse for little Tilly."

Melanie's claws dug into the earth. She would kill him. She would save her strength, and if the cyclops found Tilly before she and Brent found the Avalons, she would rip him into a thousand pieces before he laid a hand on her, no matter how many of them tore at her. What an example that would be. Even if Tilly wasn't caught, she would kill him. Someday soon. Just for fun.

"You have it all figured out, don't you, Thetis? Master's favorite dog." She saw the way he flinched at the word, and her sneer grew wider. "Head of the pack. You have all the answers, right … darling? So answer me this. These elves are very important to your king, yes? You need to deliver enough to make him happy. Now, you're so big and strong and smart, you must know how to control their magic, but, you see, you weren't around when the elves needed controlling. Those treehouses were giving you trouble." She cocked her head and pouted at him, much as he had pouted at Nathaniel. "But, you see, I'm confused. Just how do you plan to keep enough of them alive when your army broke half their jaws to keep them from spitting spells? How are they to eat? You can't turn them. Master's orders. And you're a good little doggie. You're going to have to make a lot more stops to meet your master's needs. Tell me, when are you supposed to meet him? He doesn't seem the sort of king to be kept waiting. But it looks like that's exactly what you're going to do, unless you focus all that cunning on the real problems at hand instead of on a couple of children. I know you're fond of me, Thetis, but really, you have more important things to think about. You wouldn't want Nathaniel promoted to number two, would you now?"

Thetis gaped at her, fury and fear warring on his face. Melanie laughed. He stalked toward her, but she did not shrink away. She'd gotten to him, gotten under his cold, dead flesh. He gripped her face in one hand, claws tearing into her cheeks.

"You think you're smart, don't you, pet?" he said sweetly. "What you don't seem to understand is that right now, I'm the master, and you're the dog. And I will beat you into submission and train you to follow orders one way or another."

"You forget, Thetis, you've made me just like you. True, you keep me weak, but it's usually the starving dog who bites its master's hand. Or rips out his throat."

Chapter 21

Flight

Atalanta reined in her horse so suddenly that one of her guards nearly galloped into her. Her horse bucked at the guard's as it pulled up short just behind its tail, spooking it. The guard's horse reared, drawing the attention of the rest of the party.

"We stop here," Atalanta said as Galen trotted toward her with an exasperated, beaten look.

"Princess, we are hardly five miles from Campion," he said, sounding like a tired child near tears from exhaustion.

"No one is following us. No one knows we were there. They won't come looking. It was a raid; they got what they wanted."

"We have already been delayed far too long. Your father will send another search party."

"Good, then perhaps we could chase after those beasts and free our people," said Atalanta, her nostrils flaring. "But for now, we wait until dawn breaks in a few hours' time, and we go look for survivors to take back with us."

"There are no survivors, Your Highness," said Galen, a sad sigh behind the words.

"We survived. Thanks to Bree, there could be others." Atalanta went to smile at Bree, but it quickly morphed into a frown. The elf girl was slumped against Andrew's chest, her head lolling on his shoulder, her eyelids fluttering. "She needs rest and food. We all do. We stop here, and that's final. No fires, and we keep the horses saddled."

"Yes, princess," said Galen with a bow of his head that could not hide the look of defeat on his face.

* * *

Callid walked in widening circles, both heads down, sniffing with both noses for Tilly and Brent's scents and occasionally reaching out to touch some mark in the grass. The children shrank back from him with frightened squeals as he approached on his final circle and snatched up Brent's broken shackles.

"When I return tomorrow night, I want to see the both of them waiting for me. Is that understood?" said Thetis, palming one of Callid's bald, perfectly rounded heads and forcing it around to look at him.

"Perfectly, my liege." There was clear distaste in the echoing dual voices of Callid's heads.

"Good," said Thetis, roughly shoving Callid's head away. "Now go. I have a few more fools to deal with before dawn."

Callid draped the shackles around one of his necks and took off in his ape-like run, fists pounding into the grass with dull thuds. Worry clenched Melanie's throat. He was so fast, so strong, and Brent had no weapon.

You'll have to outsmart him, Brent, she thought as she looked to the small wooded area where she'd last caught sight of them both.

Thetis' claws buried in the flesh of her forearm, and she hissed at the burning pain. He yanked her into the sky along with him. Once aloft, she pulled herself free, baring her fangs at him.

"Stick close, pet. You'll want to be nearby for your daughter's homecoming." Thetis raised his voice to address the swarm of vampires, all hovering above the ground, waiting for his orders to make their way to the nearest caves for protection from the dawn. "Who thought it a good idea to mangle the prisoners' faces? Did I not say they weren't to be seriously harmed?"

The vampires began to look at each other from the corners of shifting, frightened eyes.

"Who?" Thetis thundered. "Who was the first to play that little trick?"

The flock rippled and murmured, and then a male vampire

with long brown hair tied back with string was tossed from the mass of pearly white bodies to the forefront.

"Gregory," said Thetis with a toothy smile, "care to explain yourself?"

"They were attacking us, your grace—bringing trees to life, starting fires, and then some of them even got loose from their chains. Had we not stopped them from speaking their spells, they might all have gotten free. We only harmed the ones who were fighting with magic, and we kept them alive. They can still travel. When we convert them, their bones will heal."

"Didn't kill them?"

"N–no, your grace."

"Has it really been so long since you were mortal, Gregory? Even elves must eat, and by the king's orders, we cannot turn them until we reach Alatreon and prepare for battle. How are they to live that long with broken jaws?"

"We didn't know, your grace. We didn't know they couldn't be converted. Please, have mercy."

"He's right, you know," said Melanie, knowing it wasn't wise, but unable to stop herself. "This is your fault, really. You forgot to mention that crucial fact. Holding back to embarrass Nathaniel with your vast knowledge of your king's orders?" She clucked her tongue.

Thetis flew at her and encircled her throat in a fist. "Don't push your luck," he said, his lips brushing her ear. "You may be beautiful, but you're still replaceable."

"Are you sure?" said Melanie, cocking one eyebrow. "Why don't you go ahead and kill me then?"

Thetis' snarling face pulled back from hers and slowly softened into a lecherous grin. "Oh, no, pet. Not yet. You're too much fun for that." He pulled her to him by the throat and crushed his lips against hers in a ferocious kiss. She brought her feet up and kicked his body away, snarling like a wildcat, but he only laughed and turned back to his flock.

"Next time when I order you not to harm a prisoner, I expect that order to be followed," he said. "It is not your job to make decisions or make guesses as to what I want. Reversely, I do not have to share all of his Majesty's plans with you or explain my decisions." His eyes shifted from the nervous flock to Gregory, who was attempting to slowly make his way back into the crowd. He froze when Thetis' eyes found him. "If this cannot be fixed before dawn, you will remain here and suffer the same fate as the elves you maimed."

Gregory ducked his head, but Thetis was already gone, landing beside the rows of prisoners. He walked up and down, shaking his head as he inspected the damage on over two dozen elves.

"Is there any elf here who can still do magic?" he boomed into the crowd. "Do you wish to save your companions from the slow, painful death of starvation?"

None of the elves moved or spoke. Many deliberately looked away from Thetis as he stalked by.

"This is not a trick. King Tyrannus has wonderful plans for you. He does not wish you to die, and neither do I. Is there no one who will step up and help their fellow elves? If you do not, they will either be drained for sustenance or forced to travel along with the company until they collapse of hunger and fatigue. Will you not save them? No one?"

Two trembling hands, shackled together, rose slowly into the air.

"Ah, sweet little elfling, you shall be lauded as a hero amongst your peers," said Thetis, approaching the elf with curly black locks down her back and a petite, frightened face. "Bring her the wounded! And fetch her something to drink. She'll need her strength."

The vampires scrambled to obey, Gregory foremost among them. Melanie watched in amazement as the elf took the first victim's broken face gently in her hands and closed her eyes. A soft white glow came from her fingers, as if she'd trapped stars in her palms. She sang in a soft, humming voice, and beneath her fingers, the elf's jaw realigned. Melanie heard him sigh in relief. The elf next grabbed hold of his twisted, mangled fingers, but Thetis grabbed her shoulder.

"No, no, dear. Those shall remain to remind them all of the consequences of their misdeeds."

The elf shuddered at Thetis' touch and nodded quickly. She moved to heal the next, and the next. When she at last finished, Melanie could feel the subtle shift in the warmth of the air, the slight change of the light, and the smell of the dew that told her dawn was fast approaching. Thetis knew it, too. He looked to the horizon and then put his hand on the elf's shoulder. "You did marvelously, dear. I'm sure your fellows thank you. And you finished your task just in time, for which I myself am most grateful."

The elf said nothing and looked as though the best thanks he could give her was to remove his hand. Melanie knew how she felt.

Nathaniel slid from his horse to come and hiss in Thetis' ear. "Thetis, are you just going to leave me and my pack to deal with freshly healed spell-spewers? The full moon is too far. We will have a harder time subduing them if they rally again."

"Don't worry, my friend," said Thetis, "I'm well aware of your kind's shortcomings. Do to them what should have been done in the first place."

"And just what might that be?"

Thetis grinned at the healer elf. "Cut out their tongues."

* * *

Brent crouched low, slinking toward the tree line with his knees fully bent and his head down. He peered out from behind the large trunk of an oak and looked down the sloping hill to the village below. Black smoke blanketed the air above the houses, but the blazes lit the streets, and Brent searched them for any sign of life. Mostly, though, he searched for a glimpse of red hair or a dingy, forest-green cloak. The only movement was the dance of the flames and charred bits of the strangely shaped houses falling down in rains of soot.

At least there were no signs of the werewolves—with their crude blades, harsh voices, and unkempt clothing—or worse, vampires. Brent looked west, Melanie's instructions still clear in his head, but the night was only just beginning to fade, and in the half-light beyond the glow of the fiery village, he could see no signs of the Avalons or Erro. Thinking of Aquila, he searched the sky, hoping to see the griffin's silhouette cross the dwindling moon, but it was small and dark and obscured by clouds and smoke.

A small hand tugged on the back of his tunic. "Brent?" said Tilly.

Crouched as he was, Brent met her large eyes directly. She really was cute. A lot like Katrina. Same age, too. It made his heart hurt. He had no family any longer. His mother and father were werewolves, unable to disobey Nathaniel's orders. They'd helped start those fires, capture those elves. He'd probably never see them again. Now all he had was Erro and this little girl, entrusted to him by her mother, and he wasn't going to let any of them down. Not like Katrina.

"I'm hungry," said Tilly through a yawn.

"Me, too, child," he said, rubbing his hand over the top of her head.

She smiled at him. He could tell she'd grown attached to him during their captivity. As they'd traveled, she'd kept a tight hold on his hand. She would only speak to him and Lora. Lora was from Everly, too, and she had taken care of Tilly when Brent was still chained with the adults. But Lora had two little sisters of her own to look after, so Brent had taken up the responsibility for Melanie. He'd found it was the only thing that kept him from going crazy each day.

"What's your favorite thing to eat?" he asked her now.

"Toast and strawberry jam," she said, shoving her tongue through her lips as though savoring the taste at that very moment. Strawberry came out "stwa-berry," and Brent grinned.

"Good choice," he said. "When we find the Avalons and they take us to the elf palace, you can have heaps of toast with the best strawberry jam you ever tasted. Does that sound good?"

"Mm-hmm!" said Tilly, nodding groggily as she rubbed one eye.

"Me, I'm going to have steaks, and lamb stew and potatoes with butter and apple tarts and cherry pie and blueberries with cream."

"Can I have some of that, too?" said Tilly, wide-eyed.

"Sure," said Brent, laughing. "Anything you want."

"A pony?"

"You're going to eat a pony?" said Brent in feigned amazement.

Tilly scrunched her face into a look of utter disgust and horror. "No!" she said, shaking her head back and forth and glowering at him under sharply slanted eyebrows. "I want to have one. To ride and play with and pet."

Brent fell back on his butt and laughed at her look of outrage, until he caught himself and forced the echoing peals to stop. "I know, Tilly, I know. I was just teasing."

"That's not funny, Brent."

"You're right. That's not funny. I'm sorry." But it was most certainly funny.

The sky was turning gray. A hint of orange would appear on the horizon in just a little while. Brent looked back to the village. His heart skipped a beat, but then fell back into a regular rhythm. It wasn't a vampire, and it wasn't one of the Avalons. It was an elf woman. She was moving cautiously into the street, like a mother mouse exiting her burrow for the night's hunt. She was favoring her left leg, but Brent could see no obvious injuries. Maybe she could help them. Maybe she knew for sure which direction the Avalons had gone, or at least let him know Erro was okay. It couldn't hurt to look through the village to make sure they weren't still there after all.

"Tilly, do you see that pretty lady down there?"

"Uh-huh."

"That's an elf. Did your mom ever tell you about them?"

"Ooo, a real elf?" said Tilly, rushing past him and out of the cover of the trees to get a better look.

Brent jumped forward and pulled her back. "Whoa, hold on, child. Easy. We don't want to scare her, right?"

"Scare her?" said Tilly, perplexed.

"Yeah, you're pretty scary, you know." Brent winked, and Tilly put her hands over her mouth and giggled.

"No I'm not, silly," she said through her pudgy fingers.

"Come on," said Brent, taking her hand. "We'll go down there nice and slow and ask her real nice if—"

Something rustled behind them, no louder than the sound of a rabbit hopping into a bush, but Brent had heard that particular sound many times before, and it wasn't right. His muscles tensed, and he went back into a crouch, scanning the trees and the underbrush behind them.

"Brent ...?"

Brent shushed her, a finger to his lips. She suppressed a girlish smile, shushed him back, and playfully pressed her lips tightly together. She didn't understand. Brent thought maybe that was best.

Brent kept perfectly still, and Tilly mimicked him. Another rustling sound. Was it the same? He saw a tree limb bob under the weight of a crow, and his body began to relax. Nothing looked out of place.

"We're staying quiet so the elf's not scared. Huh, Brent?"

"Right." Brent stood up and gave Tilly a smile. "Let's go.

Keep quiet."

Tilly put her finger to her lip. "Quiet," she said.

A body as hard as a boulder slammed into Brent's back, knocking him to the ground and forcing the wind from his lungs. Tilly's scream was high and terrified. Brent tried to see if she was all right as he fought to suck air back into his burning lungs and aching chest as the weight of his attacker shifted off him, but a muscular arm put him in a strangling headlock. A torpid, echoing laugh came from both sides of Brent's head, and two separate gusts of hot breath hit both his ears. It was the two-headed cyclops, Callid.

The breath of one head left his face as it searched with its singular eye for Tilly. Brent's two eyes found her at the same time. She was shaking from the roots of her hair to her dirty bare feet, her mouth open as wide as it could go as she screamed. The hand that wasn't strangling Brent groped for her, and she stumbled backwards, hitting the grass with a soft thump.

Brent began to see spots as he yanked fruitlessly at Callid's arm. The beast was too strong. Brent shifted, recalculating, and rammed his elbow into the bulging eye of one of Callid's heads, causing a rasping cry of pain to escape both his mouths. The arm around Brent's neck loosened, and he pulled free. He positioned himself in front of Tilly and reached into the pocket of his trousers for his small hunting knife. It was a pathetic thing really, only three inches long, well-worn, and dull. It had been no good to him when he was shackled and surrounded by vampires and werewolves on all sides, and they had never searched him — they didn't need to — but one-on-one, at least it was something. Callid eyed it warily, but didn't back down.

"Bad little boy, running away," Callid said. "Callid's not scared of little boys with little knives."

"Maybe you should be," said Brent, trying to gently pry Tilly from his leg while he kept his eyes locked on Callid.

Callid snarled and jumped at him, and Brent lunged

forward with the knife. Callid moved with a speed Brent hadn't anticipated, dodging the knife easily and punching Brent in the stomach. Brent felt something crack, and doubled over in pain, once again at a loss for air. Callid laughed and reached around Brent to grab Tilly by the shoulder. Brent straightened himself and jabbed the knife at Callid's right throat. The cyclops saw the knife coming with his other head's eye and threw up an arm just in time, but the blade embedded deep in the tendons of his forearm. With a brutish cry of pain and anger Callid ripped the knife from Brent's hand and tackled him to the ground, pinning him in another headlock, squeezing his massive bicep into Brent's windpipe. Brent drilled his finger into Callid's wound, and the grip eased but did not release as Callid screamed.

"Tilly, run! Go! Find them! Do what she said!" He found Tilly's eyes, willing her to understand. He couldn't let Callid know who had freed them or where they were supposed to go.

Tilly was crying, huddled at the base of a tree, looking petrified. She looked at Brent with childish helplessness, unmoving.

"Run, Tilly, run!" he yelled, so loud his throat strained.

Callid bent Brent's hand back, pulling it from his wound and tightened his choke hold so that Brent could say no more, but his final yell had put Tilly in motion.

She ran for the village, her short legs forcing her into the unsteady, zigzagging gait of a young child. Callid looked from her to Brent, who kicked up a terrible fight, legs and arms flailing and clawing and pummeling every inch of Callid he could reach as black spots danced across his vision. Callid yelled in frustration and picked up the fallen knife with his free hand. He lobbed it at Tilly just before she left the tree line, and the blade barely missed her bobbing head. She screamed and ran harder. Brent threw wild elbows, colliding with Callid's mouths and eyes, blood sprayed on the grass and his arm. A fist collided with his temple, and his last conscious thought was, let it be enough time.

Tilly raced down the hill, her eyes on the last place she'd seen the elf, but she wasn't there. The slope was too great for her legs, and she tumbled forward with a little cry. She rolled the rest of the way, arms tucked into her body. It was almost fun, but she was still very scared. The cyclops scared her, and he had hurt Brent. She knew he would hurt her next if she didn't find the elf. At the end of her roll, she pushed herself back up to her feet and ran into the street. It was very hot, and there was a lot of fire, she looked both ways up and down the street and didn't see the elf. The fear got worse, and she ran to the left. She looked left and right as she ran, tears catching in her eyelashes. She ran from the fiery buildings, and instead went down the streets that weren't so hot.

"Elf! Elf! Help!" she called, hoping the beautiful lady would hear her.

Her calls cut off as she rounded a corner and slammed head first into something hard. It knocked her onto her bottom in the dirt, and she began to cry harder, hands over her face. The cyclops would get her now.

"My God, it's a child."

"A human child."

"What's she doing here?"

"Who cares? Can't you see she's terrified?"

Tilly felt warm arms pick her up and pull her into a hug.

"Momma?"

But when she opened her eyes, she was surrounded by lots and lots of yellow hair, and Momma's was brown.

"Are you looking for your momma?"

Tilly looked at the lady who was hugging her. She was very pretty.

"Are you an elf?"

"No, I'm a human like you."

"Are you a princess?"

The lady smiled, but her face looked surprised. "Yes, I am."
Tilly's eyes went big. "You are?"
"Yes, my name's Princess Felicity Avalon. What's yours?"

Chapter 22

Tilly's Deliverance

The girl's face glowed, and she stared into Felicity's eyes with wonderment.

"Princess Felicity, the beautiful?"

An unexpected blush warmed Felicity's cheeks. "Yes. That's what they call me."

Tilly's head turned a panoramic one-eighty, soaking in the curious faces pressing in on her.

"Princess Andromeda, the gentle," she gasped, eyes so wide they threatened to engulf her face. "Prince Michael, the strong. Prince Andrew, the trickster."

Erro's barked laugh startled the girl.

"The trickster?"

"It's a title I wear proudly," said Andrew, winking at the girl, who put a hand to her face and giggled.

In truth, the Avalons were unaccustomed to hearing the nicknames the people had bestowed on them because, though merchants emblazoned them on tapestries and paintings and bards sung them in the streets, none of the common folk dared call the siblings anything but "Highness" in their presence.

"What is that?" said the child in an awed voice, partially hiding her face with Felicity's shoulder as she stared at Aquila.

"Aquila's a griffin," said Erro, and his smile seemed to calm any fear she had of the beast. "He's very nice. So is Zezil." Erro picked the vexar up and scratched behind his ears. "He's like a puppy."

Tilly reached out a curious hand, and Zezil licked her fingers. She pulled back her hand with a happy squeal. Her eyes continued to search for more interesting creatures to meet.

"And you're an elf!" she said suddenly, a small finger aimed at Atalanta's face.

Atalanta smiled. "Yes."

"And they're elves!" The girl was pushing herself up on Felicity's shoulders now to look at Galen and his fellow guards, and Gelwyn and his family.

Atalanta turned to them, too. "Go search the village. See if you can find survivors," she told Galen. "Gelwyn, you and your family return to your home. See if you can salvage any of your belongings. We will all meet back by the stables in one hour's time."

"Sir Boris, go with Gelwyn and make sure they make it safely to their home," said Michael.

"As you wish," said Boris.

As the elves and the knight dispersed, Felicity asked the girl again for her name.

"Tilly Borsten of Glenn. Momma sent me to find you. She says you're going to save us. And I found you!"

"Save who from what, Tilly?" said Michael, moving to Felicity's shoulder.

"Glenn is on the easternmost side of the Northern Wood," said Erro, puzzled. "How did she get here?"

"Where's your mother, darling?" said Felicity, running a finger down Tilly's cheek. It was she Tilly looked to, eyes suddenly brimming with tears.

"Momma is with the bad people."

"What bad people?" said Felicity, her fingers finding their way into the rabbit-soft waves, gently loosening the many tangles.

The tenderness of the action drew Andromeda's gaze, and she watched with a curious smile as Tilly tucked her head into the crook of Felicity's neck.

"Bad people with long, pointy teeth," Tilly said into Felicity's collarbone, tears rolling off her cheeks.

Felicity's eyes flicked to Michael's. Michael urged Felicity on with a movement of his head.

"What did the bad people do, Tilly?"

"They came and took us from home. Then they hurt my daddy, and made us leave him. They bit Momma, too, but she got back up, and then she could fly.She has long teeth like them, too. She doesn't turn into a big dog, though. Some of them did that once. Brent's mommy and daddy did."

Atalanta cursed, and Felicity threw her a nasty look.

"Brent?" Now it was Erro who pressed against Felicity to get a better look at Tilly. "Did you say Brent?"

"Uh-huh," said Tilly, a finger placed nervously in her mouth. "Brent's my friend. But the man with two heads got him." Fresh tears squeezed from her eyes. "I think he hurt him. He was gonna get me, too. That's why I ran. I lost Brent, and Momma told me to stay with him."

Felicity shushed Tilly, pulling her head to her breast, bouncing her lightly in her arms. Erro's face was colorless. He pulled at the ragged end of his cloak, taking deep breaths to keep his voice steady.

"Tilly, do you know Brent's last name? Do you know where he was from?"

"He was from Everly. So was Lora. She was nice, too. But Momma didn't get her loose."

"Lora?" said Erro in a choked voice. "From Everly?"

"Uh-huh."

"And Brent's parents are ... they turn into big dogs?"

"Once, after some of the others bit them. That's what Brent said, but Lora covered my eyes so I wouldn't see. She said it was too scary."

Erro took two clumsy steps backward, breathing heavy.

"I'm sorry I made you sad," said Tilly softly.

Erro attempted to smile at the girl and couldn't. "It's all right," he whispered. Andromeda's hand found his, and he squeezed it too tight.

"When did this happen?" said Michael, roughly pulling a hand through his hair. "We were in the Northern Wood little more than a fortnight ago."

"He's got his army," said Andromeda, her face ashen.

"And he made it out of our people," said Andrew. His whole body seemed to sag, as though he was weighed down like a pack horse.

"He'll do the same to mine," said Atalanta.

"We need to get word to Father," said Felicity.

"He probably already knows the villages have been attacked," said Michael. "He sent a battalion into the wood to search for Brock."

"Brock is a bad man," said Tilly, throwing the whole street into utter silence save for the crackle of dying embers in the early morning air.

"You know Brock?" said Erro in hushed tones.

"He helped the bad people take us out of our house. He hurt Momma, too. He pulled her hair and hit her. They made him and his friends watch us when we were all chained up. He was mean. He yelled and hit us for crying or saying we were hungry."

"Did he have pointy teeth, too?" said Andromeda.

"No."

"Did he turn into a dog?"

"No."

"Filthy traitor," snarled Michael.

"He's with them," said Erro, his voice a low, vicious grumble.

"Erro?" Andromeda spoke his name like a warning.

"How far did you run, Tilly, when your mother set you and Brent loose?" said Erro, looking wild as he thrust his face into Tilly's.

The girl shrugged, looking mildly frightened. Erro took a step back and closed his eyes for a moment to compose himself.

"When did your mother release you? Yesterday?"

Tilly shook her head. "Tonight."

"They're close," said Erro, turning on Michael. "We can go find them. Hang back, check everything out. See if she's right about all of it." His cloak swished around him as he turned to Atalanta. "You might be able to free your people before they're changed."

"Erro, you heard her," said Atalanta with a look of pity. "He's changed all the humans of the Northern Wood. He has an army."

"An unwilling army. They won't fight for him. We can save all of them."

"How do you know they won't fight? They're monsters now."

"They're people! Fiona and Jeremiah aren't monsters," Erro said.

"Your friend? The one you saw tonight? He was raiding the village. He told you to stay away from him. He may not want to be, but he is one of them now."

"She's right, Erro," said Andromeda. "They won't be able to help it. The ones turned into vampires won't be able to satiate their need for blood, and the werewolves can't choose for themselves."

"What?"

"You told us Jeremiah said something about an alpha."

"Yes, so."

"I wasn't sure before, but after what the girl's told us, I have to be. Werewolves are beholden to an alpha who runs the pack, just like regular wolves. The alpha werewolf's status holds even more power. They cannot deny him. It's like a blood link, ruled by the virus that makes them transform. It's stronger at the full moon, when they are in wolf form, but it works even in their human state. They cannot disobey a direct order from the alpha. If he told Jeremiah or Fiona to kill you, they would do it."

"Then we can capture Brock, get him to tell us what their plans are," said Erro, tears still glistening in his eyes.

"We know their plans," said Atalanta. "Tyrannus wants war with my father and theirs. He's making a clear path from the mountains to Alatreon, building his army ever larger on the way. You want your revenge? We stay our course and get to Alatreon before the army does. If Brock is with them, you'll get your chance in the thick of the battle. No one will stop you. But going now is madness. We'll be slaughtered."

"What about Brent?" said Erro. "He's with that cyclops thing."

Atalanta's face softened, but she shook her head. "He could be anywhere by now. We need to keep moving and get as far away from that horde as we can. The faster we get to my father, the better."

"She's right, Erro," said Andromeda.

Tilly observed the tension with a worried brow. She cupped a hand around her mouth and whispered into Felicity's ear, "Did I say something bad?"

"No, Tilly. You've done very well. You did just what your mother told you, and you've helped us a great deal."

"We're very glad to have you, Tilly," said Andrew, his smile filled with pity for the child who had seen so much death and terror.

Aquila moved from Erro's side, his amber eyes searching the girl's face. His neck craned up to where she sat propped in Felicity's arms. Transfixed, Tilly reached down to him while the others watched the serene exchange in silence. Tilly's fingers found the golden feathers at the griffin's head and sank deep. A coo drifted up from Aquila's throat, and his eyes closed as the child touched her head to his, both of them bowing to each other.

Andromeda felt Aquila's warmth fill up her own chest. A feeling that could only be described as love came off him in waves, and deep inside her head, much clearer than any of the murmurings she'd ever heard before, a rumbling, powerful voice said, "Fear naught, sweet babe."

* * *

For the first time in a long time, Melanie's stomach was not screaming at her when she woke from a semi-slumber just as the sun was setting. The elf blood of the previous night, though she'd had very little, was still satiating her, though the extra strength she'd temporarily received from it had receded. But when her leg bumped against Thetis, curled up beside her, blocking her from the cave mouth, nausea gripped her stomach instead of hunger pains. She'd rested poorly, and her head pounded with exhaustion and the same questions that had been spinning around in it all night. Had Callid caught up with Brent and Tilly? Was her daughter once again chained and at the mercy of monsters? What would Thetis do if she was? What would he do if she wasn't?

"Pondering what you'll say to your daughter?"

Melanie's claws scraped across the cave floor. When he sat up, his eyes gleefully searched her face, lapping up any traces of fear they found. She stared back as blankly as she could manage. It had the desired effect. He scoffed dismissively in the back of his throat.

"You're going to be an utter bore until we arrive, aren't you?" he said, rising languidly from the floor, his eyes already searching for something new to quench his ceaseless tedium.

She often wondered how old he was, to find nearly everything dreadfully boring, to have seen so much of the world that everything in it no longer held any wonder. How many lifetimes did that take? She suspected it was less than many might guess. Even slaughter seemed to hold little interest for him, unless his victim made things more interesting with a good struggle.

She caught herself studying him as he woke others with rough prods of his toes, and felt her hate grow stronger. Somehow, he had become a centerpiece in her existence. He had forced his way into her life and made himself an integral part. She must always wonder what he would do, how he would act, and how she might outmaneuver him. She did not want to think of him any longer, and yet she knew she must. She had to keep watch over him at all times, learn his tendencies, his secrets. Know thine enemy. If she was to kill him, she would have to know him as well or better than herself, or she'd never get the chance, not in the state he kept her.

By the time the sun had dipped completely out of sight, the whole flock was rousted. Thetis yanked Melanie to the cave mouth by her wrist and flung her into the air ahead of him. She said not a word. Speaking would betray her fear. Suddenly, as she soared through the cool, windy night, she was certain that Tilly and Brent had been recaptured. They were no match for the beast—young and unarmed. He was too fast, too strong. She hadn't given them enough time. The chain had been discovered, ruining their chances of a good head start.

Her mind began to wander over the possible horrors Thetis could have in store. He'd said her defiance could not go unpunished. If he tried to harm Tilly, she'd make him pay. But would she be able to put an end to it? What if he decided to have Melanie herself do the harm? Starve her for a few weeks and then set Tilly in front of her. Would she be able to resist?

The flight was longer than the night before; they had to retrace the progress the party had made after the raid. It was not much of a difference—there had not been much more starlight to travel under—but the extra minutes were agony.

She smelled the others before she saw them. The scent of werewolves on the strong night breeze was dank and musky, like sopping dirt or swamp mud, with the obvious hint of dog. She could smell the elves, too. Their perfumed blood was the scent she lingered on as the flock circled the makeshift camp of a few fires and ragged blankets that the werewolves were in the process of disassembling. Her sharp eyes found Callid easily. He was cowering behind Nathaniel, who was looking more surly than usual. Hope blossomed in Melanie's chest. She scanned the knot of children. No Brent. No Tilly. The smile was uncontrollable, but she hid it from Thetis as he swooped past her. He did not slow as he dived at Callid. Nathaniel stepped deftly out of the way, and Callid squeaked and turned to run. Thetis snatched him up by his necks and hoisted him a few feet into the air before tossing him back down on his hump.

"Where are they?" he roared, landing in a crouch over the cyclops' stocky body, his fangs snapping at one of the fat necks.

"Th–th–the boy is over there," said Callid, a shaking finger pointing around Thetis' poised bicep.

Melanie's breath left her. Brent was chained with the elves. Blood trickled from a wound on his head. His right eye was a deep purple.

"And the girl?" said Thetis, pushing himself upright with the help of his wings.

"She ... she ran," Callid muttered, "when I was fighting with the boy. He had a knife!"

"I'm sure a small boy with a knife is quite terrifying," said Thetis in a deadly drone, "but I don't see how that prevented you from catching up with a babe! You run as fast as any dog, surely catching up with a child is no great feat."

"I had to make sure the boy wouldn't run away, too," said Callid, the voices coming from his heads two octaves higher than usual. "Then, the girl, she ran into the village. There was fire. Fire everywhere! You know I don't like fire, Thetis. You know! Please! I tried. She'll die on her own anyway. I got the boy! She has no one to take care of her now. Maybe ... maybe the fire got her already. Children are foolish. Perhaps she got too close, and it ate her up." He laughed wildly. "Yes, the fire! It probably ate her up already!"

"The fire?" said Thetis, fangs slurring his speech as every tooth in his mouth grew sharp. "The fire ate her up, eh?"

Callid's mouths gaped in horror and he scrambled to regain his footing as Thetis' maw grew, the jaw dislocating to fit the bed of dagger points, opening wide enough to consume one of

Callid's heads whole.

"I'll eat you up, you worthless, cowardly—"

"Thetis!" Nathaniel's voice echoed in the stillness of the watching crowd. "You ought to think twice before killing the king's favorite pet."

Thetis' shoulders relaxed and his teeth retracted slowly.

"For some reason he finds the imp entertaining," said Nathaniel. "He'll likely be displeased if he hears you killed him over a worthless human child, all because you wanted to teach your new mistress a lesson."

"She'll still learn her lesson," said Thetis, rounding on Melanie, who stood stock still, hiding her elation behind a stoic façade.

"What you do in your cave is your own business, but now we have to keep moving. I will not leave his Majesty waiting because you can't control your latest pretty distraction."

Thetis hissed low in his throat, and used Melanie's hair to pull her face to his. "We're not through."

A smile itched at the corners of Melanie's lips, but she only stared back.

With a growl of frustration, he tossed her aside and said, "Bring me the raider!"

Melanie heard the hoof beats before she found the long-haired raider in the crowd. He was laying heels and hands into his horse, and Melanie might have laughed at the futility of it had she not felt that futility herself so often as of late. Still, she felt no empathy when a chuckling vampire snatched Brock off his horse and tossed him at Thetis' feet.

"Please! Please! I can still be of use to you!" he cried, hands up to shield his neck.

"Have you been any farther than the next village you spoke of?" said Thetis, a cruel upward curl at the edge of his lips. Brock opened his mouth, but Thetis threw up a wagging finger to cut him off. "It will be far worse for you if you lie."

"N–no, but I can be of use in other ways." Brock's eyes bulged. His hands shook as he wiped strands of his dingy hair from his face.

"Pray tell."

"You still need someone to watch the children. With these elves on your hands, you need all of your people you can spare. I can watch the little ones."

"Might I remind you that you were meant to be watching the children just last night when two of them escaped? I have plenty of soldiers to watch over the children."

"Please, make me like you. I'll serve in your king's army. Please!"

"The king doesn't want the likes of you in his army," said Nathaniel.

"I'll do anything!" said Brock. Now he was screaming in the wailing voice of a terrified child. "I'll serve. I'll do whatever you say." He grasped Thetis' bare ankles and kissed his feet.

Thetis kicked him in the jaw, hard enough to send him sprawling backward in the grass, but now his micro-smile held a hint of interest.

"My lice-ridden friend is right," he said, cocking his head as he loomed over Brock. "The king doesn't want you in his army. But that doesn't mean you can't serve in other ways."

"Yes, I'll do anything," said Brock, hands together in supplication.

"Thetis, the king ordered us to dispose of him," said Nathaniel, his beard tickling at Thetis' ear as he snarled in his face.

"The king said he didn't have room for traitors in his army," said Thetis. "Perhaps he'll change his mind if the man proves his loyalty."

"Yes! Just tell me how," said Brock.

"Have you ever heard of a vampire sire?"

"No, but I'll be one."

"No you won't, fool. I shall be your sire. You will act as

my servant. You will allow me to partially drain your blood whenever I require, and in return, I shall slowly fill your veins with the venom that will make you one of the noble race."

Brock had paled at the talk of bloodletting, but he nodded vigorously at the idea all the same. "Yes, yes! I'll do it!"

"Remember, you must prove your absolute loyalty. Every command must be obeyed."

"I understand." The ghost of a smile flickered across his face, and Melanie could hear his heartbeat slowing with relief.

"Good. Now prove it," said Thetis, a true smile on his face now. "I require a token of your servitude."

"Anything."

"Take out your dagger."

The smile that had not quite blossomed vanished from Brock's eyes as he obeyed.

"I'll leave the decision up to you."

"What decision?"

"You will address me as master."

"What decision, master?"

"Which finger I shall have as a sign of your homage."

Chapter 23

The City of Green and Gold

The camp was nearly as silent as the stars. For nights now, the disheveled party of princes and princesses, royal elf guards and a knight, homeless elves and a traumatized child had sat around two small fires, eating in a sort of daze. Some stared contemplatively into the fire. Others stared at a single space in the darkness, thinking of lost friends and loved ones. Some studied their food as they brought it to their mouths. There was only an occasional murmured request to pass a water skin or inquiry about the flavor of the two-day-old meat (a complaint the elves did not have to deal with as they dined on roots dug from the earth and edible plants the Avalons had never heard of before). Even Zezil was quiet, tucked under Aquila's wing with his eyes only half-open.

Exhaustion contributed to the sullen mood. The need to reach Alatreon before their enemies urged the party on from just before daybreak to just after sundown, only slowing the pace when the horses' coats frothed with sweat.

Felicity held Tilly on her lap. The child was having difficulty tearing apart the stiff chunks of deer flesh, and the morose expression on her little face made Felicity frown. She looked around the camp and found only glazed eyes. It was no place for a child. A child ought to have time for play. A child ought to laugh and run and lay her head on a soft bed instead of a rock at night.

"Would you like to hear a story before you go to sleep, Tilly?" Felicity asked in a clear, ringing voice.

Heads raised all over the camp. Andromeda looked over with the same amused expression she'd been throwing Felicity's way since they fled Campion. The little, crooked, closed-lipped smile under those curious grey eyes irked Felicity. It was as though her younger sister knew something she didn't, some sort of secret joke. But, of course, Andromeda did know more than she—always had.

"Oh, yes please," said Tilly. "Momma tells me a story every night. Can you tell the one about Althea?"

"Who?" said Felicity.

"Althea, the farm girl," said Tilly with unabashed enthusiasm, large eyes upturned to Felicity's face. "The evil dragon comes to gobble up her pet goat." Tilly opened her mouth wide and made a chomping noise to demonstrate the danger of a gobbling dragon.

Felicity looked to her siblings for help. Andrew shrugged.

"Sorry, I don't know that one," said Felicity.

The excitement drained from Tilly's face.

"I could tell you another one," said Felicity. "Or maybe you could tell us about Althea."

"No, Momma tells it best."

"Well, would you like to hear another story?"

But Tilly wasn't listening. "Momma sings to me, too," she said, the threat of tears in her voice.

"I know lots of songs," said Felicity. "Andromeda, too. We could sing them for you." Felicity begged Andromeda with her eyes, and the other girl smiled gently and nodded.

"Can you sing 'The Shepherd's Lullaby'?" said Tilly. "That one's my favorite."

Felicity's shoulders fell.

"How would you like to hear a new song?" said Atalanta. "An elf song."

"I like the ones Momma sings," said Tilly, her voice still sad.

"Of course you do, but could your mother's songs make fire dance?" asked Atalanta.

Tilly gaped. "Your song can do that?"

"Yes. It's a magic song."

"Magic!" squealed Tilly.

Atalanta nodded. "I might need some help, though." She looked to Bree, who smiled back.

"Sing it! Sing it!" said Tilly, bouncing in Felicity's lap. When she caught everyone looking at her, she looked at her hands demurely and said, "Please?"

Atalanta raised her slender hands toward the closest fire and began to sing. The words were elvish, soft and fluid on the tongue. Atalanta's voice was ringing bells and bird song. The lilt of the melody and the beauty of her voice were enchanting. Michael's and Andrew's jaws went slack, eyes fixed on Atalanta. Erro closed his eyes and leaned back into Aquila's feathers with a sigh. Andromeda felt as though she were floating, and Felicity grew warm from head to toe. Then the fire felt the enchantment. The flames jumped and danced, tendrils waving and spitting upward in perfect rhythm with the tune. Small balls of flame escaped the stone pit and hung in midair, swirling and dancing, making fiery patterns against the black sky. Tilly leaned forward, spellbound.

Atalanta looked to Bree, who took up the song in perfect harmony, voice sweet as honeysuckle. Her fingers twirled and coaxed the balls of flame into new shapes. Fiery elves, blazing nymphs, and glowing satyrs danced together in a ring. Griffins and dragons, unicorns and fairies flew and pranced around the onlookers' heads.

The elves watched with nostalgic expressions, gentle smiles pulling at their mouths. The humans gaped in awe. Sir Boris reached out a finger with childlike wonder to touch the flaming griffin flying around his head. The fiery beast twirled around his hand and perched on the finger for a moment before swooping back in amongst its fellows.

Bree held one hand out to the second fire, and it sprang to life, birthing giants, trolls, vampires, and werewolves. Tilly gasped. Mendaline and Gelwyn took up the song, too. Now the two factions faced off for battle, playing out the story of the song. The fire elves brandished swords of flame. The griffins clashed claws with the vampires. The fairies swarmed the giants, driving them back into the pit with showers of sparks.

When it was over, a raucous round of applause broke out, and Tilly cried, "Again! Again!"

Atalanta laughed and said, "Tomorrow. Now we must get some sleep."

Felicity caught Atalanta's eye. "Thank you," she said, stroking Tilly's hair.

Atalanta nodded and gave Felicity a look not unlike Andromeda's.

Happy chatter filled the camp as the few blankets were spread out for groups of two and three to share and cloaks were bunched up into pillows. Sir Boris volunteered for first watch, as he had every night, and positioned himself close to the Avalons. Tilly curled herself against Felicity's chest and slipped a thumb into her mouth. Felicity covered the child protectively with one arm and smiled as she closed her eyes. Andromeda and Atalanta squeezed onto the blanket beside them—black, brown, blonde, and red hair fanned out across the grass. Andrew and Erro used Aquila for blanket and pillow, with Michael close by.

In the days that followed, though the travel was strenuous, the spark of comradery and hope that the fire song had ignited in the mismatched band held fast. The talk was cheerful and frequent as they rode. The elves seemed almost as curious about the humans as the humans were about the elves, and there was much discussion of culture and tradition. Felicity tried her best to explain the benefits of corsets to Bree and Mendaline, but the she-elves never really seemed convinced. Andromeda secretly agreed with them. Galen and Atalanta explained the elf High Court, though Atalanta seemed less than enthused, while Galen spoke of such authorities with a tinge of awe. Michael explained their own royal council, noting there was not much difference save the fact that the human councilmen earned their spot through noble birthright, not great deeds. Great deeds were for knights.

"Perhaps if we did it your way, my father would not be surrounded by old cowards quick to call us liars in the face of danger," Michael had said.

"At least your father values your opinion enough to heed your warnings over his advisors," Atalanta had said softly, twiddling her horse's mane through her fingers.

"Your father heeded your warning," said Michael. "He sent you an escort. I'm sure he's gathering your armies as we speak."

"Yes, he probably is, but I don't know that for sure, do I?" said Atalanta. "He sent me no letter, only a bunch of soldiers who will tell me nothing save that they have to get me home. He shares very little with me. He thinks me little more than a child." She turned from Michael to gaze out over the plains, but not before he saw the shimmer of tears in her emerald eyes. "I read your father's letter," she said, her face still averted from his. "He speaks to you as an equal."

Michael had opened his mouth several times but could not find what to say, so he, too, studied the wide expanse of lush, grassy hills that surrounded them.

Throughout their journey, they'd had little cover. The plains extended for miles in all directions, with only a few clusters of trees dotted here and there. Forests occasionally stood in the far distance to the right or left of their path, but ahead was endless grasslands. At first, Michael had complained they were too exposed with a growing army of werewolves and vampires at their backs. But Galen had insisted this path was the fastest route to Alatreon, and Michael could not argue against swift passage.

Still, the endless sea of green provided little to look at for a young girl, and Tilly had grown bored and restless. To combat this, Erro had fashioned her a toy that allowed her to play with

Zezil while on horseback. From her perch in the saddle in front of Felicity, Tilly now bobbed the toy—which was nothing but a stick and a vine of ivy tied around a bundle of acorns—in front of Zezil's quivering nose. The vexar ran alongside Felicity's horse, snapping at the acorns that dangled just out of his reach. His lolling tongue, playful yips, and acrobatic leaps kept Tilly entertained, at least for the moment.

Galen had assured them all that they would reach Alatreon that day, and moods were high all around. Tilly's high, sweet laughter served as a lovely backdrop to the last leg of the journey as the sky turned slowly purple. Silver stars showed their faces, beaming through the purple haze as the first glimpse of gold appeared, rising up into the clouds hovering above like a silver mist.

At the sight of the golden turrets peeking over the polished stone wall on the horizon, Andrew gave a cheer and urged his horse into a gallop.

"Andrew, wait!" Michael commanded, putting his heels to his own horse.

Andrew slowed and looked over his shoulder with an annoyed expression. "What?" he said, a whine in his voice.

"Last one there is the other's squire for a month," said Michael, whipping Andrew's overlong hair in a gust of wind as he galloped past.

"You're a filthy cheat!" Andrew called after him, but he was laughing as his horse picked up the pace.

"When you're both my squires, I'll have you refer to me as Lord of the Northern Wood, or there shall be consequences," Erro shouted down at the brothers as he shot over their heads on Aquila's back.

"Come on! Flying doesn't count!" said Andrew, his horse's nose dangerously close to Michael's steed's tail.

Erro reached the golden gates set into the white stone wall first, but his cry of victory was cut short as an arrow shot through the sky at his head and Aquila tucked his wings in a roll to avoid it.

"Stand down! Approach no closer! Name yourselves!"

Michael and Andrew pulled their reins back into their chests, and Erro dove for the ground.

"Well, that was horribly rude," said Erro, adjusting his cloak as he slid from Aquila's back.

"They must be unaware you're the Lord of the Northern Wood," said Andrew.

"Apparently," said Erro, raising his chin with dignity.

Andrew snickered, but Michael said, "You wouldn't be laughing if that arrow had found its mark."

"You three are a bunch of damn fools," said Felicity, cantering up to them beside Galen. "You could have been killed! This is foreign land in the middle of a pending war! You can't just storm the gates with a griffin! What were you thinking?"

"Why do you sound like mother?" said Andrew.

Felicity shot him a deadly look and said, "Somebody has to be your governess, clearly."

Andrew looked ready to stick his tongue out at her, but the guard at the top of the wall called down again.

"Announce yourselves! What is your business here?"

"Open the gate, Belin, you fool!" said Galen, waving an arm to get the guard's attention. "By your commander's orders. I've returned with the princess."

"By the land and sky!" said the elf. It seemed the outburst had been involuntary, and he visibly shook himself before calling down, "Of course, Commander Galen, at once. My humblest apologies." He leaned over the inner side of the wall and shouted, "Open the gates! Princess Atalanta has returned!"

The gate swung open to admit them without any sign of help. Guards in green breeches and tunics underneath splendid gold armor coverings, their long hair braided down their backs, appeared on either side of the gate and saluted with spears standing up from the ground and heads bowed in respect.

Atalanta urged her white horse through the gates first, her eyes searching every crevice of her home city, as if determined to memorize every detail for the next time she was shoved in a dark hole for multiple moons. Her guard followed after her, the Avalons next, Sir Boris, Erro, and Gelwyn's family trailing behind.

The houses of Alatreon did not line dirt or cobblestone roads. Grass just as lush as in the meadows outside the walls carpeted every corner of the city. Flowers grew in rows that designated paths and main streets. The houses were closely packed, but much larger than those in Campion. All were living trees with massive branches shaped into balconies and rooftops.

As the party passed through, following a street lined with tulips, elves of all ages and skin tones ran from their homes, shouting Atalanta's name. Some got to their knees and bowed so low their flawless faces touched the grass. Others, mostly children, reached out for her and called exaltations in the elvish tongue. Atalanta bent from her saddle to accept a rose held out by a young elf girl. When Atalanta tied it into the braid at the crown of her head, the girl rushed back to her mother, pointing excitedly at Atalanta to make sure she had seen.

The tulip path led through the very heart of Alatreon, straight toward the castle shimmering in the last of the sunlight. The palace rose into the clouds, its golden points caught the light of the moon and fading sun, even through the misty clouds, and twinkled along with the stars. The golden spires were long and thin, but hundreds shot up from delicate white stone towers with stained glass windows in tones of rose, gold, and soft green. The base of the castle was carved of the purest white marble intertwined with gold fastenings that rose to connect with the turrets.

Sir Boris removed his helm so that he could lean back his head and see the whole structure properly. Tilly was grinning so broadly her plump cheeks pushed against her eyes.

"Do you see? Do you see?" she whispered eagerly to Felicity, using both hands to point out every new glittering feature that caught her eye.

"My God, is your castle like this?" Erro asked Andromeda in wonder.

"This makes our home look like an exceptionally tall cottage," said Andrew, when Andromeda only shook her head, mouth hanging slightly open.

"What a shame," said Erro with a smirk. "I'm sure living there was just dreadful."

"I'm starting to wonder," said Andrew, eyes fixed on the marble stairs and the two marble stallions that reared opposite each other at the base, front hooves pawing the air.

At the top, two marble elves, one male and one female, guarded the golden doors. Both wore crowns (the male's appeared made of vines, while the females was a carved ring of flowers), but the male brandished a sword while the female held up her hands, ready to cast a spell. In front of the statues stood four real guards, two on each side.

Atalanta's smile was small, but it lit her eyes as she dismounted and gazed at the doors. The guards fell to one knee as she began to ascend the steps.

"We will take your horses to the stables to be cared for," said an elf at Andromeda's side, startling her.

He was not alone. A dozen stable hands rushed forward to take the mounts.

"Perhaps we should go with them," said Gelwyn to Mendaline.

Atalanta stopped on the third stair.

"Nonsense," she said. Gelwyn looked surprised that she'd heard him. "My father will want to speak with all of you."

The only members of the party to depart were Atalanta's escort, all save Galen. The guards at the top of the stairs pulled open the doors, two pulling at each of the large knockers.

The inner chamber was just as lovely as the exterior. Walls of polished stone decorated with elvish paintings and tapestries depicting pastoral landscapes and dense forests ran through an arched hallway with large stone beams braided along the top. The floor was smooth and flawless under their boots. Their footsteps echoed softly as they walked. At the end of the long, wide hallway, the arched ceiling opened up into a vast, square room that glittered in the lantern light. At the very center of the back wall, erected on a slab of marble, stood two thrones of gold embossed with pearls and rubies.

Upon the larger of the thrones sat an exceptionally tall elf with hair of deepest black with small braids at his temples pulled back from his face. His golden crown, which looked identical to the one worn by the statue outside, sat upon his head just above his pointed ears. His jaw was sharp and prominent, with a nose to match, but his eyes were a warming hazel.

Atalanta strode languidly into the room, head high, but her eyes searched the face of the king with desperation. King Zanthus' face transformed. The stern set of his jaw faded into a smile that lifted his cheeks and opened up his eyes, where fresh tears glittered. He stood from his throne and walked to the edge of the marble platform, watching her with a desperation that mirrored hers. Atalanta stood frozen for a moment, chest rising in slow, forcibly controlled breaths. When the first tear struck the king's cheek, she ran forward, quick and graceful as any deer, and leapt onto the platform in one fluid bound.

He caught her in his arms, his emerald robes blanketing her, and she buried her face in his gold-trimmed collar to hide her tears from her friends, crying as softly as she was able.

"My darling, my darling," he intoned in elvish, kissing the top of her hair.

"Hello, Father," she managed at last.

Chapter 24

The Black Forest

The others waited in respectful silence at the entrance to the throne room while Atalanta and King Zanthus spoke in rapid elvish. The king stood with hands clasped gently on his daughter's arms, occasionally reaching up to touch her cheek with an intonation of sympathy and despair.

"What are they saying?" Andrew whispered to Bree.

"The king is asking how she faired in captivity," said Bree.

From a wave of elvish, the name Tyrannus stood out on Atalanta's lips, disgust marring her face.

"Now he is asking her for more detail about the beast who calls himself a king," Bree said softly. Now Erro and the other Avalons were leaning in to hear her, too.

Zanthus released Atalanta's arms and gestured violently in the air, his voice hard.

"Uh oh, what does that mean?" said Andrew.

"He says he'll have the abomination roasted on a pyre," said Bree gravely. "He asked her about Tyrannus' desire for her magical power, apparently she didn't say much more in her letter. She's told him of how he tortured her."

Atalanta suddenly looked in their direction, and they all jumped apart. She smiled at them as she spoke in her native tongue. The king's face drew up in a smile, too. He held his arms out to them and switched to the common Arcamirian dialect.

"Come forth, Avalons, and your intriguing forest friend. I have much to thank you for."

The siblings and Erro walked the length of the throne room in awkward silence, Michael at the lead. Bree held Zezil back from following his master. Felicity still held Tilly at her hip, and the girl was gaping openly at the elf king.

"I don't think I shall ever be able to repay you," said Zanthus, when they reached the throne pedestal. "You've returned my daughter safely to me, and for that I give my humblest thanks."

The king bowed low at the waist, face upturned to them, one hand extended outward. Atalanta's lips parted in a tiny 'o' of surprise. Michael, recognizing the magnitude of the gesture, instantly went to one knee, and the other's quickly followed suit, looking a little alarmed. Erro tried to lean a little lower than the others, assuming it was expected of a commoner.

"Such thanks is too great, King Galechaser," said Michael. "Your daughter had already freed herself when we arrived. We did little more than escort her."

Zanthus straightened with a deep chuckle. "Still no small feat with vampires and werewolves at your heels. My thanks remains the same. Please rise; you shall be treated like children of my own house while you are here. No need for anymore bowing."

"Thank you, Your Majesty," said Michael, and the others echoed him softly.

"Your name is, Erro, yes?" said the king, his eyes suddenly on the red-haired wanderer.

"Yes, Your Majesty," said Erro with a quick bow of his head. "Please forgive my lack of proper etiquette. I know very little of royal courtesies."

"You have given no offense, young man. You simply intrigue me."

"Oh … uh, thank you?"

"I would like to address your griffin. Do you think he would agree to speak with me?"

Now it was Erro who looked intrigued by the elf king. "It would be better to ask him yourself," he said with a curious smile.

The king laughed softly. "Yes, I suppose you're right. Princess," —he addressed Andromeda, eyes flicking momentarily to the band on her arm— "would you kindly use that bracelet to assist me?"

"I'll try my best, Your Majesty, but I can only feel his emotions and disjointed thoughts."

"Ah, but the look on your face tells me you already suspect the griffin's true capabilities. Do you not?"

Andromeda appeared taken aback for only a moment. "Well, yes. He is … different."

"I think, should he choose to convene with me, he will show you the full capabilities of his mind." Without another word, he looked to where the rest of the party was standing patiently. "Master griffin, would you honor me with a word?"

Aquila's padded paws made little sound as he approached. When he reached Erro's side, he bowed his feathered head, and a deep voice rumbled in Andromeda's head, making her jump.

Your heart is noble, king. Speak as you will.

All eyes rested on Andromeda. After a moment's stammering, she repeated the message. Zanthus smiled at Andromeda before addressing Aquila.

"You have come in proximity with this hybrid king. Just what are his intentions? Can his heart be swayed?"

The one called Tyrannus has a heart black and shriveled with hate. He has known little love, and he will give none in return. He feels his cause is just. He feels his people are mistreated. To prove his strength and what he feels is his worth, he will make all feel his pain and his wrath. Those he cannot infect with his afflictions, he will destroy. The disease in his heart has little to do with venom or a poison of the blood, and I fear it is too late for a cure.

Zanthus grew grave as Andromeda translated. Erro looked at Aquila with an odd mix of amazement, elation, and something like betrayal.

"Thank you," said Zanthus with a small nod. "I feared it was so. Preparations for war are already under way. But I admit, I am at a loss for what to do about the innocents who have fallen prey to his army already. How can we distinguish them? Should we even try? They are all monsters now. It cannot be helped."

Though I cannot say what should be done with them afterward, I know of a way to distinguish your citizens, and the Avalons'.

"Name it."

Though their diseases shape their wills to crave bloodshed, their hearts' intents are still made clear to me and my kind. After decades and centuries go by, many hearts are overcome by the savagery of the diseases' desires—some much faster than that—but if you have griffins on your side, we can make it clear to you whose hearts are still fighting the afflictions.

"Then I ask that you tell me where to find more of your kind so that I might ask them to ally with our cause," said Zanthus.

There is a gathering place sacred to us where I can rally my kind, if they have not already sensed the need. I will go myself; it is a secret place. The cause is just; I shall bring you back a flock.

"I am in your debt," said Zanthus, bowing his head to the griffin.

I will leave at once, said Aquila, extending a leg to bow in return.

"And you thought I was loony for talking to him," Erro whispered to Felicity.

Aquila turned from the king and put his head under Erro's hand.

"Oh, so you really meant right now, eh?" said Erro, rubbing feathers at the crest of Aquila's head. "All right then. Hurry back."

Aquila made a soft chirruping sound.

"Why didn't you say something before?" said Andromeda, and the amber, eagle eyes found her face. "You knew I could hear you."

Aquila looked at her so long, she sighed with exasperation, thinking he'd gone mute again.

Words are necessary only when actions cannot fully convey your thoughts. Besides, you were already in my head, feeling what I felt.

Don't you think that's invasion enough, sweet one?

Andromeda was unsure what to say, but Aquila simply turned toward the exit, the brush of his tail tickling at Tilly's cheek for a moment as he did so, and loped past Sir Boris and the waiting elves, heading back the way they had come. Zezil wrestled himself out of Bree's arms and made to follow Aquila, but Erro called him back with a whistle.

Aquila's departure had brought Zanthus' attention to the small band of watchers at the throne room entrance. Galen stood straight and stiff, a soldier awaiting orders. Gelwyn and his family stood demurely, looking overwhelmed by the king's presence and the splendor all around them. Sir Boris stood with head held high, but his hands fidgeted nervously at the ends of the scroll he'd pulled from his belt.

"You have a message for me, knight?"

"Yes, Your Majesty," said Boris, bending at the knee.

"Please, bring it forth."

Boris' armor clanked softly as he rushed across the great space.

"What is your name, sir?"

"Sir Boris Cavalry, Your Majesty," said the knight, once again going to one knee, this time holding the scroll out to the elf king. "I bring word from His Royal Majesty, King Markus Avalon, in response to the troubling goings on in Arcamira. I extend this message in peace, as a gesture of alliance between our kingdoms and our species."

"Your peace is readily accepted, and I thank you," said Zanthus, breaking the seal of the scroll.

The room fell silent as Zanthus read. When he released the end of the scroll, sending it snapping back into a tight roll, it was Michael he addressed.

"I have always found your father exceptionally wise for a human. A much better man than his grandfather."

The Avalons fidgeted. Their great-grandfather, Elias Avalon, had nearly started a war with the elves in his youth. A squabble over lands.

"He speaks very highly of you, Prince Michael. Do you know of his plans?"

"I know he is rallying our armies. He told me he would send them here, should you think Tyrannus would strike Alatreon first. From what we've seen, that is the most likely."

"He has sent envoys to the centaurs in the East. I believe he has the right idea; I have ancient allies of my own I plan to call on when the time comes. The centaurs will come. Their hooves walked this land long before any feet touched it. They will fight to the last to prevent the Diseased Ones from overtaking it. I will send word to Markus, accepting his offer. I just hope there is enough time. The next full moon is less than a week away. Should Tyrannus choose to strike then, your father's host will be of no use."

"I must send a letter, myself," said Michael. "I'm sure by now his knights have brought him word that our people in the Northern Wood have been taken. I must let him know what horrors have befallen them. He will bring our armies here all the swifter for it."

"As you wish. I will have ink and parchment brought to you in your chambers. But first, I must address my own people," said Zanthus, turning his warm eyes to Gelwyn, Mendaline, and Bree, "I have already kept them waiting too long. Please, come forward." He beckoned them with his hand. "Galen," said Zanthus as the small family walked shyly toward the platform, "please find Delanie and have her show the rest of our guests to their chambers."

* * *

Melanie's hunger pains were tugging at her gut as though they'd never left. At times, the pain was excruciating, like a hook wrapped around her intestines, ready to yank them out at any moment if she did not taste blood soon. The elder vampires had not fed since Campion either, but fledglings required more blood. The ancients, like Thetis, could go months, their bodies strong and so accustomed to half-death that the thirst, the only true feeling they had left, did not touch them very often.

The captive elves looked waifish as well, though they were fed daily. At first, the werewolves had tried to force meat on them, for that was what they had dried out and preserved for their own supplies. But the elves had refused, growing thinner each day until Thetis noticed and gave Nathaniel a deep gash across the face.

Melanie gazed longingly at the dense forest in the distance—the Black Forest, Thetis had called it. It was there that they would meet this King Tyrannus whom Thetis served. We all serve him now, she reminded herself. As much as she dreaded meeting this cruel king, she needed rest. She felt ready to fall out of the sky with exhaustion.

To the east, she could see a shimmer of gold peeking over the horizon line if she allowed her eyes to focus at their full capacity from this height. It was Alatreon, the fabled elf city of gold. It was their final target.

At last they reached the edge of the forest. The vampires landed at the treeline first and walked the rest of the way. The forest was a tangle of wild foliage. The trees were larger than any Melanie had ever seen in the Northern Wood. Some of their trunks were so wide a giant would struggle to touch his fingertips together should he try to wrap his arms around them. Melanie had heard of this place in a bard song once before. It said the elves sang this forest into being when Alatreon was built, as a haven for the wildlife that would have to make way for the large city. They had made the trees so thick that no creature could level them. The name, Black Forest, was fitting. In many places, the canopy was so thick and so tangled that no light shone through. It was so dark in those places that no foliage could grow underneath the trees' shade, and only mushrooms blossomed there. The mushrooms were unlike any Melanie had ever seen—vibrant shades of red and purple and blue, some with white spots, all in different shapes and sizes. Some were as big as dinner plates, others as small as sunflower seeds. Melanie noticed the elves stumbling; they could not see through the blackness. The spaces where moonlight met the forest floor were blinding in comparison. They were also lush with life and greenery. Deer, rabbits, foxes, birds, and even a stray coyote scattered in every direction as they trudged toward the heart of the forest. Thetis halted the party in one of the places where the trees grew farther apart and the faint light of the nearly full moon tinted the surrounding forest a pale white-blue.

"We wait here for the king," he said.

There was much thumping and scrambling and agitated snarling as captives and captors settled onto the soft earth. Melanie noticed the elves running their hands reverently over the grass and the tangles of roots peeking out from the soil. Some muttered what sounded like prayers, their eyes closed and heads upturned to the moon.

Melanie shoved her way into the moonlight; it was as close to the sun as she would ever come again. There was no warmth in it. She settled with her wings tucked tight, like a second skin, to her back, resting against a thick cluster of bushes and the trunk of a sapling. She closed her eyes, trying to enjoy the pure smells and sounds of nature and shove away her hunger pains, but Thetis lowered himself next to her. A scowl pulled at her face, and she forced down an animalistic snarl.

"The perfect place, is it not?" he said.

She did not open her eyes nor look over at him.

"No more flying miles each day to find a resting place. The forest will protect us during the day. It's large enough to harbor our whole army without the elves ever knowing we are here.

They rarely venture beyond the outer tree line; they think it is an invasion into the kingdom they've created for the animals, that it's disrespectful." He made a derisive coughing noise in the back of his throat. "They think they're a superior race. They're nothing but fools, groveling in the filth of the earth, bowing to plants and dumb animals."

"At least they care for something other than themselves," said Melanie, eyes still closed.

"You think the king cares for no one else?" said Thetis.

Melanie opened her eyes and fixed him with a hard stare. She gestured at the elves, their wrists bruised and bloodied by the shackles, the rest of their bodies bruised and bloodied by their captors.

"I see no caring here."

"He cares for his children. He will care for them once they are converted," said Thetis. "He keeps us safe. He found us all when we were hunted and alone, shunned by those we once called our own kind. Many of us did not choose to become what we are, but still we were cast out and hunted down." His eyes flashed with a fervent, wild light. Only fury brought life to his face. "But the king showed us that we were hated for our strength. We are the superior races. We are more powerful, more cunning, and they fear and hate us for it. The king saw it. He sought out his powers. Asked for them."

"Then he is a worse monster than I imagined," said Melanie, her own anger rising.

Thetis struck her across the face with the back of his hand. "I suggest you rid yourself of such blasphemy before he arrives, or you will find out what true pain feels like. You think me cruel? I have been far too gentle with you. Speak such things in his presence, and I cannot protect you."

Melanie scoffed. "Is that what you've been doing? Protecting me? Why do you care?"

"You are … different," said Thetis, his head tilted as he

appraised her. "You do not cower. You have refused defeat. Your heart does not beat … yet you are still full of life. When you've existed as long as I, such … vibrancy is a rare thing."

Melanie, taken entirely by surprise, could only stare back at him, puzzled.

"So until you begin to bore me, which is inevitable, I hope you will show proper fealty to your king."

My king is Markus Avalon. But she dared not say it. She wanted only peace, to rest and think of other things in this beautiful place. She turned away and closed her eyes again. He did not disturb her but remained at her side.

And so they sat as hours ticked by. Melanie thought of Tilly, praying she had reached safety, if not with the Avalons then perhaps with the elves. Tilly would like that. She thought of Joseph as long as she dared. She'd been unable to properly grieve, and the loss was still raw, but if she did not dwell too long, she could fill her mind with sweet memories and forget the heinous ending. She found some solace knowing that he had escaped her own fate; doomed to live as a monster forever or face damnation in the afterlife for the blood she'd already spilled.

The rumbling brought her back. The earth vibrated under her hands. The leaves shook, hissing in the night. Wind, powerful gusts of wind. Wing beats. Thunderous footsteps. So many smells. The rot of vampires, the musk of werewolves, and something new. It smelled of dirt and filth and sweat. It smelled of pigs and damp and uncleanliness.

A vast shadow blocked the moon. A vampire with wings that spread longer than the tallest man alive. Lethal claws sprouted from the wing tips, larger than eagle talons. The thing attached to them smelled of both vampire and werewolf. Melanie shrank back as Thetis rose. The hybrid landed in the center of the clearing, and Melanie's growling stomach roiled at the sight of him. Dank, grey flesh covered in patches of wiry black hair. He was enormous, towering over Thetis by at least three feet. He had the face of a beast, his nose and mouth forming a muzzle. Stray fangs jutted from his jowls, glinting in the moonlight. And his eyes. Orange as a burning coal. Orange as the moon lit from behind by the setting sun. He wore a crown of bones and a flowing, tattered cape of rich purple fabric. Claws on his toes dug into the earth as he walked toward Thetis. Melanie scrambled away behind the bushes, not wanting those orange eyes to find her.

Behind and above him a hoard of vampires was circling, looking for a place to land. So many they stole away all the moonlight. Werewolves appeared amongst the trees, all armed with makeshift weapons. The ground was rumbling so violently the werewolves struggled to stay upright. The trees were rocking back and forth. Birds took flight in droves, squawking in terror. Melanie could hear the animals dashing out of the way of the owners of the monstrous footsteps. For that was what they were. She was sure of it now. The top of the first head appeared in the canopy, a scraggly tangle of blonde, matted locks. She squinted into the darkness, focusing her eyes. Giants. At least five of them. Three males, two females. And something else. Something smaller but twice as ugly. Trolls. And perhaps some of the shorter ones were ogres, but she could not tell in this light. Something low to the ground caught her eye as it darted around the legs of two trolls. Goblins. She could hear them chattering to each other now that the giants were standing still. She had never seen any of these creatures save in picture books. They had been driven out of human territory long ago by the first of the Avalons.

"You do not disappoint, Thetis," said Tyrannus, his orange eyes purveying Thetis' brood. The new recruits all looked away as his eyes fell on them, only to return a moment later, reluctantly, as if forced. "I had started to doubt you, but you've proven your worth."

Thetis bowed. "Thank you, Your Majesty."

"He didn't do it alone," grumbled Nathaniel, coming to stand beside Thetis.

"No, of course not," said Tyrannus with a revolting grin. "You have done your part well, Nathaniel. You shall be rewarded."

Callid rushed forward in an awkward, loping gate, and slobbered at the hem of Tyrannus' robes, kissing them.

"Great master, Callid has helped, too."

Tyrannus patted one of Callid's heads with a clawed hand, chuckling under his breath, but gave no response.

"I have remedied your mistakes and found replacements for our little elf princess," said Tyrannus. "It has put me in a pleasant mood. Do not spoil it with any more mishaps. I trust you have your captives and your new converts completely under your control?"

"Yes, Your Majesty," said Thetis and Nathaniel together, both looking slightly sour.

Tyrannus' eyes suddenly shifted to a spot over Nathaniel's shoulder.

"Thetis," said Tyrannus, his voice suddenly very cold, "I thought I told you to get rid of the raider and his men."

Brock bent his knees, preparing to run, but he didn't seem able. Thetis' eyes had found his, and he seemed transfixed by them. He did whatever Thetis asked now without any fuss; he couldn't help it. His skin was ashy and blue veins stood out on his neck and under his eyes. He looked weak and sickly, but Melanie had seen him throw his horse to the ground as if it weighed no more than a dog when it had shied away from his touch and refused to let him mount. The venom he received in exchange for allowing Thetis to feed whenever he willed was doing its work.

"His men are dead, sacrificed to feed the flock. He has been useful, and he showed an interest in joining your cause, your Grace. So I've made him my servant. But I will be happy to dispatch him should that be your will."

"Hmm, I suppose you are entitled your playthings after what you have done."

"He has a plaything, but it isn't that scrawny raider," said Nathaniel with a cruel sneer.

One of Tyrannus' bushy eyebrows disappeared into his thick hair. "Something pretty?" he said.

Melanie hid herself totally behind the cluster of bushes. Had her heart still beat, it would have raced. She did not want him to look at her. To even know of her.

"Very," said Thetis.

"Use caution. Pretty things can still bite. And you usually don't see it coming."

A high cackle sent shivers up Melanie's spine. Morbid curiosity pulled her head from behind the bush. From the depths of the trees, four stooped, hooded figures glided into the clearing and flanked Tyrannus, two on each side. They kept their heads low, and Melanie could only catch a glimpse of a protruding nose here and a wisp of grey hair there.

"Thetis, Nathaniel, pay your respects to my new dearest friends. They're going to make sure that when the full moon waxes, the battle is irrevocably tipped in our favor."

Chapter 25

Unanswered Questions

Andromeda woke to a soft weight on her bedcovers. Two large, blue eyes came suddenly into focus.

"Good morning," said Tilly.

Andromeda sat up, rubbing at her eyes.

"Good morning, Tilly."

Light flooded the room. Felicity had flung open the curtains. She was already dressed in the elvish custom—a long, fitted, blue linen gown free of any buttons, ties, or belts—but her eyes drooped and she yawned as she said, "It's time for breakfast. At least according to the chipmunk."

"I'm not a chipmunk," said Tilly, her indignation overridden by her giggle.

Felicity put her fists on her hips and narrowed her eyes playfully at Tilly. "Are, too."

"Am not," said Tilly, putting her fists on her own hips.

"Are, too. You look just like one, and you're always scurrying around looking for food."

"Well …," said Tilly, screwing up her face in serious thought, "you're a goose!"

Andromeda laughed so hard at Felicity's flummoxed expression that she fell back onto her pillows, clutching her stomach.

"A goose, am I?" said Felicity, as Tilly joined in Andromeda's mirth.

"Yeah," said Tilly through her giggles. "You're a big old mother goose! You say, 'Honk, honk, honk!'"

Andromeda could hardly breathe for laughter. "Wait until … I tell … Andrew," she choked out.

"Don't you dare!" said Felicity, the fun suddenly wiped from her face.

But now Tilly had jumped off the bed and was running circles around Felicity with her arms bent into wings, honking at the top of her lungs.

"Come here, you little goose," said Felicity, snatching at Tilly as a new smile tried to force its way onto her face.

Tilly dodged and said, "You said I was a chipmunk."

"Either way, you look pretty tasty to me," said Felicity, making her fingers into claws.

Tilly stopped her flapping and honking and stared at Felicity apprehensively.

"Ha!" said Felicity, pouncing with her hands up by her head.

Tilly squealed and took off into the hall. Felicity followed, yelling, "You'd better run, little chipmunk."

Still chuckling, Andromeda got up and closed her bedroom door so she could change out of her nightdress and into the lilac gown that a handmaiden had brought in the night before and folded on top of the wide windowsill dressed with a cushion for reading in the sun.

The room was rather bare of furnishings. The bed demanded most of the space. The pure gold frame had an intricate metalwork of roses on the headboard. After an inquiry of her designated handmaid, Andromeda learned the bed itself was stuffed with sheep's wool. The plush material had almost been too soft after so many nights spent sleeping on the ground. The bronze dresser was the only other furnishing. After their time spent in Campion, Andromeda found it odd seeing stone and metals adorn an elvish dwelling. The splendid metalwork and carvings were crafted by dwarf hands, though the masons had tried their best to reflect the elves' love of nature in their designs. The entire palace was a gift, bestowed upon the first elf king of Arcamira, Selwyn Faireyes, as a sign of both gratitude and alliance from the dwarf king, Gwayne Firebrand, after Faireyes' armies helped deliver Firebrand's mountainous kingdom from an invading army of giants from the southern islands. If legend held true, Firebrand had not been particularly fond of the elves, but given a choice between cohabiting their native lands with elves or giants, Firebrand proclaimed he'd take the prettier species, and built the palace and the wall surrounding Alatreon to make sure the "pretty ones" had a place to stay. Though he built it nearly as far from his own home as possible.

Andromeda had hardly gotten her new gown over her head when she heard two familiar voices outside her door. Roughly brushing her fingers through her hair, she rushed to catch up with the voices already fading down the corridor.

Erro and Andrew turned at the sound of her opening door. Erro quickly drank her in, her raven hair falling to her ribcage overtop the lilac fabric, and when his eyes came back to hers, she thought, not for the first time, that he looked surprised to see her studying him, too. His ragged green cloak was nowhere in sight. He'd been given fresh earth-colored trousers and a loose cream tunic. Both the trouser cuffs and the shirt sleeves reached the proper place on his ankles and wrists; his slender frame was well suited for elvish clothing.

Zezil was at his feet, but the vexar galloped down the hall to paw at Andromeda's legs and dance around her feet until she bent to scratch him behind the ears.

"Did I hear someone honking a moment ago?" said Andrew.

Through a laugh, Andromeda said, "Wait until you hear," as she came to walk beside them. By the time she'd finished recounting her morning, Andrew looked positively impish.

When they had at last found their way through the unfamiliar castle, after stopping two separate servants along the way, and entered the meal hall, they found Felicity, Tilly, Atalanta, and Michael already seated on large, overstuffed cushions and holding bowls of something steaming. This hall was much smaller and far less decorative than the main dining room in which they'd enjoyed a welcome home feast the night before.

There, they had sat in golden chairs with members of the court at a long, marble table. Planted, living flowers adorned the walls, and vines of ivy and the green, winding stalks of hydrangeas had been sung into shape around the stone beams supporting the high ceiling. There were no seats of gold or tables of any sort in the regular meal hall, only poufs of soft wool, dyed in rich reds, purples, greens, and golds.

"Morning," said Erro, moving to sit on a cushion next to Michael.

A serving girl peeked her head out of the adjoining kitchen and then retreated within once more.

"How are we supposed to eat on these?" said Andrew, eyeing the poufs with distrust.

"It's better than eating on the ground, and you have no trouble with that," said Atalanta, as Andromeda plopped down beside her.

Andrew scrunched his nose. "I think I prefer a solid gold chair rested firmly beneath my buttocks."

"Sit down, Andrew," said Felicity, and she sounded so much like their mother that Andrew obeyed unconsciously and nearly instantaneously.

But no sooner had his backside hit the cushion than a soft honk floated from his lips. It was so realistic, Felicity looked around in confusion. Not finding the source, her head whipped back to Andrew. She narrowed her eyes at him, one brow arching almost imperceptibly, but said nothing.

The serving girl reemerged balancing three more bowls in her arms. Inside each was a rich, hot porridge made of grains and steamed goat's milk. The star-shaped fruit and perfectly rounded yellow seeds were foreign to Erro and the Avalons. Andrew inspected one of the seeds on his spoon for a moment before shoveling in a large mouthful. A nod of his head and a soft "mmm" signaled his approval.

"So," said Erro, after a few bites of his own breakfast, "what do royals usually do in the lulls between grand battles and balls?"

"This royal has to report to her father right after breakfast for magic lessons," said Atalanta with a grimace.

"At least you'll be doing something productive," said Michael.

"Holed back up in a castle for one night and you're already restless?" said Atalanta.

"Hard not to be. Now that I'm not preoccupied with finding a stream or hunting our next meal or keeping watch for vampires and werewolves, the only thing I'm left with are my own thoughts."

"Are you being nasty to yourself?" said Andrew, pouting his bottom lip.

"Seriously, Andrew, is everything a joke to you?" said Felicity.

Andrew looked away into his porridge. Another soft honk broke the silence. Tilly looked to the ceiling for the source of the sound, her brows crinkled in confusion. This time Felicity's eyes never wandered from the back of Andrew's head, but she said not a word. Andromeda bit her lip to suppress a giggle.

Michael, also appraising Andrew curiously, unsure if he'd in fact heard the noise, said, "Doesn't it keep you awake at night? Knowing that at the next full moon we could be marching into battle. True battle, with hundreds or thousands of bloodthirsty beasts."

"They aren't all beasts," said Erro, putting his bowl aside half finished. He hugged his knees to his chest, looking anywhere but at the others.

Zezil dunked his head in the porridge bowl, and for a while his eager lapping and gulping were the only sounds in the hall. Andromeda idly swirled her spoon in the last of her porridge. Atalanta, finished with her breakfast, toyed with her hair, winding strands of it around her fingers. Tilly observed them all, keeping as still as a four-year-old could. Felicity looked down at the child, and her eyes brimmed with tears. She slammed her bowl down, spattering porridge onto the polished stone floor.

"There has to be something we can do!"

"Aquila is going to help," said Andromeda. "We'll know which of them are our people."

"They were all our people at one point or another," said Michael, eyes down as he picked at the wool of his pouf. "What use is separating the new from the old? They'll still change at the full moon. They'll still lust for blood."

"So we just slaughter them?" said Erro, red flowers blossoming in his cheeks and at his hairline. "Jeremiah, Fiona ... Brent?"

"What else can we do?" said Michael. His eyes implored Erro to give him a solution.

"Spare them!"

"So that they can kill and maim others?"

"So we kill and maim innocents who were ripped from their homes and turned into monsters against their will?"

"Isn't that how it's always been done?" said Atalanta softly. "Most of them aren't like Tyrannus. They didn't ask to walk the earth as they do. Perhaps now they enjoy it, perhaps it's corrupted them, as Aquila said, but the vampires and werewolves we've all killed for centuries were once people made prey to vampire or werewolf attacks. And yet they were hunted down."

They all watched her, but she looked at none of them. She watched her bright auburn hair slide through her fingers and said sadly, "That's why they follow him."

"But if the first extermination had succeeded, we wouldn't be in this situation," said Michael. "The only way to protect others from suffering the same fate is to eradicate those that have already succumbed to it. This war is our only chance to do it. Before, they were scattered all over Arcamira. Many of them hid once the word was spread. If Tryannus is to be believed, he's called them all together under his banner. We can end it for good."

"At the expense of hundreds forced to fight on a side they

despise?" said Erro, voice and face hard as the marble of the walls.

"They may not fight at all. He can't make them fight, can he?" said Felicity.

"He wouldn't have gone to the trouble of creating them had he not had a plan for how to use them," said Atalanta.

"When the first blood spills, the vampires will fight," said Andromeda. "And the werewolves must obey the alpha; I've told you."

"But," said Andrew, eyes suddenly alight, "if Aquila and the griffins could help us separate the werewolves from the alpha, we could spare them, right?"

"Just separating them isn't enough when they are transformed," said Andromeda. "First, you would have to take them miles and miles from the alpha so that they couldn't hear his call."

"Or we could kill him," said Andrew.

"True, but during a full moon, the human piece of them is all but gone. They feel only rage."

"We would only have to keep them at bay until the end of the full moon."

"And what of the next full moon?" said Michael.

"But that's what I'm saying," said Andrew. "Without an evil alpha forcing them to do as he wishes, they are only dangerous one night a month. The rest of the time, they're ordinary humans. Couldn't they be contained somehow?"

"Yeah!" said Erro. "Lock them away in a special prison for the night."

"Maybe," said Michael, eyes somber as he observed the other boys' enthusiasm. "But who's to say another alpha won't rise? Not every person bitten is a saint, and that much power is always tempting. And there would always be a risk that one would escape, or simply not show up to be imprisoned."

"You don't really want to save any of them, do you?" said

Erro, jumping to his feet and towering over Michael, his whole face red. "You'd rather just kill them all and have done with it. What does it matter, right? They're just monsters."

"Would you have thought any differently if you hadn't seen Jeremiah in Campion, only the carnage?" said Michael hotly.

"What if it was someone you love?" Erro shot back, looking mutinous. "What if it was Felicity or Andrew or Andromeda? Would you slit their throats with silver blades or drive stakes through their hearts?"

"It's not just about me, and it's not about you!" said Michael, rising too. "Don't you get that? We have to protect the kingdom!"

Tilly made an anxious noise and flinched back into Felicity.

"Both of you, stop it this instant!" she cried, pulling Tilly into her lap.

Both boys looked at her. At the sight of Tilly's face, Michael looked ashamed. His shoulder's drooped. Erro clenched his jaw and stormed from the room. Andromeda was on her feet in an instant, jogging after him. Zezil followed.

"Erro, wait!" she called just before he rounded a corner at the far end of the corridor.

For a moment he stared around the corner as if he meant to keep walking, but his feet remained still on the lush, embroidered rug that ran down the center of the passageway. She hurried to him and took his hand. He looked down morosely at her fingers wrapped in his.

"You oughtn't do that here. In a place as large as this, gossip has many mouths to fuel it."

"What do I care for gossip?" said Andromeda, walking on down the corridor, pulling him along with her.

"Your father is on his way here. It might reach his ears when he arrives."

"How many times must I tell you, I don't care about your title? Besides, my father is already fond of you, remember? I'm certain he'll give you a knighthood if you want it."

"He may not if he knows it will bring me closer to your station. Although, knights don't fraternize with princesses either, do they?"

"Is that what we're doing? Fraternizing?" she said, giving him a sly sideways glance.

The smile slipped through his melancholy expression, and Andromeda's heart lightened. Zezil dashed in circles around their feet, and then darted off down the winding corridor, only to look back and find they were no longer beside him and come bounding back. Zezil repeated the pattern, leading them left, then right, then left again. They followed him instinctively, having no particular destination in mind.

"I'm not sure I'm suited for castle life," said Erro.

Andromeda studied him. "Why do I feel this has to do with more than missing the woods?"

He gave her a sheepish smile. "I can't think the way Michael does. I can't be … princely. The 'kingdom' means nothing to me; it's just a word. I can't put it over people … over Jeremiah and his family."

"Not everyone should," said Andromeda softly. "Michael … he's been groomed for the throne from the moment he was born. We all have, to some extent, but Michael most of all. The king must protect the kingdom as a whole. But in order to care for the kingdom, the king mustn't forget the needs of individuals. It's hard to find a balance in times like this. Michael's scared, but he doesn't want to show it. He's holding to what he knows best, what he's been taught. It doesn't make him right. Of course, it seems there's no right answer here."

"But he was right about what he said, that I wouldn't have hesitated to agree with him if I hadn't seen Jeremiah. I've seen what leeches and moon mutts can do. I've feared them my whole life, and I've hated them from the moment I faced them with the rest of you."

"Opinions can change. And oftentimes it's for the better,"

said Andromeda.

Zezil was sitting in front of an archway that led out into sunlight. When they drew level with him, he bounded out onto the grass of a massive courtyard enclosed in a fence of bushes. Beyond the enclosure was an orchard. Inside, a lush garden surrounding a grand fountain depicting running horses stood to the left. To the right was what appeared to be a training ground. Archery targets lined the far side. Two elves were utilizing the space to practice their swordplay. They never glanced from each other's faces and blades. Erro and Andromeda wended their way through the garden. The beauty momentarily interrupted their conversation. They walked hand in hand along a spiraling stone path that led them through flowerbeds planted so that the petal colors created images. Some spelled out elvish words with purple blossoms in the midst of a yellow field. Another depicted a beautiful female face with pointed ears. Hedges shaped like centaurs, unicorns, griffins, and fairies towered over them, but Andromeda knew no blade had ever touched their leaves.

"I think there's something we all ought to learn from all of this," said Andromeda at last.

Erro looked at her expectantly.

"Don't you think it's rather disturbing how easily we've always cut down vampires and werewolves? Killing them was never questioned, at least not by the majority. We feared them, so we ignored their humanity. Yes, they do awful things that must be punished, but no one ever stopped to ask why."

"What else is there to do, though?" said Erro, eyes shining with the beginnings of tears. "Their diseases make them kill, and it also makes them impossible to control. Vampires are already dead, aren't they?"

"I don't know. But don't you think more people ought to have asked those questions? Maybe if they had, we would have a cure by now."

"You think there's really hope for a cure?"

Andromeda sighed. "I don't know. Hardly anyone ever really bothered to look for one. Anyone turned was automatically labelled inhuman. People slaughtered their own loved ones. Some had no choice; they were being attacked. Others killed them before they even fully changed because they told themselves it wasn't really their loved one anymore. It was a beast."

"I bet if a prince or princess was ever changed, they would have found a way to spare them," said Erro, bitterness making his voice cold. "But princes and princesses get to live behind strong walls and never leave shelter alone." He looked over at her and blushed. "Sorry."

"Don't be," said Andromeda, looking out into the orchard. "You're right, you know. The closest we ever came to a cure was when Princess Georgina Valentine was bitten by a werewolf nearly eight hundred years ago at the age of sixteen."

"I've never heard that," said Erro, brows raised. "Of course, you hear very little of history living on your own in the woods."

"Her father called together healers and alchemists from all over Arcamira and paid them mounds of gold and jewels to help him find a cure. He paid them to keep quiet, too, but like you said, a castle is full of gossiping mouths. Three of his own knights slew her while she slept, then killed themselves for their betrayal."

"My God."

Andromeda nodded. "He quit seeking a cure, though one of the alchemists' whose writings were preserved felt they were close. He had wanted to wait until Georgina's next full moon transformation and collect her saliva and her fur. He thought the key lay in her wolf form. But the knights killed her the day before the full moon. She had nearly escaped her bonds during her last transformation, and they had feared she would succeed sooner or later. King Valentine's wife had died two years before, and he had Georgina late in life. He had no desire for another child, just as he had no desire for a cure. Truth be told, he had little desire for anything after her death. He took the son of one of his most favored nobles under his wing and raised him to take over the throne. His name was Harold Avalon."

Erro looked at her, startled.

"Lovely bit of family legacy, isn't it?"

"Why has no one done anything?" said Erro. "They were close! Why has no one finished what they started?"

"Three other healers' and alchemists' writings were preserved. I've read them. They mention the hopeful alchemist, and none are very fond of him. They chide him in their writings, calling him a fool. It seems none of the others were as … optimistic as he was. He was written off as a kook. One of the accounts even calls him a dark sorcerer, and the writer suspected he was actually trying to make the princess stronger so that she could free herself. Who knows, they could have been right. Even if he wasn't a sorcerer, there's a pretty big chance he was wrong. None of the others thought they were anywhere close to a cure."

Erro slumped on a bench formed from a tree root poking up from the soil of the garden.

"But somebody must have read his account and wanted to at least try to find a cure, even if they didn't use his methods."

Andromeda shrugged. "The need was gone. I'm sure there were many families who hoped for a cure after their loved ones were taken. But what could they do? Harold's brother had been killed by a vampire right in front of him. He wasn't too keen on helping them or showing them mercy. Not many people ever even knew about Georgina or her father's search for a cure. They only knew she had died. Of course, rumors circulated, but they were only whispers. Public opinion never changed. It fueled the extermination, and then everyone thought it was all over."

Erro raised an eyebrow.

"Okay, not everyone, but everyone who could do something about it. And even the common folk turned a blind eye for centuries."

Erro nodded, face grim. "It's easier to believe your loved one got lost in the woods or attacked by a wild animal."

"Right."

Erro sighed. "But we should be finding a cure now, shouldn't we? At least trying."

"I think we should go talk to Zanthus."

"Uh, you mean you should talk to Zanthus."

"Oh, that's right," said Andromeda, putting a finger under Erro's chin and using it to coax him to his feet. "The Lord of the Northern Wood is afraid of the court. Anyone wearing a crown makes him shake in his boots."

His roguish smile set her heart thumping madly.

"Is that a challenge, princess?"

She leaned into him and rested her hand on the back of his neck.

"You really oughtn't do that," he said, his face slightly pained at the thought, but he leaned his head down toward hers all the same. "There are wandering eyes everywhere."

"I'm not afraid," she said, her lips brushing his as she spoke.

"That makes one of us," he said, and he took her face in his hands and drew her lips against his.

Chapter 26

Consulting the Veil

With only three days until the full moon, tensions in the castle thickened the air, and occupants wore the hard, strained expressions of people carrying great weights on their chests. The lower levels of the eastern wing were hot and stuffy from the forges beneath. Atalanta explained that the underground forges hadn't been used since the Extermination. Outside forges had been created long ago to better suit the preferences of the elves, and those were in use, too, but the old, dwarf-crafted forges were larger and better equipped.

Somewhere within the untraveled recesses of the palace, elf alchemists and healers were gathered in rooms piled with books and ingredients, searching feverishly for a cure. Zanthus had taken to the idea quicker than expected, though he warned them all it was most likely a fruitless effort.

After Erro and Andromeda had shared their idea with the others, they had all petitioned Zanthus together. Atalanta had not waited for a servant to request her father see them in the throne room. Instead, she marched them all to his private study, where they found him sitting at the window engrossed in a scroll so long it trailed the length of the room.

He had listened to their proposal with unwavering, quiet attention, Atalanta inserting bold admonitions like, "It would be nothing short of neglect of duty not to at least try." And, "We ought to have thought of it before," while Erro and the Avalons—mostly Andromeda—did their best to make their case in dulcet and what they hoped were persuasive tones, feeling awkward at barging in on the king as they had. When they had finished, he set aside his scroll, which he had kept in his lap while they spoke, and stood.

"Your compassion is to be admired, and the wisdom you all show at such a young age should be praised, but I fear you are investing too much of that precious asset, hope, in this idea."

The Avalons hung their heads, thinking they had failed. Erro had looked as though he wanted to protest, but under Zanthus' steady gaze, he shut his mouth. Atalanta, though, looked mutinous, but Zanthus held up a hand to silence her.

"The fate of our people," —he looked to the Avalons—"and yours, has troubled me since you told me of their capture yesterday. In truth, I had come to the same conclusion. An attempt for a cure is the only solution available to us. Still, it is a feeble solution, with little hope for success. I will gather all of the healers in Alatreon and send messages to those outside its walls, but time is short. The battle will come before any solution is found. It could take years, if it's possible at all. We are still faced with the same dilemma. What shall we do in the heat of battle? How can innocent lives be spared once our griffin allies have identified them? That is what you must put your minds to now."

But try as they might, they'd fallen short of any sort of solution.

"What if we had the forges create extra strong chains? Perhaps out of dwarvish chainmail, like in our armor," said Andrew now as they sat under the sun in the orchard, the smell of familiar and exotic fruits perfuming the air.

They had gone round and round with the idea of restraining those the griffins marked as unwilling victims of the werewolf disease and vampire venom, but the strength of the two species and the logistics of trapping them in the midst of battle kept getting in the way of a satisfactory solution.

"Dwarvish chainmail isn't just lying around," said Atalanta, her frustration making her snappish.

"Everything else around here is dwarvish!" said Andrew, his own brain thumping against his skull.

"Quit yelling," said Michael, close to a shout.

"What if they just make refortified chains?" said Felicity, one eye on Tilly as she ran through the trees in a wild, rule-free game of chase with Zezil. "Extra thick, double linked."

Andromeda sighed. "We've been over this. Even if we can find some way to bind them for the entirety of the battle, we have to figure out a practical strategy for doing so. Is every soldier supposed to lug around a chain? Or should there be a special battalion designated only for restraining them? How will they be protected? How will they carry around that many chains? Will the griffins somehow corral them into one group, or will they just point them out to us one by one?"

"Hey!" said Felicity, only half listening, for Zezil had just pounced on Tilly's back, tackling her into a pile of fallen leaves and squishy fruit, but Tilly only squealed with joy as Zezil licked the remnants of an orange from her cheek. Felicity sat back down, having risen halfway off the ground.

"Be gentle, Zezil," said Erro. "You don't want to ignite the wrath of the mother goose."

Andrew honked.

Felicity had quickly figured out that the boys knew of Tilly's impromptu nickname for her after Andrew had honked under his breath every time she spoke at dinner, so much so that a few of the servants had started looking for the animal at the window. Erro had been silently crying into his rice cake with suppressed laughter. When the two boys accidentally locked eyes, they burst into gales of laughter so loud they hardly heard Felicity's thunderous scolding.

Now she surprised them all by sighing resignedly and ignoring them.

An eagle cry made them all look up, shielding their eyes from the sun with their hands. Zezil whined and spun in circles, his eyes upturned to the clouds where a flock of griffins soared, their wings filtering the sunlight in tones of gold and copper.

Andromeda closed her eyes and concentrated.

Hello, dear one.

Andromeda smiled. Erro was already on his feet, sprinting through the orchard after the flock. She raced after him, Zezil at her heels. Atalanta flew past them both, her bare feet making no noise as they floated over the grass. She said, "Humans," in a pitying voice as she passed.

Minutes later, they all came to a sliding stop in the hall outside the throne room. Atalanta's hair whipped around her shoulders as she pulled up first, nearly causing a collision of bodies behind her. Zezil's nails scratched at the floor, trying in vain to find a grip on the smooth surface of the stone. As he tried to come to a halt after his frantic flight down the hall, his short, muscular legs back-peddled frantically and he panted with effort, his red tongue hanging from the side of his mouth. He stopped his unwilling slide by grabbing hold of Andromeda's boot with his claws. Erro, on the other hand, did not even attempt to stop.

Three of the griffins had beaten them to the throne room and stood before Zanthus, Aquila at the center. Aquila turned at the sound of Erro's footfalls and rose up on his back paws to catch the boy in an embrace with his front paws on Erro's shoulders and his wings encircling him. The eagle head bowed to meet Erro's, and Aquila cooed as Erro stroked the feathers at his neck.

Andromeda, concentrating hard on Aquila to see if he would speak, instead felt the griffin's surge of love and relief at the sight of Erro, and she wondered if they had ever been separated since the day the griffin had found him as an orphaned child, alone in the woods.

During this exchange, Atalanta walked to her father, inclining her head to the two new griffins as she passed.

"Princess Andromeda," said Zanthus, when Atalanta had taken her seat beside him. "Would you join me so that I may speak to our guests?"

Andromeda crossed the room and stood at the foot of the

platform. Aquila released Erro and turned to face the king.

"Your alliance in this war is an honor. Might I know the names of my allies?" said Zanthus.

Vendita, guardian of the Silver Forest, said the griffin on Aquila's left. Andromeda immediately identified the voice in her head as female, cool and delicate. Vendita was smaller than Aquila and leaner in build. Her lion's pelt was a soft, creamy beige. Her rich brown feathers were loose on her neck and head, almost fluffy, and at the top of her head the dark feathers stuck up in tufted points like cat's ears. Her beak was hawk-like, smaller than Aquila's and curved down at a sharp angle, but the tip looked sharp enough to prick a finger at the slightest touch.

Andromeda introduced her to Zanthus.

Jaculo, guardian of the Eastern Mountains, said the griffin to Aquila's right.

His voice was much like Aquila's, steady and baritone. His pelt was black as Andromeda's hair. His black and silver feathers created a thick mane around his head and neck, even covering the full width of his chest and trailing onto his underbelly. His silver eagle's beak clicked as he introduced himself, and his orange eyes flicked curiously to Andromeda as she relayed his words.

"Do you have a title?" Erro asked Aquila. Then, remembering where he was, looked at Zanthus and mumbled an apology. Zanthus gently shook his head to show there was no offense, but Vendita's head turned nearly one hundred and eighty degrees on her neck to look at Erro.

Until the day life leaves you, he is Aquila, guardian of Erro. You are his title and his purpose now. Her yellow eyes found Aquila's. I feel why you chose him. His soul calls to me, too. He will do great things if only he can put away his hate.

Erro waited until Vendita turned away to look expectantly at Andromeda.

She mouthed "later," for Jaculo was speaking.

All who are able will fight with you, elf king. Your cause is just. Aquila has told us of your people's dilemma. We will do all that we can, though it's very little.

"It is my greatest concern," said Zanthus. "I would ask that you join my council to discuss the matter further, but first, let me know of any accommodations you might require."

Your orchard will serve as a nesting place for our flock, said Aquila. *We require nothing more.*

We will speak to your council whenever you wish, said Vendita.

"Then I shall assemble them at once."

"Will you require my presence, then?" said Andromeda.

"Not this time, princess. Elder Arameus will act as my translator at council. Thank you for your assistance."

Andromeda bowed her head and quickly rejoined her siblings after greeting Aquila with a quick stroke on the head, Erro at her side. Atalanta descended the platform and made to join them, but Zanthus called her back.

"I would have you join us at council," he said. "It is your rightful place."

"As you wish, Father," said Atalanta, surprise readable on her face.

The others left without her, heading back toward their chambers.

"They'll figure it out," Felicity said, breaking the silence. "The griffins will know what to do."

"Yeah," said Andrew, but Michael remained solemn.

"I hope you're right," he said.

"Your Highnesses!"

Sir Boris jogged toward them, a falcon perched on his shoulder and a small scroll pinched between three fingers.

"Father replied?" said Michael, eagerly taking the message.

"He sent Dax," said Boris, scratching the falcon's chest with one finger. "He must be on the move."

The others waited impatiently as Michael squinted at the tiny scroll.

"I don't think he received our last message, but he knows about the villagers," said Michael. "They found the ruins of the villages while searching for Brock, just as I thought they might. He's already headed this way; he set out as soon as he got word from the Northern Wood. He says he hopes to reach Alatreon by the full moon, but he's not certain. He doesn't want to wear down the troops."

"Let's hope Tyrannus isn't done gathering his own troops," said Andromeda. "We need more time."

* * *

Melanie's eyes shot open. There was no longer any delay in sleeping and waking. No weariness, no yawning, no stretching. The moment her eyelids parted one another's company, she was alert, a predator ready to strike. But she did not feel strong. Her stomach screamed at her; it was her gut that had shaken her awake. The hunger pains tore at her. She had never been forced to go this long without food. She often found her mind wandering to the next full moon, longing for it and dreading it at once. The predator inside was eager for the feed, and yet her rational mind rebelled against the idea so severely she became sick at the thought. It did nothing for her troubled stomach.

She could sense the sun more than see it, the canopy was so thick. She raised up on one elbow. All around her, vampires slept like statues cast aside on the ground and in the limbs of trees, never breathing. Thetis lay at her back, and she inched away from him before getting to her feet.

Fiona and Jeremiah would be up. The thought took away some of her discomfort. Brent's parents had shown her great kindness, thanking her for trying to release their son. She found their mature, parental presence calming. Jeremiah reminded her very much of her own father.

She unfurled her wings and used them to hover silently over the sleeping horde of vampires. She connected with the rest of the army quicker than she would have liked. She guessed their ranks somewhere between fifteen hundred and two thousand strong. Not the largest army that ever marched across Arcamira, but made plenty formidable by the nightmarish appearance of its troops. Figures of all sizes and forms moved through the trees, some resting, some ripping at raw hunks of flesh scavenged from kills, some squabbling, and some laughing together—at what, Melanie did not wish to know.

Melanie scanned her surroundings for Fiona's red curls, a rare, distinct feature amongst the musky grays, dingy browns, and cruel steel. She swept over the strange green and blue sea of goblins, chattering and gurgling in their strange tongue. They bore the banners and emblems of various tribes but differed little in their features.

The trolls and the ogres had banded together. The trolls were bigger, with bulging, misshapen bodies covered with tough, charcoal skin. The ogres were of the same build, but slightly smaller, with skin the color of dishwater. The trolls' facial features were flat, small, and smashed into their heads, as if each one was bashed with a club at birth. The ogre's facial features appeared stretched, as if their mothers had constantly pulled on the skin of their cheeks, noses, and ears. Both species' arms dragged the ground as they walked, trailing fat clubs along behind them. They rarely put down their clubs, preferring to use them as an extension of their hands, pointing and gesturing with them, or occasionally thwacking each other on the head for some reason or other.

There was no sign of Fiona or Jeremiah from where she stood, so Melanie shoved her way further into the crowds. This part of the forest was not quite as dense as the vampire nesting grounds, and little cracks and fissures of light penetrated the top layer of leaves. They stung her eyes if she looked at them directly, and her skin felt itchy and inflamed as she pushed through the crowd. She welcomed the new pain—a nice distraction from her stomach. Still, she kept well away from the two clearings in the distance, to the north and west. Even being near the outskirts of the area began to burn her flesh. She'd tested it two days before, stretching her arm into residual light from the clearing, wondering what it would feel like to die by sunlight. The small taste she'd gotten had been excruciating. That would not be how she ended her days as a vampire.

She passed the group of minotaurs, avoiding their black eyes. The other species had learned quickly that the minotaurs were a confrontational species, quick to assert their dominance at the smallest of threats. A vampire and a troll had been gored already. The minotaurs' bodies were all clearly male, their muscles larger than any humans Melanie had ever seen, and she wondered what their mates and offspring looked like. Some had the head of bulls, while others had the wide faces of buffaloes. Each was equipped with a set of lethal horns. Though she did not look at them, the minotaurs blew short, menacing snorts through their nostrils as Melanie passed.

Just beyond their ranks, she spotted a shock of curly red hair.

"Fiona!" Melanie called, raising her hand.

Fiona shuffled toward her carrying a large wooden bucket full of water.

"Hello, Melanie, dear," she said, grunting as she set the bucket down, sloshing water over the side.

"Need some help with that?"

"Oh, well, if you wouldn't mind. I do feel a little stronger, with the full moon coming and all, but that's about the fifth bucket I've lugged around in the last hour, and I'm tuckered. I don't exactly have the physique of your typical werewolf." She gestured down at herself, all of her edges softly rounded. Melanie smiled.

"Where is this one headed?" she asked, hoisting the bucket

with only two fingers.

"Show off," said Fiona. "It's going to the children."

Melanie's face fell. "Well, I can take it most of the way for you."

"Brent would love to see you," said Fiona, pity in her eyes.

"The trouble is, I'm afraid I'd be a little too happy to see him." Fiona nodded.

"Where are they keeping them?" said Melanie. "Not in the middle of this lot, I hope."

"He's keeping them close. Doesn't want anyone getting any ideas now that it's getting close to the end, I suppose."

"He? You mean …?"

"King Tyrannus," said Fiona, speaking the title with disdain.

"How close is he keeping them?"

"Just a few paces off from where he's set up his camp," said Fiona, starting off toward the heart of the forest. "He keeps them under guard, but if I go when the werewolves are on duty, they let me talk to Brent for a few minutes if I bring food or water."

"So, have you seen him? Up close?"

"He walked by a few times, yeah," said Fiona, studying the ground. "He's … he's not much to look at, is he? Didn't look at me, thankfully."

A rumbling moan and a crack like lightning caused Melanie to duck instinctively, sloshing water down her front. She hissed irritably, ringing out her ragged dress.

"Giants," she spat through her freshly sprouted fangs. "What did they do this time? Every time they move it's a natural catastrophe."

She spotted them easily in the distance, seated together on the forest floor, legs and arms wound between trees.

"Looks like one of them needed something to pick his teeth with," said Fiona.

The giant's hands were the size of wagons; their noses resembled boulders. Beady black pupils stared out of their pale eyes. Coarse hair sprouted in thick, matted tufts on their heads. The females, whose filthy hair was arranged in knotted braids, were no smaller than the males, though perhaps less broad. One of the males held the thick lower branch of one of the trees between his fingers. He studied it, slack-jawed, as though he'd entirely forgotten why he snapped it loose in the first place. All of them were dressed for battle, in rough armor that looked pieced together from random scraps of different metals and hundreds of boiled leather pelts. Swords the size of trees hung at their waists. The largest of the five also carried a mace big enough to smash the head of a dragon.

"Not much farther now," said Fiona, pulling Melanie's attention from the giants.

The children materialized out of the darkness a few minutes later, bathed in light from an opening in the canopy. No doubt to free vampire parents such as herself from temptation. Still, three werewolf sentries ringed the chained children. One bared his teeth at Melanie, even though she hung well back from them. Even at this distance, the smell of the children's blood was almost too much. She took an extra step back, focusing instead on the foul, wet dog scent emanating from the werewolves' veins.

"Back away, traitor," the snarling werewolf said. "Fiona, you dare bring her here?"

"Leave her out of it," said Melanie. "I'm going."

She set the bucket gently on the ground. Brent studied her, but she did not betray that she'd noticed him. Still, from the corner of her eye, she saw him raise his hand to her. She smiled a fraction of an inch to let him know she'd seen.

She nodded to Fiona and turned back the way they'd come. She'd only gone a few paces when her enhanced hearing picked up on a soft rustling in a thicket. She would not have cared, had it not been for the smell. Callid. The little beast was walking a straight shot into the darkest, deepest part of the forest. There was a purpose in his step, and Melanie itched to know what it was.

She had little else to do. She followed silently, concentrating on the ground, avoiding any twig or gathering of fallen leaves that might betray her presence. She was as silent as death, keeping a safe distance from the cyclops, hearing him more often than seeing him. He led her to the very heart of the forest where the trees grew closest together.

Melanie froze, listening for him, but he seemed to have stopped. She squinted through the darkness, swiveling her head left and right.

"I did not call for you, Callid."

The voice sent fear racing up Melanie's spine. She crouched low, praying she would see him before he saw her.

"No, master. Callid's apologies. I will return when you are done with your ... guests."

"Speak your piece, you worthless thing. Let this not be a complete waste of my time."

The voices came from her left, and Melanie, suddenly sure Callid's news was about Tilly or the Avalons—or better, both—crept closer, careful to keep trees between herself and where she believed the voices were coming from. After rounding the second massive tree, they came into view, and Melanie ducked back behind it, her back pressed against the bark. Tyrannus indeed had guests. The four hooded figures she hadn't seen since the night of Tyrannus' arrival stood behind him as he sneered down at Callid.

"There is an elf village ripe for the taking just three miles south. They are farmers, with fields and fields of crops on all sides of them. Nowhere to run." Callid let out a breathy laugh from both heads.

Melanie's heart fell.

"Tell Thetis. I want it done tonight."

"Yes, master."

Callid rushed back through the trees not twenty paces from

where Melanie stood. She ought to turn back. The imp would wake Thetis, and he would realize she was gone.

"Alone at last, sweet ladies," said Tyrannus.

A high, cackling laugh answered him. "It has been many lifetimes since we were called sweet, Your Majesty."

Lured by curiosity, Melanie slowly peeked around the tree. Just who did Tyrannus believe could tip the war, how had he put it, irrevocably in his favor?

The four figures had tossed back their black hoods, revealing wild, wispy grey hair and identical dull, blue eyes. Hags, witches, sorceresses, or something of the sort, twisted by the black powers that dwelt in their souls.

Tyrannus addressed the tallest of the four whose nose was even more hooked and beak-like than her fellows'. She clutched a jagged bone knife in one hand.

"Ah, Porphyria, but you are all sweet as ambrosial nectar to me," said Tyrannus, giving the hag a small bow, "for with our powers joined together, what elf or human king will not quail on his high throne?"

"Flattery is sweet, but it is not why you summoned us," said Porphyria. "We will fight at your side, as promised. What else do you require?"

"I wish to know."

Melanie sensed the fervor in his voice, each word spoken slow and deliberate, his tongue caressing the last. It was almost lust.

"Ah," said Porphyria. "Many before you have sought to breach the future, but I warn you, noble king, that many have been displeased with what they learned. Many have learned nothing at all. The veil that hides the future is often thick, with very few holes to peek through."

"I trust in your abilities."

The shortest of the four hissed, and it took a moment for Melanie to realize she was laughing. Her back was so twisted, she was two heads shorter than her sisters. Her cheeks puffed out from her skull, like a child with the mumps, instead of sinking into the hollows of her face like the others.

"Our abilities allow us to approach the veil, nothing more," she said. "You will find none who can find it swifter or cast it aside more often, but all the black magic in the depths cannot make it reveal whatever you wish, little king."

Melanie saw a shadow pass over Tyrannus' face at her address, but when he spoke, it was just as silky as before.

"Then please, lovely Typhoid, do your best to cast it aside for me. I will not fault you should the revelation be unpleasant."

"What would you have it reveal?"

"Which side victory favors."

Typhoid limped forward, pulling a ball of opaque white glass from an inner pocket of her cloak.

"Porphyria," she said, holding out her hand without looking back at her sister.

Porphyria slid the knife across Typhoid's palm. Typhoid sucked in a sharp breath, but when she held the hand in front of her face, a sort of ecstasy danced in her eyes. She rubbed her injured hand over the surface of the ball, smearing it with crimson. She began to hum, and her eyes rolled back in her head. Her tongue danced over her yellow teeth as she chanted. She examined the ball with the whites of her eyes. The blood began to seep into the glass, forming a crimson smoke within its now translucent surface. Her chanting reached a fever pitch, and then suddenly cut off. She gulped in a shuddering breath and pulled the ball against her chest, her blue irises rolling back to the forefront of her eyes.

"Victory is undecided. The elf king still ponders many decisions. The choices hold the key."

"What choices?" said Tyrannus, his purple cloak billowing around him as he took a predatory step toward Typhoid. The witch didn't flinch.

"He wishes to save those you have recently transformed. Those unwilling but forced to serve you. If he finds a way, your forces will be weakened."

"Save them?"

Melanie ducked back behind the tree as Tyrannus paced wildly, orange eyes dark with fury.

"Save them?" he bellowed. "From what? From power? From immortality? He never cared to save them before. None have ever cared to do anything but slaughter us."

"Never before have so many of their subjects been taken at once," said Typhoid. "You have caused this."

Tyrannus growled, a true beast's cry of rage. "Let them try. It cannot be undone. They must slaughter their precious subjects or bow to me."

"There you are right. They have no hope in succeeding before the full moon. But they seek to separate their subjects in some way. The method is undetermined, but the choice will sway the outcome. As will the involvement of magical allies."

"What allies? Elves and humans have no allies but each other, and even they rarely mingle."

"Once again, you have caused a newfound need. The griffins have already labeled their fight against you just. The elf king plans to call on ancient allies, those who only join their cause in times of great need, the guardians of nature. And the humans have a weak alliance with the centaurs. The king has called them to his side. They all rally against you. Should their numbers swell large enough, your victory will be hard won."

"I will crush them no matter their numbers. Half my number cannot bleed."

"As I said, victory is undetermined. It is unclear if the human and centaur forces will arrive in time. Should they be late, the battle will most assuredly end in your favor."

"I must send troops to delay them. Will that change the outcome?"

"I cannot say until the decision is made, but should you send part of your forces away and the ball reveal it to be the wrong course, there will be no way to undo it. The scale can tip either way. You would be wise to not blindly toss weight onto it."

"We can help you weigh the decision, sweet king," said the third witch.

She and the fourth were nearly identical. They appeared younger than their counterparts, with thicker, longer hair and fresher faces. The one who spoke still had one thick strand of black hair at the crown of her head, stark against the silver of the rest.

"I would be in your debt, Malaria," said Tyrannus.

"You already are," said the fourth witch, who pointed the head of her staff at him. "No matter what the future may reveal. It would not do to forget our bargain."

"You and your sisters have nothing to fear. You shall have enough babe's blood to fill the elf king's royal baths."

Malaria giggled, a high, girlish sound, far more frightening than Porphyria's cackle or Typhoid's hiss. "See, Anemia, he's a sweet little beastling."

Tyrannus' heinous attempt at an indulgent grin made Malaria giggle some more.

Malaria pulled a squirming ferret from the sleeve of her cloak. Anemia smashed the butt of her staff into the earth, and a rough stone bench appeared from nothing but air. Malaria forced the squirming rodent flat on the bench, one hand strangling its throat and the other wrapped firmly around its tail. Porphyria slashed the creature's soft belly from end to end and dug two fingers into the opening. She pulled the entrails from the wound, trailing them through her fingers inches from her nose. Anemia and Malaria looked over her shoulders.

"Do not divide your troops," said Porphyria. "The human king has a great force with him. Sending a battalion to delay him would lead to a disastrous loss to your numbers."

Anemia dug into the ferret's corpse and pulled out its heart. She turned it in front of her eyes before popping it in her mouth like a sweet. Melanie stifled a gag.

"One in your number contemplates mutiny. A new recruit, one of the human villagers," she said after chewing the organ with a contemplative look.

Melanie ducked back behind the tree, her brain screaming at her to run.

Tyrannus laughed. "Only one?"

Malaria took her turn with the ferret's innards and examined its remaining organs.

"This one is more important than the rest. He or she can deal you a major blow."

"You cannot say who it is?"

"Temper, temper," crooned Malaria, for Tyrannus had leapt at them in frustration. "We told you the veil is not always thin."

It was time to leave. Melanie did not catch what Tyrannus said next, for she was once again focused on the ground ahead, keeping utterly silent. As she made her way back to the nesting grounds, she cared very little that Thetis would be up and waiting to punish her for wandering off. The witches' words replayed, filling her with real hope for the first time since she'd watched Tilly running free with Brent. For there was no doubt in her mind that she was the one the witches spoke of. When the time came, she would make sure her final act counted.

Chapter 27

The Song of the Fae

Michael's broadsword slashed at Andromeda's right shoulder in a downward arch. Her two rapiers crossed in front of her to meet it, catching the blunted steel blade between them. With an adept twisting of her wrists, she nearly wrenched its handle from Michael's grasp, but he held tight. Pulling his blade free of hers just in time to block her quick flurry of short slashes at his torso.

Their real blades, silver-coated, shining, and sharp enough to detach a limb at a single blow, were locked away in their chambers. The plain steel blades they sparred with—dark, ugly things with thin scratches down the length and many dents and chips on the edges from years of play battle—were from the small, marble building at the edge of the courtyard where all manner of training equipment was held: straw dummies, dulled weapons, battered shields, and painted targets.

Michael's next swing caught Andromeda off-guard, and though she just managed to block the blow, it sent her poorly planted feet skidding through the grass, offsetting her balance. Michael aimed the flat side of his blade at her back, intending to swat her while she wobbled and knock her to the grass, but a loud noise to his left made his eyes flick away from her. Andromeda planted one rapier into the earth to steady herself, knocked Michael's lazily swinging blade aside with the other, and delivered a kick to the center of his chest. His breath escaped him with a deep "oof," and his backside was the one to hit the ground. He looked up at her from the grass, surprised, and then threw his head back laughing.

"I suppose that's what I get for taking my eyes off you," he said.

"You underestimate your littlest sister," said Andromeda.

"Not in the slightest," said Michael. "I'm not a fool. It's just that my elder little sister distracted me."

The sound that had pulled Michael's eyes from Andromeda's blades was Felicity's shriek of fury.

"You suggested they train together," said Andromeda with a sigh, looking across the courtyard at her quarrelling siblings.

Felicity's swords were cast off in the grass, and Andrew's broadsword hung at his side while she raged at him.

"You're such a child!" Felicity yelled.

"What? What did I do?" said Andrew, palms up.

"Yes, what did he do?" said Michael loud enough that they both turned their heads.

"Nothing!" said Andrew.

"He isn't taking this seriously!"

"Well I'm not exactly trying to take your head off. It's just sparring."

"Oh, aren't you? You're swinging that thing around like a mad man." Felicity addressed Michael. "He's flailing it around like he doesn't even know how to use it. He's bruised my wrist and nearly broken my toe."

"I know how to use it!" said Andrew, anger crossing his face for the first time. "You just don't like losing."

"Losing? Ha!" said Felicity.

"Stop it," said Michael. "I paired you together because I thought we could do with a switch up, learn someone else's combat style. Andrew, how many times did Archimedes tell you to control your swings? That wild slashing might back down your opponent at first, but a smart one will realize you leave yourself too open when you charge in like that."

"I wasn't—" Andrew began.

"Felicity, do you really think a vampire's going to apologize for stepping on your foot?" said Michael.

"See," said Andrew. "I'm training you."

Felicity kept her eyes locked on Michael, but the heel of her right boot crunched Andrew's instep.

"I'm only training you," she said with a smirk as he howled in pain and rage.

"I thought," Michael began loudly, startling them all, "that after all we have faced these past moons, we would be beyond this childish bickering! Do you remember how hard we fought to make Mother and Father allow us to begin this journey? They thought us children. Let's not prove them right—not now, when we are two days from the full moon that may well bring the most important battle ever fought, certainly the most important in nearly a century."

Felicity's smirk morphed into an abashed frown. Andrew hung his head and fiddled with his sword hilt.

"Have you been away from Archimedes so long you've forgotten his teachings? Have you been in this castle so long you've forgotten what awaits us? Have you forgotten our people?"

"No!" said Felicity and Andrew together.

"How could we forget our people?" said Felicity. "It is all I think about as I lie in bed at night, when I'm eating rich food and sleeping in a bed full of soft wool, while they are in an unimaginable hell! Tilly's mother! Accuse me of childishness all you want, Michael—I fear you are right in that—but never say I've forgotten my duties to my people."

Between the council, the king, and the griffins, a plan for protecting the captured villagers had at last been agreed upon, but no one was entirely happy with the outcome. Zanthus himself had warned them all that should the plan go awry—which many feared likely—and the lives of those who were not transformed were put into jeopardy, it was to be abandoned, and all vampires and werewolves slaughtered.

"Then think on them now, and get back to work," said Michael.

"I think I'd like a go at Erro's training," said Andrew, pointing a finger to the sky.

High above them, Erro rode between Aquila's wing joints, practicing aerial maneuvers: diving, rolling, and zigzagging through the clouds, occasionally dipping down into the orchard, where Erro practiced throwing his knives at two targets he'd set up between the trees.

"How about a new game here on the ground?" said a voice.

Atalanta was striding toward them from the palace, her auburn hair pulled back in a large braid made of smaller braids wound together. Her armor was thick, elvish leather, dyed pale-pink and green. Her pink wrist guards extended over her hand in a petal-like design, and a green archer's glove blossomed like a stamen from the center. Over the leather on her torso was a shining breastplate with the Galechaser crest engraved in exquisite detail. The personified cloud in the center had the almond eyes, thin, sharp nose, and bow-like lips of an elf. Those perfect lips pursed into an O from which a gust of wind, carrying rose petals inside it, blew across her breast. The silvery metal was thinner than any breastplate the Avalons had ever seen, but it was doubtless incredibly strong if its purpose was to protect the only living heir to the throne of Alatreon.

"What game is that?" asked Michael.

"I need to practice magic, and you need to learn how to fight against it. We've no idea if the vampire elves can do magic, but Tyrannus is bound to have sought out some form of replacement for me. He was determined to have some form of magic on his side. I doubt he would have given it up easily. So, the four of you against me."

"That hardly seems fair," said Michael. "Perhaps one of us ought to join your side."

"If you're that concerned for my well-being, you can play my bodyguard if you wish," she said tilting her head as she studied him. "My father will doubtless assign me a number of them in the real battle."

"And you will doubtless make their post incredibly difficult," said Michael.

She smiled at him. "You know me well."

Michael failed to hide his delight as Atalanta made for the equipment house.

"You oughtn't pine for her the way you do," said Felicity softly when Atalanta had entered and shut the door behind her.

Michael sputtered. "I'm not ... Pining? Who said ...?"

"There has never been a marriage between an elf and a human. Not even to strengthen alliances. They think us lesser," said Felicity, sadness etched in the lines of her face.

Michael ceased blabbering and looked solemn. "You don't know what you're talking about."

"I don't want to see you hurt," said Felicity.

"How can I be hurt by something I never wished in the first place?" said Michael, going red at the temples.

Andrew and Andromeda stood together, their dark heads down as they looked anywhere but at Michael. Felicity, though, held his gaze and sighed.

"There is no hope in it, Michael." Pity dulled her eyes and her tones. "Protect your heart, or she is sure to break it."

Atalanta came out of the equipment house carrying a rapier. A bow was slung over her shoulder and a quiver was strapped to her back. She carried the detached head of a straw dummy under one arm.

Michael, who had been glowering at Felicity, nearly tripped over his own feet in an attempt to look nonchalant. Andrew rumpled his hair with one hand and gave Andromeda a look that said he was glad the moment had passed.

"Why do you all look as though you've just been told to return to your rooms without supper?" said Atalanta when she reached them.

"You're not going to shoot us with arrows, are you?" said Andrew, knocking his knuckles against her quiver.

"No," said Atalanta, shrugging off the bow and quiver, "those are for later." She looked around at them all, still perplexed by their sudden gloom. "Let's get started then."

"Sure. What's with the dummy head?" said Andromeda.

"It's our prize," said Atalanta, tossing it up and catching it like a ball. "We place it in the middle of the courtyard, and both teams start at opposite ends. The first team to carry it back to their side wins."

"Sounds fun," said Andrew.

Atalanta walked a few paces, studying the hedge lines, judging the distance. When she was satisfied she was at the heart of the courtyard, she dropped the head and signaled Michael to follow her to one side. When both teams were in their places, knees braced and ready to spring forward, Atalanta shouted, "Go!"

The two parties raced toward each other, drawing their weapons. When both teams had each gone no more than ten paces, Atalanta held out her hand and said, "Arboris ascendium." Roots sprang from the earth in a wall of uniform arches, perfect for tripping and trapping an unsuspecting foot. Felicity, in the lead, tumbled to the grass, cursing. Andrew vaulted the little wall, while Andromeda paused to help Felicity hack at the root withdrawing into the ground, trapping her boot beneath it. It took their dull swords a few tries, but the moment Felicity was free, Andromeda pulled her to her feet, and the two girls charged together. Michael and Atalanta had reached the head, and Andrew was closing in. Michael picked up the straw-filled ball while Atalanta stretched her arm out toward Andrew, fingers splayed and palm out.

"Ignis circumfrum."

Andrew cried out as a knee-high ring of fire encircled him.

Andromeda, eyes on Michael, picked up a sizeable rock from the ground as she ran, and cocked back her arm. The rock struck Michael between the shoulder blades, staggering him as he turned to run back to the hedges. With his armor to protect him, it only stopped him for a moment, and Andromeda took chase while Felicity charged Atalanta. The two girls' training swords clashed together with high, ringing notes. As Felicity drew Atalanta's concentration with her two dancing blades, the flames around Andrew receded. He stepped over the burning ring of ash, but hesitated, trying to decide which sister needed his assistance most. He made his decision as Atalanta knocked Felicity backward with a well-placed blow and turned her hand toward Andromeda.

Sheathing his sword, he slammed into the elf from behind, tackling her to the grass where he attempted to pin her hands. Felicity advanced to hold the elf at sword-point just as Andromeda thrust a rapier between Michael's racing legs, entangling them and sending him to the ground.

Andromeda sheathed one sword, picked up the head, and started back with it. Andrew's yell of triumph turned into a cry of pain as fire ignited in Atalanta's palms, singeing his hands as he held hers in place. With his weight off her, Atalanta rolled adeptly away from Felicity's blade and leapt to her feet with her retrieved sword in hand.

She met Andrew and Felicity in swordplay, her brow furrowed as she contemplated the next spell to use while trying to parry their flurry of attacks. Andromeda raced past the dueling threesome, Michael hot on her heels. But she pulled up short at the sight of King Zanthus in her path.

"As much as I would love to watch this battle through," he said, smiling at Andromeda and Michael's sweaty, red faces, "I think I can provide you all with a bit of entertainment of my own." As Andrew, Felicity, and Atalanta approached, Zanthus asked Andromeda, "Would you mind getting our young commander's attention?"

Andromeda put her thumb and index fingers at the corners of her mouth and whistled high and long, reaching out to touch

Aquila's mind at the same time. Erro and the griffin alighted on the grass a few moments later.

Erro looked nervously at Zanthus, and Andromeda smiled internally. He was not completely comfortable with the new title Zanthus had given him. King and council had decided, after much debate, that Erro command the rescue battalion, due to his close relationship with Aquila.

"Aquila's the one who convinced them in the end," Erro had said when he had returned from the council room, looking a bit pale. "I haven't the damnedest idea why. Zanthus had said it should be me the whole time, but a lot of the other elves didn't think I could do it. Not sure I blame them. But Aquila said I was the only one he'd take orders from, and that sort of made it impossible for them to say no." He had shrugged, looking a little helpless. "So I guess I'm it."

"Are we finally going to call on the Fae?" said Atalanta now.

"Yes, my dear. The council does many great things, but making swift decisions isn't one of them. We ought to have asked their help the moment you arrived, but aging elves are a proud bunch, and politics are dreary, petty business. So now we call on them with little notice and pray they accept."

"They will accept, Father. If not for us, then for themselves."

"I believe you are right, but nothing is guaranteed." He smiled at the group. "Would you follow me to the orchard? Regardless of whether our alliance is accepted, I don't think you will be disappointed by what you see."

"Lead the way, Your Majesty," said Michael.

Zanthus led them to a part of the orchard they had not yet traversed. A large stream ran over rock steps and wound in curves between the trees.

"I must ask all of you to remain still, and utterly silent," he said when they had all gathered at his back. "Nymphs are a gentle and timid race."

"Then why do we ask their help?" Erro said, and almost

immediately bit his lip, wishing he hadn't, as Zanthus looked at him.

Zanthus chuckled, a soft, rhythmic sound from deep in his chest. "Your questions are cutting, young man, but well placed. We ask their help for, though they are naturally peaceful, they possess the powers of the elements—earth, wind, water, and even fire, though there are no fire nymphs in this region—and they are a literal force of nature when provoked."

He turned his back on them before Erro could give a bashful reply.

"Now, wait and watch," he said, and with that, he began to sing.

His clear voice seemed to possess its own mass. It seemed to add weight to the breeze. The first verse was smooth and rolling like living water.

The river began to bubble and swirl. Out of the foam rose the forms of twelve maidens. They had faces and bodies as perfect as elves. Their skin was palest blue, almost transparent. They seemed to shimmer in and out of focus like reflections in rippling water. Thick hair of black so dark it appeared blue cascaded in waves down their backs. They were robed in dresses of silver. They began to sing along with Zanthus. Their voices rippled like their skin.

Zanthus' song changed, and the words seemed to float away on the wind, barely a whisper. But the wind answered back. A gust of cool wind blew through the trees, and beautiful faces appeared, merely outlines against the sky. Twelve maidens then alighted next to their watery sisters. They were just as slender and fair, but their robes were of white and their skin and hair of silver.

When the third verse broke out, whimsical and carefree, the twelve wood nymphs emerged, giggling and dancing among the trees, robed in green, with long tresses of gold and brown crowned in wreathes of leaves.

Zanthus stopped his song, but only long enough to incline his head to the nymphs, who curtsied back.

Then Zanthus took up a new song, this one's tones deep and hard. The trees creaked and moaned. Then, out of every tree within sight, figures pushed against the bark from the inside. The trees appeared to breathe as the figures pushed again and again against the bark. Then, dryads of all varieties began to spring forth. All had skin like bark, but some had hair of orange and cherry blossoms. Other's had hair of different leaves. Hundreds, male and female, stood in front of every tree in the orchard. Even those the party could not see added their voices, whispering and creaking their song to its conclusion.

"Atalanta, darling," said Zanthus, after bowing his head to the dryads. "I think you'd best lead the next song. They do prefer a female voice."

Atalanta cleared her throat and then struck up a new tune, this one wild and moody, undulating between happy and sad notes, shifting pace in the midst of a line.

Flashes of colored light glittered amongst the trees. Dozens of butterflies made a shimmering rainbow all around the small party. Andromeda and Felicity both gasped in delight as the tiny creatures fluttered past. They were not butterflies at all. Tiny faces appraised the company as they swirled around their heads. Then the fairies began to grow, shifting size until they were just as tall as the nymphs. They looked more like elves than either the nymphs or the dryads; they even had pointed ears. They glowed and glittered in the sun. Their bodies were draped in garments of different rich colors. The females had long, beautifully curled tresses of every color of the rainbow. The males braided their shoulder-length hair down the bases of their necks. Gorgeous wings, curved at the base but needle-pointed at the ends, sprouted from their backs. The colors of their translucent wings shifted and changed as the sunlight caught the threadlike veins.

Zanthus bowed at the waist as the most beautiful of the fairies, tall and slender with ivory skin and curling hair that shifted from red to orange to yellow as she moved, hovered toward him over the stream. A thin crown of flame sat atop her head.

"You certainly waited until the last possible moment to ask our help, Zanthus," she said. "Think you could defeat him all on your own?"

"My apologies for the delay, Iris," said Zanthus. "I came to you as swiftly as I could."

"If this is swift, your age is showing," said Iris.

Atalanta made an affronted sound in her throat, but Zanthus stayed her with a single look. Iris did not spare her even that.

"I have no doubt it is," Zanthus said with a gentle smile, and the fairy queen returned her own. "But here I am, and my plea is still the same. I suppose I should not be surprised that you know why I make it. Will you join me?"

"I have little choice."

"But if you did?" said Zanthus.

Iris gave him another shadow of a smile. "I would cast my lot with you."

"You flatter me."

"Always."

Atalanta looked as though she might gag.

Zanthus bowed his head to Iris one more time and then turned to the nymphs and dryads.

"I would be most honored if my nymph and dryad cousins would add their powers to mine, and that of the human king."

One of the water nymphs stepped forward. When she spoke, though her voice was clear, she sounded as though her head was underwater. "It is our honor to join you, noble king. Whenever the cause is just, we nymphs shall always come to the aid of our elf brethren."

"We, too, give you our service," rasped a willow dryad with long leafy tresses. The other dryads nodded and stomped their consent. "An enemy most dreadful gathers in the Black Forest, putrefying that sacred place of trees. We will fight at your side until it is wiped clean."

"The Black Forest, you say?" said Zanthus. "I should have known."

"No matter where they hide," said Iris, flames suddenly dancing in her hair as her already glowing skin shone with the light of a distant star, "we will scorch them from the face of the earth."

"I hope you are right, my lady," said Zanthus. "I hope you are right."

Chapter 28

When Angels Weep

The earth seeps blood
When angels weep.
In death's black hood
Do warriors sleep.
The nameless man
Is buried deep,
When heaven cries
And angels weep.

The words repeated themselves in Andromeda's head, a poem written in the time of the Extermination, carried to her from childhood memories by the cool night wind. Summer's days were waning, and autumn's wind broke free at night, howling at the full moon already visible through the clouds in the darkening sky. She had read that warrior poem in the safety of her home when it was merely pretty, woeful words on a page, but now it chilled her blood as her mare's shoes clopped softly through the streets, mixing with the thousands of other hoof beats of the army sifting through the city behind her.

As she and her siblings had donned their armor, they'd murmured words of comfort to each other. "It may not even happen tonight," became a sort of prayer. No one fully believed it. It all rested on the scouts Zanthus had sent to stalk the edges of the Black Forest. Should they see any sign that the army hidden among the giant trunks was readying for battle as the sun fell behind the horizon line, they would gallop back on elvish horses swifter than the wind. For now, the army gathered behind the gates, cavalry, infantry, and aerial troops spread out in two-by-two lines through the silent streets. The citizens of Alatreon watched the procession without celebration. Some of the children waved and tried to run alongside the horses, but their mothers and grandmothers snatched them back. Many houses stood empty and silent, as all the occupants now marched with their king. Zanthus had an army of trained warriors, and battle-trained elves from all over the region had flocked to Alatreon in the past fortnight, but still the council had worried their numbers were not sufficient—a worry that grew all the more urgent when it appeared Markus Avalon and his army would not arrive in time. A call had gone out for volunteers, and many elves, both male and female, had answered it.

Markus had still not arrived, and his children ached for his gentle face and steadying words.

The nymphs radiated iridescent light that cast heavenly glows over the homes lining the streets. The fairies were little bright lights dancing on the backs of horses or making ornaments in the hair of their elf cousins. A particularly bright light, its glow shifting through the colors of the rainbow, hovered around Zanthus' ear. The griffins soared overhead in a V formation, Erro and Aquila at the flock's forefront, Vendita and Jaculo flanking them. The Avalons rode just behind Zanthus, Atalanta, and the high elf general, Valarion. Behind them, Bree sat at the head of the elf mages. Her extraordinary magical power, and a good deal of persuasion on Atalanta's part, had earned her a commanding spot amongst the rescue battalion. Andromeda breathed a little easier knowing she would be helping Erro with his mission.

Zanthus brought the army to a halt at the glittering gate, and all eyes that were able watched the rolling hills for any sign of approaching scouts.

* * *

The screams rattled around in Melanie's brain, maddening,

thrilling. She wanted to sprint toward them almost as much as she longed to flee in the other direction. The blood was calling her, even from this distance. The elder vampire guards tensed, watching the group of starving fledglings with claws and fangs drawn as a reminder of the pain they would face if they disobeyed Thetis' orders. It would be useless to test the boundary of elders, this batch freshly fed on the first wave of elf blood while many of the fledglings swayed on their feet. Now it was the werewolves' turn. The full moon was bright and clear, and the transformations had begun before dark fell completely. Fiona and Jeremiah would be among them now, ripping and tearing at that perfect elf flesh, getting stronger as they lapped up the blood with rough, pink tongues. The thought gave her a strange, horrible thrill up her spine—an intermingling of revulsion and desire.

When the screaming turned to moans of pain and gray dusk turned into night, Thetis appeared from the trees.

"Come and meet your new brothers and sisters," he said, zeal in his eyes. "They are magnificent to behold. The elf army will quake before their own."

He led the flock to a stretch of forest where the grass was stained black with blood. The smell made Melanie dizzy. Her fangs emerged from her gums, but a new scent fouled the heavenly scent of elf blood. Dog. A musky, dirty scent was racing through the veins of the beautiful elves littering the ground, spattered with their own blood from monstrous wounds that were already healing. A few of the fledglings fell to hands and knees to lap up any blood left undried. An elder embedded his claws in the head of a female fledgling near Melanie and tossed her bodily into a tree. Melanie heard her back snap in two, and the fledgling shrieked in agony as the bones healed slowly. With growls and cruel swipes at their faces, the elders forced the fledglings back from the bloodstained ring of grass while a new species, vampire elves, began to toss the bloodied elves into the break in the trees where the light of the full moon shone through. Melanie was transfixed by the vampire elves, keeping her eyes on them as the elders forced her back with the others.

They were the most beautiful things Melanie had ever seen, so gorgeous it almost hurt to look at them. Their unblemished skin now looked hard and smooth as polished stone—so white, it gleamed like fresh snow in the moonlight. Their hair seemed alive, the tresses swirling around their bodies with the slightest of movements. Their black wings, melted into their backs like a second skin, shimmered with iridescent colors—blue, purple, and yellow. Their eyes ... their eyes raised the hair on Melanie's neck. The irises glittered with the colors of gemstones—ruby, garnet, emerald, amethyst, sapphire, and even diamond—but the irises had overtaken the pupils, and all that was left was a hard, beautiful, blank stone eyeing their fellow elves, who were battered and bleeding, without compassion. The vampire elves picked up their unchanged brethren by limbs or hair and tossed them toward the waiting jaws of the werewolves. With a jolt, Melanie saw Tyrannus watching the elf vampires from the other side of the bloody transformation grounds, his orange eyes burning with excitement.

In the light of the moon, the wounded elves' moans turned once again to screams as the transformation ripped apart their bodies. Flesh split down their backs, peeling away to make room for fur of purest white. Their bones cracked and crunched as their skeletons elongated and changed shape. And they just kept growing, taller than even Nathaniel who stood at over ten feet on his back legs. When all was said and done, they looked down at their alpha with solid black eyes from a height of at least thirteen feet.

Nathaniel, the bushiest of the gathered wolves, with fur drawn together in mattes in many places, stalked around his new pack members, flaunting his vast muscles with strong, languid strides. Occasionally he rose to his back legs to tower over the crouching white beasts and sniff the air. At last, he threw back his head and howled the cry of the alpha. The white wolves, a few hundred of them, sank into bows, one forepaw extended, furry heads bent. All but one.

The beast was the most monstrous of his fellows, and instead of bowing, he rose to his back legs to stand like a man, bushy tail swinging behind him, hackles raised in a razor-straight line down his back. He pulled up his muzzle in a challenging growl. All eyes watched the pair. The white wolves raised their heads. A small pack of werewolves gathered at Nathaniel's back, their own hackles raised, fangs dripping saliva as they snapped and snarled at their alpha's challenger. The white wolf sniffed the air, seemingly uncertain. Nathaniel, now on his back legs as well, took a step toward the white wolf and growled deep in his chest, but it seemed a bad move. From so close, the white wolf had to look down at Nathaniel, and it seemed to give him confidence. He snarled back, and a paw swiped at Nathaniel's muzzle, swift and powerful, a blow that would surely send Nathaniel sprawling. But suddenly Nathaniel's fangs were at the white wolf's throat, sinking deep and staining the white fur in a spray of crimson. The white wolf yelped like a pup, and with a powerful yank of his great head, Nathaniel flung him to the ground and pounced on him. The white wolf whimpered and snarled, ears back as his teeth snapped at air, but Nathaniel raked four bloody lines down the white muzzle with his claws. He bent his shaggy brown head to the challenger's white one and howled the alpha howl right in his face. The other wolves were whipped into a frenzy, howling and barking, and the white wolf whined, averting his black eyes from Nathaniel. The white wolf licked at his jowls, soft whines coming through his nose. Nathaniel stepped off of him and gave another triumphant howl. This time, all the white wolves bowed.

Tyrannus laughed as he approached Nathaniel—a hellish

sound that could not decide if it was a rasping guffaw or a cruel, high cackle. The Black Sisters flanked him, and Callid danced around his feet, singing from both heads.

"Death, death to the pretty elflings. Death, death to the puny humans."

"Indeed, my little imp," said Tyrannus. His orange eyes turned to Nathaniel. "I see I have chosen my wolf general well."

The great brown dog bent his head to his master.

Tyrannus turned to Thetis. "And what of my vampire general? Can you lead your newest fledglings? Will they fight for you?"

Thetis soured at the challenge hidden in the words. "I have no magic dog whistle to make them bend to my command, but they are newly reborn and hungry just like the rest. You can ask them for yourself. Their answer might amuse you."

Tyrannus narrowed his eyes at Thetis but said nothing. Instead, he turned to the nearest vampire elf, a male, with white blonde hair that touched his shoulders, and eyes of sapphire.

"You are the hybrid king?" the elf asked.

"Indeed. I have brought you here. Made you what you are."

"For that, at least, I thank you," said the elf with a wicked smile. "Now I am a god."

Tyrannus laughed, eyes alight with a greedy fervor—he looked as though he might lick his deformed jowls. "Yes, we are all gods now."

The elf stayed frozen, and Melanie thought he looked a bit doubtful at the inclusiveness of the statement.

Tyrannus raised his voice and cried, "We are all gods here!"

A cry went up from the army, and the Black Sisters cackled.

"After today we shall reign as gods for eternity! We will crush the elves and humans underfoot and tear them with our teeth. After today they will bow before us while we sit on the thrones from which they ordered us slaughtered, from which they sought to destroy us!"

Now the whole army, filling up the spaces between the trees

as far back as Melanie could see, were spreading the message and sending up a cry. Minotaurs bellowed. Goblins chittered and whooped. The giants banged their clubs on the ground, shaking the trees from their roots to their highest leaves. Ogres and trolls yelled and stomped. Wolves howled. All around Melanie, the elder vampires filled their mouths with fangs and cried out in high, predatory shrieks.

"Will you fight with me?" Tryannus asked the vampire elf.

The fledgling's beautiful visage was defaced by the twisted smile that overcame his lips.

Melanie strained to hear his reply over the thundering army.

He nodded his head once, and the army roared, drowning out his words, but Melanie watched the shape of his mouth. "For now."

Tyrannus held himself tall and raised his arms in triumph, but Melanie saw the curl of his muzzle and the flicker of what might have been fear in his eyes.

Something cold brushed Melanie's back, and she jumped. Thetis traced a finger up her spine and cupped his hand around the back of her neck.

"After today, I shall be a god king, and you,"—he used the hand hidden under her hair to shake her ever so slightly as his clawed fingers bit into her skin—"shall be my queen."

She turned to face his smile, and one of her own broke through her icy expression. Thetis looked surprised, but pleased. The hand came loose around her neck and rested at the small of her back while the army roared around them.

Today, her last day, she would slay a god.

* * *

A horn blast—three short, urgent blows—made heads snap to attention.

"The scouts, Your Majesty," shouted one of the hundred

archers stationed atop the marble wall. "They're returning. Fast."

The announcement was unnecessary. At the head of the procession, Zanthus and the Avalons could see the three scouts flying over the gently rolling hills, their horses' manes and their own braids whipped behind them by the wind. The steeds tossed their heads, nostrils wide. One of the scouts blew again on his horn, looking over his shoulder as he did. A vampire, skin so white it seemed to glow, crested the hill behind him, flying low. Its wings shimmered and shifted color in the moonlight as it swooped over the horn-wielding scout and snatched him from his horse by the neck.

"Tonight is the night!" Zanthus cried. "Remember what you fight for! Win your freedom! Open the gates!"

Andromeda's legs felt unsteady in her stirrups as a wave of black figures crested the far hill. Werewolves ran low to the ground, some throwing back their heads to howl at the silvery moon that seemed to have been pulled closer to earth during the day. Goblins ran around their paws, brandishing their bone spears and swords. Trolls and ogres lumbered behind them on unsteady feet as they tried not to topple down the hill. Minotaurs lowered their horned heads into the charge. Vampires held aloft by bat wings blotted out the sky. As the golden gates swung open, the head of a giant appeared, and the ground rumbled. Then another stomped into view, club resting on its shoulder.

Someone atop the walls said, "Arrows at the ready!" as the Avalons put their heels to their horses, leading the charge with Atalanta and Zanthus.

"Protect the king!" came a shout to Andromeda's left.

As they galloped through the gates, a wall of elves on horseback enclosed the royals. Zanthus was forced to slow his horse, prompting the others to do the same.

"Bree?" said Andrew, looking over his shoulder for the elf, but she had been cut off from the Avalons. At the sound of her name, she met Andrew's eyes, and then kicked her horse to follow the other mages as they raced to the front, a battalion of cavalry forming a protective ring around them.

Bree's voice joined a hundred others in a chant that echoed over the battlefield, closing the gap between the two charging armies. On the eastern side of the field, saplings sprouted from the soil—a small forest in a perfect ring, coiling upward in a strange dance as they grew taller and wider until they were strong, thick oaks and maples. Their limbs interlocked as they reached for the sky to create a dome, and their trunks crashed together to form a living cage of bark.

In the sky, beaks and talons crashed with claws and fangs. Feathers fluttered toward the ground and shrieks filled the night air as the vampires and griffins collided, silhouetted by the moon. The dark wings blocked most of the moonlight, and the battlefield was plunged further into darkness. Then, the soft, tiny lights of fairies dispersed among the elf army, glowing brighter and brighter until they resembled miniatures suns, illuminating the army's path as it surged forward, ready to meet the enemy in the middle.

The wind nymphs took to the air, sending Andromeda and Felicity's braids swinging around their heads in a gusting breeze. They swirled like tornadoes as they propelled themselves through the flock of vampires, tossing them end over end. The vampires flapped wildly to stay aloft, but many crashed into each other with bone-crunching force, dropping them to the earth where they were quickly dispatched by elf troops armed with silver stakes.

Andromeda frantically searched the sky for Erro and Aquila. She spotted them. Aquila and another griffin had a vampire gripped in their beaks and claws. As Andromeda watched, the two griffins flew in opposite directions and ripped the head off the vampire's shoulders. Rolling and diving, Erro low on his back, Aquila dodged the claws of one vampire and seized another by the wings. But this time, he shifted directions, heading for the tree prison. Once he was hovering above the domed cage, the limbs parted just wide enough for a human to fit easily. Aquila used his paws to shred the vampire's wings and then dropped him into the hole, where the trees swallowed him up. More griffins followed him, circling the cage with their prey in their talons, kicking and writhing.

"It's working!" said Andrew, but the clang of metal and the cries of death nearly drowned him out.

The front lines of soldiers had at last collided with Tyrannus' horde. A snow-white werewolf barreled through the line just in front of Zanthus, ripping elf throats and bashing others aside with its massive paws as it leaped over swords and shields alike. Zanthus raised his sword, signaling Atalanta to get out of the way as she tried to position herself in front of him. The werewolf seemed to only have eyes for him, but silver-coated blades sank into its snowy pelt from all sides. Even as it died, it tried to pull itself to the king through the host of soldiers protecting him.

Zanthus watched it until it had breathed its last and begun to change back into an elf. Then he scanned the horde before his forces.

"The white wolves are our brothers and sisters!" he called to his closest generals, and they in turn spread the word throughout the troops.

"Look!" said Felicity, pointing into the battle where three griffins were diving toward a white wolf. "The griffins already know."

One of the griffins protected the other two, dispatching a handful of goblins and grappling with a black wolf as his fellows lifted the white wolf into the air and headed off for the cage of trees. The mages had it surrounded now. The outer ring sent flashes of light and fire and ice flying out from their hands as they guarded their makeshift prison, while the inner circle kept their eyes on the skies, opening and closing the top limbs each time a griffin came to deliver an innocent soul.

"Valerian," shouted Zanthus to his high general, "I want more troops protecting the mages!"

"Yes, Your Majesty," said Valarian, waving his standard to gain the attention of a nearby general.

The Avalons continued to watch as the two griffins attempted to deliver their white wolf. A vampire forced its way out of the small opening. Another griffin swooped in to snatch it back out of the sky.

Michael groaned. They had anticipated that containing the vampires would be nearly impossible for that very reason, but no one had been able to invent a solution. Atop Aquila, Erro glided low to the ground, shouting something at the mages, gesticulating wildly with his arm.

Andromeda screamed as a bloodied, gutted griffin crashed into two elves in Zanthus' inner circle, tossed there by a vampire with eerily perfect features, cold, pupiless diamond eyes, and iridescent wings. Her black hair writhed like snakes behind her as she dove for Zanthus, arms outstretched as if for an embrace, her mouth alight with a wicked, unfeeling smile. Michael raised his arm in a fist, and a stake shot from his wrist at the vampire's heart, but she rolled, and it caught her in the shoulder. She pulled up and hovered out of range, still smiling. She thrust out a hand and spoke an incantation in elvish. Nothing. She cursed.

"Our magic is tied to life, to nature," Zanthus shouted up to her. "You are a dead, unnatural thing now."

The vampire elf flipped backward and dove into the throng of elf soldiers, snatching one by his hair. She ripped into his throat like a rabid dog. Blood dripping down her alabaster throat, she grinned at Zanthus.

"Then death shall feed my power," she said.

She again drew the dying elf to her mouth and drank deeply. She thrust out her hand, and a black, burning bolt of energy knocked Zanthus from his horse. The vampire elf dove, and another appeared at her side—an emerald-eyed male with tawny hair that curled around his pointed ears. As Atalanta leapt from her horse to kneel at her father's side, Michael shot a stake. Zanthus' and Atalanta's horses reared and whinnied as the female vampire elf crashed at their hooves, her shimmering wings crumpling and snapping underneath her. Valerian maneuvered his horse to guard his king and met the male vampire elf with a stake of his own to the heart.

With a sound like a swarm of giant mosquitoes or the swishing of a hundred horse tails, the archers on the wall released a hail of projectiles. But no silver-tipped arrows rained down on the surging crowd of enemies. Andromeda whipped her head around to see a wave of vampires that had escaped the flock of griffins and headed toward the walls crash into the troops in the back of the elf army, stakes from the giant crossbows set into the crenels of the wall embedded in their hearts.

Zanthus was on his feet. He smelled of burnt hair and a red burn marred his chin, but he mounted his horse unassisted.

"Were those truly our people, Father?" Atalanta asked, her eyes transfixed by the terrible beauty of the dead vampire before her. Her voice, usually sure and strong, was timid and tremulous.

"Yes, my child. It is just as the ancient writings depicted."

A singular howl, barely heard over the fray of the battle, made the ears of every werewolf in sight prick up at full attention. The howl spread through the ranks until it was all the Avalons could hear. Tyrannus' army began to shift. Wolves jostled goblins, minotaurs, trolls, and ogres aside as they came together in the center of the fray. Their eyes reflected yellow in the dark of the night as they formed an uneven line. Hundreds of yellow eyes, perhaps thousands, fixed on a singular point—the center of the elf army where the royals sat encircled by the Royal Guard, the best of the best.

"They're going to try and break through to you, sire," said Michael, color draining from his face as he looked to Zanthus.

"To us."

"There's a whole army in their way," said Atalanta.

"They don't mean to take on the whole army," said Michael. "They're going to make a path straight to us."

Even as he spoke, the wolf pack charged, shoving through their own troops. The first wave smacked into the front lines of the elf army like a battering ram. Moon mutts went down with yelps of pain, but those behind leapt over their fallen brethren, tearing into the elf soldiers with mouths full of teeth as sharp as swords.

Andromeda reached for her twin, her fingers brushing his wrist guard. Instinctively, without taking his eyes from the charging werewolves, Andrew twisted his fingers around hers and gave them a gentle squeeze. The soft, familiar pressure worked to slow her fluttering heart.

"Swear you won't leave my side," she said just loud enough for him to hear, ashamed at the weakness in her voice, like the plea of a child.

He turned to face her, tossing a lock of his overlong hair from his forehead. His attempt at his usual mischievous grin was lackluster at best. "I swear it," he said, giving her fingers another squeeze before letting go.

"They're going to break through," said Felicity, a quaver in her unusually high voice.

The sheer concentrated force of the werewolf pack was indeed overwhelming the elf troops. Perceiving the threat to their king, the elves tried to concentrate their forces on the pack, but only those in front could reach the tight cluster of wolves. Those in the way were mowed down. When one wolf was dispatched two more leapt forward to take its place. The griffins were swirling over the fray, diving in to grab the unwilling souls, but only one could be carried off at a time. It took two griffins to carry the white wolves. Worse still, only temporarily impeded by their own allies, the giants had almost reached the front lines of the elf troops.

The ball of light at Zanthus' shoulder began to grow as the fairy queen, Iris, took her full form. The fairies nearest her did the same, watching their queen as she hovered on her delicate wings next to Zanthus' horse.

"Protect the king!" she shouted, and as she pointed to the oncoming pack. Fire erupted from her palms, creating balls of flame that she tossed into the wolves, setting fur alight.

The closest fairies swarmed the pack while those on the outer regions continued to light the battlefield. Balls of fire slammed into werewolves with enough force to stagger the giant beasts, who howled in pain as the flames spread along their bodies, fueled by their thick, matted fur. But still, they pressed on.

"We have to separate!" said Michael. "If we are their target, they will have to disperse with us."

"Split up! Are you crazy?" said Felicity.

"He is right," said Zanthus.

"Father?" said Atalanta, incredulous.

"He is right," Zanthus repeated, voice and eyes stern.

"Andromeda, Andrew," said Michael, "go west. Felicity and I will go east. Your Majesty, you and Atalanta move back toward the walls. You are more important. Without you, the army will scatter."

"I will not flee while my people die!" said Atalanta.

"Do as he says," said Zanthus. "His reasoning is sound."

"I—"

With a ferocious snarl, a white wolf broke through the last line of defenses, leaping over the Royal Guard, black eyes fixed on Zanthus. Behind the royals, the wood nymphs stomped the ground. A wall of thorns erupted from the earth in front of Zanthus, ensnaring the wolf and bloodying its pelt.

"Now!" said Michael, putting his heels to his horse.

"Make a path!" Andrew shouted at the Royal Guard as he turned his horse east.

The message carried down the line of troops, and a narrow passage opened to allow Andrew and Andromeda's horses to pass through. But it wasn't long before the forward surge of the army caught them up and forced them to stop their flight. Andromeda looked back to the center and saw only an indistinguishable sea of bodies. The wolf pack was yipping and howling to each other, scattering in different directions.

"I think we—"

Andromeda's horse reared, nearly unseating her, as a vampire crashed to earth beside her, shot down by the elves on the wall.

They were surrounded by infantry, and the shoving of bodies as the army pushed back against its foes pushed Andrew's and Andromeda's mounts along with them. Their wild, zigzagging flight had taken them closer to the front lines, and by the blue light of the moon and the orange glow of the fairies, they could see the whites of their enemies' eyes. Goblins hacked at elf ankles, moving low to the ground, undetected. Minotaurs lowered their heads and crushed their adversaries' shields. Ogres swung their clubs in long, sweeping motions, obliterating any skull they came in contact with. But the elves were not without their own strengths. They dodged the wild, brutish blows of their foes, moving like water, spinning, jumping, parrying, jabbing, and shooting spells from their palms. The front lines ebbed and flowed, no one side gaining the upper hand for long.

"Suppose it's time to get our swords bloody?" said Andrew, and his attempt at a grin was stronger this time.

"I don't see why not," said Andromeda, trying her best to return the look.

She gripped her horse with her legs and urged it forward, drawing both swords, doing her best to steady her breathing, summoning Archimedes' commanding voice to her ears. *Breathe calm and strong, and you will be. Focus, child. Concentrate on your blades. They're part of you now. Think only of them.*

Andrew matched his horse's speed to hers, raising his

broadsword in one hand and holding his reigns in the other.

A grey werewolf galloped through a gap in the infantry directly at them. With her left knee Andromeda sidestepped her horse to the right just as the beast pounced, claws outstretched. With her left arm Andromeda swung her sword and slit the beast's throat.

She nearly fell from the saddle as her horse's right leg buckled. Andromeda looked down to see two goblins circling her horse. One of their white bone daggers was stained red with her horse's blood. Urging his horse with his heels and a cluck of his tongue, Andrew trampled one of the goblins under the hooves of his mount, and Andromeda decapitated the other with a downward slash of her sword.

"Look out!"

Andromeda looked up just as the black werewolf collided with her horse, ripping it from under her. Her only thought was to keep her swords away from her body during the inevitable impact with the ground. She held the swords down and at her sides, and they embedded in the earth, keeping her head from smacking the ground. Her legs were not so lucky, and she cried out when her kneecaps hit the dirt.

She could hear the monster's claws digging into the earth as it spun to lunge at her again, and she used her swords to pull herself up, yanking them from the ground as she spun. A shower of warm blood spattered her face as Andrew's broadsword severed the werewolf's jugular. The beast fell at her feet, and Andrew's arm appeared in front of her face as she used a sleeve to wipe blood from her eyes. She grabbed his wrist in one hand and his saddle in the other and hoisted herself up to sit behind him. As Andrew drove his horse onward, Andromeda turned to look for her mare. She saw it stagger to its feet, blood spilling from a wound on its side. With a toss of its head, it made off for Alatreon, scattering troops as it went. She felt a pang of loss watching the animal go and prayed the wound wasn't fatal.

When she turned her head back to look over Andrew's shoulder, she saw he had his steed's head aimed right for a troll that was wildly swinging its club at the end of its long arm, sending elves flying into the jaws of waiting werewolves.

"Flank him," she said in Andrew's ear. "If we charge him from the front, he'll unhorse us before we get close enough to touch him with our swords."

Andrew redirected his horse's head to obey her orders. A loud bray and a threatening snort made Andromeda whip her head to the right. A minotaur was lowering its head, eyes fixed on their horse, its foot scuffing up dirt as it perfected its aim. Andromeda sheathed her swords.

"What are you doing?" said Andrew, as she freed his crossbow from the strap on his back.

"Just keep riding!"

The minotaur charged, twisted horns aimed right for their horse's belly. She had to stop his momentum before he came too close. She snatched an arrow from Andrew's quiver and took aim. The arrow shot free with a soft thwunk and found its mark in between the minotaur's horns. It crashed into a werewolf as it fell dying, impaling the wolf's chest.

"Get ready!" said Andrew.

"You get ready," she said, stringing another arrow. "I'll get its attention."

The arrow shot through the troll's palm, making it drop its club on the backswing. As it turned, pain and confusion deforming its ugly face, Andrew's broadsword freed its head from its shoulders.

Andrew raised his sword in a triumphant cheer, and a foot the size of a small house crashed down mere feet from them, crushing elves beneath it. The earth shook under their horse's hooves, and it brayed in terror.

"Go, go!" Andromeda screamed, digging her heels into the stallion's flank as Andrew swore colorfully, looking up at the giant's trousers far overhead. As the giant's left foot moved to meet its right, its boot scattered the elves, who were forced to press against Andrew's horse. Surrounded on all sides and wild with fear, the stallion reared, but the fleeing troops collided with its flank, sending it and the twins sprawling in the dirt.

"Damn!" said Erro, his yell hardly audible even to his own ears over the screeches of griffins, the roar of the wind nymph's powers, and the cries of vampires.

He had turned his immediate attention away from the skies once again to try and catch a glimpse of Andromeda, trusting Aquila to protect him, but instead he saw two of the giants break the elf army's lines as easily as taking a stroll. The elves atop the walls shot everything they had at the massive foes: arrows, stakes, and giant boulders launched from catapults. Only the boulders did any real good. One struck the lighter haired giant in the chest and staggered it, but Erro wondered how many had been killed underfoot in that one gesture. The giants raised their weapons. One had a sword, the other a mace. They swung them in broad sweeping motions, sending dozens of elves on a long fall to their deaths.

A dark silhouette in his periphery made Erro look around just in time to stop the vampire reaching for his neck with a swipe of his borrowed sword that severed its wing. It dropped five feet in an instant, but caught itself by flapping wildly with its uninjured wing. It tossed its head and hissed at him, and he noticed the pointed ears and the blank amethyst eyes. Aquila grabbed the elf vampire in his talons and shot off toward the cage of trees. Erro risked another look back at the wall. The giant with the mace was slamming his weapon into it, breaking off a large chunk of white stone that went crashing into the elf troops. The second giant kicked at the wall with his great foot, sending a crack snaking across its surface. As the giant drew back its foot again, thick, rope-like vines grabbed at its ankle. Erro squinted through the night. It was the wood nymphs.

An angry roar turned Erro's attention to the mace-wielding giant.

Water nymphs were attempting to beat him back with a flood made from their own bodies. They battered the giant's head with a wave shaped like a fist. It roared again, spitting blood from its broken jaw. It groped at the twelve nymphs as they swirled around him, forming a liquid blanket, but they simply slid through his enormous fingers. They filled the giant's mouth, nose, and ears with water. It clutched at its throat as it drowned from the inside.

"They have to get out of the way!" Erro shouted to the night sky as the giant began to fall, ready to crush hundreds beneath his corpse.

Aquila rolled, and Erro had to dig his fingers into the griffin's feathers to keep from plummeting toward earth. He felt the wind from a vampire wing ruffle his hair. The cage was just below them, and it opened ever so slightly as Aquila dove for it and shoved the struggling elf vampire inside.

A great rumbling again captured Erro's attention. The dead giant had toppled forward, and his corpse had crashed into the wall, sending stones falling into Alatreon. A cry of triumph went up from the enemy, and Erro yelled in dismay.

He searched for the other giants. The wood nymphs were working to restrain one, wrapping his arms and chest in strong vines and pulling in toward the ground, forcing him into a crouch. Vines snaked around his throat, and his face began to purple.

There were three more giants, two of them female, still struggling to make a path to the wall without decimating Tyrannus' troops. As Erro watched, a vampire hovered next to one of the female's ears and then flew off to the male. The female fixed her eyes on the cage of trees and readjusted her course. Just behind her, the last male did the same.

"Aquila!" said Erro, heart pounding in his ears. "I have to speak with Bree. Now!"

Aquila tucked his wings to his sides and dove toward the ground.

Chapter 29

Clash of the Titans

Michael's and Felicity's knees knocked together as the giant crashed into the wall only fifty feet from them.

"It's created a breech!" said Michael.

The water nymphs rushed out from the giant's orifices in small streams, taking their female form when they reached the ground. They sent up a wail at the sight of what their heroic actions had done.

"Zanthus needs to concentrate the troops at the opening," said Michael, aiming a stake from his wrist at a vampire flying low, looking for a loose elf braid to snatch.

When it found its mark, he risked a glance toward the golden gates where the sky-blue Galechaser standard waved in the night breeze. A horn blew a quick, four-toned song, and the elf army shifted, moving from east to west, clumping closer together to converge upon the breach.

"We ought to get closer, too," said Felicity, eyeing the massive corpse with a mix of curiosity and trepidation

"Your Highness! Watch out!" came a call from the throng of battling elves.

Felicity's mare saw the threat before she did and reared. Its hooves battered the skull of the leaping russet werewolf. It hit the dirt with a whine, and the elf who had called the warning sank his sword into its back. Felicity gave him a breathless thanks before pushing her mare toward the wall, Michael just behind her.

"Damn, there's another one coming!" said Michael, looking over his shoulder.

Another male giant was gingerly picking his way through Tyrannus' army with slow, wavering steps. He hovered each foot over the ground as he took a step, waiting for those beneath to scramble out of the way, but his balance was rather lackluster, and anything still lingering when he wobbled forward was decimated beneath his tattered boots. The two females walked in much the same way, but they were headed for the tree prison. Those would be Erro's problem.

"Felicity," said Michael, loading another stake, "you go on, lead the troops at the wall."

This far from the front lines, they were moving amongst allies, but the skies were still filled with scattered vampires keeping just out of range of the elves on the wall. Michael punched the air above his head and loosed another stake. It missed the heart, but embedded in the lower torso, and the vampire writhed in pain in midair. A willow dryad snapped one of the branches that made up its hair like a whip that wrapped around the vampire's neck and slung it to earth to face the stake-wielding elves.

"And what exactly are you going to do?" said Felicity.

"I'm going to stop that giant before it gets to our lines."

"What?" she yelled in an eerie impersonation of their mother. "You'll do no such thing! Come with me."

The cry of an eagle made Michael look up. A tawny griffin snatched a vampire out of the air just above him and headed toward the cage, but that was not the griffin Michael watched. Jaculo was circling overhead, and at the sight of his black and silver mane of feathers, Michael's face split in a grin. He put two fingers in his mouth and whistled to get the griffin's attention. Jaculo fixed his orange eyes on Michael and dipped one wing to pull in closer.

"I need your help," he said, as Jaculo glided around his horse. "I need to get into the sky."

The elves parted beneath his paws, and Jaculo landed. As he tucked in his wings, he cocked his head to one side and clicked his beak. Michael wished Andromeda was there to translate, but he pressed on. "We've got to stop that giant," he said.

Jaculo's screech made Michael put a hand to his ringing ear.

"Sorry, but I'm not sure what that means."

Jaculo extended one wing and placed it on the ground like a ramp as he bent one knee.

"Thank you!" said Michael, sliding from his horse.

"Michael!" said Felicity as he swung his leg over Jaculo's back.

"I'll be fine," said Michael.

Elves sidestepped as Jaculo began to pump his wings. When he sprang into the air like a cat, Michael was almost unseated. He dug his hands into Jaculo's thick feathers and held as tight as he dared.

"I'll be fine," he called down to Felicity. "Get to the wall!"

The rush of excitement was inescapable as Jaculo's wings caught an updraft, and he rose high above the army, gliding on the breeze, and Michael almost felt guilty at the smile that lifted his cheeks. He bent forward toward where he guessed the griffin's ears must be and said, "First, we have to get the nymphs."

Aquila swiped at the muzzle of a werewolf as he came in for a landing next to the mages. The wolf's head whipped back, bloodied, but it bared its fangs and growled, turning its yellow eyes back on Aquila. Erro readied his sword, but a ball of pure white light blasted the werewolf off its feet, and an elf soldier finished the deed for him.

"Come, quick!" A hand pulled at Erro's elbow. Bree's face glittered with sweat. Her large brown eyes studied him, looking for injuries. "Get behind the line," she said.

Aquila crouched and Erro tightened his legs around the griffin's back just in time. Aquila leapt over the line of mages, and Bree shoved her way through to meet them on the other side.

"I thought elf magic could only control trees and plants and stuff," said Erro. "What was that thing you just did?"

"Our magic is attuned with nature. Light and energy are just as natural as trees and flowers."

"Oh, well that was—"

"What do you need?" she said, a little impatient.

"Oh, yeah, damn," said Erro. "There's—"

Behind Bree, a clawed fist burst from the tree prison, sending bark flying. The bloodless, white hand grabbed the hair of the nearest mage and slammed him against the prison. The elf vampire's head burst through next, and she sank her fangs into the mage before Bree could do more than turn around. The mage's blood gushed from the ragged wound as the vampire elf turned her amethyst eyes on Erro. Tongue lapping at the mage's blood, she placed her hand on the tree prison and set it alight with purple flame. Bree's spell doused the flame with water that shot from her hands like a fountain, but the vampire elf broke free and shot into the sky. Erro braced himself, assuming Aquila would follow, but the griffin stayed grounded. If the vampire elves could do magic, attempting to cage them was a lost cause.

The mages scrambled, and Erro tried to stay out of the way, taking nervous glances over his shoulder at the giants. The mages used bolts of energy to blast back the werewolves who tried to push through the opening and sang the prison back into shape.

"Bree," said Erro, arresting her attention when the worst of the damage was repaired.

"What do you need?" she snapped.

"There are two giants headed our way."

"Yes, I can see them quite well." She massaged her temple, and Erro noticed the purple bags under her eyes.

"So what are we going to do?" said Erro, an embarrassed flush rising in his cheeks. "They'll smash this thing to bits." He patted the closest tree trunk. "They've been given orders. I saw the vampire that delivered them."

"I think I know of a way," said Bree, putting a finger to her chin. "I've never done something that big before, though."

"You're some sort of prodigy, right? I bet you can do it, no problem."

"You're kind ... I think," she said with a small laugh that didn't reach her eyes, which were narrowed in thought.

"Can I help?"

She eyed the borrowed armor that didn't quite fit him and the sword at his belt.

"Not this time," she said. "Get back in the sky. Save as many as you can."

"You heard the lady, Aquila."

The griffin spread his wings.

"Good luck," said Erro as Aquila took flight.

She gave him a small wave, and then he heard her say, "I need energy!" as she pressed back through the ring of mages.

When he was above the cage, Erro looked down to see three mages encircling Bree. One laid her hands on Bree's head, the other two on both her shoulders. Their hands glowed from within, illuminating Bree's face in the dark.

A griffin called out in distress as a vampire elf slammed into it, making it drop the human vampire it was carrying. Another griffin swooped underneath the falling wolf and snatched it to safety. The vampire elf, a male with white-blond, shoulder-length hair and sapphire eyes, and the griffin grappled in the air, and Aquila veered toward them.

"Save or kill?" said Erro.

Aquila's tail whipped around his body to swat Erro's boot and the stake strapped to it.

"Really? Are you sure? That's one of the elf captives."

Aquila's tail swatted the stake again. Erro pulled the smooth, pointed piece of wood free.

"Ready when you are."

Aquila slammed into the vampire, knocking him away from

the other griffin. He snarled like a cat and swiped at Aquila's face, but Aquila snapped his beak over the hand, severing the fingers. Aquila swerved to give Erro a clear shot, but the vampire dove beneath them. The griffin they had saved grabbed the vampire's wing in its beak and hauled it back up. Erro blocked the vampire's flying claws with his left wrist guard and jabbed with the stake. Missed. The vampire swiped again, but this time his black claws raked through the thin bone and membrane of his own wing, severing it and releasing him from the other griffin's grip. The vampire fell like a seed blown from a tree, his remaining wing flapping to slow him while the severed wing regrew. Aquila circled, trying to bring Erro close enough to plunge the stake home, but the vampire elf fought like a cougar, gnashing teeth and slashing with claws on hands until he dropped into the fray of battle in the middle of Tyrannus' horde. Aquila flew upward, searching for a new target. Erro was nearly unseated by a bump from beneath. Aquila screeched in pain and rolled out of further harm's way, Erro hugging his neck. The vampire elf flashed his fangs in a grin, hovering in front of them.

"Stop this," said Erro, searching for a sign of humanity in the vampire's gemstone eyes. "I know you don't want to do this. Tyrannus turned you into this, but we can help you. King Zanthus has the whole kingdom working on a cure."

"A cure?" said the vampire. His voice was siren song, like a refreshing drink of cool water filled with deadly shards of glass. "So that is why you try to cage us?"

His laugh raised the hairs on Erro's arm. Aquila clicked his beak in a threat.

"My kind and I want no cure," said the vampire.

"So you will fight for Tyrannus and destroy your people?" said Erro, fighting down the fear the vampire's deadened eyes spawned in him.

"We have no people, and we fight for ourselves and our rightful place."

With a mighty pump of his wings, Aquila shot toward the vampire. Erro held the stake out like a javelin in a joust, but the vampire moved too fast to see and the stake only sliced through air. Erro heard him laugh as he dove toward the front lines in search of spilled blood.

Chanting pulled Erro's attention back to the tree prison. Bree rose toward him, lifted up on a tree trunk pedestal. Her eyes were closed, her arms raised around her head in a gesture of supplication to the heavens, chanting along with the mages below her. A vampire dove for her. Aquila swerved to chase after it, but a spout of fire from below sent it careening toward the ground like an asteroid. The tree trunk grew branches that wrapped around Bree like a cage. It was not until two thick branches sprang from the top of it that Erro realized it was a torso. The trunk split in two, and the roots became feet. The branches at the shoulders grew hands with fingers that grew to deadly points. Hundreds of thin branches formed a head and face, sprouting a thick mop of mossy hair. It was a giant formed of branches interlocked like sinews, with Bree as its heart.

The two giants of skin and bone hesitated, looking at each other in stupefied wonder. Bree studied them with a tiny smile from the gaps in between the interlaced branches of the torso, her eyes glowing with a strange, soft, green light. She flexed her arms and put one foot back on her trunk pedestal in a fighting stance, and the tree giant did the same. She pumped her legs in place, and her giant trudged forward through the horde, crushing the goblins, trolls, ogres, and werewolves the two female giants had been so careful to avoid. The giant in front took a surprised step back, squishing a particularly fat troll underfoot. Then she and her fellow drew their weapons—a sword the length of three men and a chain and ball mace.

"Think we can help her?" Erro asked Aquila.

The griffin screeched and glided on an updraft over Bree's head, circling like a vulture. Erro kept low to his back.

Bree's giant met the sword-wielding foe first. The giantess swung the weapon in a wide sideswipe. There was nothing hasty about the movement, as if it was a chore for the giantess to move her own weight. Bree's giant didn't move much faster as it stuck out a hand to grab the swinging wrist. The force of the block pushed Bree's giant sideways, and it wobbled on one foot as Bree struggled to stand upright inside her protective cage.

"Now!" cried Erro. "Go for the eyes."

Aquila dove, claws extended. The giantess went cross-eyed just before Aquila plunged both front feet into the murky, muddy pupil. Liquid sprayed onto Erro's face, and he stifled a gag. The giantess roared, vibrating Erro's eardrums, and the gust of foul breath that poured from her mouth caught under Aquila's wings and tossed him backward. They rolled out of the freefall just before Aquila's back slammed into Bree's giant, who was swinging its free arm. Its sharp fingers gouged its foe's face, and blood rained down onto the battlefield. Bree pulled out of the move and slammed her giant's elbow into the wrist holding the sword, wrenching the weapon free. She raised a knee, and her giant did the same, slamming into its flesh-and-bone cousin's gut. Bree brought the sword up and swung it in a wide arc that pruned the giantess' head from her shoulders with ease. The massive skull plunged to earth and rolled through the army below, scattering troops.

Just as Erro let out a triumphant cry that he couldn't hear over the ringing in his ears, a mace slammed into the head of Bree's giant, splintering the wood into a thousand pieces. Inside the tree giant's chest, Bree was flung sideways and slammed against the branches of the torso. The tree giant fell with her, landing precariously close to the ring of mages. Instead of falling back, the mages raced forward, hands glowing, to touch any part of the giant they could reach, but Bree was already getting to her feet, one arm outstretched for the fallen sword. Her tree giant, half its face missing, mimicked her movements and rose once more. The last giantess swiveled her wrist in circles, swinging the spiked ball of the mace around on its chain, building a steady momentum. Aquila and Erro dove in from the left to avoid the swinging weapon in the giantess' right hand, but she was ready for them. Her slow, dirt-smeared hand, as wide as a barn, swatted at them. Erro pressed himself into Aquila's back with a cry of fear. Aquila pressed his wings flat to his side, encasing Erro's legs, and shot through the gap between two fingers.

Bree's giant swung the sword, but the mace was ready. The two weapons collided with an earsplitting clang, and the sword flew free of the tree giant's hand. The mace swung again and slammed into the tree giant's shoulder, but Bree grabbed onto the wrist holding it and kept her giant upright. Erro saw Bree slash her hand upward in an open-fingered uppercut, and the tree giant's claw-like hand plunged into the soft spot under the giantess' jaw. As the giantess screamed, Bree pulled the mace free and finished the job.

"Only one more to go!" said Erro, looking for the last of the giants. "Never mind," he said when he found the giant entwined in the wood nymphs' thick vines, a griffin circling his head. As Erro watched, the water nymphs poured into the giant's mouth.

"Is that Michael?" said Erro, squinting at the griffin he thought must be Jaculo.

Whoever was sitting atop the griffin waved his arm in a forward motion as the giant turned blue. Wind nymphs slammed into the giant, propelling it backward as it died so that it fell behind enemy lines.

Erro punched the air, but Aquila screeched in alarm, diving so suddenly that Erro was almost unseated.

"What the—?"

But then he saw it. The tree giant was falling backward, the branches rotting away, exposing an unconscious Bree. Aquila crashed through the rotted wood of the torso, and Erro snatched Bree up just before she slid off her crumbling pedestal, pulling her into his lap. Blood streamed from both nostrils, and her eyes were rolled back to the whites. Erro called her name and shook her as Aquila glided toward the ground, but she didn't stir.

A great cry of jubilation went up from Zanthus' army as the mages pulled Bree away from Erro.

"I don't know what's wrong," he said. "I didn't see her get hit."

"The spell has drained too much of her life force. She knew it might happen," said an elf whose wizened voice betrayed his years better than his smooth skin.

"But you can heal her, right?"

"We can try, but we must keep our powers on the task at hand. You, too, young sire. Get back in the sky. We will do what we can."

Erro chewed at his lip as the elf laid Bree in the grass at the base of the tree prison. Aquila flapped his wings.

"All right. I know." He shook his head. "Andrew's going to kill me."

* * *

Melanie flinched, shrinking away from the sound of Tyrannus' roar. The cry of fury awakened something primal, something that screamed at her to run. Thetis had claimed keeping her in Tyrannus' inner circle at the back of the army would keep her safe, but she felt more like a prisoner than ever, and the danger felt no less with the hybrid king close enough to touch and his dark sorceresses brewing something vile in a cauldron big enough to bathe a man. Despite her fear, Melanie harbored a smile as she watched the last of the giants fall.

"I thought you said if the human king did not arrive, my victory was assured!" Tyrannus bellowed at the hags. "I do not see him, and yet I do not sit on the golden throne!"

"Patience," said Porphyria. "The battle has only begun."

"We warned you the veil is not always thin," said Typhoid.

"No matter, no matter," said Tyrannus, his forked tongue sliding over his jowls. "We've breeched the wall. Is that potion almost ready?"

"It's finished," said Malaria with a giggle. "Bring us the king, and you'll have all the magic of an elfling."

Melanie, who had been staring at the strange tree prison wondering, not for the first time, if it was really what she thought it was, pricked her ears and studied the angry red fumes of the bubbling potion with renewed interest. A hybrid king with the magic of an elf. Arcamira would stand little chance.

"Thetis!" said Tyrannus. "It's time to prove your worth. Rally the vampires. Storm the breech. I want so many bodies converging on that spot that the few archers left up there don't even know where to shoot. Hopefully Nathaniel isn't daft enough to miss the message. I want the whole army concentrated there. Forget the field. Take the city!"

"Your Majesty, I am your last line of defense," said Thetis with a bow. "Do you wish me to return when the troops are in motion?"

"Do you think me a helpless pup, Thetis?" said Tyrannus, a dangerous smile curling his misshapen lips.

"No, Your Majesty, I merely—"

"I have an army at my front and sorcery at my back. I can fare without you. Do as I say, and take your whorish plaything with you. It's time she proves her worth."

Tyrannus' orange eyes found Melanie, and she shuddered. He knew; she was certain. He knew that she was the mutinous recruit the hags spoke of. For just an instant, she contemplated throwing herself at his feet and begging for mercy, but the urge was gone as swiftly as it came when Tyrannus' eyes moved from her, bored and impatient. He could not know. None of them knew. Not even the witches. Or she would surely be dead or in immense pain.

"Go!" Tyrannus roared, his eyes on his army.

"Come," Thetis whispered, and Melanie opened her wings as he did, more eager than she'd ever been to take flight.

If Tilly had found the Avalons, she was in the city. She could find her. See her one last time. But never be with her, not anymore. Unless … Her eyes found the tree prison. What did it mean?

Just in front of her, Thetis unstrapped a horn from his belt and put it to his lips. The sound was high and wailing, and the wind caught it up and carried it across the battlefield as he flew. Beating wings encased Melanie and Thetis as the vampires rallied.

"We take the wall at the gap!" Thetis cried between horn blasts.

The closest vampires spread the word through the growing flock. Melanie searched the surrounding faces, trying to recognize them. Surely these were all the elder vampires, those who chose this war. If she was right, all of those who had been forced into Tyrannus' army ought to have been flying off toward the tree prison. In fact, she'd seen a few do just that as she stood behind the lines, aching to do so herself. Even if it was not meant to save them, as she hoped, it would keep them from doing harm.

Cold, ruby eyes startled her. The elves were rallying around their captors, attacking their own people of their own accord. After the initial shock wore off, Melanie found she was not all that surprised. The vampire elves scared her just as much as Tyrannus did.

Melanie realized she was lightheaded when her fangs pricked her bottom lip. The smell of blood was far stronger here. She looked down and saw a heaving mass of bodies. The blood stood out bright on her retinas. She heard the beating of a hundred hearts at once. The sound filled her head, pounding against her skull. Her stomach cramped, demanding her attention. She felt her jaw dislocate to accommodate a maw of growing teeth.

A sharp pain at her neck brought her back just enough to realize that Thetis was flying underneath her and his fangs were in her flesh. But then he pulled back.

"You cannot go into a frenzy yet, my sweet," he said.

"Thetis," she moaned, hearing the animalistic growling whine in her voice, like a wolf fighting with its brother over a hunk of meat, but she didn't care. "I have to have it. Please, Thetis."

He pondered her for a moment. "I can't have you flying blindly into the fray," he said, and in a flash, he was diving down to the battlefield.

Realizing what was about to happen, Melanie shook her head violently and bit down on her own lip, trying to come fully back to herself, but all she could hear was a hundred pulses, all she could feel was the growling of her stomach, and all she could think about was the smell, the glorious smell. Suddenly it was incredibly strong. She saw a beautiful face screaming in terror, and her head bent to the elf's neck. The gush of the warm, perfumed blood exploded on her tongue, and her eyes rolled back in ecstasy. But then it was gone. The elf was plummeting to earth.

"Prove yourself today, and I will no longer keep you from a full meal," said Thetis. "Now stay alert, we're nearly there."

Melanie flexed her hands in front of her face. She felt good, marvelous even. Her muscles felt tight and strong. Pitiful meal or no, the elf blood was working its magic. Thetis had made a mistake. It would be his undoing, if she had any say. But then a horrible thought struck her. What if killing Thetis was not enough? What if this was not how she was meant to fulfill the hags' prophecy? Tyrannus himself had seemed unconcerned by Thetis' absence. The hags' potion. That had to be the key. She should have killed them, tipped over their cauldron, something. Or perhaps she was supposed to kill Thetis before he gave Tyrannus' order to storm the wall, but she had failed there, too. All she had been thinking about was Tilly.

"Brace yourselves!" Thetis said.

A boulder from one of the catapults on the palace wall crashed through the flock, sending bodies slamming into Melanie's wings as the vampires tried to get out of the way. There was a faint cacophony of sounds much like the twang of a bow, and the flock surged the other direction, some screaming in pain. Melanie saw two bodies drop, stakes embedded in their chests. As she watched their descent, nervous fear gathering in her gut, she saw the werewolves, the whole pack galloping underneath them, biting and clawing their way through the elf soldiers, all headed toward the fallen giant and the gap in the wall.

Chapter 30

The Tipping Scale

Felicity knew all was lost when she looked at the crumbling remains of the wall. It did not matter how many elf soldiers were on the ground, surging together to crush the werewolf pack beneath the weight of swords, shields, and mail. It did not matter that the griffins were circling, snatching away unwilling souls—of which it seemed there were not many left. The griffins sank their claws all the way through the necks of many wolves and the wings of many vampires, tossing them to the elves to finish with silver and stakes, but there were not enough of them. The vampire hoard was flying straight for the wall, never stopping to fight. The wolf line was breaking, but the shifting ball of black wings surged forward. It didn't matter that the fairies were tossing fireballs into their midst. The pain didn't kill them. It hardly slowed them down. The only real line of defense, the elves of the wall, was decimated. There were barely twenty left after the sweep of the giant's sword and the fall of the wall. Many of them were wounded. Only a handful had their crossbows still intact. The surviving archers from the other end of the wall were running toward the gap; Felicity could see their gold-painted armor flashing in the light of the torches set atop the merlons. But they weren't going to make it.

Felicity stood next to the booted foot of the fallen giant, rapiers at the ready, but the blades felt useless in her hands as she tilted her head back to watch the flock as it soared over her head. The elf next to her cocked back his arm and threw his stake with a cry of rage, but it fell back, useless, to the ground.

Iris screamed in fury, too, two fireballs blazing in her palms. She brought her hands together, combining the flames into a roaring ball the size of one of the catapult boulders and threw it with all her might, hovering over Felicity's head on her iridescent wings. The fireball exploded into the back of the flock, but it only propelled them—their light garments, hair, and wings alight—further past the wall.

A snarl brought Felicity's attention back to the ground and forced her into a fighting stance. Thirty odd werewolves had broken the line. A great black beast with gobs of bloody drool dripping from its jowls leapt for her. And suddenly she was in the air, held aloft by her armpits.

She screamed and kicked, certain she was in the clutches of a vampire, until she heard her brother's voice.

"Quit that! Do you want me to drop you?"

Michael hoisted her into his lap so that she could sheathe her swords and throw her leg around Jaculo's back.

"We're too heavy for him," said Felicity.

Jaculo had sunk closer to earth, his black wings laboring to keep him aloft.

"You have to put me down."

"Find her a horse," Michael shouted toward Jaculo's head.

Jaculo landed behind friendly lines, startling the white, riderless horse with a brush of his wings. Felicity jumped off and soothed the beast.

"My God, is he opening the gates?" she cried as she swung her leg over the steed.

Michael looked to the golden gates and found them propped halfway open. Zanthus' steed paced beside it as the king shouted orders.

"He'll need troops inside now that they've breached the wall."

"But he'll let more in!"

"Not if they can hold the line."

"Michael … we're … we're going to lose, aren't we?"

"Not if we cut off the head of the horde," said Michael, looking across the battlefield.

"Oh no," said Felicity, her jaw clenched in anger. "No way."

"Felicity, there's no other way. Just look!" He jabbed a finger at the vampire horde now spreading out over Alatreon.

Ice pierced Felicity's heart. The vampires dove and circled, bringing children and the infirm back into the air with them, but they never stopped moving forward, toward the white marble palace.

"Tilly," she breathed.

"What?" said Michael.

"Tilly! She's in the palace."

"She's safe, Felicity."

"Nobody's safe!"

Michael snapped his mouth shut, watching her with sad eyes.

"The only way to save her is to win this war," he said. "Kill the hybrid king, and the army dies with him."

"Michael, I have to go find her," said Felicity, tears brimming in her eyes. "I can't leave her by herself."

Michael looked at the ground and nodded his head. "I know."

"And I can't leave you by yourself. Don't go. You don't have to be the hero."

"Who says he's the hero?" said Atalanta, trotting up behind Felicity on her own white steed.

Michael gaped like a fish for a moment and said, "You need to stay with your father."

"My father needs to command his army within the walls. I need to have Tryannus' head on a pike. I'm coming with you."

Felicity never looked at Atalanta. Her head swiveled from the darker mass in the night sky that was the vampire horde to Michael's face, where it at last came to rest.

"Be safe," she said.

"You, too."

Felicity put her heels to her horse and headed for the gates.

"Get back in the sky," said Atalanta, pulling Michael's gaze from his sister's back. "Find Erro. I'll find the twins."

"They'll probably find you," said Michael, making Atalanta

smirk as Jaculo launched into the sky.

"We'll be right behind you!" she called after his silhouette against the moon.

* * *

Tilly set the straw doll down, its curly, red yarn hair falling over its face, and turned her head slowly toward Zezil, her heart suddenly beating very fast. The funny doggy was growling on top of the bed. The hair on his back was sticking up like spikes. But he wasn't looking at her. He was looking out the window.

"Zezil?" she said, scooting away from the doggy on her butt.

He didn't act like he heard his name. He was growling louder. Something was happening to his shoulders. They were getting taller. There was an ugly cracking noise. The funny doggy's whole body started to change. His teeth got bigger, his claws got longer, and by the time he grinned over at her, he was the size of a wolf. Tilly wanted to scream, but she couldn't.

"Good puppy," she whispered.

The window shattered, and the monster that crawled through the window wrenched the scream free of Tilly's throat. It was like the ones that got Mommy and Daddy; people with long teeth and ugly black wings. The monster man licked his lips when he saw her, but then his eyes got big when the doggy growled again.

"Devil d—"

Zezil jumped on the monster and bit him in the neck. Tilly screamed with the monster and shut her eyes tight, punching her fists into them. Then there was fur on her face, and something was pulling her up by her dress. Screaming, she opened her eyes and swatted at her attacker, and she felt a wet puppy nose. Zezil ran out the door, holding her dress in his mouth. Her legs scraped on the cold floor, and she pulled her knees up to her chest. She could hear the monster coming, but Zezil was running fast. So fast Tilly could not tell where she was, bouncing along in his mouth, his slobber dripping down on her back. Her armpits ached where her dress pulled, and she couldn't hold her legs up much longer.

Then another monster jumped out from behind a wall, and Tilly shut her eyes as Zezil swerved to the left. When she opened them again, they were in the kitchen. Then something slammed into Zezil. The collar of Tilly's dress ripped, and she went spinning across the smooth floor while Zezil was tossed out the kitchen door into the cobbled street beyond. She started to cry when her back hit a hard counter, and a yellow-haired lady with bone-white skin and pointy teeth said, "There, there, sweet thing, don't cry. I'll take the pain away."

Zezil's ferocious bark made the lady whip around just in time to meet his teeth with her face in a gruesome, flesh-ripping kiss. She staggered backward, fingers exploring the tatters of her flesh and the bone peeking through, and Zezil slammed into her with his shoulder, sending her careening backward into the lit fireplace. Tilly shrank back as Zezil pounced at her, jaws wide, but he only snapped at the back of her dress again. But this time, as he raised his head to lift her, her dress only tore more. His great head nudged her to her feet, and with one hand gripped in the fur at his neck, now sticky with his own blood, she ran out into the street with him, away from the terrible screams of the burning lady.

* * *

At last, Melanie was alone with Thetis, flying slightly behind him as he circled around a golden palace turret, observing his troops as they pulled servants out of windows and dropped them to their deaths. He wasn't looking at her. The elf blood was still filling her up. It was time, but part of her wanted to flee. If Tilly was here, she was in the palace. She could be the next body tossed from a window. The thought made her want to dive through the window in the turret and search every nook of the grand palace for her daughter. But Thetis would notice. Thetis would follow, and then what? Could she ever really be with Tilly again? No. She knew that. But, just to see her, one last time. Melanie tensed when she noticed Thetis looking at her.

"Thinking of doing something foolish, pet?" he said, his dark-blue eyes hard and cold. "Just remember, I am all you have left."

"Yes, you made certain of that, didn't you?" said Melanie, the words breaking free in an exhilarating rush. "First my husband, then my unborn child." The rage struck her with the force of a giant's club as she traced her fingers over her stomach, now thin and toned, as cold and perfect as the marble of the palace walls. "But you didn't get, Tilly. No. I made certain of that."

"Did you? You left her alone in a burning elf village. She is ash or rotting flesh," he spat, pumping his wings once and holding them close to his sides to zoom toward her. "You are eternal, and it is I you have to thank," he said, hovering in front of her. "Even now, I protect you. I kept you at my side in a place of honor. I kept you safe as we crossed the wall." His hand encircled her throat. "And I will have gratitude, pet. Now stick close, or I will throw you to the elves myself."

He tossed her aside and continued his circling, his eyes flicking to the lightening sky with just a trace of apprehension.

Melanie watched him, and this time, she did not attempt to stopper the rage. Her nails slid out from their beds and became claws. Her jaw popped and reformed to fit her new rows of fangs. He was flying underneath her now, and he didn't look up until an animalistic snarl burst from her chest as she dove for him. He tucked his wings and rolled, but not fast enough. They tumbled together, but Melanie stayed crouched on his back, wrenching his wings from their sockets. She let him loose just long enough to right herself and give him a sharp, crushing, two-legged kick in the spine that sent his diaphragm straight through the golden point of one of the lower spires. Impaled, he sank down a few more inches until the spire became too wide. He cried out like a wounded wild cat, his hands groping at the spire that should have been slick with his blood. She had meant to spear his heart, but the sight of him floundering there, unable to heal himself, was almost more satisfactory. She dove in close, just far enough to stay out of reach of his clawing hands, her mouth shrinking to accommodate just two fangs.

"I am not your pet," she said, her face twisted with an intermingling of fury and delight. "I am not your plaything. I am the beast you created. I am the one the hags' prophecy foretold. I am your undoing."

Thetis regarded her with agony in the lines of his face, his eyes wide in disbelief, and his mouth curled in fury. A roar, a hellish scream, and the smell of charred flesh rising from below made his eyes flick downward, and a sneer brightened his face.

"No, my dear, she is your undoing," he said.

If she had been breathing, it would have caught in her throat. A scent so strangely familiar tickled her nostrils, demanding her attention even in the midst of the sounds and smells of war all around her. Her head moved slowly. The brown waves bobbed beside a large, gray, dog-like beast, and for a moment, her heart felt alive.

Tilly.

The name filled her up, set her senses on fire. But even as it rang in her own head, someone screamed it in the distance. Melanie found the princess easily through the dark and the running elf bodies, just as she had in the elf village. She was mounted atop a white steed, her bright golden hair stained pink with blood on one side, her eyes fixed on Tilly and the dog as she galloped through the street, closing the distance fast.

"She is why you fight," said Thetis. "She is why you cannot accept my gift."

Melanie pulled her eyes from her daughter just as Thetis used his hands, feet, and newly healed wings to thrust himself off of the spire, soaring out of her reach.

"What if I give her the same gift?" he said, his eyes full of mad light. "Perhaps then you will be mine."

"No!"

She shot toward him, but he dove, ducking under her swiping claw. She threw herself into a backflip and plummeted after him.

* * *

Felicity yanked back on her horse's reins and slid off as it reared in protest, but she had only taken a step when Zezil threw himself in front of Tilly, snapping and snarling. His eyes were wild and fixed on her drawn rapier.

"Zezil ..." she said, apprehension tautening her voice as she moved to sheathe the weapon.

He pounced without warning, jaws wide. She rushed to meet him, but hit the cobblestone in a slide, one foot extended, the other tucked underneath her. He soared over her, and his claws skidded for purchase on the stones as he tried to whirl around and lunge again. She sheathed the weapon and faced him with arms out, palms up, and fingers splayed wide. Zezil stalked toward her, crouching low, growling deep in his throat.

"Oh hell," Felicity mumbled. "How does Erro do this ... uh, good boy, Zezil? It's me. You remember me."

"Felicity!"

Short arms wrapped around Felicity's leg and squeezed it tight. Zezil stopped, ears twitching forward. Felicity looked down to see Tilly, now with her legs wrapped around her calf as well.

"Tilly," she said with a sigh of relief.

Then Zezil growled and leapt high into the air. Felicity looked just in time to see his teeth close on air just below Thetis' foot as he dove right for her. Her fingers wrapped around her sword hilt just as Thetis' foot slammed into her nose, crushing it, and sending her sprawling backward in a spray of blood. Her head cracked hard on the cobblestones, and her vision went blurry. Miniature suns blazed in front of her. She groaned, only half aware of a weight leaving her leg.

"Felicity!" The high scream made terror grip at her chest, but she wasn't entirely sure why. She shook her head and blinked up after the sound.

"Tilly!" she cried, trying to leap to her feet, but her stomach churned and she fell hard on her backside, watching helplessly as Tilly was carried off in Thetis' arms.

Tears filled her eyes as panic set in. She called Tilly's name again, screaming so loudly her throat felt raw with the effort. Zezil was already gone, streaking off through Alatreon, head tilted upward, barreling through anyone who stood in his path. Felicity ran to her horse, which was tossing its head nervously. She jumped into the saddle and spurred it after the receding shape of Zezil, back toward the battlefield, her eyes on the sky.

* * *

"I'm in," said Erro before Michael had even finished his explanation. "Where's Andromeda?"

They were gliding over the tree prison, entirely alone in the night sky. The griffins and vampires battled over Alatreon now.

"Atalanta's gone to find her and Andrew," said Michael. "We'll pull in closer and circle until they catch up. We attack together."

Erro nodded, and the two griffins dipped their right wings in an about face, raptor eyes on the far side of the battlefield where a semicircle of guards protected the hybrid king.

"So that's him," said Michael, when they'd gotten as close as they dared, squinting down through the brightening dark at the beast with a crown of bones atop his dark head. He was lit from behind by a strange red glow, but his features were hard to make out from a distance. "What's that behind him? Is that a …?"

"Dark magic," said Erro. "Some sort of … potion. He's got hags with him. Four of them."

"This is going to be more difficult than I thought," said Michael.

"You thought it was going to be easy?" said Erro, snickering.

Michael grinned and shrugged. "More or less."

Erro started to laugh, but broke off, head turned back toward Alatreon. "There they are," he said, pointing to a white horse barreling through enemy lines.

Fairies illuminated the landscape and the horse as it cantered past the tree prison, its gait hampered by the weight of three people — Andromeda, Andrew, and Atalanta. Though both armies were depleted, their ranks spread thin over two battlegrounds, the elves had plenty of foes to overcome, and that charging steed had plenty of foes to dodge. Goblins ran amok in tight packs, sneaking around elf lines and swiping at shins. Ogres, trolls, and minotaurs charged the ranks. The howls, barks, and yips of werewolves still carried on the night breeze, but a quick scan of the field showed that their ranks had taken the biggest losses. The naked bodies of fallen werewolves were piled atop one another around the wall. So many that the elf soldiers had to split ranks to get around the corpses. Michael easily found the alpha. He was the largest of them all, now that the white wolves had all been captured. His umber fur was wild, long, and bushy. A small group of four ran behind him, leaping in front of any elf soldier who tried to put a silver blade to him.

"He's got all the important ones around him," said Erro. "Look. That troll has gold bands on his arms. The ogre has an iron crown. That minotaur is the biggest I've seen yet."

"He's even got the new goblin king," said Michael. "Or is that a queen?"

"Hard to tell with goblins."

"So they're all royalty. Makes sense. The kings always stay at the back. Strange he doesn't have any vampires or werewolves guarding him, though."

"He might," said Erro. "There's a man down there. Maybe he's a ..."

The tremor in Erro's voice made Michael look over to find him paler than the moon. But even as Michael watched, a flush rose in his cheeks and high on his forehead.

"Erro, what?"

"I don't believe it," said Erro, looking at Michael with something like dismay. "It's ... it's him."

"Who?"

Erro looked down again, and the muscles in his jaw flexed. "Brock."

"Erro, it can't be."

"It's him. Go, Aquila!"

Aquila clicked his beak.

"Erro, don't! We have to wait for the others."

"Now, Aquila!"

Aquila screeched and backpedaled in the air.

As red as his hair now, Erro cried out in frustration. "Fine! I'll just go without you." And with that, he crossed his arms and slid sideways off of Aquila's back.

Michael could find no words, no warnings to shout. He gaped in disbelief as Erro dropped like a stone, arms still folded stubbornly over his chest, never making a sound. Aquila cried out in alarm and dove for him, wings pressed to his sides like a second skin. The griffin zipped past his plummeting companion and maneuvered himself under him, opening his wings and catching the boy on his back, feet from the ground. Michael let out the breath he'd been holding in and called Erro a few colorful names.

Below him, Erro stroked Aquila's head once and jumped the rest of the way to the ground, ducking under Aquila's swiping paw and running straight for a man with long, disheveled hair, wedged neatly between the troll and goblin kings, feet from the hybrid king himself.

"Erro, you damned fool!" Michael screamed, hoping the other boy could hear him down there. He put a hand to his forehead to rub at his throbbing temples. He looked from Erro to the white horse, still too far away, at an utter loss for what to do.

* * *

Melanie sucked in panicked breaths she did not really need, her wings beating as fast as she could drive them, but Thetis was bigger, stronger, and he shot through the air just out of reach. She flew with one arm outstretched, and when she got hold of him, she would rip him to shreds. Tilly was screaming for the princess. "Felicity! Felicity!" Over and over.

"Tilly! It's okay, sweetheart. Momma's coming for you."

Thetis laughed, high and cold, but Tilly's screams ebbed. "Momma?"

Melanie could not see her daughter, pulled tight to Thetis' chest, but she heard her. She could hear her heartbeat, her breath, the swish of her dress as the night air caught the lower hem.

"Yes, Tilly! I'm here!" she called.

"Momma! Momma!"

Melanie caught a glimpse of a kicking black shoe as Tilly wriggled in Thetis' arms, trying to see past him.

"Best tell your daughter to stay still, pet. I'd hate to drop her," said Thetis, never looking back, never slowing as he approached the wall where elves with crossbows stood watch. There weren't many, but now they would have fewer targets.

"Tilly, do as he says! I'll come for you!"

"Momma! Momma!"

The wall was upon them. Two elves took aim. When the stakes were loosed, Thetis encircled his torso in his wings and barrel rolled, diving straight for the elves. One of the stakes ripped through the membrane of his wing, but it didn't slow him. Melanie dropped a few feet to dodge the stake that missed him entirely. Thetis opened his wings just when it looked like he was going to slam into the wall and knocked the two elves backward with his wing joints. One fell over the ramparts, screaming.

The maneuver had slowed Thetis, and Melanie streamlined her wings and dove in for the kill, but just as she shot over the wall, she pulled back. She couldn't. Tilly would fall.

She cried out in frustration, and Thetis returned the sound with a laugh. Melanie looked over the battlefield, trying to think straight, and saw Nathaniel below, his head thrown back in a howl to rally his scattered troops. As he did, he caught sight of Thetis, and his ears pricked to attention. He started snarling and barking at the wolf closest to him, giving some kind of order, no doubt.

She fixed her eyes back on Thetis, not knowing what else to do but keep her wings propelling her forward. He was headed for the hybrid king, with her daughter in his arms.

* * *

Felicity's horse nearly sent two elf soldiers sprawling as she charged back through the golden gates. She swiped at the blood dripping into her mouth, struggling to breathe through her broken nose.

"Princess Felicity!"

Zanthus' call would not have broken through Felicity's concentration had he not positioned his horse right in front of hers, causing it to plant its hooves and toss its head in fear, nearly sending her flying over its neck. Zezil, who had been running just ahead of her, never stopped. He launched himself into the fray, savaging a werewolf's face.

"How fares the city?" said Zanthus. "The palace? I've split

the troops in two, but I fear we are now spread too thin."

"They have Tilly!"

"What? The little girl? Where?"

Felicity thrust a finger at the diminishing shapes of the two vampires.

"Please ..." she said.

Zanthus' horse sidestepped out of her way at his command.

"Be careful, young Avalon. The alpha is rallying his moon mutts again."

Felicity set her heels to her horse, and the wind whipped around her ears. She thought she heard Zanthus say something very like, "your brother," but she had no time to stop; the vampires never slowed. She searched for the werewolf alpha and found it was not so dark on the battlefield as before. If they could hold a few more hours, the sun might save them, at least for a day. Or perhaps the vampires would just take up roost in the palace, away from the deadly light of the sun, and hold it as their own.

She saw the bushy-furred alpha off to her right. If she wanted to follow right behind the vampires, she would have to pass close to him. She stayed on her course, swords drawn, hacking at the goblins threatening to trip her horse as she broke past the furthermost elf soldiers. There was no real front line anymore. The two armies had bashed against one another so many times that they melded into an ever-shifting but united entity, but now she was in the dark belly of the beast. Felicity's racing heart fueled the adrenaline that hardened her muscles and sharpened her focus, but still it pitter-pattered in fear as she realized she was now far outnumbered on the field, her allies behind her. She had Zezil, but he wasn't exactly staying close. The vexar fought wildly, only focusing on one enemy long enough to satisfy his blood lust before pouncing on another. Felicity's elvish horse was strong and battle trained, and it never stopped its charge. It leapt over a speared and dying wolf, crushing a goblin under its hooves as it went. A troll thundered toward her, club lifted high over its head. Suddenly there was elf cavalry at her back. An arrow pierced the troll's makeshift boiled leather armor at the weak spot at the throat.

"The king would have us escort you, princess," said an elf with hair of midnight and eyes of ocean-blue, his braided hair flying free from his golden helm. "Your siblings head in the same direction, our princess with them. He fears your brother means to kill Tyrannus himself."

"He is right."

The elf looked stunned for only a moment, and then a charging minotaur grabbed his attention.

"We intend to help him," said a red-haired elf on Felicity's left.

Felicity meant to give her thanks, but the black-haired elf cried out in agony as a wolf snatched him from his horse. The wolf bit deep into the leg, tearing until a spray of blood drenched its muzzle. Felicity turned her horse to attack, but now three wolves faced her, teeth bared, but not lunging. They formed a circle around the screaming elf. Between their legs, Felicity watched the elf writhe. Not one of the wolves moved in for the kill. The nearest one, a grey beast with a bloodied eye, snapped at Felicity's ankle, but she brought her blade down across its nose. The elf screamed louder, his cry comingling with the horrendous cracking sound of his spine breaking and reforming. But his leg was no longer pooling blood around him. His black braid was shrinking and turning white. She had no time to stay and fight, but the realization of what was happening held her in place for a few seconds longer. A wolf yelped behind her, pierced by the blade of one of her escort.

"We need to keep moving, princess!" said the red-haired elf. "If we don't, they'll surround us."

Felicity turned her horse and obeyed. One look at the elf beside her told her she understood, too. The werewolves were replenishing their numbers.

* * *

Erro pulled his dagger from an ogre that had tried to block his way, stepping on its chest to wrench the blade from its skull, and when he looked up, Brock's eyes had found him. There was recognition in his face, shock, but no trace of fear, only curiosity. Erro stared back, forcing air through his nose and grinding his teeth.

They had crossed paths before. The first time Erro had ever found Brock, only a few months after his parents' deaths, the raider had been in the marketplace in Glenn, scoping out the livestock and wealth of the town no doubt. He'd rushed him blindly with nothing but a large stone, screaming a small boy's battle cry, his face slick with angry tears. He'd split the raider's forehead with the rock, but a rough backhand had sent him sprawling, mouth bloodied.

Brock had cursed and stamped and picked him up by the collar, and for a wild moment, Erro had been sure he would strangle him, but then his eyes found the spectators, drawn in by a young boy's sudden rage. Brock had set him down and given him an excruciating kick in the tailbone that made him curl up on the ground in agony.

"Get out of here, kid," he'd said, spitting on the back of Erro's head. Then he'd looked to the crowd and said, "The boy's lost his mind. You ought to have him locked up. Which one of you fools does he belong to?"

But no one had claimed him.

Lying there in the dirt he had realized he would never get his vengeance unless he made himself strong and quick—a man. So he'd bided his time in the forest. Aquila had appeared to him only a few days later, a golden, terrifying angel that had walked through the trees and bowed his head to a half-starved, bedraggled boy with hate and despair in his heart. With Aquila at his side, Erro learned from travelers, hunters, and trappers. He found his way to Everly, where Fiona and Jeremiah had taken him in. But he could never stay long. Word would come that raiders were back in the forest. Erro would track Brock down, but each time he was surrounded by more and more men.

Then, a year ago, he'd finally gotten his chance. He was strong and quick. He had a griffin on his side. Brock had fewer men surrounding his tent than usual. Erro and Aquila had snuck through the dark and cut their way through his defenses, but the cries of his men had rousted him from his tent before Erro got close, and the sight of Aquila had put fire to Brock's heels. He was gone into the night, the only one to survive. Aquila had been injured, unable to pursue him.

Not this time. Erro's boots dug into the earth as he sprinted, dodging a werewolf that snapped at his arm and jumping over a goblin that swiped at his shins. Dark shapes moved around him. He was behind Tryannus' main line of defense, but some of them were realizing that an enemy had somehow flanked them and was headed straight for their kings. Erro sliced at the groping hand of a troll, and Aquila's wings brushed his face as the griffin flew in front of a leaping werewolf, tossing it aside with a nasty gash in its neck. Erro never stopped moving. He sensed the presence of Tyrannus nestled behind his line of kings—a dark shape, a bone-white crown—but he kept his focus on Brock. The raider now held a nervous frown on his face, but that shifted to terror when Aquila zipped over Erro's head and dove straight for him. Aquila snatched Brock into the air with his beak before the troll king had time to turn his head to the right and ponder lifting his club. Brock screamed in pain and fear as Aquila's beak dug into his shoulder. Erro shifted course, following Aquila away from Tyrannus' inner circle, away from the din of the battle behind him, and into open field. Aquila tossed Brock into the grass, where he floundered, clutching at his arm. Erro spared the line of kings one look, just long enough to realize Tyrannus apparently cared little for the raider as no one was coming for him, before closing in, a grin on his face. His heart beat erratically. His lungs burned from exertion. A wild giddiness plastered the smile on his face, a rush of adrenaline and nerves and elation. In truth, he felt slightly sick. His hands shook on his dagger hilts. His father's daggers, preserved for this moment. But it was his mother's face that swam before his eyes as he closed the distance, her voice in his head as Brock got to his feet and drew a short sword. *Don't move. Don't make a sound until they go away. Promise me, Erro. Promise your mother.*

And then the screaming. As the years passed, it had grown harder and harder to remember her singing, but the screams, the screams had stayed. His hands shook harder, and he ground his teeth and clenched his hands around the hilts until his jaw and fingers hurt. But then Katrina's face came unbidden. Her voice was at his ear.

I'll be the princess and you'll be the knight. Okay, Erro? Okay?

But her knight had not been there when she'd needed him most. He had been as useless to her as he'd been to his mother, cowering in the cellar while she screamed.

Erro scraped at the stray tears with his knuckles. Brock saw, and he laughed.

"Still a sniveling boy, I see," he said, pointing the tip of his blade at Erro's chest.

Erro stopped just out of reach and held his daggers ready, elbows tucked into his sides, and circled slowly. Brock followed. Each looked for an opening. Aquila landed next to them and tucked his wings, watching, still as stone. Erro didn't need to look at him to know he would not interfere unless necessary.

"Just who are you?" said Brock.

"You won't know my name, so why should I give it?"

"I don't care about your name, boy. Why do you pursue me?"

"There was a house, in the farmland between the Northern

Wood and the palace. A clay-brick house with a thatched roof, on a hillside, and a barn painted as red as a woodpecker's head."

"I see lots of barns, boy." He grinned to reveal rotted, yellow teeth. "Burn lots of them, too."

"There was a man with hair and nose like mine. You slew him on his doorstep when he tried to defend his home. One against a dozen."

"Ah, so this is about revenge—"

"There was a woman," Erro shouted over him, blood high in his face, fighting to control the tremble in his hands and voice, "hiding in the cellar. Hair like the chestnut coat of a mare and eyes like the sea. You dragged her out by her hair and slaughtered her, too. Just because you wanted to."

"Oh, yes, I believe I do remember her," said Brock, his grin turning more malicious. "About eight years ago, wasn't it? Around the time we first met. She was a pretty thing for a common farmer's wife. As I recall, I didn't … how did you put it … slaughter her right away."

Erro launched himself at Brock, forgetting that his blades were best as long-range weapons, that they were a third the size of Brock's short sword. The fury of his attack was what saved him. Brock had little time to react. His sword went up in a guard rather than lashing out for a strike. Erro's right blade, meant to slash open Brock's cheek, scraped along Brock's sword, sparking as it went. Brock's fist collided with Erro's face and sent him into the dirt. Horrible sharp pain. He couldn't see. A wave of black ink was washing across his eyes. Aquila screeched, and Brock cried out. When Erro shook his head and cleared his vision, Brock was sprawled in the grass, clambering to his feet, and Aquila was once again still as a statue, watching.

Brock laughed as Erro examined his immediately swollen jaw gingerly with his fingertips. Two of his teeth had come loose, and he spat them onto the grass. It was no ordinary punch. He couldn't understand it. Brock had never been a particularly strong man.

"Without your pet you would already be dead, boy," he said, but despite the mockery in his voice, he eyed Aquila with fear. "I am no mere man any longer. My master has made me strong. Soon, I shall be immortal."

"Soon, eh?" said Erro, rising to his feet. "But not yet."

The dagger left his fingertips as Brock charged him. The movement was so fast, so fluid, so natural, that Brock didn't see it in time to block with his sword. Instead, he tried to duck the blade, but it struck him high in the shoulder. The force slung his left arm backward, spinning him off balance.

"Erro!"

Everything in him demanded he look back at the sound of Andromeda's voice, but Brock was still coming, sword raised. Erro held his ground until the last possible moment, and then sidestepped around the charging man, slicing his side below the armpit with his remaining dagger as he did so. Now he was behind Brock, and he gave him a hard kick in the buttocks that knocked him flat on the ground, driving the embedded blade all the way through Brock's shoulder. It was only then that Erro looked.

Andromeda was wedged between Atalanta and Andrew atop a white elf horse. She was trying to dismount while the horse was still moving, her eyes locked on him. But just as she got her leg over, nearly kicking Andrew in the face, a massive brown werewolf, the alpha, collided with the horse, claws and teeth first. The horse brayed in terror and toppled under the weight, its riders with it. Erro took a single, purposeful step forward without thinking, but then his eyes found Brock, moaning as he tried to lift himself from the ground with only one arm.

When he looked back up, the alpha, Nathaniel, had Atalanta's hair in his jaws, dragging her away from the horse toward Tyrannus' inner circle. The minotaur king, armed with a double-sided axe, and the ogre king, armed with a spiked club, advanced on the chaos. Andrew's leg was pinned beneath the flailing, dying horse. Andromeda, blood trickling from a busted lip and forehead, rushed to her twin and began to tug him out, her arms under his armpits. Jaculo swooped down and mangled the alpha's ear with his beak. As he swerved and dove again, the alpha released Atalanta's hair, pinned her to the ground with a paw, and snatched Jaculo's front paw in his jaws, tossing the griffin and Michael to the ground.

Erro's eyes returned to Brock just in time to duck his swinging blade.

"Aquila! Help them!"

The griffin clicked his beak in protest as Erro and Brock began to dance around each other in a circle once more.

"Go, Aquila! Their fight is more important than mine. You know it is! Go!"

Aquila's call was sorrowful as he took to the sky, and Erro felt his absence like a weight in his gut.

"That was just about the stupidest thing you could have done," said Brock.

Erro did not want to draw the borrowed sword at his belt. It felt clumsy in his hand, and he wanted the kiss of his father's blades to end Brock, but with only one dagger against a sword, close range, and no Aquila to help him, he had little choice. Brock attacked in a flurry of blows, and Erro was forced to sheathe his remaining dagger to hold the sword with both hands and ward off Brock's inhumanly strong slashes and thrusts. Had he been able to use both arms, Erro did not think he would have stood a chance, but the dagger was still embedded in Brock's shoulder. Erro's sword was bigger, but he was unsure how to use it. Each slash he made felt slow, his jabs wobbled in their forward thrust. This blade was much heavier and clumsier than Andromeda's thin rapier. That had felt like an extended dagger. This felt like a club. Shifting strategy, he aimed for the legs, but the move left him open, and Brock's sword caught him in the side. His elvish armor slowed the blade, but agony lanced up his body as the steel parted flesh. Brock yanked the blade out, and Erro watched his own crimson blood drip from the tip. Warm blood wet his trousers, leaking in a steady stream from the wound. He staggered, using all of his strength not to hit his knees. He managed to block another thrust of Brock's sword, but Brock brought up his foot and kicked him in the chest. Erro's ribs screamed at him, on fire. One or more was surely broken. The pain was twofold when his back slammed into the earth. The sword fell from his hand, but he reached across his body for the dagger. As he drew it out, Brock caught his arm at the wrist and twisted. He felt and heard his right forearm crack. The pain blinded him with white light. His stomach heaved, but nothing came up. All he could hear was Brock laughing. No, something else. It was her, calling his name. She was scared. Very scared. His mother? No. Andromeda.

It was only then that he realized he was screaming. Through Brock's legs, he saw her running, black braid swishing around her shoulders, rapiers drawn. She was too far. And she was alone. He tried to call to her, but it only came out in a whisper. Brock looked over his shoulder.

"She's lovely," he said with a lecherous grin as he stomped Erro's broken sword hand into the ground, setting off fresh explosions of pain that turned his stomach. "I'll be sure to comfort her when you're gone."

As Brock raised his blade with his uninjured arm, the tip pointing at Erro's heart, rage boiled from Erro's belly into his brain. He bent his knees, sending shooting pain through his ribs, and kicked Brock in the kneecap with both feet with all his might, mumbling, "For Katrina." The knee bent backward with a sickening crunch. Brock tried to keep his footing, but the broken knee crumpled, forcing him into a lopsided kneel. Erro wrenched the short sword free of Brock's loosened grip and tossed it into the grass before using his left hand to wrench his father's dagger from Brock's shoulder. "For my father," he said, his voice drowned in Brock's scream. He rammed the dagger to the hilt in Brock's chest, and this time his voice was clear as he grimaced into Brock's dying eyes. "For my mother."

Chapter 31

The Call of the Alpha

Tilly's feet dangled between Thetis' in midair. He had one arm wrapped tight around her waist. Some of Melanie's fear momentarily gave way to shock when she saw the Avalons below, battling with Tyrannus' collection of hellish kings. Only one was missing, the eldest girl, the one left behind in the city. The younger princess was running toward a boy battling with Brock ... and losing. There was an elf, too. The princess Atalanta, perhaps, the one the Avalons had gone to save? Nathaniel had her hair in his jaws, dragging her to his master, careful not to pierce her flesh with his fangs, lest she turn under the full moon. But why? Melanie did not know. At the moment, she couldn't bring herself to care.

Thetis was slowing down, but still she could not grab him. To her surprise, he did not head for the ground. Instead, he circled, and as he turned his profile toward her, she realized he was unsure, scared even. Now it was Melanie's turn to laugh.

"Your master's not going to be happy you abandoned your post for me and my daughter, is he?"

Thetis turned lazy eyes on her, quickly masking what she had thought she saw in his face.

"I haven't abandoned anything," he said with a growing smirk. "I've brought him the mutineer in his precious prophecy."

"You wouldn't," said Melanie, fighting to control the panicked timbre of her voice. She took a soft, steadying breath and did her best to adopt Thetis' own haughty, unconcerned affect. "For some reason, you're infatuated with me. You might even think you care about me. That's why you have her, isn't it?" She nodded at Tilly, dangling in his arms and looking wide-eyed at Melanie, her voice tired and spent from all her yelling. "You want me to be with you. You think turning her will force me to stay, force me not to end my own life, as you know I want to. But you're wrong."

"Am I?" said Thetis. His words were mocking and defiant, but his eyes flicked down toward Tyrannus, who still had not looked up at them; his focus was on the Avalons and the elf. It was then that Melanie realized Thetis had no real plan. Something in him truly cared for her, or at least lusted for her so strongly he mistook it for love, and it had driven him to act blindly. Grabbing Tilly had been an act of desperation to keep Melanie close, but now he was beginning to see the flaws in it, the trouble it could cause him. If she could only say the right thing now, he might abandon any thought of converting Tilly.

"Yes. You're wrong. If you turn her, I will hate you forever. I won't hesitate to kill you. I will never be yours."

"If you tried to kill me, I would kill her faster."

"Are you sure? I've nearly done it once. Next time I'll be more careful with my aim."

He began to snarl, and she quickly shifted directions. "If you let her go, I … I could perhaps learn to love you. Letting her go would be an act of kindness, of mercy. I cannot love a man who is incapable of mercy."

"I am not a man. You are not a woman. We are gods, you and I, and she could be, too."

"Your zealotry will not win you my affection! Let her go, and I will stay with you. We can turn around right now, before Tyrannus ever sees us. We can go back to the palace, and if you let her go, I will stay with you. I will rule at your side in whatever kingdom Tyrannus has promised you. I swear it."

"If I let her go, you will kill yourself and squander my gift at your earliest opportunity."

"No! No, she keeps me alive. I will live for her."

"No, pet, you will kill yourself with the misguided happy notion that she is free—though she will actually be chained by her own mortality and weakness. You will feel you have saved her. That you have nothing left to do."

Melanie was stunned into silence.

"I know you better than you think, pet. You are strong, but your strength is misplaced. If I make your daughter one of us, you will stay with me, for her. She will not die. She will not age. She will be a child forever, in need of a mother."

Melanie wet her lips, feeling her grip on him slipping away. "She won't be my daughter anymore," she cried in desperation.

Thetis' stunned expression urged her on.

"You wouldn't allow the children to be converted. You said they were too dangerous. She won't be my daughter anymore. She will be a wild, bloodthirsty, unnatural beast. I don't want her to suffer as I have suffered. I don't want her to know what it's like to take a life. She is a baby, Thetis, only four. Can you even begin to remember youth like that, with all your years behind you? I don't think you can. I don't think you can feel much of anything anymore. But I remember, and I will not allow my baby to be forced to drink life from other human beings. I won't allow something so perverse. I'll kill her first, and then you, and then myself."

She tried her best to convince herself of the truth of the words as she spoke them. Part of her knew what she said was sound, but even she heard the hesitation in her voice when she spoke of killing Tilly. Thetis' face hardened. His small, crooked smile was colder than she'd ever seen it. But before he could speak, Melanie heard something, carried to her enhanced ears over the rushing of the wind. It stood out because it held the weight of love, both to her own ears and, by the sound of it, to the speaker. It was her daughter's name, a scream that was nothing but a faint whisper when it reached Melanie, high in the sky. The eldest Avalon princess. She had fought her way across an entire battlefield for Tilly. Melanie was filled with a surge of love for Felicity Avalon, but she kept her eyes locked on Thetis so as not to betray her quickly forming plan.

"You'll do no such thing," said Thetis. "Her conversion is the only way. I see it plainly now."

Melanie braced herself. Below, Felicity called Tilly's name again. She was getting closer. Soon, Thetis would hear her, too. Still, she held back. Could she free Tilly from his grip without harming her?

"We need not trouble the king with it now, either," he said. "This is a private affair."

He was really going to do it, and he wasn't going to wait for firm ground beneath his feet.

"Wait! Thetis, please! Shouldn't you put her down first? Doesn't it require concentration?"

The terror in Melanie's voice made Tilly begin to cry and reach out her hands for comfort.

"A great amount," said Thetis, that icy smile still etched into his face as he shifted Tilly into one arm, "so you'd best not interrupt me."

His fingers brushed Tilly's hair from her neck. Melanie closed the distance in an instant and snapped every finger that had touched her daughter backward. Her fangs ripped into his face, and then her fist crushed his left cheekbone. Just as Tilly began to slip from his grasp, Melanie snatched her up, used both feet to kick Thetis backward, and dove for the ground. The smell of Tilly's blood was heavenly, but Melanie was no longer hungry. She found the princess' white horse and adjusted her course.

Below, Felicity drew her silver stake from her boot as the vampire holding Tilly flew straight for her, but what started as a sure and steady movement became a half-hearted gesture. The female vampire was holding Tilly out like an offering. She had attacked Thetis, who now streaked after her. Why? Felicity made her decision, shoving the stake back in her boot just in time to catch Tilly as the female vampire shoved her in her arms, her black wings flapping around the horse's head and making it sidestep in fright. Felicity pulled Tilly tight to her breast with one arm and steadied the horse with the other, her eyes never leaving the female vampire's wild, wide eyes—a startling blue, the mirror image of Tilly's.

"Run!" said the vampire, and then her head snapped backward, Thetis' fist wrapped in her hair.

Felicity dug her heels into her stallion and took off, but Tilly reached out, nearly toppling out of Felicity's grip.

"Momma!"

Felicity's stomach somersaulted, and she looked over her shoulder. The two vampires were locked in a vicious, animalistic battle, clawing and biting and tearing at one another in the air. But she never slowed her horse. She couldn't. She maneuvered the stallion so that it ran along the outskirts of the battle and adjusted Tilly more snuggly in her lap.

"That's ... that's your mother?" said Felicity.

Tilly wiped at her eyes and nodded her small head, and Felicity burst into tears.

* * *

Atalanta could not see Michael. She knew he had been thrown out of the sky, had heard the crash, the tumble and smack of his and Jaculo's limbs rolling across the grass, but all she could see was the grass sliding beneath her hands and knees as she was forced to crawl. Nathaniel tugged on her braid, and if she planted herself into the earth, he would surely scalp her. She had lost her sword; the small dagger at her belt was her only hope. She pulled it free, but the loss of one arm threw her off balance, and she fell face first into the ground. Nathaniel tugged mercilessly, and she felt hairs rip at her crown. She grabbed behind her head, seizing her long braid in her left hand and slicing it with the dagger in her right. As soon as the pressure was gone from her head, she sprang up like a cat and faced the werewolf.

"Hello, scruffy," she said, knees bent, short blade pointed at Nathaniel.

Nathaniel growled and sank into his own crouch, but he did not spring.

"No cage between us now. No hunger to make me weak," said Atalanta.

The bottom of her braid lay in a hunk on the grass between them. She could feel the rest of her hair coming free and swishing around her shoulders. Not ideal.

"How many hacks do you think it will take to get your head off with this thing, hmm?" she said, jabbing the dagger in his direction.

"Such violence from one so beautiful," said Tyrannus.

The voice sent an unwelcome chill through Atalanta's blood. She realized she was very alone. Nathaniel had dragged her into Tyrannus' inner sanctum. The sounds of Michael's and Andrew's swords clashing against club, horn, and bone seemed far behind her. The griffins' battle cries were miles and miles overhead. His voice, the one that snuck into her nightmares, was all around her, much too close. Nathaniel lowered his head and slunk out of his master's way like a battered hunting dog.

"Still fancy yourself a king, I see," said Atalanta, her voice breathy.

The crown of bone was held in place by his pointed, dog-like ears. He had added a ring of rabbits' fur to the collar of his purple cloak. Someone had done their best to sew and patch up the tatters on the bottom. His white shirt and trousers were freshly cleaned. Callid hovered behind him like a pup, both mouths hanging open in a dopey grin, his fat tongues lolling.

"I command an army, do I not? That is all being a king really requires."

"You and I both know that isn't true. You've sold them promises to buy their loyalty. The moment you can no longer deliver, they will cast you down from your imaginary throne."

"Imaginary? Perhaps. But not for long. My army overwhelms your city. Your allies do not come to your aid. I will sit atop Alatreon's golden throne by sunrise."

He licked his forked tongue across his jutting fangs at the thought. Atalanta made a show of looking at the sky.

"You'd best hurry then," she said.

Tyrannus grinned, an awkward movement for his strange mouth. It made him look even more deformed. He looked over his shoulder, and Atalanta noticed the hags for the first time. Two, decrepit, bent, and wrinkled, the other two slightly more youthful, but weathered. Each wore hoods of black and carried staffs carved of hemlock.

"You heard the princess. When will my potion be ready?" he asked, a note of danger slinking through his dulcet tones.

"It is ready now," croaked the fat, squat one.

"And you did not tell me?" said Tyrannus, the anger creeping to the forefront, making him sound petulant.

"You did not ask," said the tallest of the four, whose nose jutted far outside of the protection of her dark hood.

With a snarl from the back of his throat, he loomed over Atalanta again. "No matter. The time has come. Once I have your father, nothing shall stand in my way."

Atalanta laughed. "My father? None of your troops have touched him. He is better protected than even you."

"Oh, I wouldn't send pawns for such an important task. I've learned my lesson well. I'm going to fetch him myself."

The purple cloak rustled and then was thrust back as if by a tempestuous wind as enormous, black wings unfurled from his back. Claws of bone long enough to impale a man grew from the upper wing joints nearest his shoulders, and two more dragged along the ground at the bottommost tips. Atalanta took two steps back and cursed herself for her fear.

"But first ..." Tyrannus turned to the hags. "Will the potion only work once?"

"Now that it's finished, it will boil until we put out the flames ourselves," said the tallest hag.

"Toss in as many little elflings as you want," said one of the younger hags with a girlish giggle. "All their magic will be yours."

"Your father will be no easy foe," said Tyrannus. "Perhaps it would be best to take what you would not give me before. Even if you are truly as hopeless at magic as you claimed, even a small drop can be turned against him. He won't be expecting it."

Atalanta eyed the bubbling red potion as she took another shaking step back and clenched her dagger hilt until her knuckles shone bone white.

"Bind her," said Tyrannus, and the second of the younger hags pointed her staff at Atalanta.

There was a bang and a flash of green light. Atalanta threw up her arms to protect her face, and a wall of thorns sprang up from the earth to shield her instead. But the thorns exploded in every direction when the green light struck them.

Tyrannus' grin was broader now. "Excellent," he murmured, and licked the drool from his jowls.

* * *

Andromeda fell to her knees in the grass and rolled Brock's body off of Erro. Her trembling hands hovered over Erro, unsure where to alight. His eyes struggled to focus on her face.

"Andromeda?" he muttered, searching the sky.

"We have to get you to the elves," she said, examining the wound in his side as best she could through his mail. "They can fix you."

Her face was wiped blank by fear as she pulled her hand back, the ivory of her skin obscured by crimson.

"I can't get up," said Erro.

"Yes, you can," she said. "I'll throw you on Aquila's back myself if I have to."

"Aquila," he said, eyelids fluttering. "Where's Aquila?"

Andromeda searched. Andrew and Michael battled the dark kings. Jaculo, forepaws bleeding and one wing crumpled, and Nathaniel circled each other. Aquila was grappling with a werewolf that had broken free from the main battle lines. Andromeda scanned the field. While most of Tyrannus' army surged ever forward, heading toward Alatreon's walls, the noises of battle were beginning to draw unwanted attention. Even as Andromeda watched, a small pack of werewolves perked their ears and ran toward their alpha and their king. They rushed past an ogre, who turned his great, bald head to find his own king in distress, bleeding from a slice of Andrew's blade.

"This was so foolish," Andromeda whispered, mouth agape in wonderment at the absurdity of it all. "We're all going to die."

A frosty numbness closed a fist around her heart and the tears that had threatened to spill from her eyes began to dry. The feathery touch of Erro's fingertips on her face startled her.

"Run," he commanded, his voice stronger. "Get on Aquila's back and fly far from here."

Storm clouds brewed in her smoky eyes. "And leave you and my siblings here to be ripped apart? Just who do you think I am?"

"Fight or fly," he said, "but don't just give up."

She looked him over, his shattered arm lying useless and horribly misshapen in the grass at his side. Blood soaked the grass underneath him. She cursed herself for wasting time.

"Come on, get up," she said, and a small smile broke his lips.

She put one arm under his good arm and the other at his back and shoved him to his feet. His scream brought the tears back to her eyes, but she forced him to stand upright.

"Aquila!" The scream tore at her throat, but one of Aquila's amber eyes found her instantly. He disentangled himself from the werewolf and rose into the sky, but the wolf's teeth clamped around his tail.

A growl at her back chilled Andromeda's blood. Erro reacted first, pushing her away from him with the last of his strength. The werewolf's furry side brushed her face as it embraced Erro in its paws and buried its fangs in his shoulder. Andromeda's cry caught in her throat, but she managed to draw a rapier.

The werewolf leapt off Erro's back and turned on her, nearly catching her left arm in its jaws. She thrust her sword at its chest, but it leapt back. Erro began to scream as if he were on fire, and the sound filled Andromeda's head, disorienting her. She barely managed to lift her sword in time when the werewolf pounced. The air rushed from her lungs when her back hit the ground, and spots danced in her eyes when her head followed suit. The werewolf's weight crushed her, and its blood wet her hands, chest, and neck. Only when it began to shrink and become a woman once more was she able to get herself free. She struggled to her hands and knees, ragged breaths shaking her chest.

The blare of a war horn snapped her head toward the east. The thunder of hoof beats rumbled through the night.

"Father," she breathed, hope giving her voice the intonation of a child.

The army crested the horizon—a black mass of galloping legs, tossed manes, and helmeted heads. The centaurs had renewed the ancient alliance.

"Father!" She leapt to her feet, waving like she had as a young girl when her father had returned from a journey, waving like he could see her. A wild giggle escaped her when she realized what she was doing.

"Err—"

The hope faded along with her voice. He wasn't screaming anymore. He was breathing. Strong, sure breaths. She turned her head ever so slowly. A shaggy red wolf flexed its shoulders, as if testing its muscles, its muzzle pointed at the ground. The tail swished experimentally.

A sob slipped through Andromeda's lips—a helpless sound. The werewolf's ears flicked backward and a guttural growl bubbled in its chest. The growl never ceased as it turned to face her. Its lips drew back from moon-white fangs.

"Erro?" Andromeda took a shaking step back, tears pouring freely down her cheeks now.

She could feel its blind rage. She could sense no trace of the boy she loved. It licked its gums and snapped at her. Fingers trembling on the hilt of her rapier, Andromeda lifted the bloodied blade to guard herself.

"Erro, please. It's me."

The wolf sank low on its front legs, shimmying its shoulders like a barn cat lining up a mouse. Andromeda's tears blinded her, and she swiped at her eyes with her wrist guard.

"Don't ... don't make me do it. Please. I can't."

The wolf flexed its haunches, and then Aquila was shielding her, golden wings spread wide, body upright, all four paws swiping the air in a threat. Andromeda heard his eagle cry from a distance as his voice boomed in her head, *REMEMBER YOURSELF, BOY!*

Erro cowered, whining softly, eyes averted, head bowed under the griffin's sharp gaze. The rage in his head lessened, and fear momentarily replaced it, but Andromeda could sense little else from him. Still, she stepped around Aquila's wing and sheathed her rapier.

"Erro?"

Erro raised his shaggy head and met her eyes. Aquila's paws found the ground. Andromeda extended a hand to the wolf. He sniffed it, whining. He licked her hand and then closed the distance to do the same to her face. Andromeda put a hand to her mouth and stifled a sob.

"You're going to be okay," she whispered. "I swear it."

"Atalanta!" Michael's cry carried across the battlefield.

The monstrous fear in her elder brother's voice made Andromeda's feet itch to run to him, but she only looked his way. At their backs, the whole battlefield was shifting. Tyrannus' army, which only moments ago had been driving the elves against their own walls in a relentless assault, was now in chaos, rushing to meet Marcus Avalon's new horde without being crushed betwixt them and the elves at the walls. The elves had found new heart at the blare of Marcus' war horn, and they sent up shouts of their own. But at the back of the field, a small battle still raged, untouched, and in this one, the Avalons did not have the upper hand.

Strange lights flashed green, red, and blue in the night. Michael and Andrew battled the troll and minotaur kings, the goblin and ogre dead in the grass around them. Jaculo bled on the ground, his wings flapping weakly as Nathaniel moved in for the kill. Aquila cried out and flew to his fellow, but even as she began to run after him, Andromeda knew it was too late. Cold despair and dread closed like a fist in her chest when the great black griffin cried his last, and from behind Nathaniel's bent head, Andromeda caught her first real glimpse of the hybrid king. His wings bore spikes as big as swords, and a laugh widened his misshapen mouth as he watched Atalanta struggle against bonds that had formed from thin air, conjured by one of four hags cackling around a cauldron. In the sky, two vampires grappled like feral tomcats. Just as she vaguely began to wonder why they had turned on each other, a furry body brushed her arm. Erro ran twice as fast as Andromeda's legs could ever hope to take her.

Aquila circled Nathaniel's head, waiting for an opening, but Erro never stopped moving. He crashed into the alpha with audible force, tearing into the scruff of his neck. Nathaniel was enormous, standing at least two heads taller than Erro, and he shook the smaller wolf from his back easily. His claws raked Erro's muzzle, and his teeth buried in his upper leg. Then

Nathaniel stood up like a man on his back legs and howled, black eyes on Erro. Erro cringed at the sound, whining and writhing in the grass. The alpha howled again, and Erro got to all fours and began to extend one leg in a bow, but at Aquila's screech, Erro drew the foot back. Nathaniel cocked his head and went down on all fours so that he was snarling in Erro's face, their noses centimeters apart. He snarled and yipped, and Erro turned his head in shame. Andromeda froze a few feet from the two wolves. A small voice yelled at her to help her brothers, but she could not look away.

Aquila called again, and Andromeda heard him in her head. *Fight, Erro. Fight! All alphas can be challenged. I will help, but you must make the first move.*

Erro faced Nathaniel, who cocked his head once more, but neither wolf made a move.

Little one. Andromeda started when she realized Aquila was speaking to her. *Tell him. I do not know if he hears me. He is still a man somewhere inside; he will hear you.*

Andromeda wasted no time.

"Fight, Erro! Fight him!" The red werewolf's ears flicked back at her. "You have to become the new alpha. Challenge him! He must accept."

Erro bared his fangs, the hackles raising on his back like spikes, and growled in Nathaniel's face. Nathaniel leered back, and in an instant snapped for Erro's neck, but Erro caught his opponent's muzzle in his jaws.

Andromeda, Aquila's voice permeated her skull. *Save the elf princess, or all will be for naught!*

* * *

Felicity gasped when she heard her father's war horn, and Tilly whined uneasily. Felicity hugged her tighter.

"Things are going to get better now, Tilly. My father is here to help us."

Tilly only sniffled.

Heavy panting made Felicity point her sword at the ground rushing under her stallion's feet, but she drew it up quickly.

"Hello, Zezil."

The vexar shrank as she greeted him, and she slowed her pace enough to allow him to jump up and climb her leg. He stopped briefly to lick Tilly's hair and then clambered up Felicity's armor to wrap around her neck like a stole. Felicity checked that her horse was holding its course to a small grove of trees untouched by the battle and then stole her first glance back. The human and centaur army spilled over the gentle slope of the land and spread like an ocean wave. More than she had expected. Surely now the battle was won. But bright lights pulled her eyes to the plight of her siblings and their friends. While all other heads turned to the east, the shapes at the back of the field faced only each other. Above it all, she could still see the battling forms of Tilly's mother and her opponent. She set her sights on the grove with new determination. She could not bring Tilly back to the palace, but she could not stay hidden with her in the grove either. When she reigned in her horse, Zezil slithered off of her. She pulled Tilly off as she dismounted and held her on her hip. She kissed the little girl's forehead and then got to her knees in the thick of the calm, cool grove.

"Tilly, you have to stay here with Zezil, all right?"

"No!" Tilly latched herself onto Felicity's arm.

"No one will come to hurt you here, I promise. But you must stay in these trees."

"Don't go, Felicity! Don't go! I'm scared." Tears shimmered in Tilly's eyes, and Felicity bit her lip.

"I know, but you don't need to be scared anymore, Tilly. You have Zezil to protect you. Remember how he protected you in the palace? He won't let anything touch you."

Felicity scratched behind the vexar's ears, and he rolled over for a belly rub. Tilly looked uncertain.

"I don't want to leave, but my brothers and sister need help. So do Atalanta and Erro. What kind of princess would I be if I didn't help them?"

"Are they fighting the bad king?"

"Yes."

"Bad kings always lose."

Felicity smiled. "Yes, but only if all the heroes fight together. Do you see why I must go?"

Tilly nodded morosely. "But you'll come back, right? You promise?"

"Of course I'll come back, just like I did in the palace, except this time when I come back, it'll all be over."

"Okay," said Tilly, plopping into the grass with a soft huff, belling out her dress around herself.

Felicity gave her another peck on the forehead. "I love you, Tilly."

Tilly's rosy lips lifted in a sweet smile. "I love you, too, Felicity."

Felicity jumped back on her horse and pointed at the vexar, who had looked up at her with expectant black eyes. "Stay, Zezil."

Zezil made a circle in the grass and fallen leaves and then rested his head on his front paws next to Tilly.

"Felicity?"

"Hmm?"

"Will my momma come back, too?"

Felicity froze, her horse's head already turned toward the battlefield.

"I hope so, Tilly."

* * *

Andrew jumped out of the way of the minotaur's horns, but its muscled arm caught him in the torso, and he was thrown back on his butt. When he tried to get up, it slammed its fist into his chest, forcing the air from his lungs and sending him sprawling. Then he was in the air. His surprised cry was weak from lack of oxygen. He looked up to find, not a vampire, but Vendita. She circled and set him back down just long enough to allow him to jump on her back. The minotaur bellowed in frustration, but Andrew suddenly bubbled with mirth. He laughed with relief when he sheathed his great sword and got his bow in his hands once again. He reached behind his head and groped for his arrows to find he had only three left. It was enough. Vendita lined up the shots, dipping her wing out of his way. The first arrow sunk between the minotaur's horns. As Andrew strung the next, Michael parried the troll king's club, embedding his sword in the thick wood, but when he tried to pull it out, it wouldn't come. Vendita dipped lower, and Andrew shouted, "Michael, duck!"

Michael rolled out of the way, leaving his sword behind, and the arrow toppled the troll king. Michael rushed in and wrenched his sword free. He saluted Andrew without looking at him and ran for Atalanta, who was being reeled in by the hags, her whole body wrapped in black cord. Andrew pulled his final arrow from the quiver and took aim for the hybrid king, who was fixing his orange eyes on Michael. Andrew sucked in a breath, steadied his aim, and on the exhale let the arrow fly. Blood that was nearly black gushed from Tyrannus' neck, and Andrew whooped in triumph, hardly able to believe it.

But his jubilation came too soon. Tyrannus ripped the arrow free, peeled back his grey, hairless muzzle to reveal a wolf's maw with vampire canines, and roared like a lion, orange eyes ablaze. He sprang into the air with incredible speed. Vendita positioned herself upright so that her body shielded Andrew and tried to backpedal, but a spike on Tyrannus' wing embedded in her side, and his long, yellow nails slashed her head. She flapped as she fell to earth, slowing herself, and Andrew held onto her neck to keep from sliding off her. She turned her body so that she took the brunt of the fall, and Andrew heard her wing snap beneath her. He rolled from her back and reached for his sword, eyes wide and searching for Tyrannus in the sky, but he had not pursued them. Andrew crawled to Vendita and cradled her head. She cooed when he stroked her beak. She managed to roll herself upright, but she did not attempt to stand. Blood seeped from the wound in her pelt.

"Thank you," said Andrew. The words sounded lame, so he kissed her feathered head instead.

Behind him, Michael brought his sword down on the cord binding Atalanta, severing the hags' connection. Atalanta wriggled lose enough to use her dagger on her bindings. Andromeda raced up behind them but was pushed backward by the force of Tryannus' wing beats, her hair flying back as if caught in a high storm wind. Tryannus tossed Michael aside, splitting his ear with his claws and ripping through the elvish leather on his arm and back. Tyrannus hoisted Atalanta into the air and shook her like a ragdoll. Already, the wound from Andrew's arrow had closed, leaving only a drying waterfall of blood down his neck and onto his cloak.

"You have fought your last, princess," he said, spittle flying from his jowls. "No more running. I will have your magic."

Andromeda looked for a place to strike while Michael rolled in the grass, trying to catch his breath, but Tyrannus' wing shielded his body. There was no way to go but through it, so she hacked a hole in the sinuous skin and rushed through it, batting it aside like curtains. Tyrannus' foot met her chest and knocked her on her back. Atalanta squirmed in his grip, but he had her arms pinned to her sides. The lower spike of his wing hovered over Andromeda's head. She rolled, and the spike pierced the ground. He slammed it down again and again, giving her no time to right herself. She rolled once, twice. The third time, she found one of her swords in the grass and sliced the spike from its hollow bone nest.

"Into the pot, beasty," said one of the hags. "Drain her magic and be done with these pests."

"Into the pot," echoed the one that might have been her twin.

Above, Melanie spun her body in a backflip, her foot catching Thetis under the chin. He tugged his jaw to pop his neck back into alignment and slashed at her face. She bit at his neck, but he caught her head in his palm and slammed her face into his kneecap. Melanie hardly noticed the pain anymore, nor the hot tingling as her body healed itself. Fury still drove her, but she could feel exhaustion creeping up on her. She had to end it now, but how?

She skirted his next attack, thinking. Tyrannus yelled something, and she looked down. He had the elf princess. He was going to dump her in the hag's potion.

Here was her second chance to fulfill the prophecy. The potion; the potion was his last plan to steal the throne. She dove.

Andrew jumped over Andromeda and swung, but something solid plowed into his legs, whipping and popping his neck.

"Eugh!" he cried when the two faces, connected at the base of their necks to a hunched, heavily muscled body, leered over him.

He drove his fist into Callid's right eye and kicked him backward as he howled, hands over his face.

Andrew dislodged both heads from the odd cyclops' body in one swipe.

Michael found his feet and ran to Atalanta's aid, but two vampires crashed at his feet, blocking his way as they ripped at each other like cats. The female beat the male off with a flurry of slashes to his head and chest.

"Michael!" Atalanta screamed, her green eyes wide as she kicked and thrashed in Tyrannus' arms.

Michael ran around the battling vampires just as Tyrannus held Atalanta over the bathtub-sized cauldron.

Two furry bodies slammed into Tyrannus from the side, and Atalanta was sent flying.

"Erro!" Andromeda cried.

"What?" said Michael.

"The red wolf is Erro."

Michael swore but peeled his eyes away from the wolves to go to Atalanta.

The two wolves trampled Tyrannus underfoot as they grappled. Erro was on top, half riding on Nathaniel's back as he tore at him with his teeth. With a roar, Tyrannus yanked his wing free of their dancing paws and dug his claw-like nails into Erro's back. Erro whined and retreated, but Aquila swooped in and slashed Tyrannus' face with his paw and tore into the top of his head with his beak.

Nathaniel pounced, but Erro leapt out of the way, and whipped his head around to catch Nathaniel's throat in his jaws. Nathaniel's whine was high and fearful as Erro clamped down with all his strength and the blood began to flow freely. Nathaniel struggled, but his breathing was harried, his tongue lolling from the side of his mouth, and he could not pull free. This time his yelp sounded like supplication. Erro tossed Nathaniel to the ground with a shake of his head and stood over the defeated alpha, jaws dripping blood as he snarled. The fight was over. Nathaniel no longer wielded the power of the alpha. Nathaniel bowed his head under Erro's gaze, whining, and Andromeda moved in to finish the job, silver-coated swords ready to take off his head.

Aquila savaged Tyrannus' left wing and used it to hoist the hybrid king into the air.

As Tyrannus' feet left the ground, Melanie dove for the cauldron, hands outstretched to tip it over, but Thetis caught her ankle and yanked her body into his, where he held her in a vice-like hug. He squeezed, and her ribs began to crack.

"You have denied me for the last time," he hissed in her ear. "I gave you the gift of eternal life, but I can take it away."

"You gave me nothing but death! Now I shall give it back to you."

Melanie jumped, taking Thetis with her, and slammed onto her back, crushing him beneath her. She broke free of his grip and rolled herself so that she straddled his torso and took his head in her hands like a lover, and for a moment, Thetis' eyes softened. His mouth popped into a surprised 'o' when she dug her nails under his jaw and heaved with all of her strength. The head did not pop free cleanly, but still it came. The head bared its fangs like the severed head of a snake, but there was no real life in the eyes. Still, the body flailed, grabbing for her.

Her mouth curled in disgust, and she tossed the head into the cauldron while the hags stared in curiosity. The bubbling red liquid swallowed it and began to froth. Thetis' body went still and then crumbled to ash.

Only a few feet off the ground, Aquila bled from a fresh gash in his haunches, and Tyrannus' wing was beginning to knit back together. But Erro leapt up and grabbed Tyrannus' leg, yanking him down, where Andromeda ran him through with both of her swords at once, pinning him to the soil. He roared in agony, but his feet, so much like the back paws of a wolf, caught her under the breastbone as she extracted her stake from her boot. Erro leapt for Tyrannus' throat, but Tyrannus' clawed hands beat a rhythm on his face and neck, and he fell aside, whimpering and bleeding. Then Tyrannus' chest began to give off a faint, red glow, as if he had a heart of fire. Tyrannus licked his lips and chuckled as he yanked the swords from his gut. His muscles felt hard as steel. He inclined his head to the hags.

"Thank you, ladies."

But they did not acknowledge him.

Typhoid eyed Melanie with dread. "The last of the signs."

"At your service," said Melanie.

The other three Black Sisters, though, turned their staffs on Michael and Atalanta as they ran for the cauldron.

"Ignis displodere!" said Atalanta.

The fire underneath the cauldron whooshed to life and exploded in a ring, catching all four hags ablaze. They screamed only for a moment before dousing the flames with a swirl of their black cloaks.

Anemia thrust her staff in Michael's direction, and a flash of light hit him like a shockwave. His sword flew from his hand, and a large, stinging cut appeared on his wrist. Another slash sliced through the top layer of his armor, but could not pierce flesh. Malaria swirled her staff above her head and then pointed it at Atalanta. The elf screamed as oozing sores sprang up on the exposed skin of her neck, hands, and face. Malaria giggled. Michael bent to pick up his sword, and another blow like a corded whip sliced at his back and sent warm blood trickling down from his hair. Typhoid's spell hoisted Michael upside down into the air. Typhoid twirled her finger, and Michael began to spin out of control. He could hear her cackling as the world became a swirling blur.

Atalanta flung her dagger at Malaria's head. The blade sank deep, and the painful sores vanished as the hag hit the ground. Porphyria threw a blade of her own, and the sacrificial dagger caught Atalanta in the shoulder, staggering her, pain like a firebrand.

Melanie sprang at Typhoid. The squat witch saw her too late and had only time to screech before Melanie picked her up and threw her head first into the side of the cauldron, breaking the hag's neck and making potion slosh over the cauldron's edge.

Melanie ignored the burns and finished the job, upending the whole thing so that the bubbling potion spilled over the grass, blackening it. Melanie hovered over it, careful not to touch it. The potion sizzled and sparked before evaporating into steam or sinking into the soil. She smiled to herself.

Michael, freed from the spell, rolled out of the fall, but fell sideways when he tried to stand upright. He shook his head, trying to shake off the dizziness.

Anemia wailed for her fallen sisters, and Porphyria's cloak billowed around her like a living thing in her rage. She turned her staff on Atalanta, but the elf was quicker.

"Terra vorare!"

Porphyria shrieked in terror as the ground opened beneath her. She fell into the chasm, groping in vain at the sides, which only opened wider. The earth closed up again with a suctioning sound like the slurping of soup.

Melanie tore into Anemia with her fangs and silenced the wails of the last of the Black Sisters. Her sour blood made Melanie's tongue tingle.

"Who are you?"

Melanie found Michael staring at her.

"Your humble servant," she said, taking a step back from him. The smell of his blood was suddenly powerful. She felt drained.

Michael took a step toward her, and she hissed, making him reach for his stake, tucked into his belt.

"Michael! Don't hurt her!" Felicity leapt off her horse and jumped in front of Michael, arms wide.

"Where did you—?"

"She's Tilly's mother."

Michael's breath left him, and he couldn't say a word. He only gaped.

"Please, don't come any closer," said Melanie, backing up until her legs hit the overturned cauldron. "I can't control it."

Felicity began to extend a hand, and then pulled it back,

fingers closing in a fist.

"There are so many things I want say ..." said Felicity.

"Is she safe?" said Melanie.

"Yes."

"Thank you."

Andromeda's cry of "Andrew!" forced Felicity's and Melanie's eyes apart.

Andrew flew backward, launched by a blow from Tryannus' hand, and his ankle crumpled beneath him, making him grit his teeth against the pain. Andromeda lunged for Tyrannus, swiping both her rapiers together in an X, hoping to catch his body between them, but Tyrannus leapt back on all fours. He fought like a beast, back legs crouched, wolf paws dug into the earth, hands in the grass so that he moved on all fours, his black wings poised above him, the spikes ready to sink into anyone who got too close. He lunged for Andromeda, muzzle wide, but Erro leapt in the way. Tyrannus savaged his shoulder with his teeth, and Erro howled. Aquila dove and grabbed Tyrannus' neck in his beak, yanking him off so that Erro could slink away. But a wing spike jabbed for Aquila's side, and the griffin, already bleeding from his last bout with Tyrannus, was forced to retreat.

Melanie took to the sky, circling with Aquila. Atalanta and Michael raced into the fray, and Michael stopped only to help Andrew to his feet. Andromeda sheathed one of her swords and drew her stake from her boot. The silver chinked as the mechanism freed the point from the cylinder. Tyrannus moved back and snarled when he saw it, his orange eyes betraying the slightest flicker of fear.

"Wooden stakes and silver blades don't kill you, do they?" said Andromeda. "But put them together ... What do you think, Your Majesty?" She dipped in a theatrical curtsy as the title dripped off her mocking tongue.

"It's rather useless if you're unable to drive it home, mortal," said Tyrannus. "Try to pierce my heart, I beg you. I'll taste your flesh first."

Michael, Andrew, and Felicity drew their stakes, too, and gathered at Andromeda's sides. Tyrannus' eyes flicked from tip to tip, and he gnashed his teeth.

The Avalons attacked together, but Tyrannus fought like a savage, cornered animal. He moved in a flurry of claws, teeth, and spikes, faster than any human. Faster than even a vampire. Andrew and Andromeda moved in a unit, attacking from the left, but Tyrannus spun on his hands, knocking their legs from under them with his feet. His spikes slammed in a rain of blows that had them rolling and scrambling out of the way. Atalanta sent thorns up from the ground to seize his wing and stop the onslaught, and Andromeda found her footing and rushed to Erro. Something was wrong.

Blood still ran from the punctures and gashes Tyrannus' teeth had made in Erro's hide. He panted on his side, unable to stand. The wounds weren't healing. Andromeda looked at the moon, still bright and perfect in the graying sky.

"I don't understand," she said, her hands hovering over the wounds.

Erro whined when she touched him to part the fur and examine the wounds.

Behind her Felicity and Michael attacked from the right, but before they could get close enough for the short stakes to do any damage, Tyrannus tore himself free of the thorns with his claws and teeth and jumped over them, using his wings to propel himself behind them. The two Avalons spun to meet him, but a wing joint pierced Michael's side in the spot in his armor weakened by the hags. His grunt of pain as the spike dislodged itself sent fear pounding through Felicity's heart. Tyrannus lunged for her, mouth wide, but Melanie dove from the sky and took Felicity's place. Tyrannus' teeth sank into her neck, and his wing spikes pierced her from both sides. She sucked in a surprised breath—a soft, almost delicate sound that only Felicity heard.

"Traitor," Tyrannus snarled in her ear.

"Mutineer," Melanie whispered back. "I have completed the prophecy. You cannot win."

With a cry of rage, his spike pierced her heart, and he let her fall to the ground while Felicity screamed, high and long. Melanie rolled over in the grass, feeling at her wounds with curiosity. There was no tingling sensation. No healing. She put her hand to her eyes to examine the dark blood that spilled from her chest.

Atalanta blasted Tyrannus off his feet with a ball of light and energy, and Felicity rushed in to kneel at Melanie's side.

"Take care of Tilly," said Melanie.

"I swear," said Felicity through a sob.

Melanie's final breath escaped through a small, soft smile.

Andromeda ran her hands through Erro's fur, despair overtaking her once more. She looked over her shoulder. Felicity sobbed as she held the hand of Tilly's mother to her face. Andrew, Atalanta, and Michael circled Tyrannus, but Michael had been forced to abandon his sword because the wound in his side made it impossible to lift, and Andrew limped on a broken ankle, and Atalanta wielded nothing but a dagger and spells that could not kill the hellish beast that snapped and clawed at them.

Erro tried once more to get to his feet, and this time he managed it, though he wobbled on his paws. Suddenly, Andromeda saw the way.

"Erro, you're the alpha now! You can command them. You can turn them against him."

His eyes, the same rich brown, studied her for a moment, and then he threw back his head in a howl that battered her eardrums. He howled again, and a third time. The werewolves began to howl back.

"It's working!" said Andromeda.

All throughout the battlefield, werewolves changed their courses, leaving their allies to the mercy of the two armies, heeding the call of their alpha. The closest of the pack were there in an instant, half a dozen strong from the start, with more trailing after them. Erro howled again, and his pack raced past him, yipping and howling and snapping playfully at one another, happy to be free of the battle. Atalanta and the Avalons were pushed roughly aside as the pack zeroed in on their target. Tyrannus tried to leap into the sky, but the pack caught him before he ever left the ground. They grabbed pieces of him and shook their heads like pups practicing the kill. They tugged him between each other like a plaything. Those that could not get a piece whined at their siblings for a turn.

Tyrannus screamed in agony and fear, all attempts to fight back futile as more and more wolves piled on. When Tyrannus was totally blocked from view by a frenzy of fur, Erro barked—a single, strong, commanding sound. The wolves backed off in a ring. Tryannus crawled across the grass, struggling to right himself. His purple cloak was but a rabbit fur collar and a few tattered strings of fabric. His crown of bone was gone, settled into the stomachs of a few lucky wolves. His wings were ripped to shreds. His black fur and ashen skin were stained red with blood. But even as Atalanta moved toward him with slow, sure steps, Michael's stake in her fist, his wounds began to knit back together, though the process was slowed by the sheer damage.

"I told you they would turn on you," said Atalanta. "You have no truly loyal servants. Look,"—she tossed her arm back in the direction of Alatreon—"your vampires flee the city. They know all is lost. They know you are no king. They do not even come to save you, to make sure you are unharmed. They care only for themselves. You cannot deliver your promises. You are alone. You have always been alone."

Tyrannus braced his hands and knees underneath himself, preparing to pull himself up.

"Your kind forced me to be alone," he said. "You shun us because you fear us, our power."

"No one forced your hand. Your desire for power and your bloodlust brought you here at my feet. But perhaps you are right in one regard. We never sought to help your kind. We slaughtered blindly. But now we seek a cure."

"What? No! It's impossible," said Tyrannus.

"Perhaps, but there is hope. And that is all we need," said Atalanta. "We will wipe out the vampires and werewolves, but not with blades."

She kicked him as he tried to rise, sending him back to the ground.

"I told you I would kill you," she said. "For all your talk of immortality, you seem to have forgotten that it is only a mirage." She turned the stake this way and that in front of her face, examining it in the moonlight. "Do you fear the other side of death, Tyrannus?"

Orange eyes wild with fear, Tyrannus sprang from the ground, claws outstretched for Atalanta, but she met him in a violent hug and rammed the stake home. His final cry was a high shriek, not of pain, but of terror.

The wolves howled in triumph as their former king sank to the ground. Atalanta looked back at her friends, a half-smile on her face.

"Is it really over?" said Andrew, sword hanging limply at his side.

They all looked toward Alatreon. Tyrannus' army was scattered, the elf, human, and centaur armies in hot pursuit. Arrows shot into the sky like reverse rain, sending fleeing vampires crashing to earth. The griffins carried more to the tree prison.

"Yes, I think it is," said Michael, hugging Felicity to him. She buried her wet face in his shoulder.

Aquila's cry mingled with the triumphant blare of the Avalon and Galechaser victory horns.

"Now the real work begins," said Andromeda, walking toward her siblings with her arm slung over Erro's furry shoulder.

Chapter 32

Werewolf Ball

Andromeda waited in Barion's castle courtyard for her knight to return. The lush green space full of her mother's favorite pink roses was not as splendid as the one in Alatreon, but tonight it was even more peaceful than usual. Everyone was readying themselves for the ball. It was to be the second celebration of the war's end. The first had been a wild, raucus thing that spilled into the streets of Alatreon even as parts of it smoldered and the wall still bore its scars. This would be a more formal event, a time to renew and celebrate old and new treaties, establish friendships. There would be elves, fairies, nymphs, dryads, centaurs, and even werewolves in attendance.

Many of Tyrannus' willing followers still refused to mingle with elves and humans, to willingly allow themselves to be chained and confined at the full moon, but some had wanted nothing more than to be accepted back into the culture they had been shunned from, and all it took to win their loyalty was simple kindness.

At first, the plan had been to use the unwilling werewolves for the alchemists' tests, but so many willing volunteers from the group of transformed villagers came forward, there was no need. It was safer that way. Each time Erro changed, locked in the dungeons, his back paws chained to the floor, Aquila was in the cell with him. The griffin's presence quelled the blind rage brought on by the disease and had been able to bring Erro to himself all three times thus far. Once the alpha was quelled, the others were easier to contain, but some of the older werewolves still snapped at whoever came too close. It was much safer to take hair and saliva samples from the more docile, willing werewolves. The alchemists had moved their workshop from

Alatreon to Barion because Erro had refused to stay in the elf city after he had been made a knight of the Avalon house. He was not the first peasant to rise to the status of knight, but he was the first werewolf.

A month previously, the head alchemist had spread the news that they were becoming optimistic about the werewolf cure, though any hope for the vampires still looked grim. The werewolves' hearts still beat and pumped blood through their bodies. Their werewolfism was merely a disease of the blood. The vampires' hearts were cold and still, coagulating blood at their center. Venom ran through their otherwise empty veins. They were more like reanimated corpses, and the alchemists feared there was no way to reverse the process. Recently, there had been talk of creating an enclosed city for them, but creating something of that scale that actually functioned would take time. For now, those of Tyrannus' old order were kept in the human and elf dungeons, while those who had been turned against their will for the sake of swelling Tyrannus' numbers now stayed outside of Alatreon in tree prisons much like the one that had saved their lives in the war. It was not an ideal space, but they now had eternity ahead of them, and waiting half a century for their own city did not seem quite so bad.

While the call of their alpha had held the werewolves in place until the sun rose the day after the war was won, many vampires had escaped when they'd seen that the battle was lost. A small few had presented themselves in Alatreon when they heard that none of their captured fellows had been slaughtered, but most did not. Many of those who had escaped were the dreaded elf vampires. Garrisons of knights had been sent out over the human and elf kingdoms to search for them. Their orders were to capture, not kill, if possible. At a court gathering in Alatreon, it had been decided that the Extermination of seven hundred years ago had sparked what was now being called, The Tyrant's War. The young Avalons and Atalanta had spoken of all they had learned on their long journey from the northern mountains to the defeat of Tyrannus at Alatreon, and together they had moved even the elf elders. The plight of their own villagers had been the key to swaying their hardened, frightened hearts. There would be no more blind slaughter. If aid could be given and accepted, a helping hand would always be extended before the blade. There were still some who protested, but they were outvoted. Still, Andromeda knew their dissent would be felt for many years to come. It would take time.

"Andromeda!"

The call came from a high window directly above her. Felicity's golden head leaned out of it.

"You'll miss the ball if you don't come get dressed now," she said.

"I'll be in in a moment," she said with a dismissive wave.

Perhaps if she was late, there would be no time for incessant corset tugging. In that case, she would have to thank Erro, if he arrived tonight.

The trumpets sounded just a few minutes later, and the garrison came through the castle gates. Oxen pulled wagons laden with steel cages reinforced with elf magic. The cages were covered in heavy, wool blankets to keep the sun from burning the occupants who rattled the bars.

Erro rode at the head of party, gliding low over the ground atop Aquila. He glittered in silver armor, his breastplate emblazoned with the Avalon eagle. His helmet was a griffin, complete with outstretched wings and a razor beak that descended his nose. Andromeda could see he wore the dour, moody expression he often adopted when the time of the full moon drew near, but when he saw her waving to him, he brightened.

When Aquila landed before her, he nuzzled his head under her arm and clicked his beak affectionately while Erro climbed off. When he had removed his helmet, Andromeda threw herself in his arms. He had been gone since two days after the last full moon. He hugged her, but his head swiveled to the garrison, still marching on toward the dungeon entrance.

"Oh, Erro, honestly!" said Andromeda.

She grabbed his chin and pulled his mouth to hers. He relaxed into the kiss and then pulled back smiling.

"You're going to make absolutely sure my head rolls from my shoulders, aren't you?" he said.

She chuckled, but then turned stern. "You really must stop that. It drives me crazy."

"I'm sorry," he said. "I still feel a bit out of place. And I'm almost certain it's not proper to kiss a princess unless you're known to be courting."

"I can't fathom how you've convinced yourself that everybody doesn't already know," she said.

"But I haven't asked your father yet."

"And whose fault is that?"

He smiled sheepishly and rubbed at the back of his head, mussing his long hair. "I was just hoping … You know …"

"No, I don't."

He sighed. "I was just waiting for … for a way to impress him." His embarrassed grin turned into a playful one. "You know, an opportunity for a daring act of heroism. I think he'd be more likely to say yes if I'd just saved his life, don't you?"

She snorted. "So, my father must be in mortal peril for you to ask for my hand, is that it?" she said. She tapped her chin. "Hmm, another vampire at a ball might do it. Think one of the guards would give me his keys?"

They laughed together, and Andromeda brushed his face with her fingertips. "You have nothing more to prove."

"And still I worry," he said, catching her hand and pressing it to his cheek.

Her brows pulled together in mischief. "As an unbetrothed princess, I'm required to dance with all the eligible noblemen's sons tonight."

Erro's face became sour.

"Who knows," said Andromeda. "Perhaps one of them might ask my father for my hand tonight. Lord Harrigan's son, Tristan, has always been rather fond of me."

"But you would say no," said Erro, brushing the hair from her forehead as nonchalantly as he could.

"Well, if father approves, I would have to at least go through the formalities of giving it a try, I suppose."

"I thought you said before your father liked me better than all the noblemen's sons."

"He does, but he also likes a man of action."

"I am a man of action. I'm a knight."

"Yet you still have not asked for what you want most."

Gray and brown irises locked, silently studying, memorizing. He took her face gently in both hands and kissed her hard and long, never once stopping to see who was watching.

"Ewwww!"

The two pulled apart while Felicity laughed, Tilly propped in her lap in the window seat of Tilly's bedroom. The little girl feigned a gag, and Felicity tossed back her curls and laughed harder.

"You like it just fine when the princess kisses a knight in your bedtime stories," Andromeda called up. "Why is this any different?"

"'Cuz it's real! Ewww! Are you gonna get married?"

"You bet your bonnet, little goose," said Erro.

"Does that mean you're going to ask?" Andromeda said softly, and Erro nodded and pressed his forehead to hers.

"She's the goose," said Tilly, poking Felicity in the chest. "Hey! Don't start that again," said Felicity. "Andrew's only just grown bored of honking at me."

"Come on, let's get inside before anyone else calls me gross," said Erro.

As they made their way inside with arms around each other,

Erro said, "So, this Tristan. I could beat him in combat, right?"

"Tristan is ten."

Erro's laugh carried over the courtyard.

* * *

Felicity's laughter rang down the hall to where Michael and Atalanta strolled side-by-side. There was not much mirth on Atalanta's face, though. She had been sullen for three days, and Michael could not, for the life of him, figure out why.

The two of them were already dressed for the festivities. Michael sported his finest doublet of black velvet, embroidered in gold thread. The black tunic he wore beneath had eagles flying around the cuffs. His tall boots made a solid thump each time he put his feet to the stone floor. Atalanta wore an uncoreseted silk dress without a hoop or any sort of undergarment, as was elvish custom. The lilac fabric clung to her in ways that made Michael fear looking at her too long. Her hair had been pulled back from her crown with a silver headdress that resembled a band of ivy climbing up a castle wall, but the rest of it fell free in loose curls down her back and brushed her waist.

They walked in silence. Michael had tried to strike a casual conversation as they made their way to the throne room, where they were to stand with their parents to meet their guests as they arrived, but Atalanta had cut off every attempt with a curt single-word answer.

He glanced sideways at her, and her beauty hurt his heart. Only the sour frown spoiled it, and he was not sure spoiled was even the right word. It didn't make her any less beautiful; it only made him feel as though he'd done something wrong.

"What's troubling you?"

"Nothing," she said, not looking at him.

"There is something. You've been upset for days."

"I just don't like balls."

478

"Somehow, I don't think that's it."

She slowed and studied the ground.

"Please, just tell me. I cannot help if you don't tell me."

"You ought to know," she said with a ferocity that startled him.

"How am I to know?" he said, shaking his head in angry disbelief. "Should I read your mind?"

"It's what you want, too, isn't it?" She rounded on him, her face angry but her eyes pleading.

"What? What are you talking about? You're not making any sense."

She made an exasperated noise at the back of her throat. "Must I really tell you?"

"Yes!" said Michael, utterly bewildered. "You must."

"You didn't ask me to the ball."

"What?" said Michael, his hand going to his forehead in disbelief. "Ask you to the ball? You're already going to the ball. Why should I ask you?"

She sighed, looking again at the ground. "That's not what I really meant to say. Oh, what's wrong with me! You make me act like one of the foolish elves I used to laugh behind my hand at, twittering around after soldiers."

Michael's shoulders slumped, and he looked at her totally perplexed. "Atalanta, please, I have no earthly idea what you're talking about."

She turned her eyes up to him without lifting her head.

"I thought ... I thought you felt something ... for me."

Michael's head buzzed. "What?" He couldn't have heard her correctly.

"Do you not?" she said, angry again. Roses blossomed on her cheeks, and she raised her head to face him.

"Feel something for you?"

"Yes! By the elders, Michael, I thought you were smart."

"Yes, I ... I'm smart," he babbled, and then shook his head. "I mean, yes, I do."

"Do what?" she said, a hand on her hip.

He closed his eyes and took a calming breath.

"From the moment I first saw you I was fascinated," he said. "What man wouldn't be? But then you spoke and you fought and you never wavered from your convictions, and all the time I watched, and I knew you were stronger than I could ever be. You were the leader I wanted to be. You teased me mercilessly," — she laughed softly — "and still I followed at your hemline. You have had me from before you ever wanted me."

He was astonished to find that she was blushing.

"Then why didn't you ever say something?"

"Because I thought you were the type of woman who prefers to take what she wants for herself. I couldn't force you to want me, and I wasn't sure if you did."

She took a step toward him, and his breath caught.

"You are mostly right," she said, her thin fingers coming up to meet his hairline. "But you've forgotten, I am not a woman. I am an elf. I will never be like the human girls you're accustomed to."

"None of them ever caught my fancy anyway."

She smiled a disbelieving smile. "Oh, I'm sure." Then her face grew sullen again. "I will not age as you do either. Will you be all right with that?"

"Will you is the more important question," said Michael, his breath trembling on his lips as she began to trace the outer lines of his face. "You will have to watch me grow old. Can you do that?"

"I don't know," she said. "That is still a long time away. We don't know who we'll be then. But I know who you are now, and I would have you for my own."

She pressed herself against him, and his head swam as his arms went around her and the silk caressed his hands. She kissed him fiercely and took his breath completely. He lost himself in it, and he did not stop kissing her even as he pulled aside an old tapestry to push her into a hidden corridor beyond. She slammed him against the wall and slung her arms about his neck. She was everywhere around him. She smelled of lilac and tasted of honeysuckle. It seemed impossible that he could be holding her this way, and when he at last pulled back for just a moment, he said, "Felicity says you'll break my heart."

"Oh, does she?"

"Yes." There was a plea in his voice that he hoped she would answer.

"I fear it's you who'll break mine," she said, studying him closely as her hand pushed back his hair.

"What are we to do, then?"

She shrugged and bent toward him so that her lips brushed against his as she said, "I'd like to do this."

They emerged, a bit disheveled, sometime later and nearly ran into Andrew. Andrew raised an eyebrow.

"Well, hello there," he said through a smirk. "Taking an innocent stroll through a dead-end corridor, are we?"

"Keep moving, Andrew," said Michael.

"Yes, all of you keep moving," said Felicity from down the hall. She was fully decked in a rose and copper gown, complete with corset and hoop. Tilly wore a belled blue dress that matched her eyes. A little tiara sat atop her head. She held Felicity's hand and mimicked her scolding expression with astounding accuracy.

"Mother and Father have sent me to fetch you. You're all late," said Felicity.

"You're very, very late," said Tilly, tapping her foot.

"I was trying to find Bree," said Andrew. "I know she's around here somewhere."

"Want to find her? She'll be at the ball. Let's go," said Felicity. She turned back and mouthed as she counted. "Where's Andromeda?"

"She and Erro ran by me not long ago," said Andrew.

"Did you happen to notice if she was dressed yet?"

"Nope," said Andrew, totally unconcerned. "She did say something about Governess Hattie strangling her with corset strings, though."

"Brilliant," said Felicity, but the hint of a smile appeared in a crack in her stern expression.

Andromeda ran into the throne room where the royals traditionally held audience with their guests, heavy violet skirts swishing, nearly half an hour late. Isabelle gave her daughter a scathing look over top of the bowing head of a nobleman. Andromeda smiled sheepishly and skidded into her place next to Andrew just in time for the nobleman to extend his hand to her. She curtsied as she placed her hand in his and allowed him to kiss the back of it.

"Did I miss most of it?" Andromeda whispered to her twin when the nobleman had been escorted off toward the ballroom.

"Yes, the centaurs and all the fae have been through here. I believe all of the elves are here, too. Now just our noblemen are left."

"Oh good."

"Lucky," Andrew said out of the corner of his mouth. "I tried to lose track of time myself, but Felicity caught me."

"She's good at that."

"I caught Michael and Atalanta in the throes of passion."

"What?" Andromeda's voice echoed off the stone walls, and Isabelle looked absolutely livid.

Andromeda mouthed, sorry, to her mother and then whispered back at Andrew. "What?"

"Yeah, caught them coming out from behind that tapestry in the corridor just outside Tilly's room." He stifled a snicker. "You should have seen Michael's face. Lucky dog. Speaking of which, how's your dog? Catch anything on his trip?"

Another nobleman came down the line, forcing Andromeda

to spare Andrew her look of scorn. She tromped on his toe instead. He only held back another snicker.

"Your Majesties, Your Majesties!"

The servant came charging through the side throne room door.

"This is highly irregular, Claudius," said Marcus.

"We have guests," said Isabelle, as though that explained absolutely everything inappropriate about the situation.

"My apologies, Your Majesties," said Claudius, "but my orders were to inform you the moment it was done."

"You don't mean ...?" said Marcus.

"Yes, Your Majesty. The werewolf cure, it is finished! Of course, we'll need to test it at the full moon, but they say they've done it. They've cleared the disease from the blood specimens."

A cheer rang through the room, drowning out the last of Claudius' words, and Andromeda cheered loudest of all.

"Enough with these formalities, don't you think, brother?" said Zanthus, clasping Marcus' hand in both of his.

"To the ballroom!" cried Marcus, his voice booming through the room and out into the corridors. "Let's celebrate!"

In the Northern Wood, vampires were taking up old, solitary perches. In the mountains, the goblins returned to their caves, dancing and sacrificing to Olga to select the new king. Minotaurs sharpened their horns on the trees in the Black Forest. Trolls and ogres parted ways on their journeys home to the swamps and caves of the south. Each to his own. In the western hills, giants quarreled with their fists and clubs over minor injustices. But inside Barion's castle walls, many species were united in dance and feast and celebration. Andromeda danced with her knight. An elf princess and a human prince lost themselves in each other's gazes. Commoners reveled in the splendor of the food, the mirror-lined dance hall, and the colorful creatures that had always stayed apart from them. There would be no more separation. No more myths. Instead, there would be connection and intermingling and dancing. It was the dawn of a new age, when orphaned peasant boys could become knights, when werewolves could dance amongst lords and ladies, when the terror of the unknown began to lift and morph into understanding. All hearts within the castle felt the change, and they danced fiercely and with abandon.

THE END

Acknowledgements

Thank you to Krystina Kellingley and Dominic C. James for taking a chance on a massive debut novel from young gal down in Tennessee. And for your kind, insightful guidance the first time I submitted it (long before it was ready); you gave me the kick in the pants I needed to get it right.

Thank you to the entire Cosmic Egg Books team for making this book a reality.

Huge thanks to my mentor, Russell Helms, for spending months beta-reading this monster even though fantasy isn't exactly your bag. Sorry I didn't manage to give Callid a backstory; I find it endlessly amusing that he was your favorite. Maybe I'll write you a short story.

To my husband, Stephen, thank you for reading not only every version of Arcamira, but everything I write. And for allowing my 14-year-old self's tragic, orphaned fantasy version of you to be immortalized in print. Sorry I didn't give him a guitar, but hey, you got a badass backflip scene. And a freaking griffin!

Elizabeth Sills, you're the OG. Thanks for geeking out about the original ninth-grade version and encouraging me to keep writing. This one's way better, I promise.

Mom and Dad, thanks for saying, "You go, babydoll!" instead of, "Really? You're sure about that?" when I decided to make writing my career.

COSMIC EGG
BOOKS

FANTASY, SCI-FI, HORROR & PARANORMAL

If you prefer to spend your nights with Vampires and Werewolves rather than the mundane then we publish the books for you. If your preference is for Dragons and Faeries or Angels and Demons – we should be your first stop. Perhaps your perfect partner has artificial skin or comes from another planet – step right this way. If your passion is Fantasy (including magical realism and spiritual fantasy), Metaphysical Cosmology, Horror or Science Fiction (including Steampunk), Cosmic Egg books will feed your hunger. Our curiosity shop contains treasures you will enjoy unearthing. If you have enjoyed this book, why not tell other readers by posting a review on your preferred book site.

The Gawain Legacy
Jon Mackley
If you try to control every secret, secrets may end up controlling
you.
Paperback: 978-1-78279-485-1 ebook: 978-1-78279-484-4

Readers of ebooks can buy or view any of these bestsellers by
clicking on the live link in the title. Most titles are published
in paperback and as an ebook. Paperbacks are available in
traditional bookshops. Both print and ebook formats are
available online.
Find more titles and sign up to our readers' newsletter at
http://www.johnhuntpublishing.com/fiction
Follow us on Facebook at https://www.facebook.com/JHPfiction
and Twitter at https://twitter.com/JHPFiction